Prince

RAVEN

THE PIRATE PRINCESS

Year Three: Monsters of the Deep

Chapter One: Date Night Part 1

Written By: Jeremy Whitley

Pencils By: Xenia Pamfil

Inks By: Christine Hipp

Colors By: Lexillo

Lettered By: Justin Birch

Edited By: Nicole D'Andria

Cover By: Sorah Suhng
and Eddy Swan

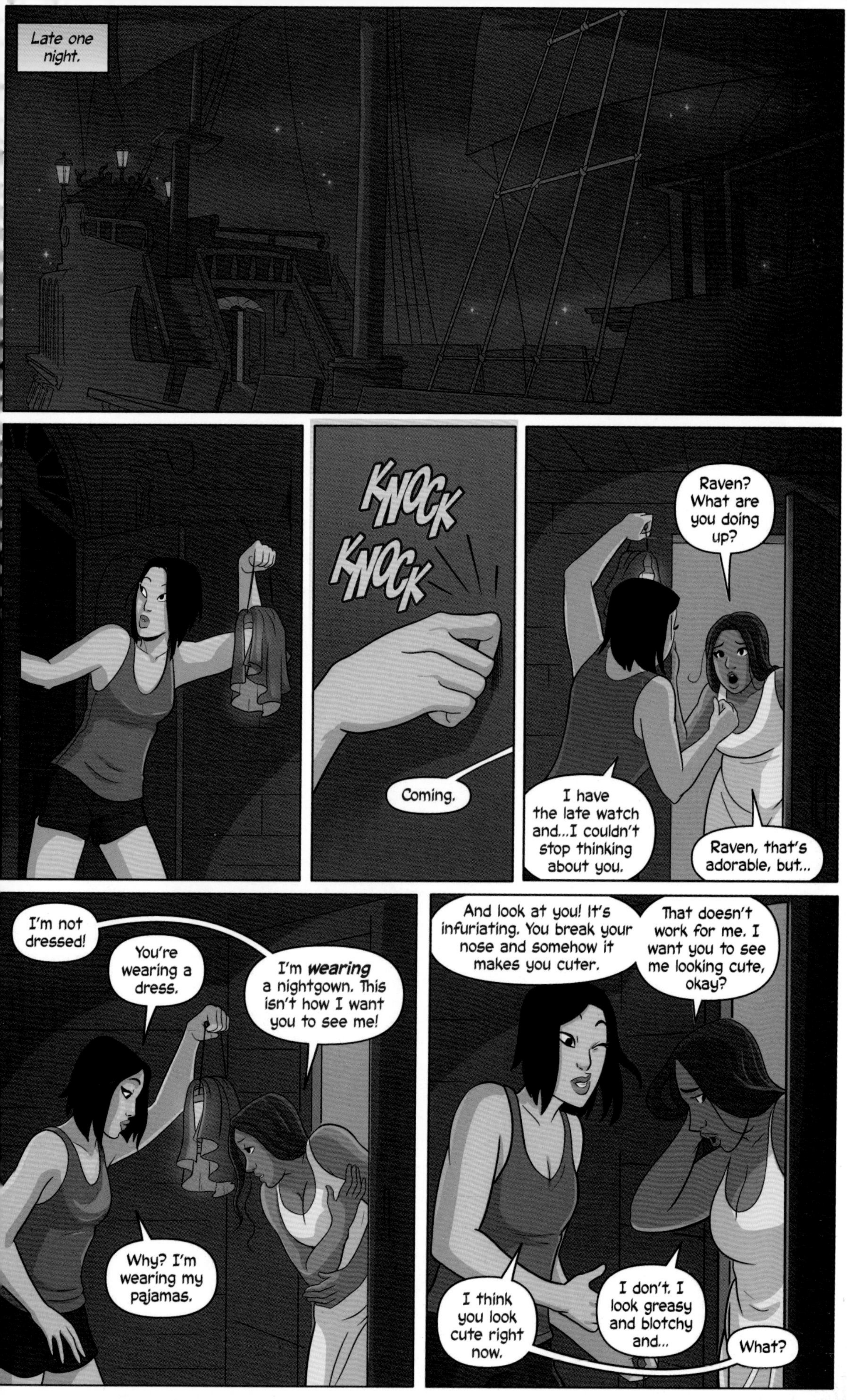
Late one night.
KNOCK
KNOCK
Coming.
Raven? What are you doing up?
I have the late watch and...I couldn't stop thinking about you.
Raven, that's adorable, but...
I'm not dressed!
You're wearing a dress.
I'm *wearing* a nightgown. This isn't how I want you to see me!
Why? I'm wearing my pajamas.
And look at you! It's infuriating. You break your nose and somehow it makes you cuter.
That doesn't work for me. I want you to see me looking cute, okay?
I think you look cute right now.
I don't. I look greasy and blotchy and...
What?

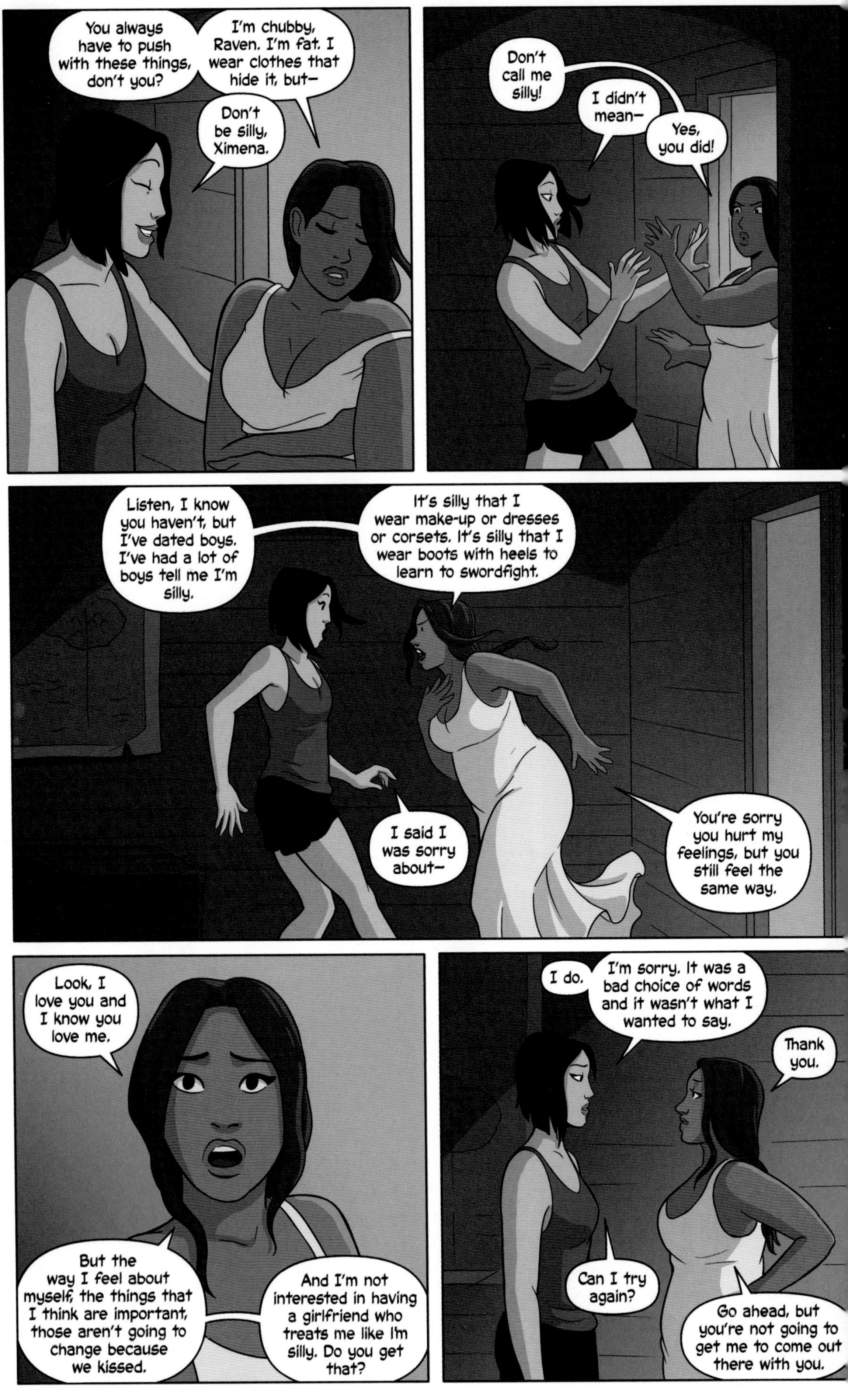
You always have to push with these things, don't you?
I'm chubby, Raven. I'm fat. I wear clothes that hide it, but—
Don't be silly, Ximena.
Don't call me silly!
I didn't mean—
Yes, you did!
Listen, I know you haven't, but I've dated boys. I've had a lot of boys tell me I'm silly.
It's silly that I wear make-up or dresses or corsets. It's silly that I wear boots with heels to learn to swordfight.
I said I was sorry about—
You're sorry you hurt my feelings, but you still feel the same way.
Look, I love you and I know you love me.
But the way I feel about myself, the things that I think are important, those aren't going to change because we kissed.
And I'm not interested in having a girlfriend who treats me like I'm silly. Do you get that?
I do.
I'm sorry. It was a bad choice of words and it wasn't what I wanted to say.
Thank you.
Can I try again?
Go ahead, but you're not going to get me to come out there with you.

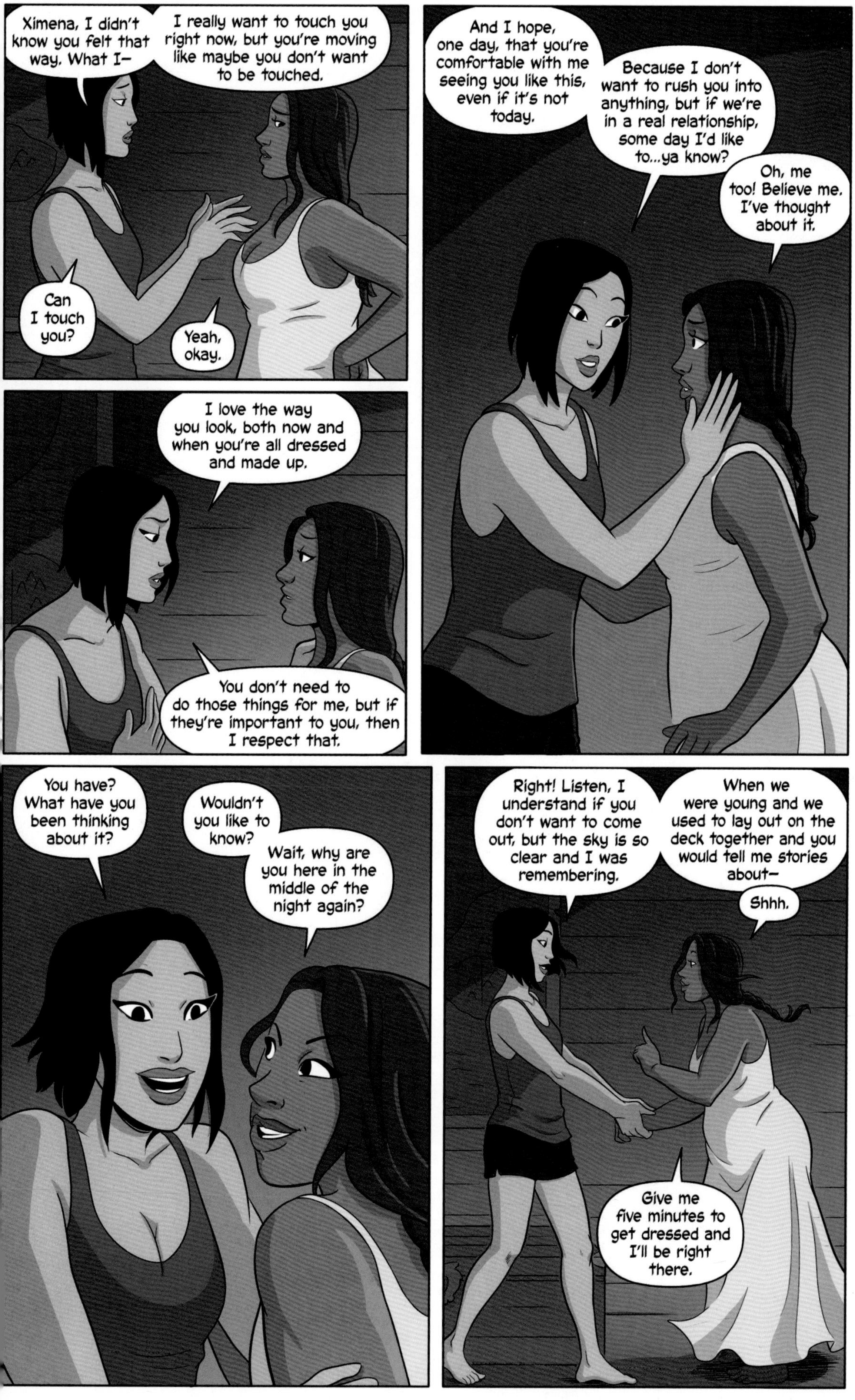
Ximena, I didn't know you felt that way. What I—
I really want to touch you right now, but you're moving like maybe you don't want to be touched.
Can I touch you?
Yeah, okay.
I love the way you look, both now and when you're all dressed and made up.
You don't need to do those things for me, but if they're important to you, then I respect that.
And I hope, one day, that you're comfortable with me seeing you like this, even if it's not today.
Because I don't want to rush you into anything, but if we're in a real relationship, some day I'd like to...ya know?
Oh, me too! Believe me. I've thought about it.
You have? What have you been thinking about it?
Wouldn't you like to know?
Wait, why are you here in the middle of the night again?
Right! Listen, I understand if you don't want to come out, but the sky is so clear and I was remembering.
When we were young and we used to lay out on the deck together and you would tell me stories about—
Shhh.
Give me five minutes to get dressed and I'll be right there.

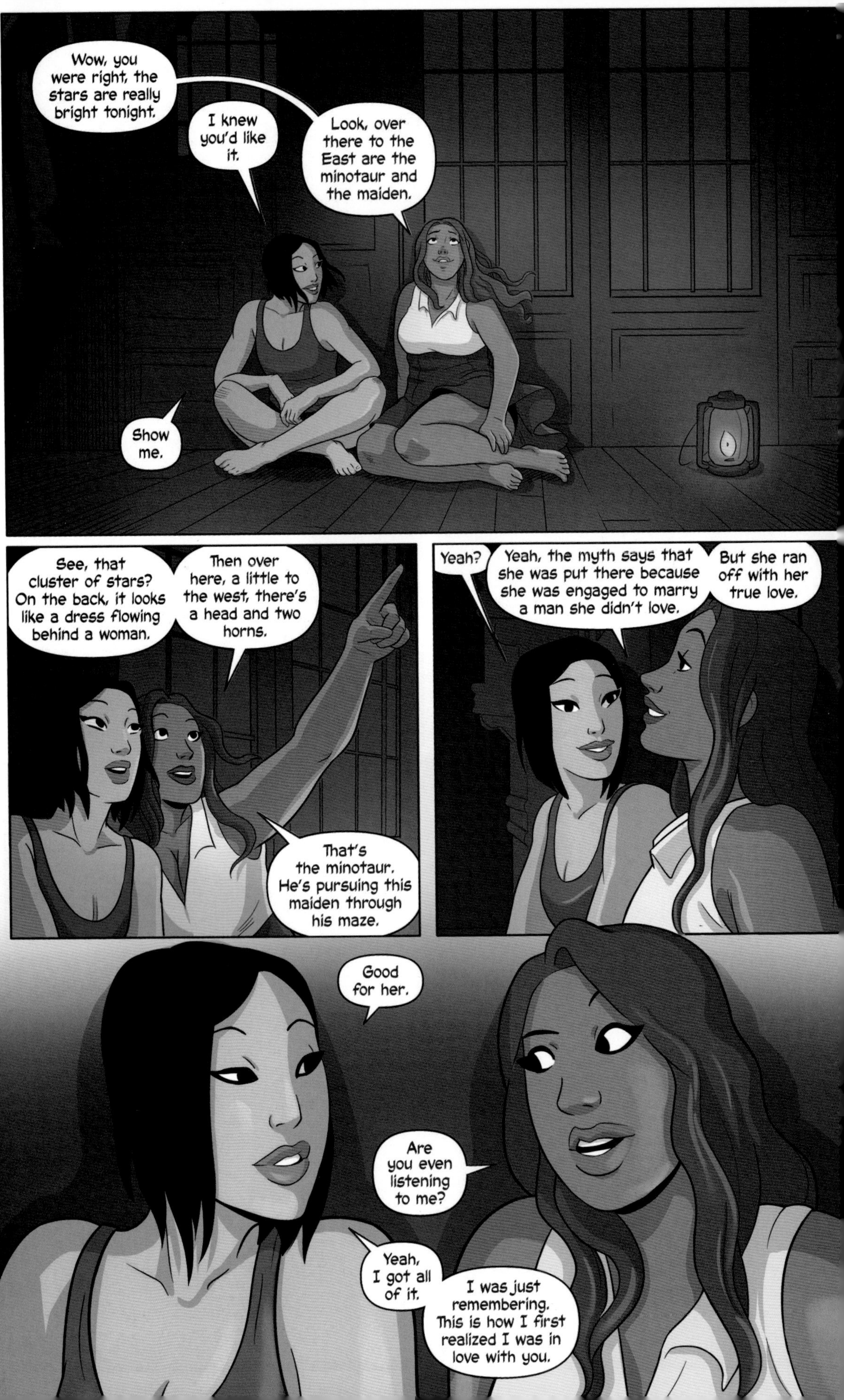

Wow, you were right, the stars are really bright tonight.
I knew you'd like it.
Look, over there to the East are the minotaur and the maiden.
Show me.
See, that cluster of stars? On the back, it looks like a dress flowing behind a woman.
Then over here, a little to the west, there's a head and two horns.
That's the minotaur. He's pursuing this maiden through his maze.
Yeah?
Yeah, the myth says that she was put there because she was engaged to marry a man she didn't love.
But she ran off with her true love.
Good for her.
Are you even listening to me?
Yeah, I got all of it.
I was just remembering. This is how I first realized I was in love with you.

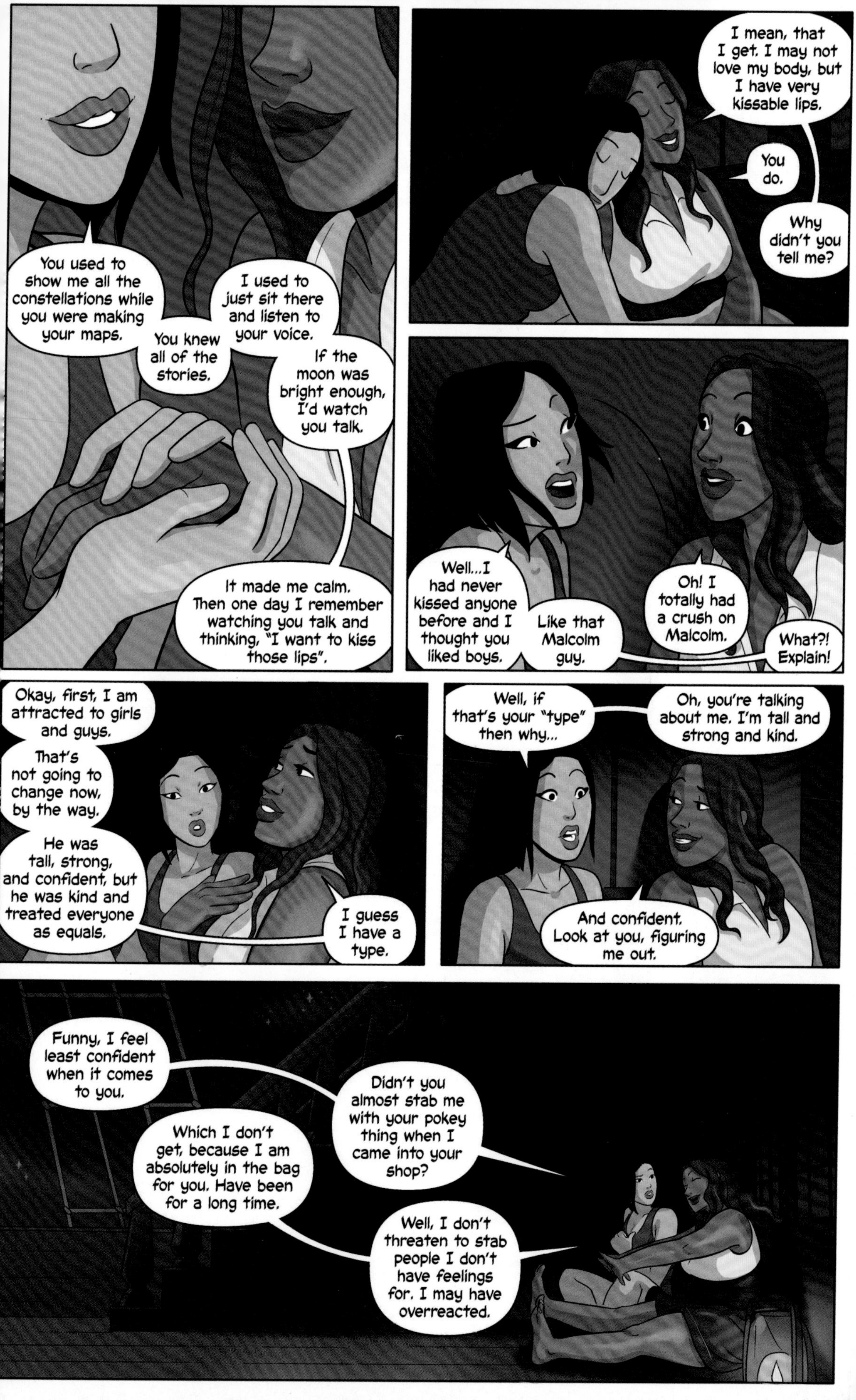

You used to show me all the constellations while you were making your maps.
I used to just sit there and listen to your voice.
You knew all of the stories.
If the moon was bright enough, I'd watch you talk.
It made me calm. Then one day I remember watching you talk and thinking, "I want to kiss those lips".
I mean, that I get. I may not love my body, but I have very kissable lips.
You do.
Why didn't you tell me?
Well...I had never kissed anyone before and I thought you liked boys.
Like that Malcolm guy.
Oh! I totally had a crush on Malcolm.
What?! Explain!
Okay, first, I am attracted to girls and guys.
That's not going to change now, by the way.
He was tall, strong, and confident, but he was kind and treated everyone as equals.
I guess I have a type.
Well, if that's your "type" then why...
Oh, you're talking about me. I'm tall and strong and kind.
And confident. Look at you, figuring me out.
Funny, I feel least confident when it comes to you.
Which I don't get, because I am absolutely in the bag for you. Have been for a long time.
Didn't you almost stab me with your pokey thing when I came into your shop?
Well, I don't threaten to stab people I don't have feelings for. I may have overreacted.

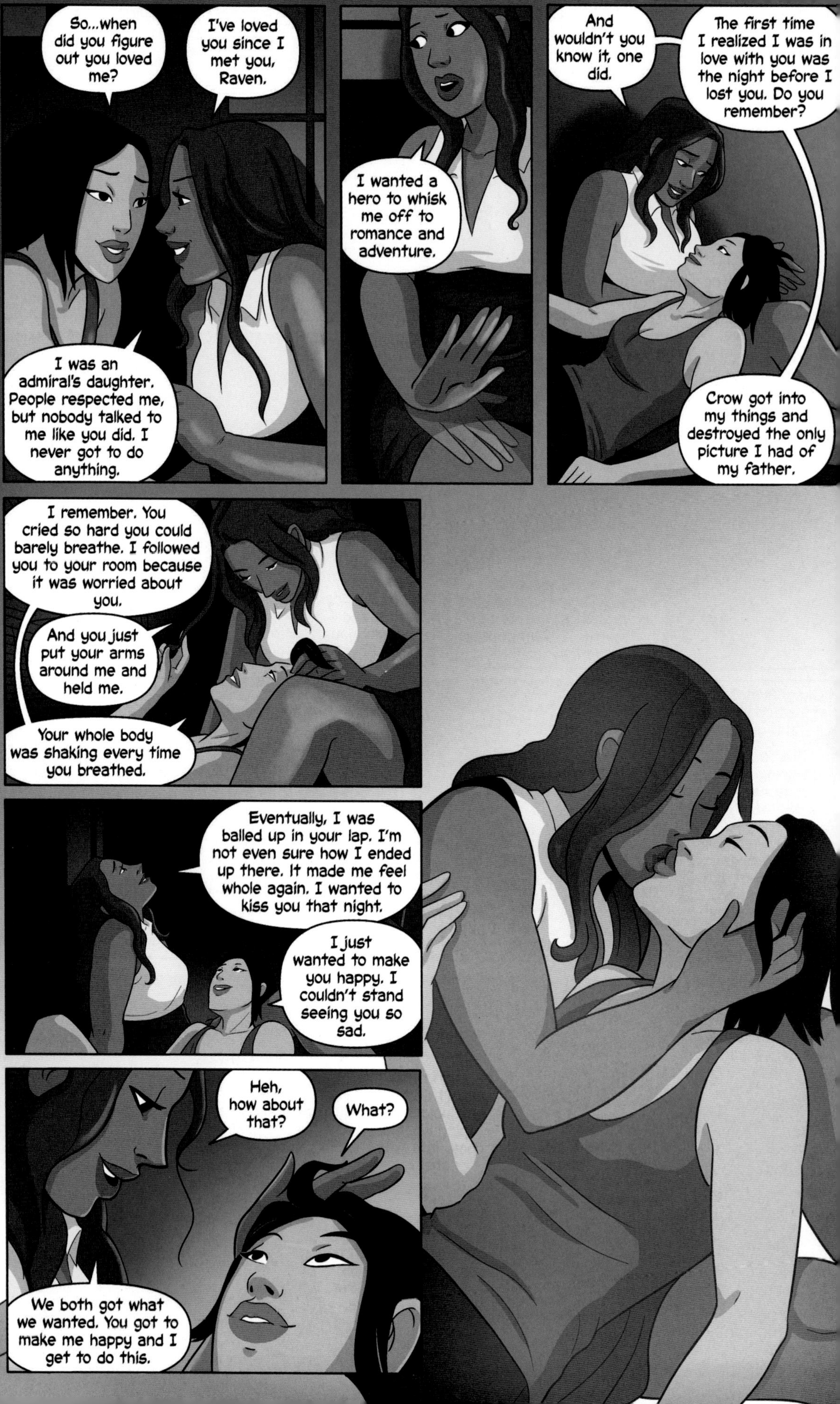
So...when did you figure out you loved me?
I've loved you since I met you, Raven.
I was an admiral's daughter. People respected me, but nobody talked to me like you did. I never got to do anything.
I wanted a hero to whisk me off to romance and adventure.
And wouldn't you know it, one did.
The first time I realized I was in love with you was the night before I lost you. Do you remember?
Crow got into my things and destroyed the only picture I had of my father.
I remember. You cried so hard you could barely breathe. I followed you to your room because it was worried about you.
And you just put your arms around me and held me.
Your whole body was shaking every time you breathed.
Eventually, I was balled up in your lap. I'm not even sure how I ended up there. It made me feel whole again. I wanted to kiss you that night.
I just wanted to make you happy. I couldn't stand seeing you so sad.
Heh, how about that?
What?
We both got what we wanted. You got to make me happy and I get to do this.

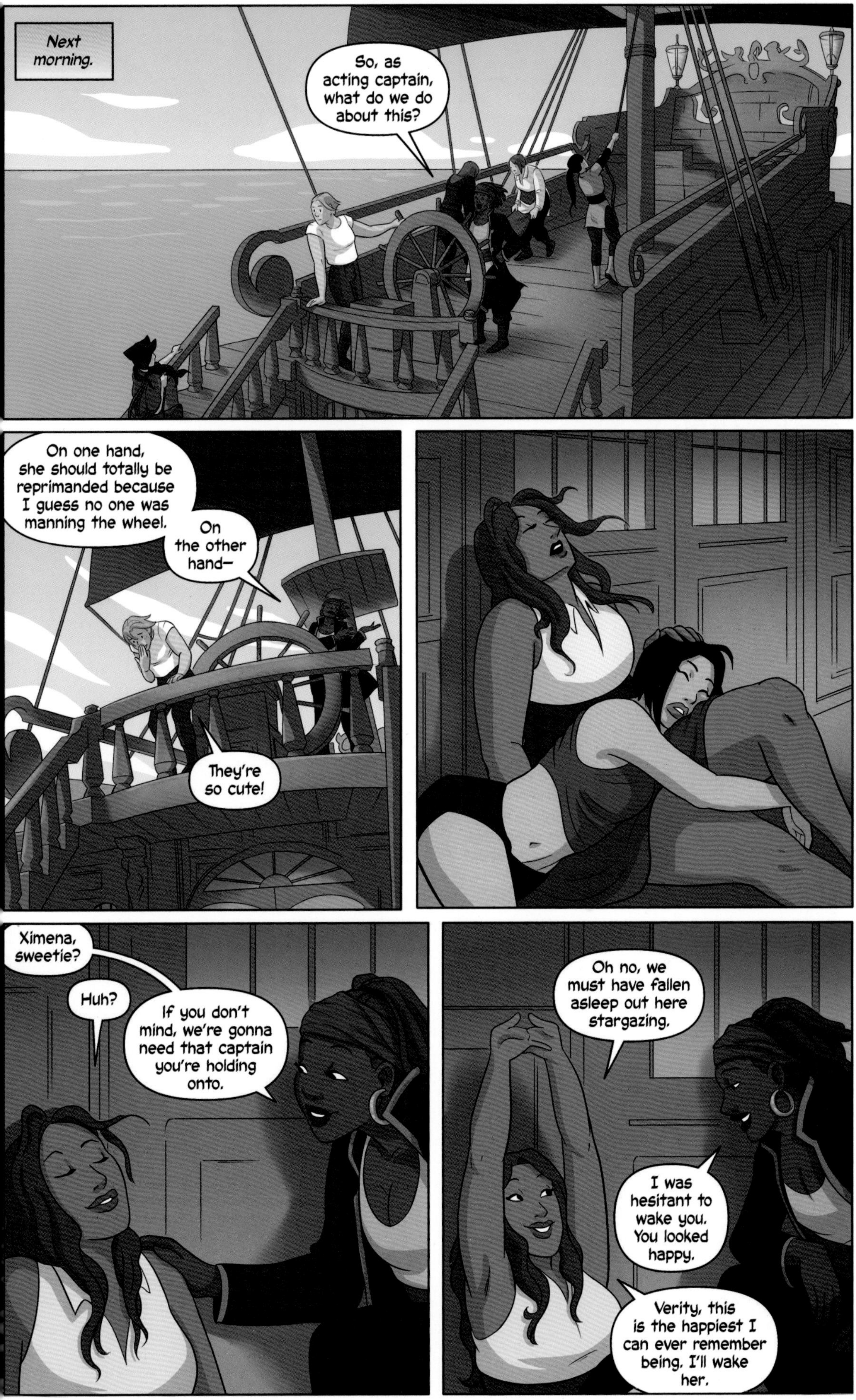
Next morning.
So, as acting captain, what do we do about this?
On one hand, she should totally be reprimanded because I guess no one was manning the wheel.
On the other hand—
They're so cute!
Ximena, sweetie?
Huh?
If you don't mind, we're gonna need that captain you're holding onto.
Oh no, we must have fallen asleep out here stargazing.
I was hesitant to wake you. You looked happy.
Verity, this is the happiest I can ever remember being. I'll wake her.

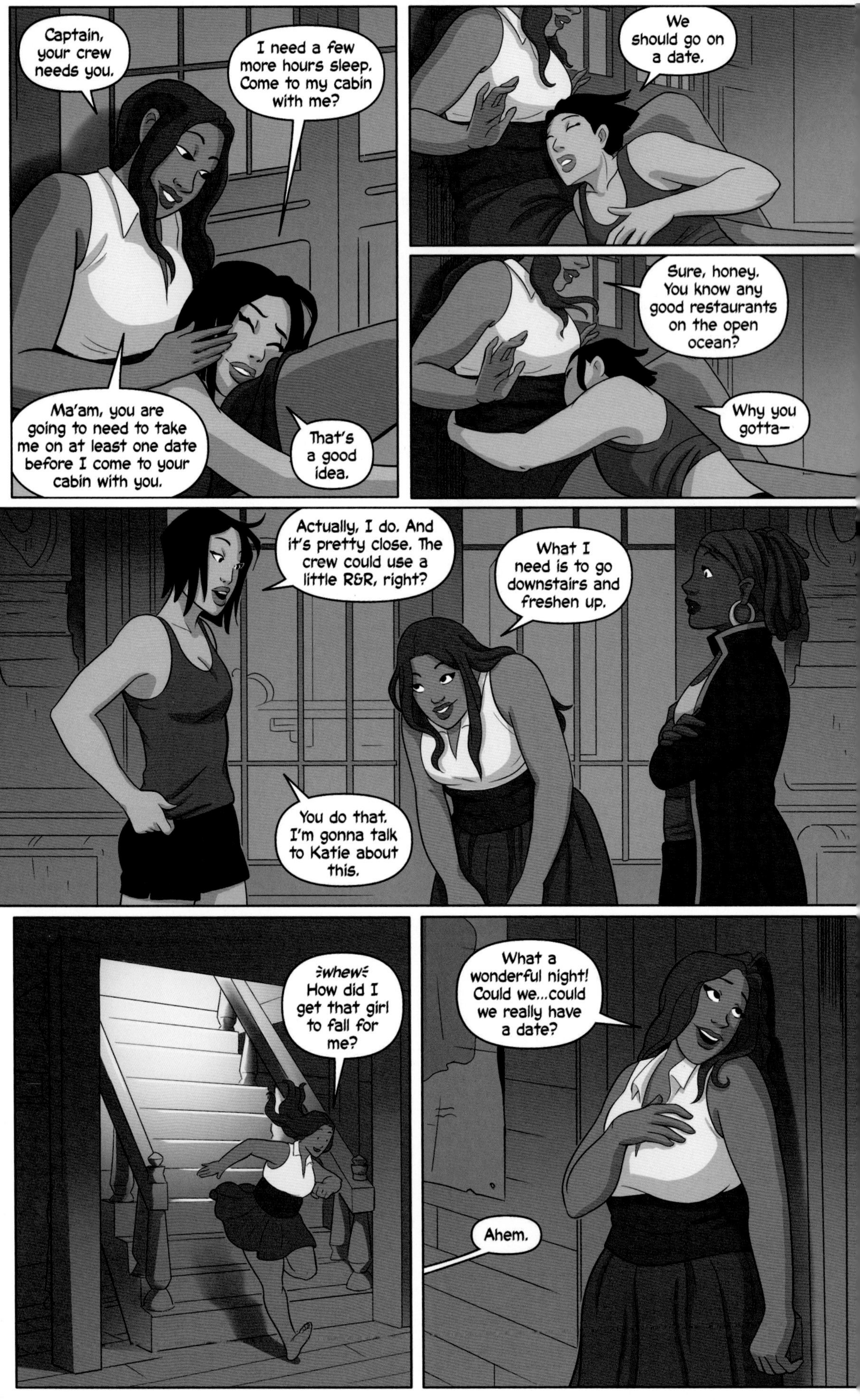
Captain, your crew needs you.
I need a few more hours sleep. Come to my cabin with me?
Ma'am, you are going to need to take me on at least one date before I come to your cabin with you.
That's a good idea.
We should go on a date.
Sure, honey. You know any good restaurants on the open ocean?
Why you gotta—
Actually, I do. And it's pretty close. The crew could use a little R&R, right?
What I need is to go downstairs and freshen up.
You do that. I'm gonna talk to Katie about this.
whew How did I get that girl to fall for me?
What a wonderful night! Could we...could we really have a date?
Ahem.

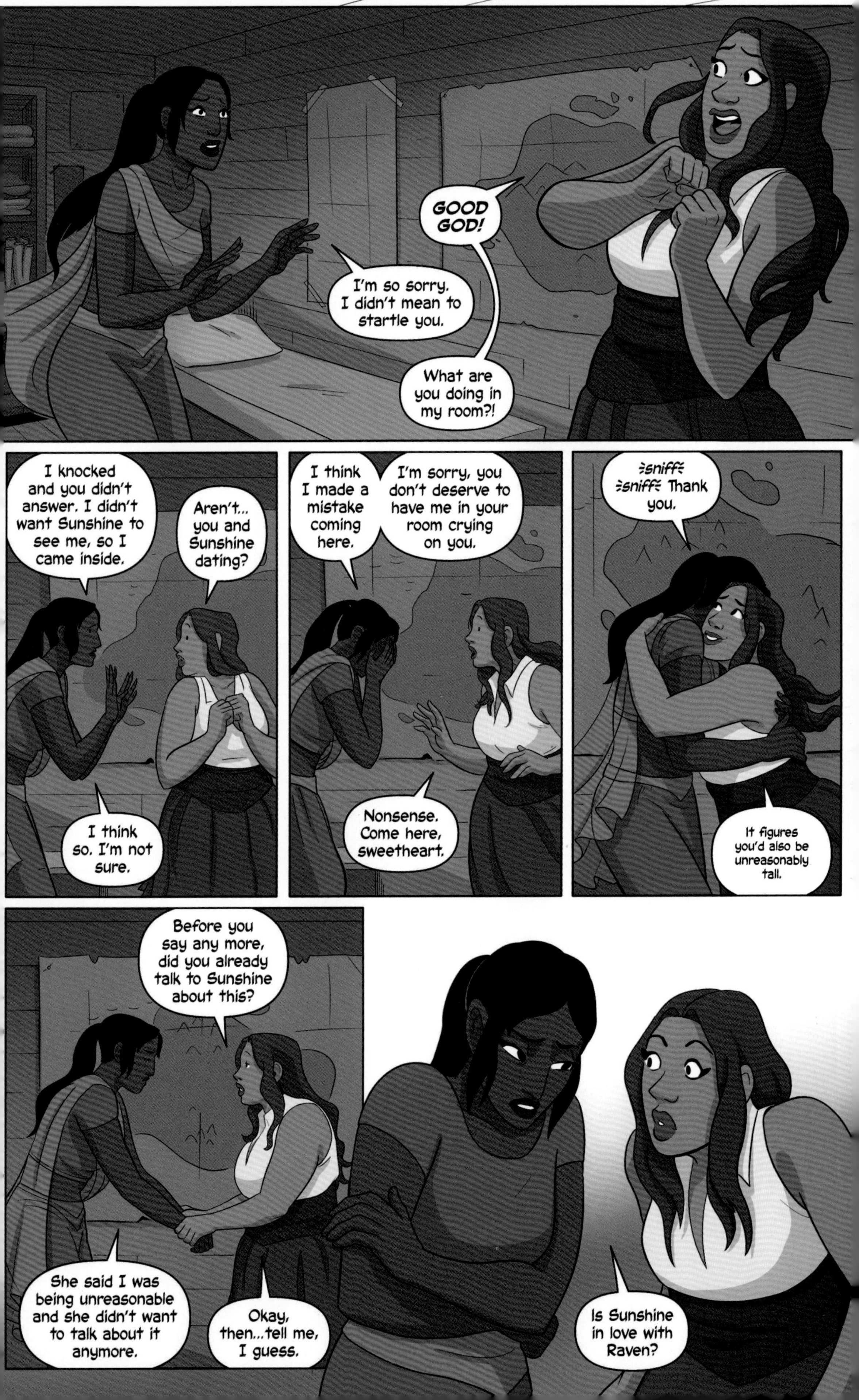
GOOD GOD!
I'm so sorry. I didn't mean to startle you.
What are you doing in my room?!
I knocked and you didn't answer. I didn't want Sunshine to see me, so I came inside.
Aren't... you and Sunshine dating?
I think so. I'm not sure.
I think I made a mistake coming here.
I'm sorry, you don't deserve to have me in your room crying on you.
Nonsense. Come here, sweetheart.
sniff sniff Thank you.
It figures you'd also be unreasonably tall.
Before you say any more, did you already talk to Sunshine about this?
She said I was being unreasonable and she didn't want to talk about it anymore.
Okay, then...tell me, I guess.
Is Sunshine in love with Raven?

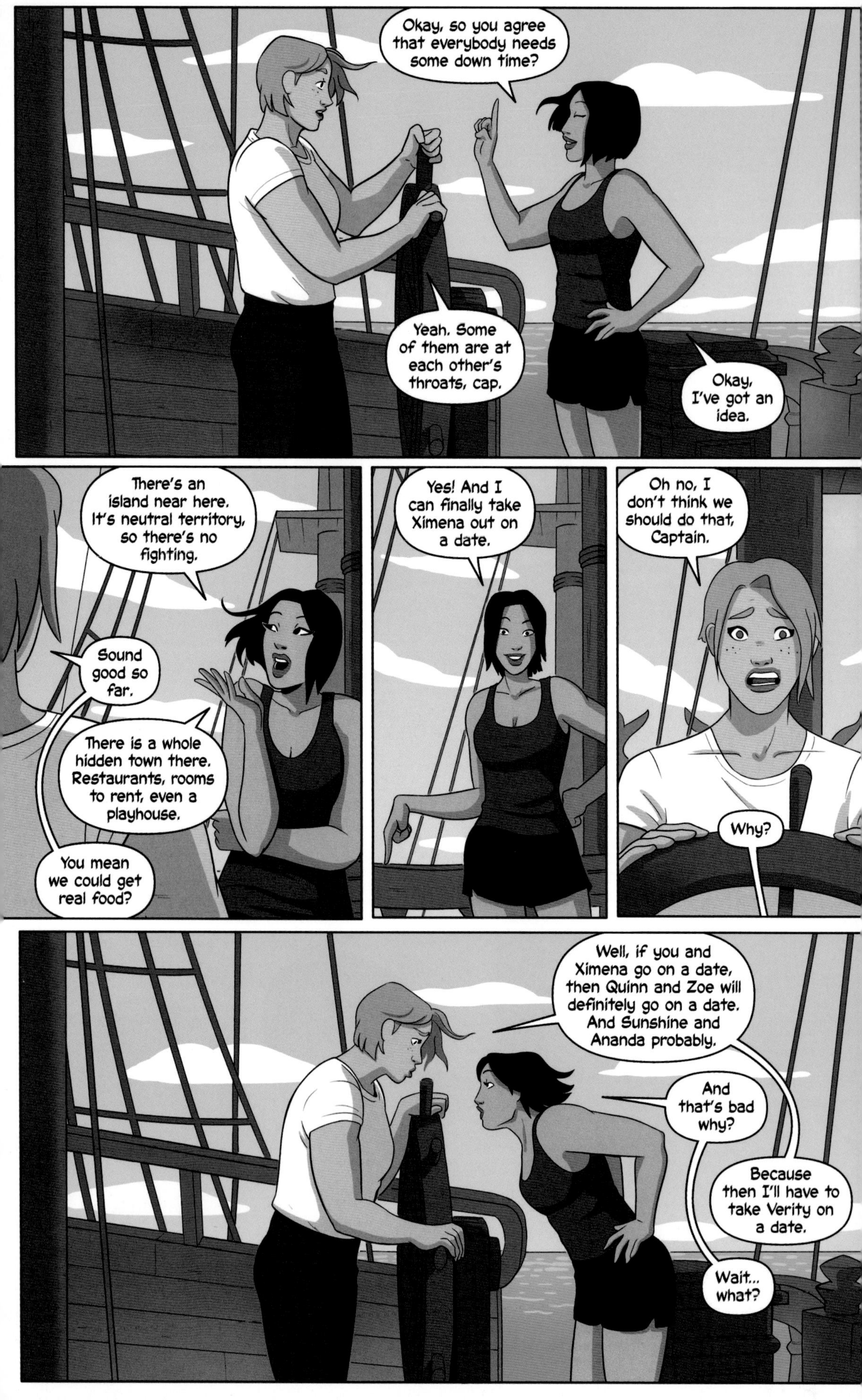
Okay, so you agree that everybody needs some down time?
Yeah. Some of them are at each other's throats, cap.
Okay, I've got an idea.
There's an island near here. It's neutral territory, so there's no fighting.
Sound good so far.
There is a whole hidden town there. Restaurants, rooms to rent, even a playhouse.
You mean we could get real food?
Yes! And I can finally take Ximena out on a date.
Oh no, I don't think we should do that, Captain.
Why?
Well, if you and Ximena go on a date, then Quinn and Zoe will definitely go on a date. And Sunshine and Ananda probably.
And that's bad why?
Because then I'll have to take Verity on a date.
Wait... what?

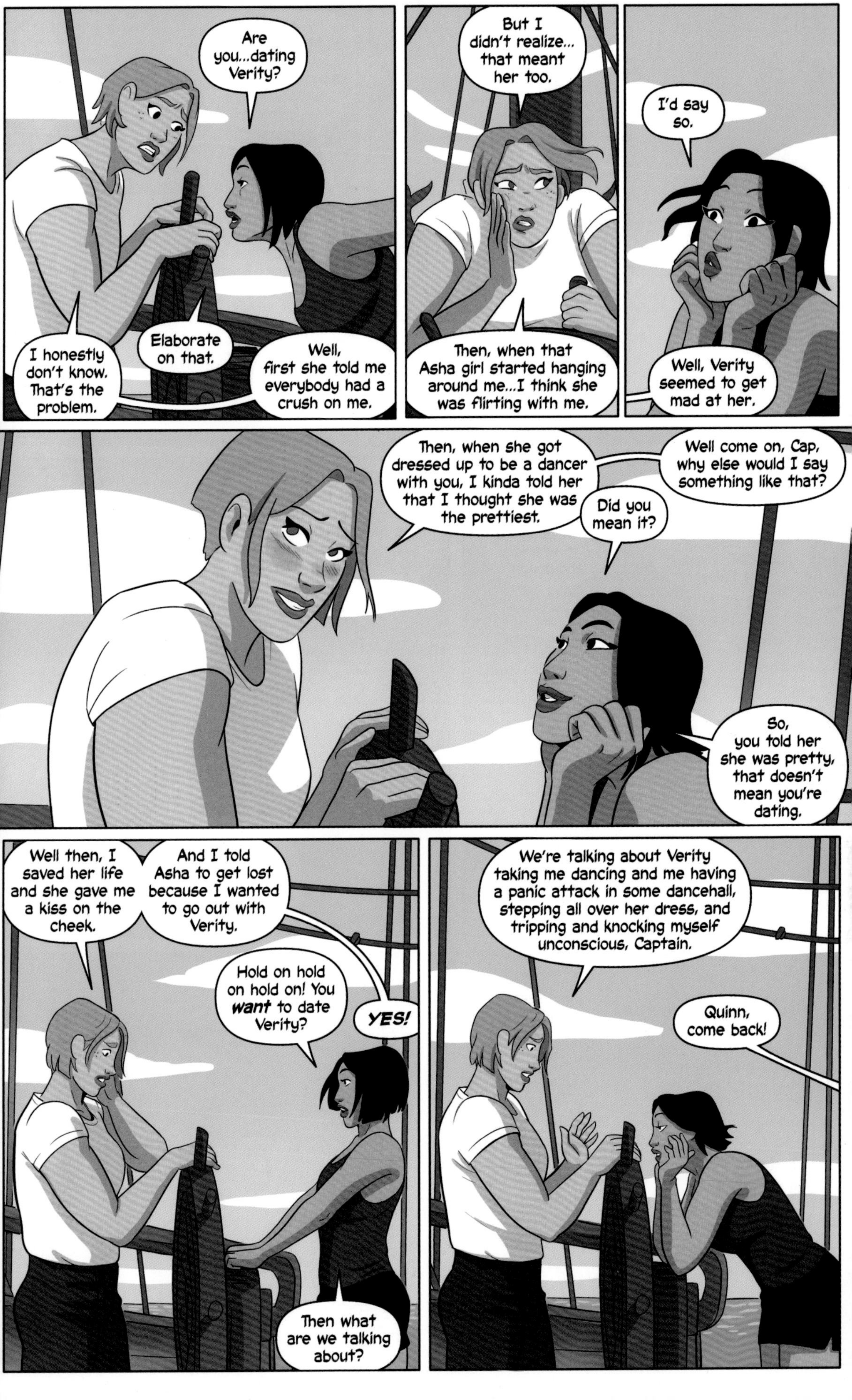
Are you...dating Verity?
I honestly don't know. That's the problem.
Elaborate on that.
Well, first she told me everybody had a crush on me.
But I didn't realize... that meant her too.
Then, when that Asha girl started hanging around me...I think she was flirting with me.
I'd say so.
Well, Verity seemed to get mad at her.
Then, when she got dressed up to be a dancer with you, I kinda told her that I thought she was the prettiest.
Did you mean it?
Well come on, Cap, why else would I say something like that?
So, you told her she was pretty, that doesn't mean you're dating.
Well then, I saved her life and she gave me a kiss on the cheek.
And I told Asha to get lost because I wanted to go out with Verity.
Hold on hold on hold on! You *want* to date Verity?
YES!
Then what are we talking about?
We're talking about Verity taking me dancing and me having a panic attack in some dancehall, stepping all over her dress, and tripping and knocking myself unconscious, Captain.
Quinn, come back!

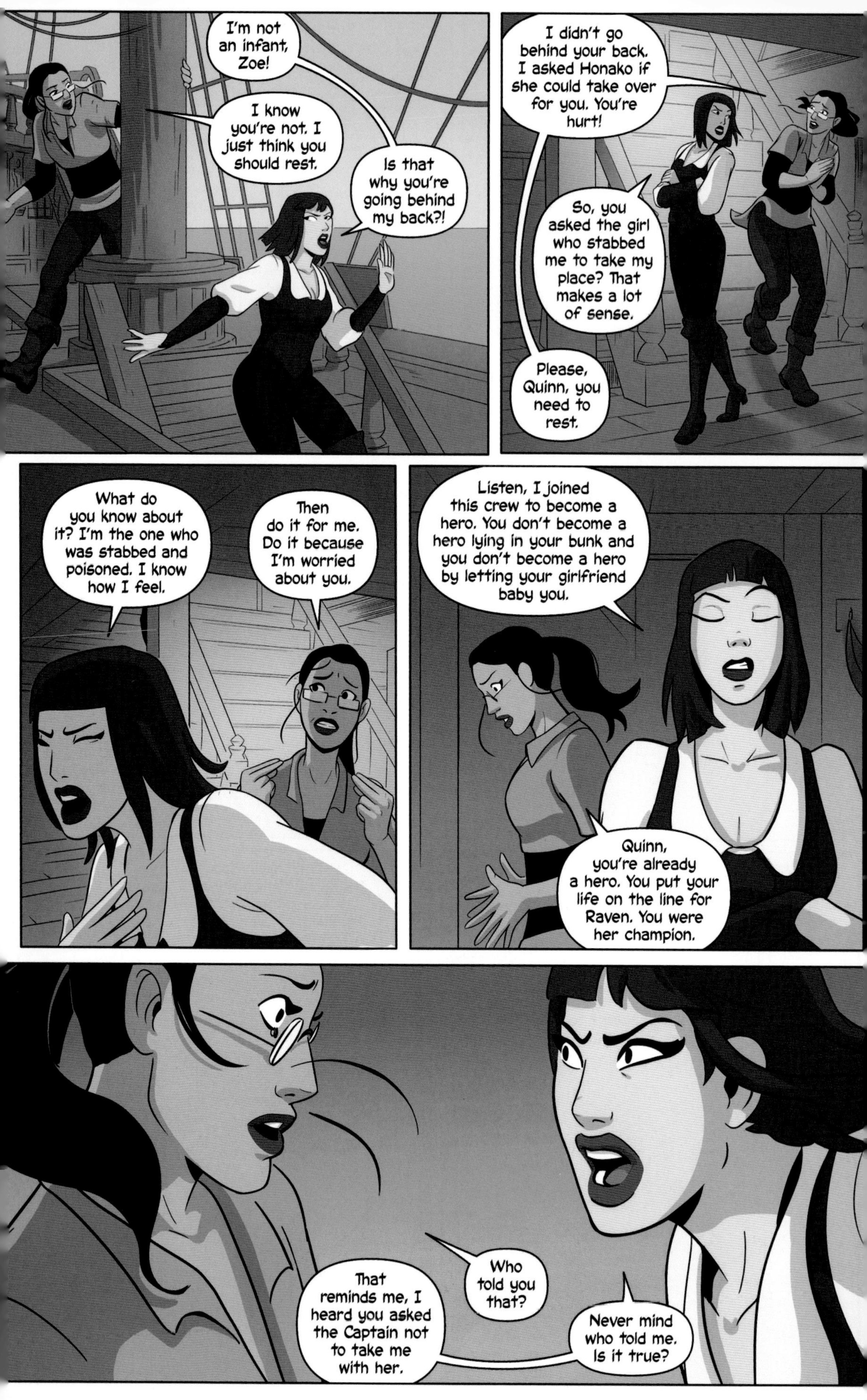
I'm not an infant, Zoe!
I know you're not. I just think you should rest.
Is that why you're going behind my back?!
I didn't go behind your back. I asked Honako if she could take over for you. You're hurt!
So, you asked the girl who stabbed me to take my place? That makes a lot of sense.
Please, Quinn, you need to rest.
What do you know about it? I'm the one who was stabbed and poisoned. I know how I feel.
Then do it for me. Do it because I'm worried about you.
Listen, I joined this crew to become a hero. You don't become a hero lying in your bunk and you don't become a hero by letting your girlfriend baby you.
Quinn, you're already a hero. You put your life on the line for Raven. You were her champion.
That reminds me, I heard you asked the Captain not to take me with her.
Who told you that?
Never mind who told me. Is it true?

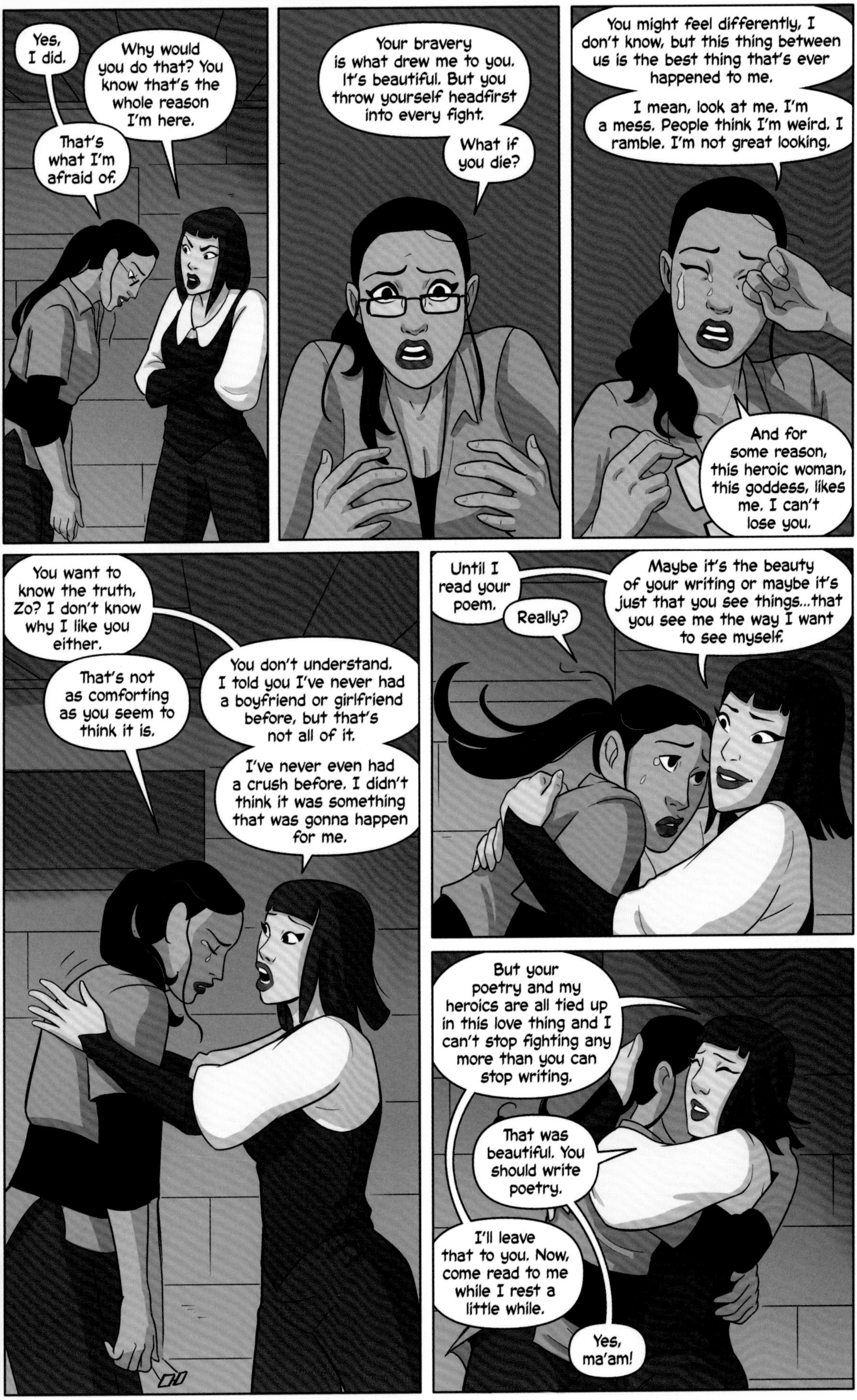
Yes, I did.
Why would you do that? You know that's the whole reason I'm here.
That's what I'm afraid of.
Your bravery is what drew me to you. It's beautiful. But you throw yourself headfirst into every fight.
What if you die?
You might feel differently, I don't know, but this thing between us is the best thing that's ever happened to me.
I mean, look at me. I'm a mess. People think I'm weird. I ramble. I'm not great looking.
And for some reason, this heroic woman, this goddess, likes me. I can't lose you.
You want to know the truth, Zo? I don't know why I like you either.
That's not as comforting as you seem to think it is.
You don't understand. I told you I've never had a boyfriend or girlfriend before, but that's not all of it.
I've never even had a crush before. I didn't think it was something that was gonna happen for me.
Until I read your poem.
Really?
Maybe it's the beauty of your writing or maybe it's just that you see things...that you see me the way I want to see myself.
But your poetry and my heroics are all tied up in this love thing and I can't stop fighting any more than you can stop writing.
That was beautiful. You should write poetry.
I'll leave that to you. Now, come read to me while I rest a little while.
Yes, ma'am!

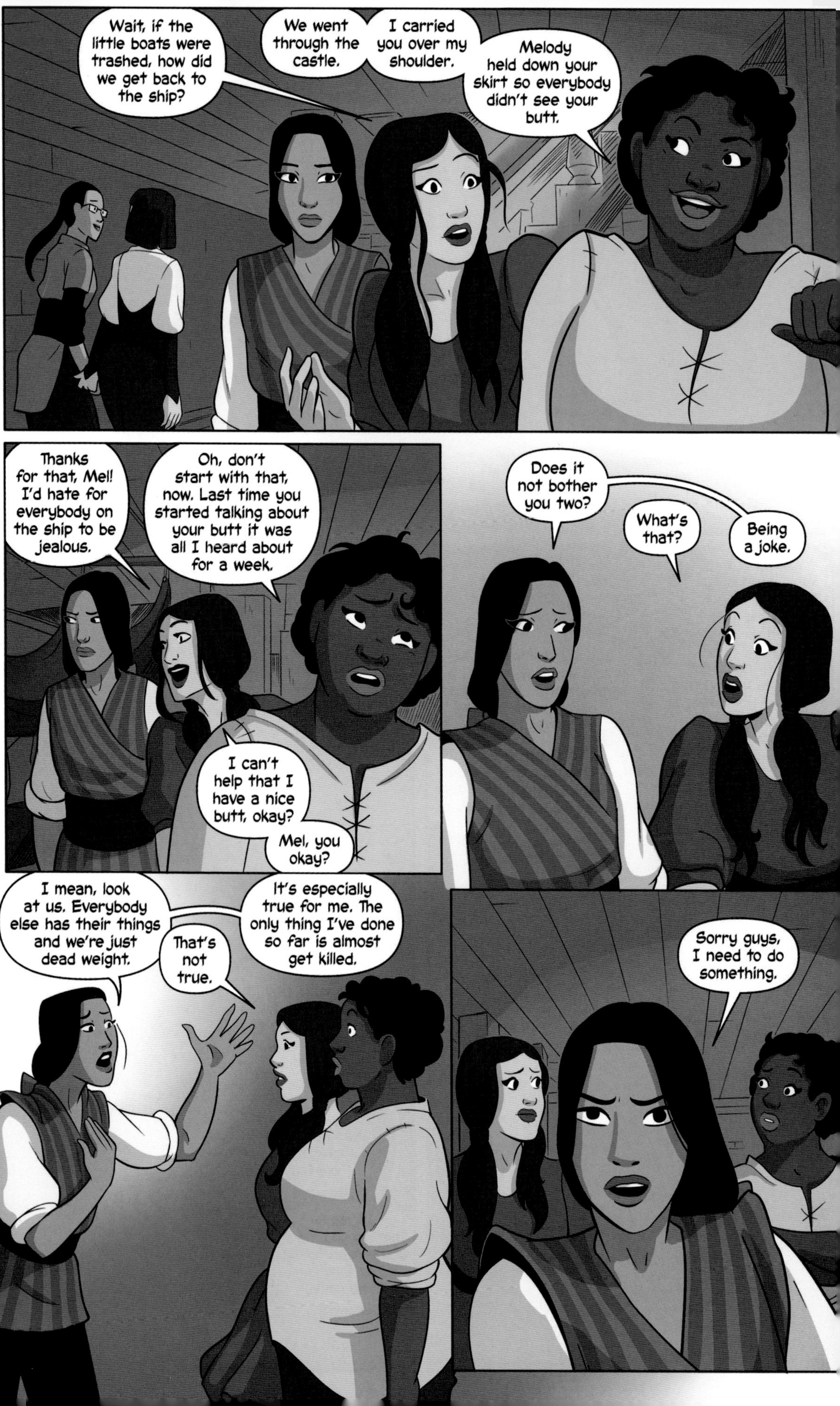
Wait, if the little boats were trashed, how did we get back to the ship?
We went through the castle.
I carried you over my shoulder.
Melody held down your skirt so everybody didn't see your butt.
Thanks for that, Mel! I'd hate for everybody on the ship to be jealous.
Oh, don't start with that, now. Last time you started talking about your butt it was all I heard about for a week.
I can't help that I have a nice butt, okay?
Mel, you okay?
Does it not bother you two?
What's that?
Being a joke.
I mean, look at us. Everybody else has their things and we're just dead weight.
That's not true.
It's especially true for me. The only thing I've done so far is almost get killed.
Sorry guys, I need to do something.

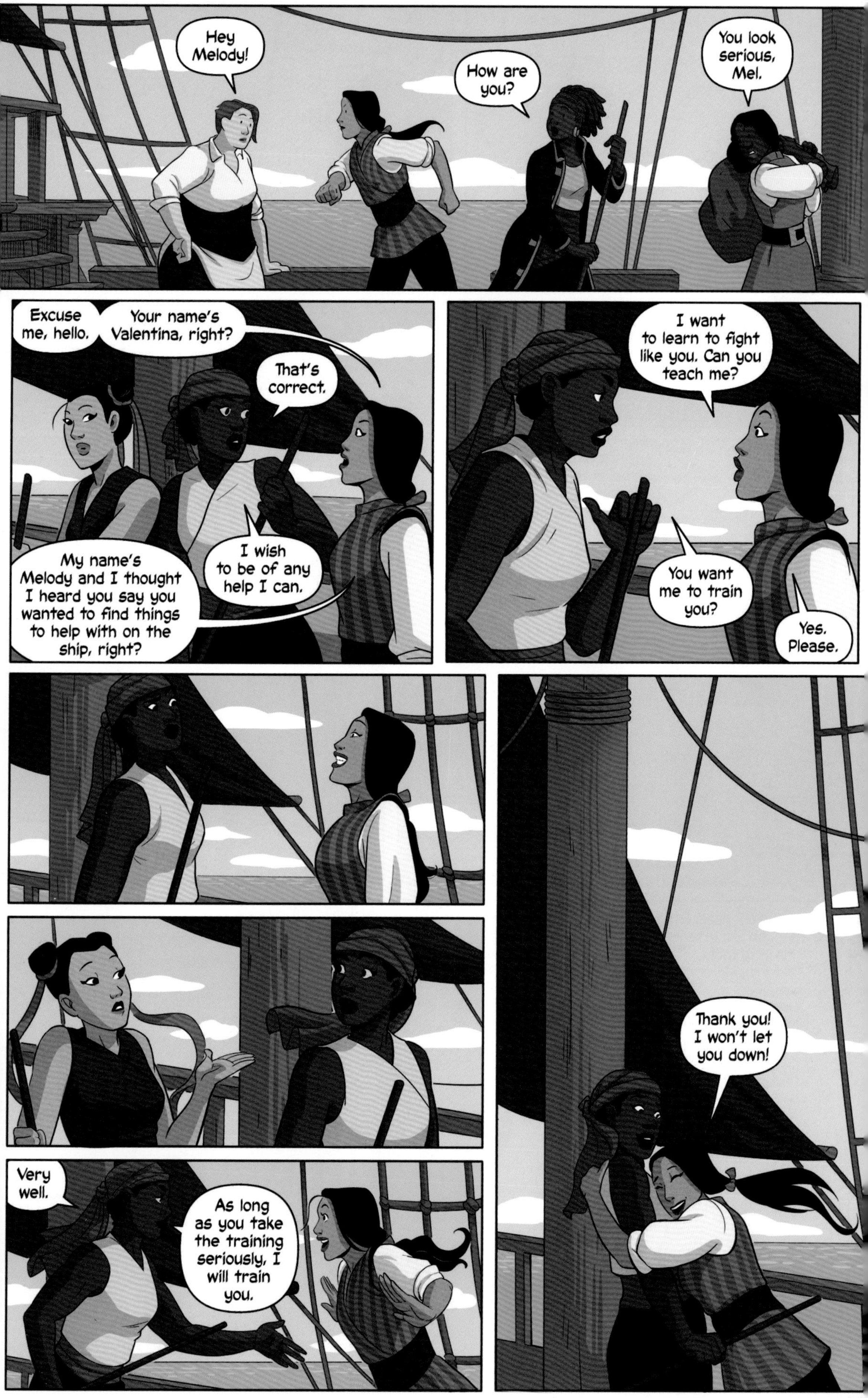
Hey Melody!
How are you?
You look serious, Mel.
Excuse me, hello.
Your name's Valentina, right?
That's correct.
My name's Melody and I thought I heard you say you wanted to find things to help with on the ship, right?
I wish to be of any help I can.
I want to learn to fight like you. Can you teach me?
You want me to train you?
Yes. Please.
Very well.
As long as you take the training seriously, I will train you.
Thank you! I won't let you down!

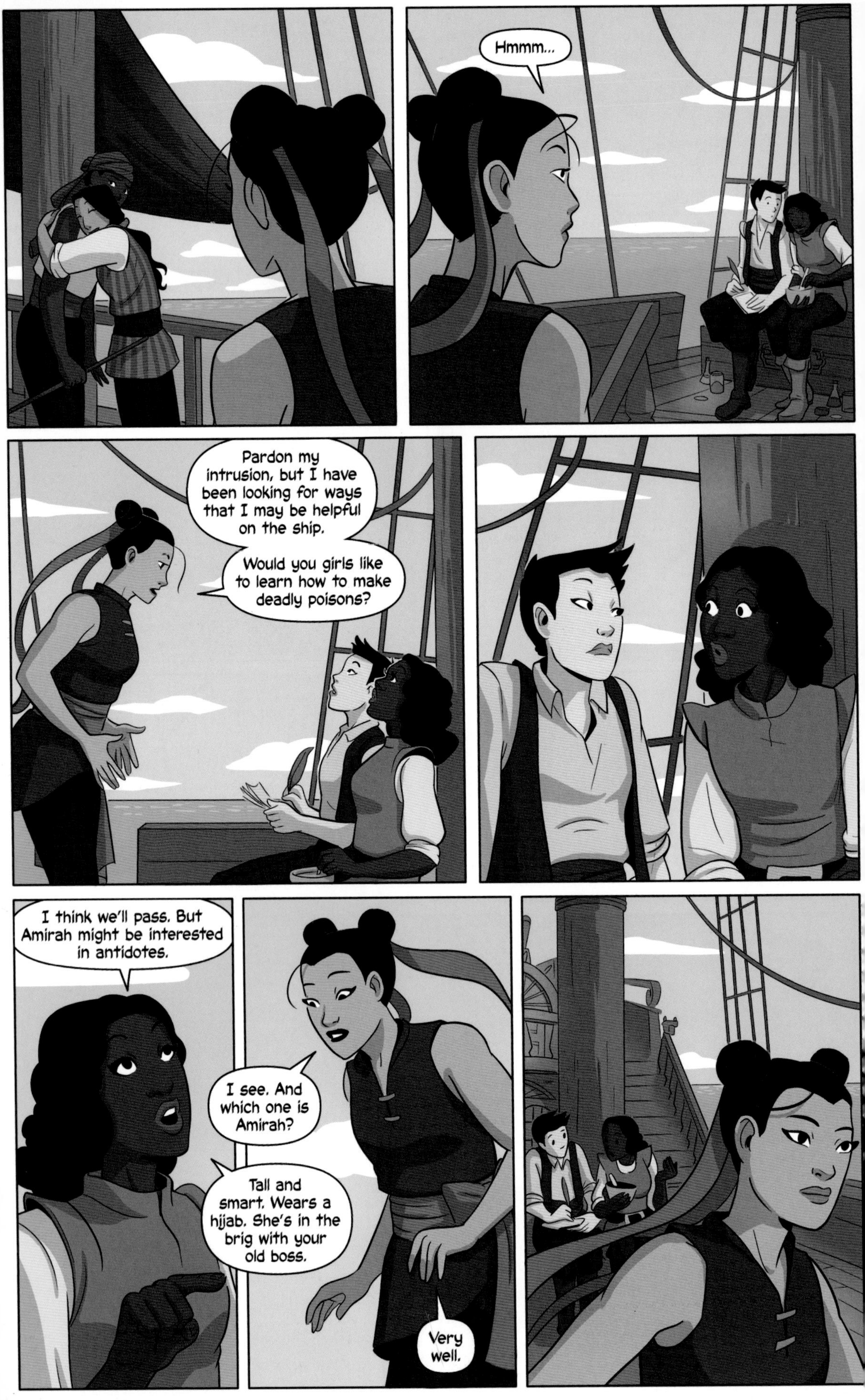
Hmmm...
Pardon my intrusion, but I have been looking for ways that I may be helpful on the ship.
Would you girls like to learn how to make deadly poisons?
I think we'll pass. But Amirah might be interested in antidotes.
I see. And which one is Amirah?
Tall and smart. Wears a hijab. She's in the brig with your old boss.
Very well.

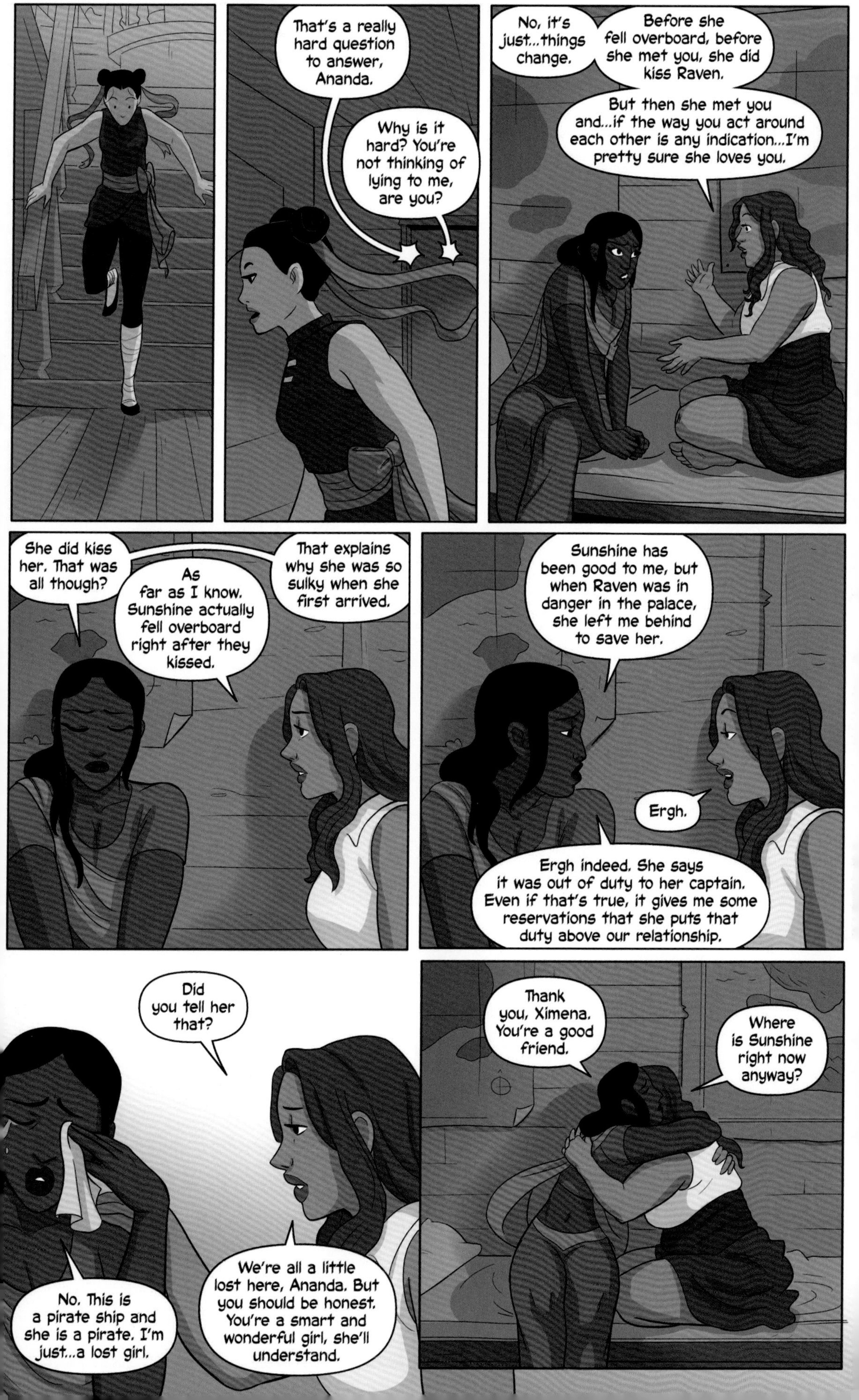
That's a really hard question to answer, Ananda.
Why is it hard? You're not thinking of lying to me, are you?
No, it's just...things change.
Before she fell overboard, before she met you, she did kiss Raven.
But then she met you and...if the way you act around each other is any indication...I'm pretty sure she loves you.
She did kiss her. That was all though?
As far as I know. Sunshine actually fell overboard right after they kissed.
That explains why she was so sulky when she first arrived.
Sunshine has been good to me, but when Raven was in danger in the palace, she left me behind to save her.
Ergh.
Ergh indeed. She says it was out of duty to her captain. Even if that's true, it gives me some reservations that she puts that duty above our relationship.
Did you tell her that?
No. This is a pirate ship and she is a pirate. I'm just...a lost girl.
We're all a little lost here, Ananda. But you should be honest. You're a smart and wonderful girl, she'll understand.
Thank you, Ximena. You're a good friend.
Where is Sunshine right now anyway?

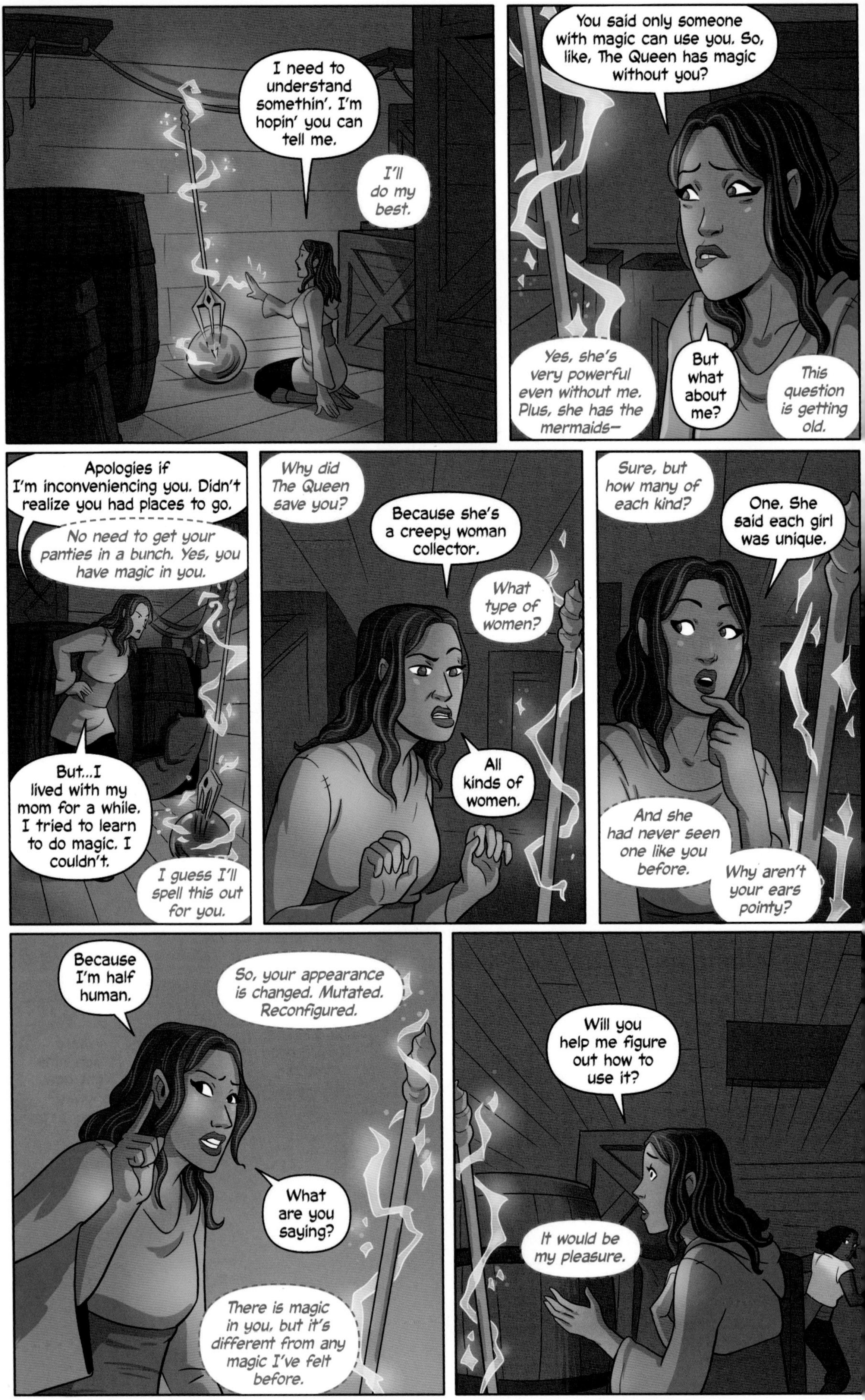
I need to understand somethin'. I'm hopin' you can tell me.
I'll do my best.
You said only someone with magic can use you. So, like, The Queen has magic without you?
Yes, she's very powerful even without me. Plus, she has the mermaids—
But what about me?
This question is getting old.
Apologies if I'm inconveniencing you. Didn't realize you had places to go.
No need to get your panties in a bunch. Yes, you have magic in you.
But...I lived with my mom for a while. I tried to learn to do magic. I couldn't.
I guess I'll spell this out for you.
Why did The Queen save you?
Because she's a creepy woman collector.
What type of women?
All kinds of women.
Sure, but how many of each kind?
One. She said each girl was unique.
And she had never seen one like you before.
Why aren't your ears pointy?
Because I'm half human.
So, your appearance is changed. Mutated. Reconfigured.
What are you saying?
There is magic in you, but it's different from any magic I've felt before.
Will you help me figure out how to use it?
It would be my pleasure.

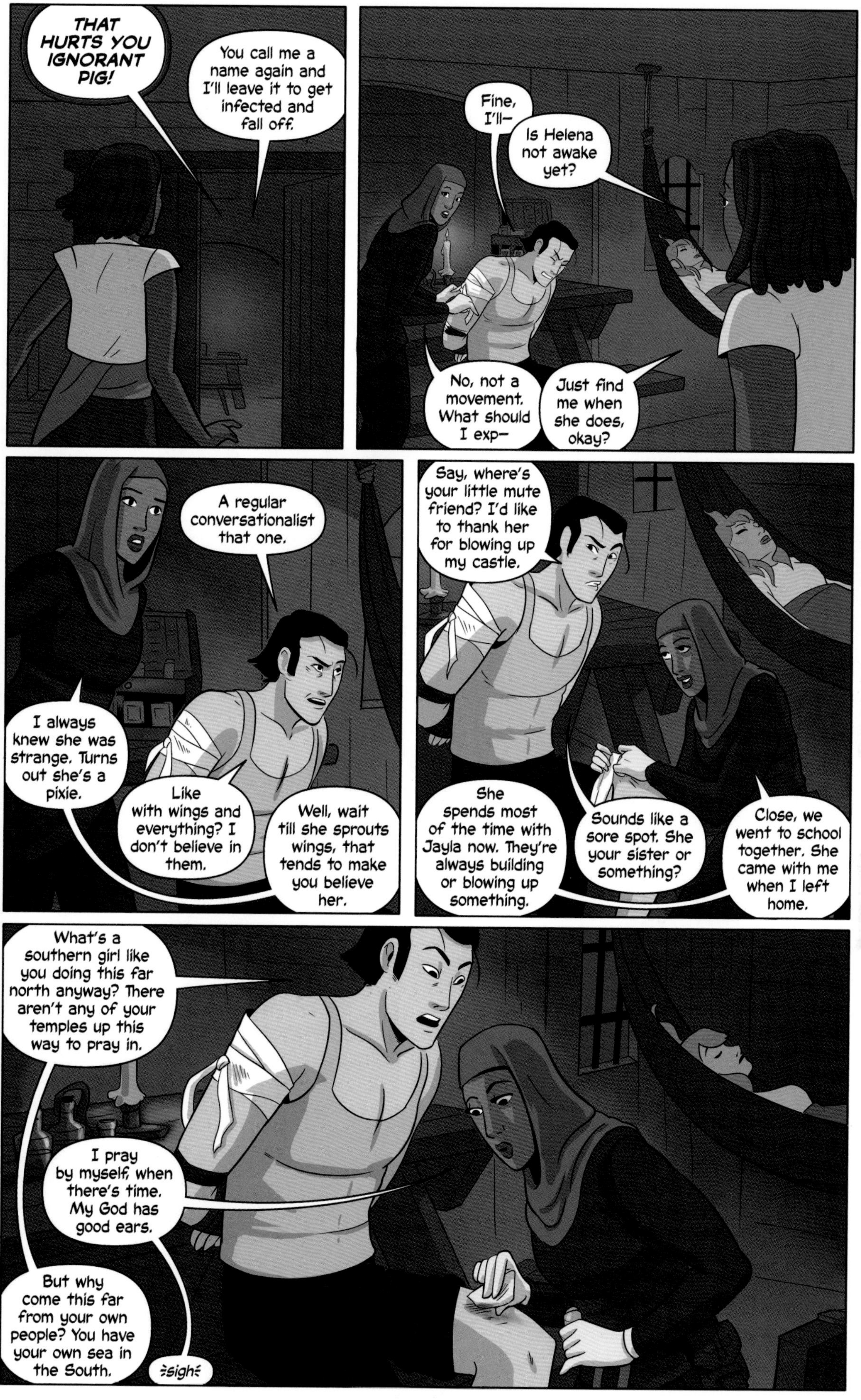
THAT HURTS YOU IGNORANT PIG!
You call me a name again and I'll leave it to get infected and fall off.
Fine, I'll—
Is Helena not awake yet?
No, not a movement. What should I exp—
Just find me when she does, okay?
A regular conversationalist that one.
I always knew she was strange. Turns out she's a pixie.
Like with wings and everything? I don't believe in them.
Well, wait till she sprouts wings, that tends to make you believe her.
Say, where's your little mute friend? I'd like to thank her for blowing up my castle.
She spends most of the time with Jayla now. They're always building or blowing up something.
Sounds like a sore spot. She your sister or something?
Close, we went to school together. She came with me when I left home.
What's a southern girl like you doing this far north anyway? There aren't any of your temples up this way to pray in.
I pray by myself, when there's time. My God has good ears.
But why come this far from your own people? You have your own sea in the South.
sigh

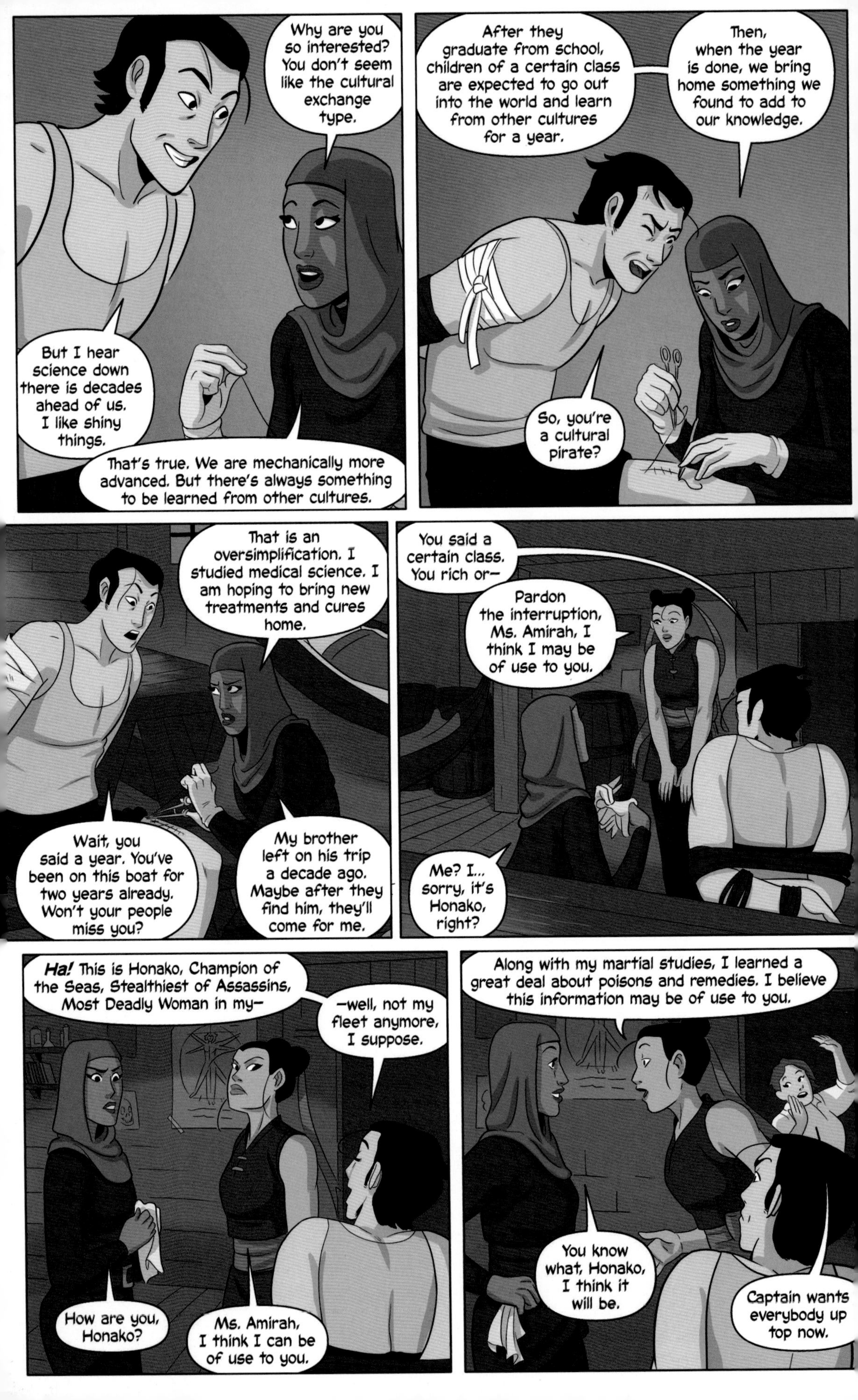
Why are you so interested? You don't seem like the cultural exchange type.
But I hear science down there is decades ahead of us. I like shiny things.
That's true. We are mechanically more advanced. But there's always something to be learned from other cultures.
After they graduate from school, children of a certain class are expected to go out into the world and learn from other cultures for a year.
Then, when the year is done, we bring home something we found to add to our knowledge.
So, you're a cultural pirate?
That is an oversimplification. I studied medical science. I am hoping to bring new treatments and cures home.
Wait, you said a year. You've been on this boat for two years already. Won't your people miss you?
My brother left on his trip a decade ago. Maybe after they find him, they'll come for me.
You said a certain class. You rich or—
Pardon the interruption, Ms. Amirah, I think I may be of use to you.
Me? I... sorry, it's Honako, right?
Ha! This is Honako, Champion of the Seas, Stealthiest of Assassins, Most Deadly Woman in my—
—well, not my fleet anymore, I suppose.
How are you, Honako?
Ms. Amirah, I think I can be of use to you.
Along with my martial studies, I learned a great deal about poisons and remedies. I believe this information may be of use to you.
You know what, Honako, I think it will be.
Captain wants everybody up top now.

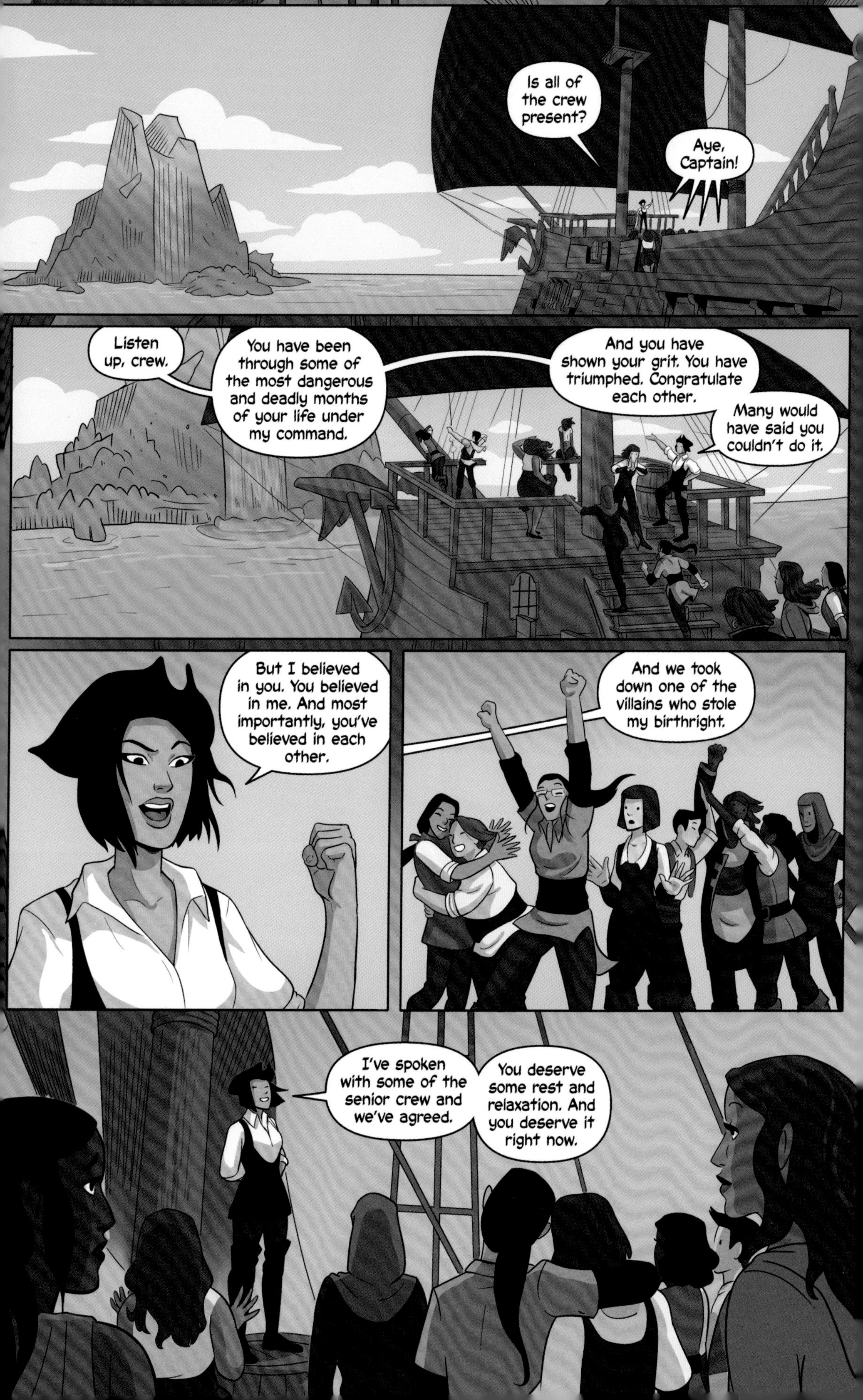
Is all of the crew present?
Aye, Captain!
Listen up, crew.
You have been through some of the most dangerous and deadly months of your life under my command.
And you have shown your grit. You have triumphed. Congratulate each other.
Many would have said you couldn't do it.
But I believed in you. You believed in me. And most importantly, you've believed in each other.
And we took down one of the villains who stole my birthright.
I've spoken with some of the senior crew and we've agreed.
You deserve some rest and relaxation. And you deserve it right now.

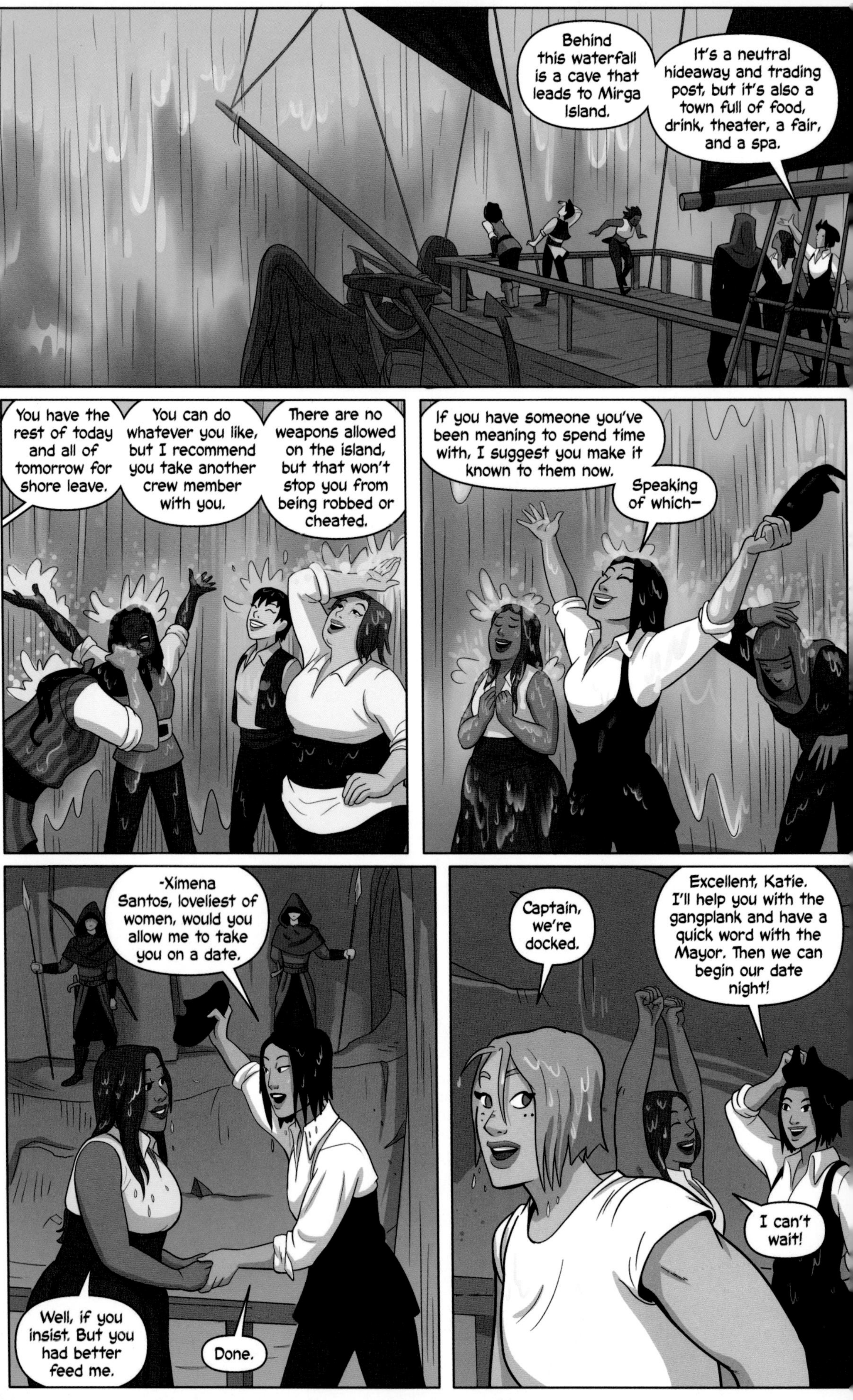
Behind this waterfall is a cave that leads to Mirga Island.
It's a neutral hideaway and trading post, but it's also a town full of food, drink, theater, a fair, and a spa.
You have the rest of today and all of tomorrow for shore leave.
You can do whatever you like, but I recommend you take another crew member with you.
There are no weapons allowed on the island, but that won't stop you from being robbed or cheated.
If you have someone you've been meaning to spend time with, I suggest you make it known to them now.
Speaking of which—
-Ximena Santos, loveliest of women, would you allow me to take you on a date.
Well, if you insist. But you had better feed me.
Done.
Captain, we're docked.
Excellent, Katie. I'll help you with the gangplank and have a quick word with the Mayor. Then we can begin our date night!
I can't wait!

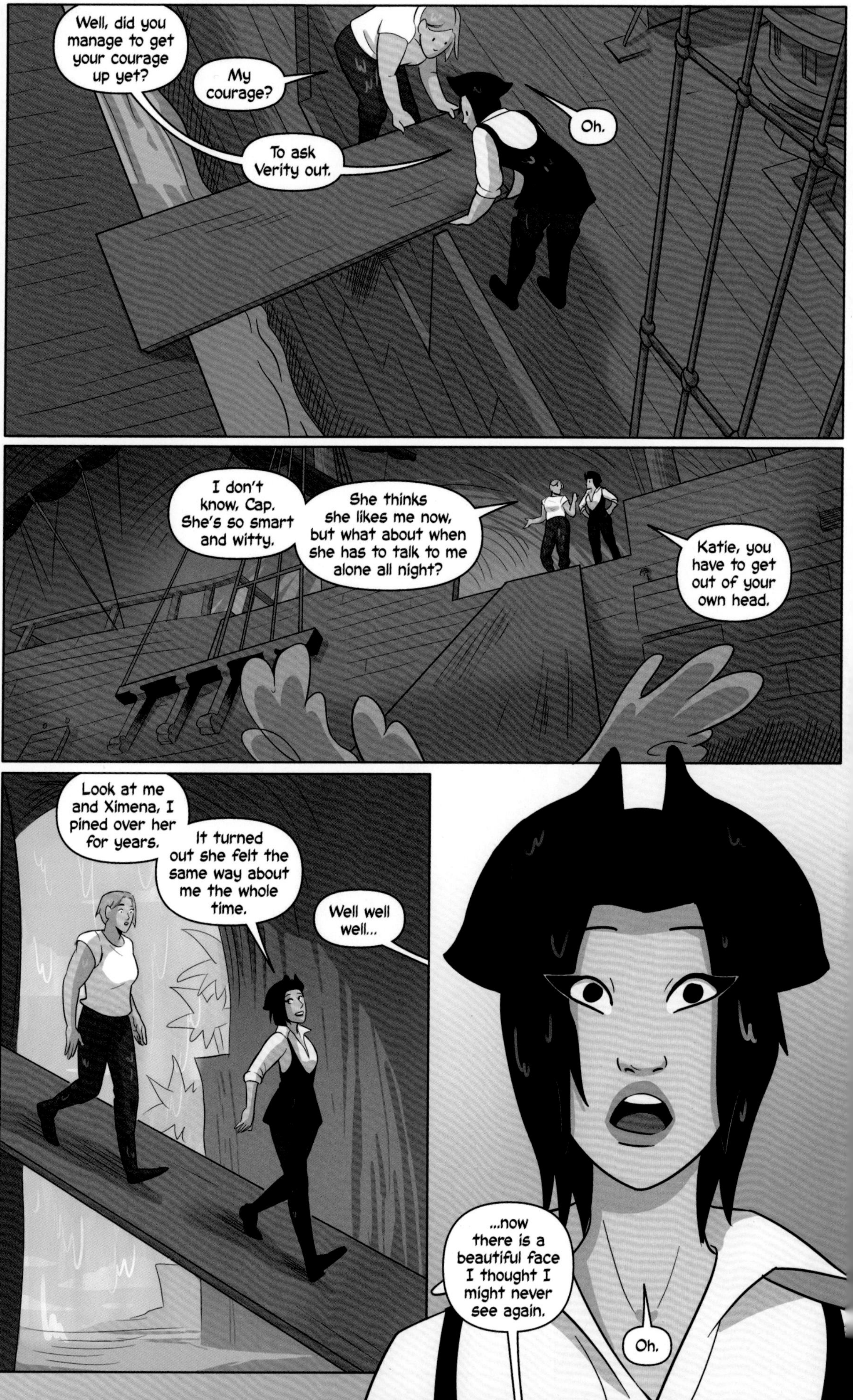
Well, did you manage to get your courage up yet?
My courage?
To ask Verity out.
Oh.
I don't know, Cap. She's so smart and witty.
She thinks she likes me now, but what about when she has to talk to me alone all night?
Katie, you have to get out of your own head.
Look at me and Ximena, I pined over her for years.
It turned out she felt the same way about me the whole time.
Well well well...
...now there is a beautiful face I thought I might never see again.
Oh.

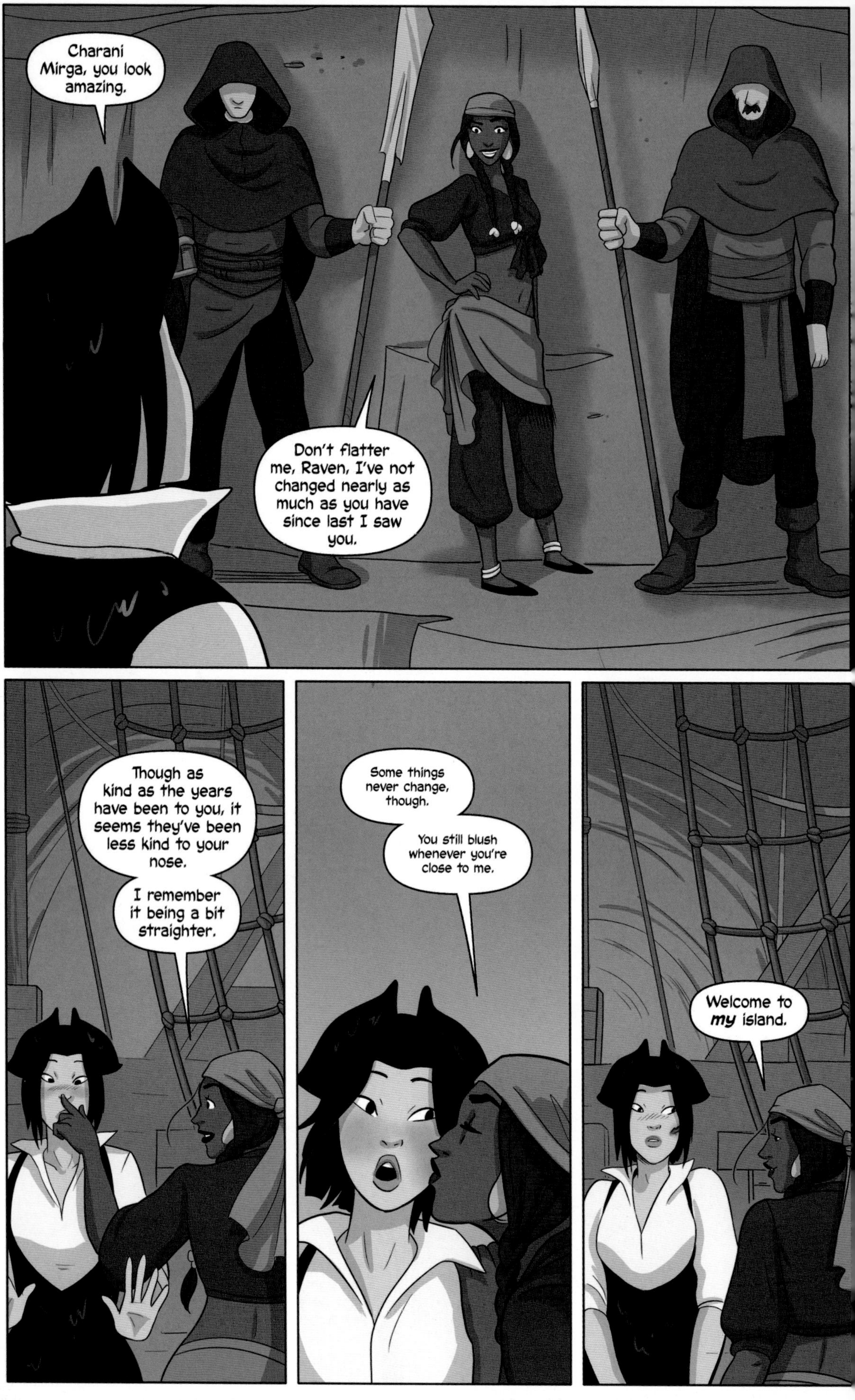
Charani Mirga, you look amazing.
Don't flatter me, Raven, I've not changed nearly as much as you have since last I saw you.
Though as kind as the years have been to you, it seems they've been less kind to your nose.
I remember it being a bit straighter.
Some things never change, though.
You still blush whenever you're close to me.
Welcome to *my* island.

Princeless

Raven: The Pirate Princess

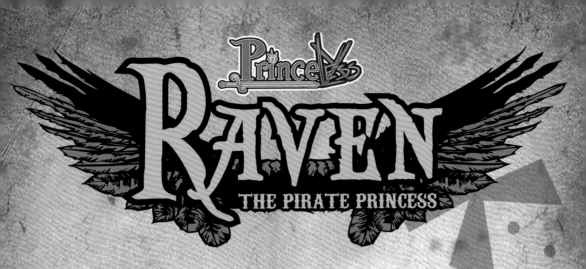

Year Three: Monsters of the Deep

Chapter Two: Date Night Part 2

Written By: Jeremy Whitley

Pencils By: Xenia Pamfil

Inks By: Christine Hipp

Colors By: Lexillo

Lettered By: Justin Birch

Edited By: Nicole D'Andria

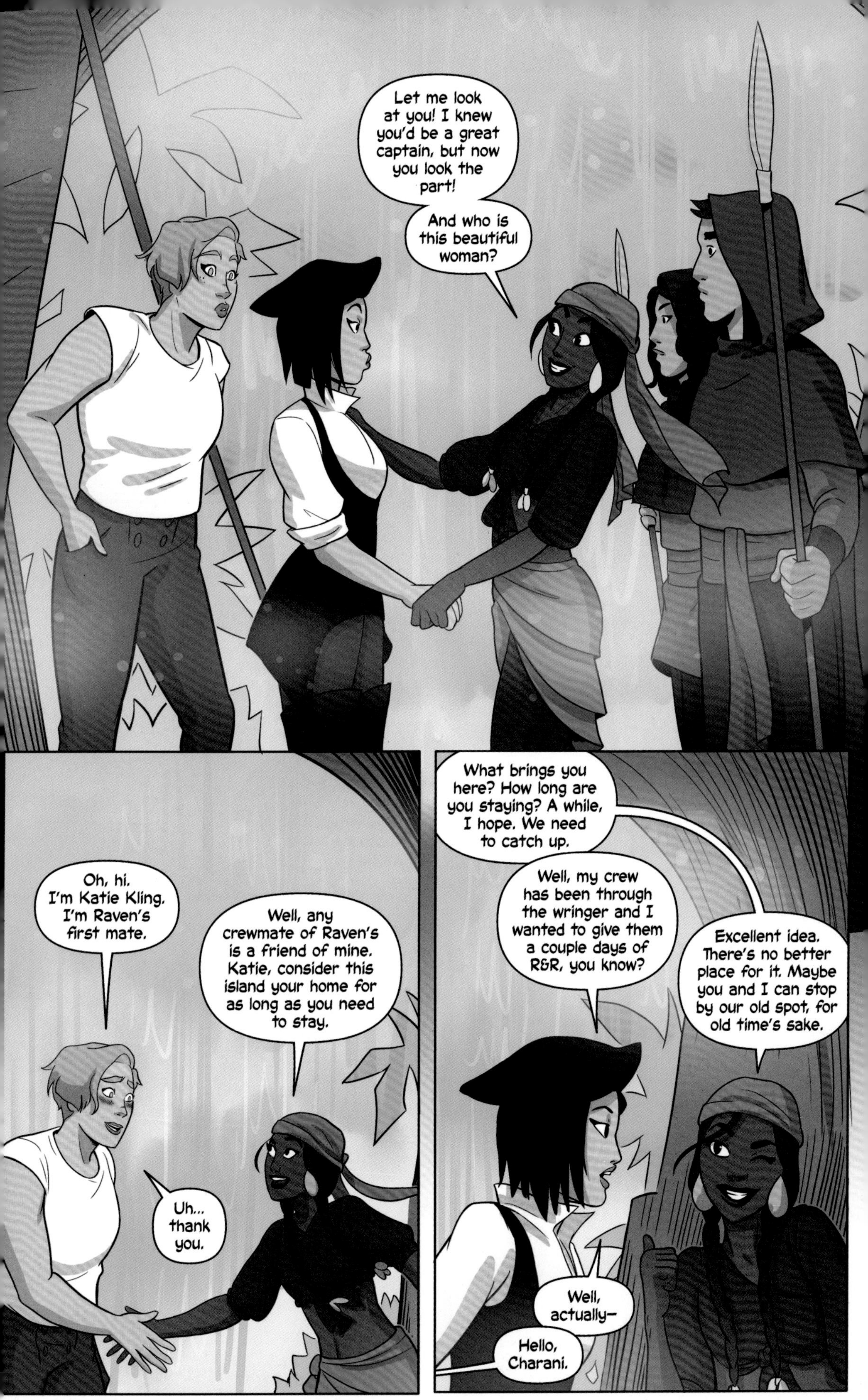
Let me look at you! I knew you'd be a great captain, but now you look the part!
And who is this beautiful woman?
Oh, hi. I'm Katie Kling. I'm Raven's first mate.
Well, any crewmate of Raven's is a friend of mine. Katie, consider this island your home for as long as you need to stay.
Uh... thank you.
What brings you here? How long are you staying? A while, I hope. We need to catch up.
Well, my crew has been through the wringer and I wanted to give them a couple days of R&R, you know?
Excellent idea. There's no better place for it. Maybe you and I can stop by our old spot, for old time's sake.
Well, actually—
Hello, Charani.

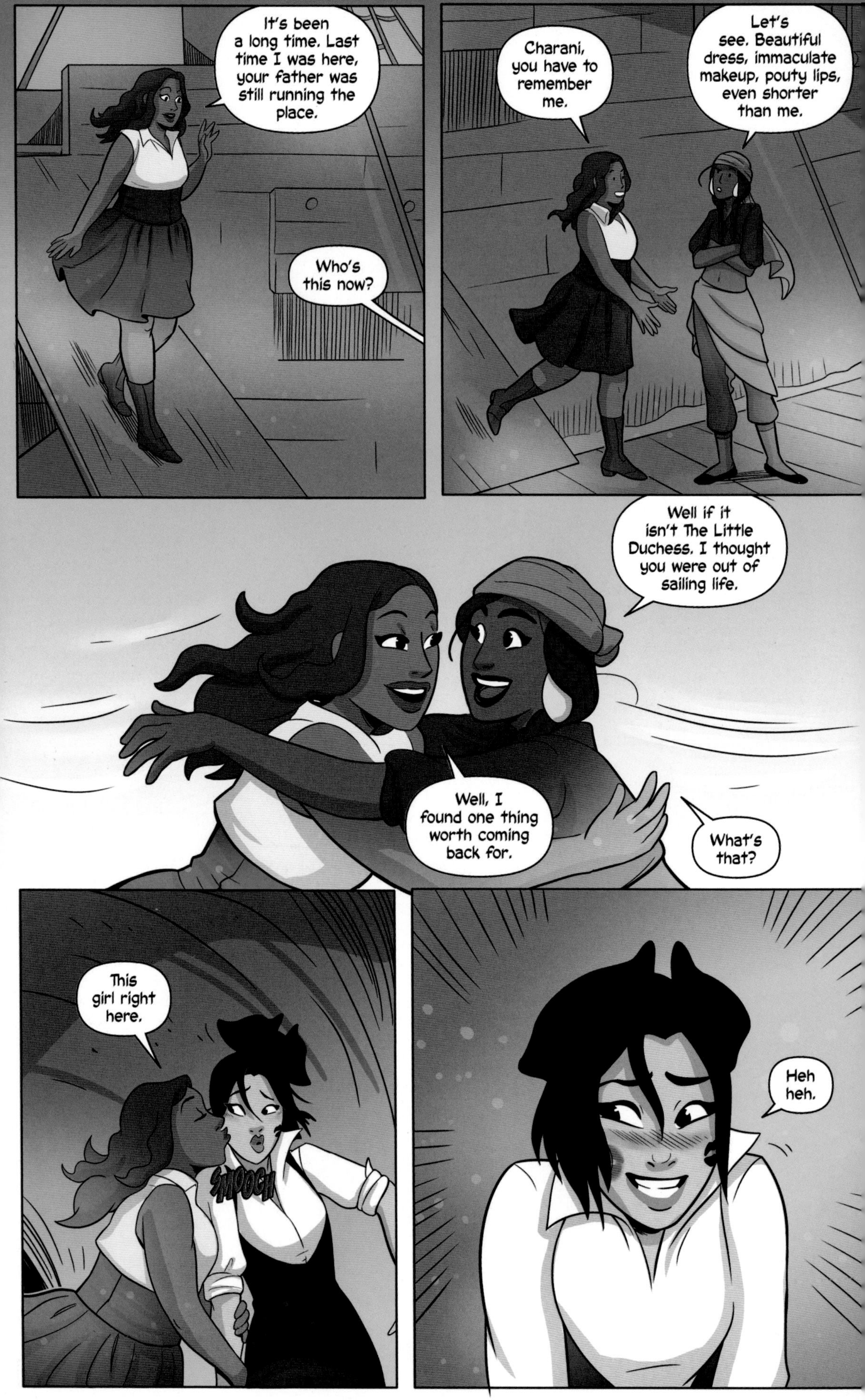
It's been a long time. Last time I was here, your father was still running the place.
Who's this now?
Charani, you have to remember me.
Let's see. Beautiful dress, immaculate makeup, pouty lips, even shorter than me.
Well if it isn't The Little Duchess. I thought you were out of sailing life.
Well, I found one thing worth coming back for.
What's that?
This girl right here.
SMOOCH
Heh heh.

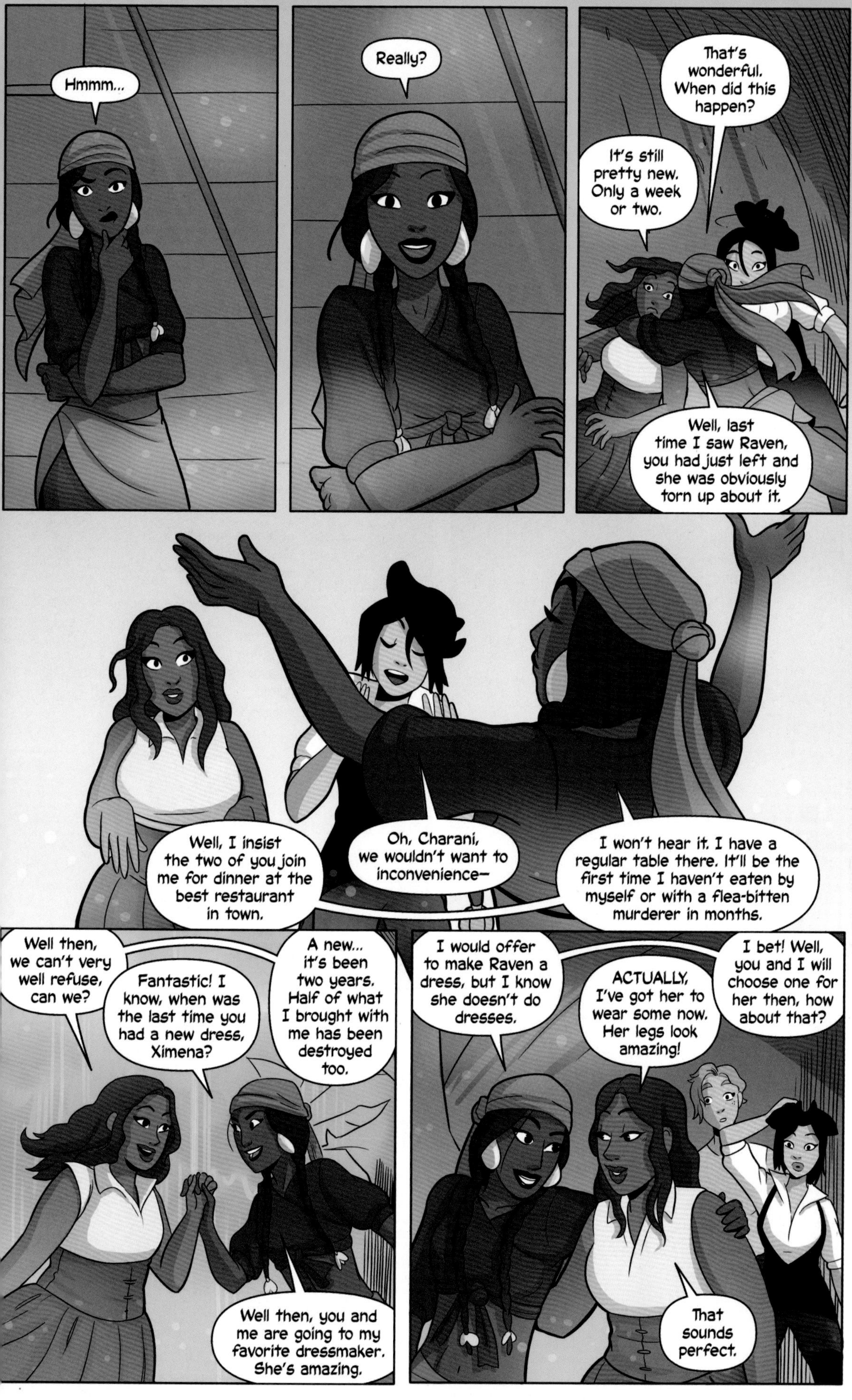
Hmmm...
Really?
That's wonderful. When did this happen?
It's still pretty new. Only a week or two.
Well, last time I saw Raven, you had just left and she was obviously torn up about it.
Well, I insist the two of you join me for dinner at the best restaurant in town.
Oh, Charani, we wouldn't want to inconvenience—
I won't hear it. I have a regular table there. It'll be the first time I haven't eaten by myself or with a flea-bitten murderer in months.
Well then, we can't very well refuse, can we?
Fantastic! I know, when was the last time you had a new dress, Ximena?
A new... it's been two years. Half of what I brought with me has been destroyed too.
Well then, you and me are going to my favorite dressmaker. She's amazing.
I would offer to make Raven a dress, but I know she doesn't do dresses.
ACTUALLY, I've got her to wear some now. Her legs look amazing!
I bet! Well, you and I will choose one for her then, how about that?
That sounds perfect.

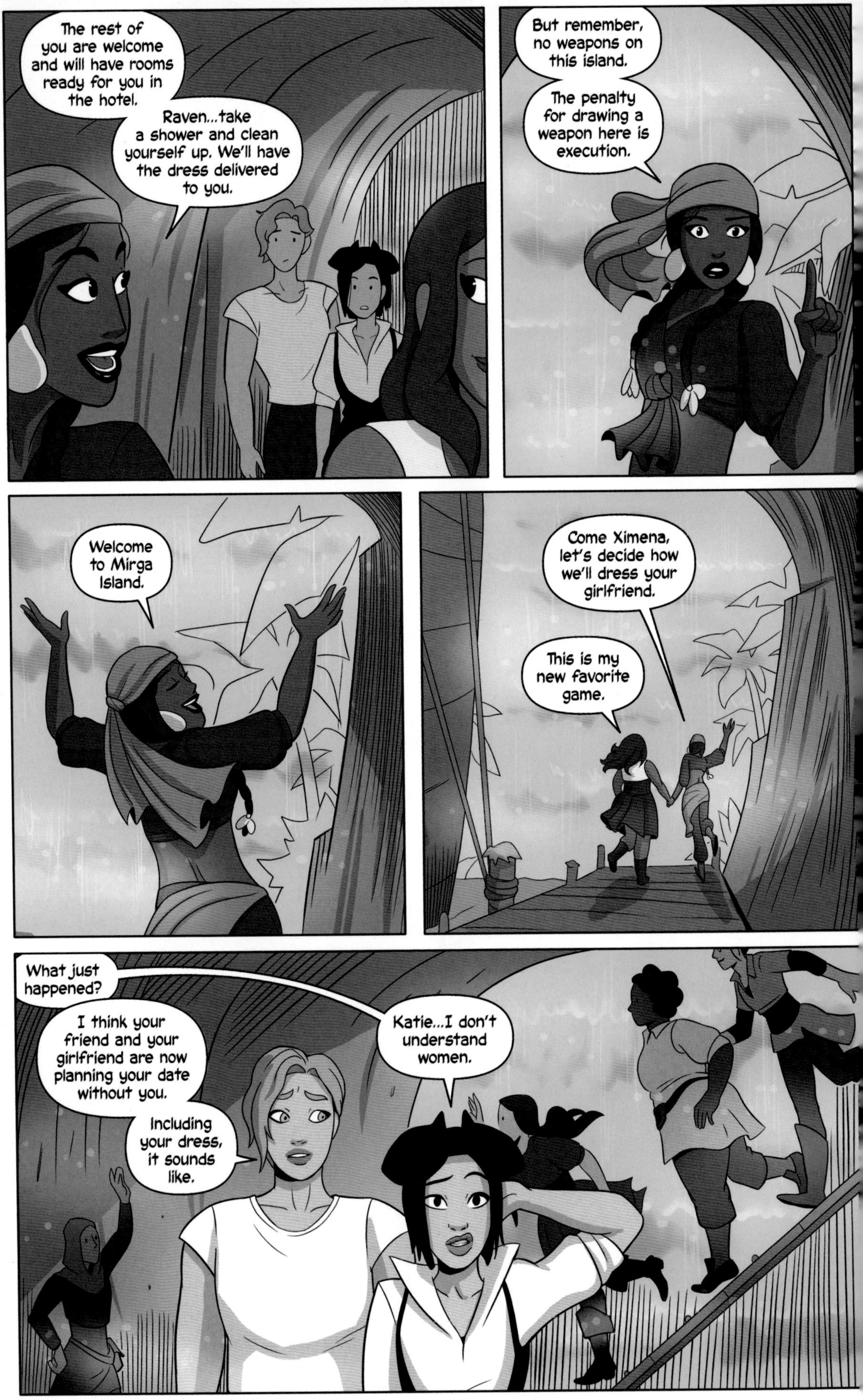
The rest of you are welcome and will have rooms ready for you in the hotel.
Raven...take a shower and clean yourself up. We'll have the dress delivered to you.
But remember, no weapons on this island.
The penalty for drawing a weapon here is execution.
Welcome to Mirga Island.
Come Ximena, let's decide how we'll dress your girlfriend.
This is my new favorite game.
What just happened?
I think your friend and your girlfriend are now planning your date without you.
Including your dress, it sounds like.
Katie...I don't understand women.

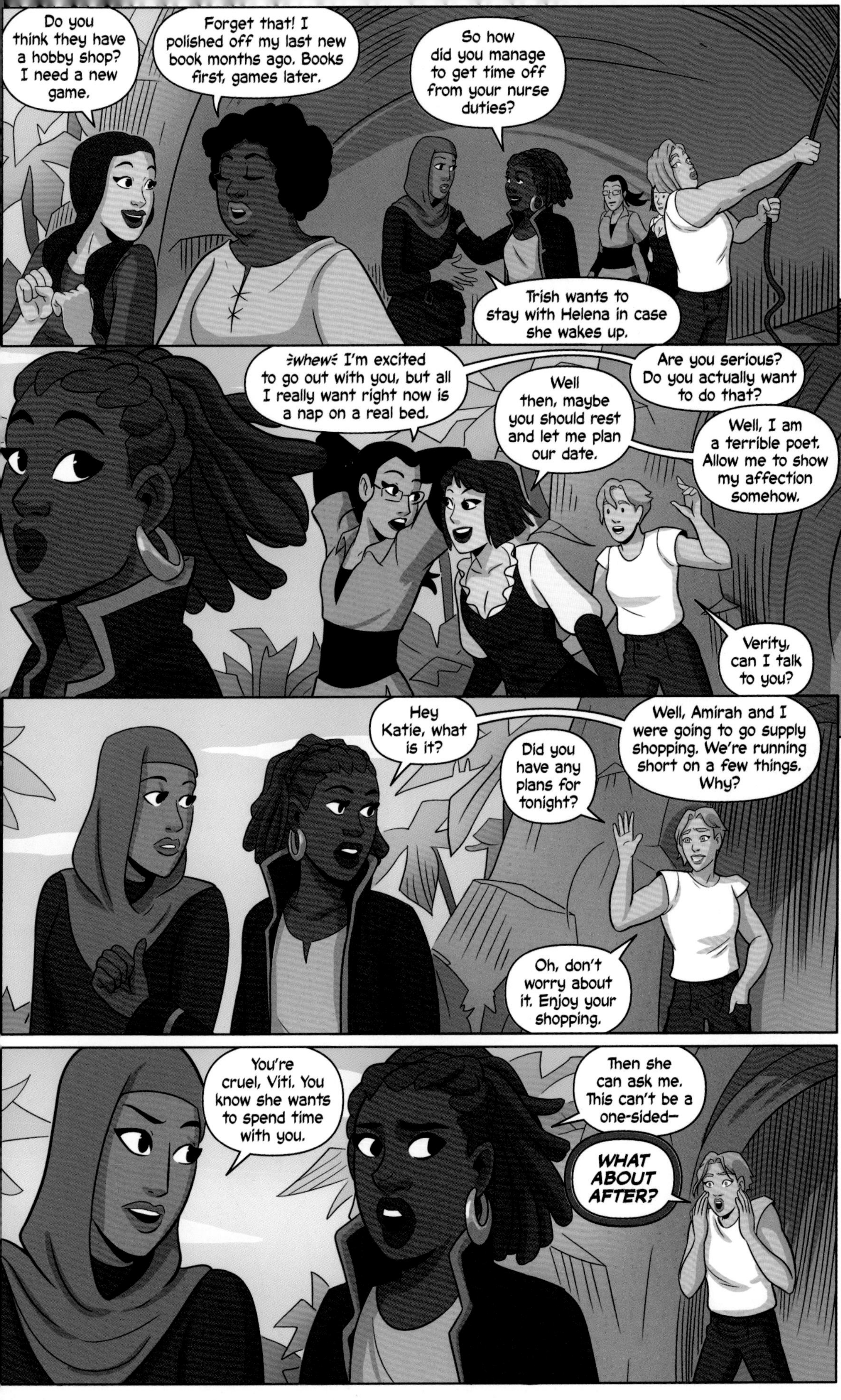
Do you think they have a hobby shop? I need a new game.
Forget that! I polished off my last new book months ago. Books first, games later.
So how did you manage to get time off from your nurse duties?
Trish wants to stay with Helena in case she wakes up.
≈whew≈ I'm excited to go out with you, but all I really want right now is a nap on a real bed.
Are you serious? Do you actually want to do that?
Well then, maybe you should rest and let me plan our date.
Well, I am a terrible poet. Allow me to show my affection somehow.
Verity, can I talk to you?
Hey Katie, what is it?
Did you have any plans for tonight?
Well, Amirah and I were going to go supply shopping. We're running short on a few things. Why?
Oh, don't worry about it. Enjoy your shopping.
You're cruel, Viti. You know she wants to spend time with you.
Then she can ask me. This can't be a one-sided—
WHAT ABOUT AFTER?

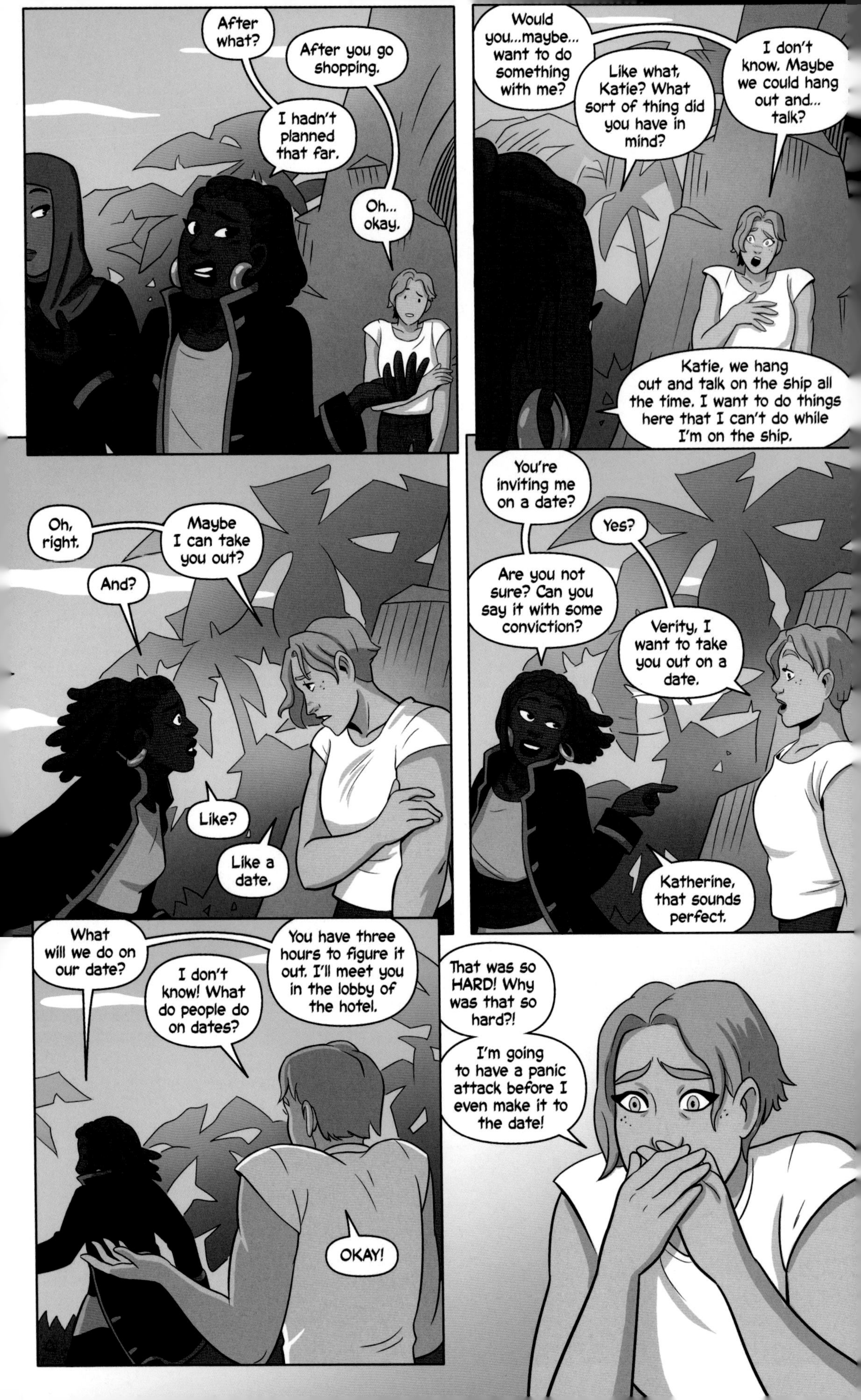
After what?
After you go shopping.
I hadn't planned that far.
Oh... okay.
Would you...maybe... want to do something with me?
Like what, Katie? What sort of thing did you have in mind?
I don't know. Maybe we could hang out and... talk?
Katie, we hang out and talk on the ship all the time. I want to do things here that I can't do while I'm on the ship.
Oh, right.
Maybe I can take you out?
And?
Like?
Like a date.
You're inviting me on a date?
Yes?
Are you not sure? Can you say it with some conviction?
Verity, I want to take you out on a date.
Katherine, that sounds perfect.
What will we do on our date?
You have three hours to figure it out. I'll meet you in the lobby of the hotel.
I don't know! What do people do on dates?
OKAY!
That was so HARD! Why was that so hard?!
I'm going to have a panic attack before I even make it to the date!

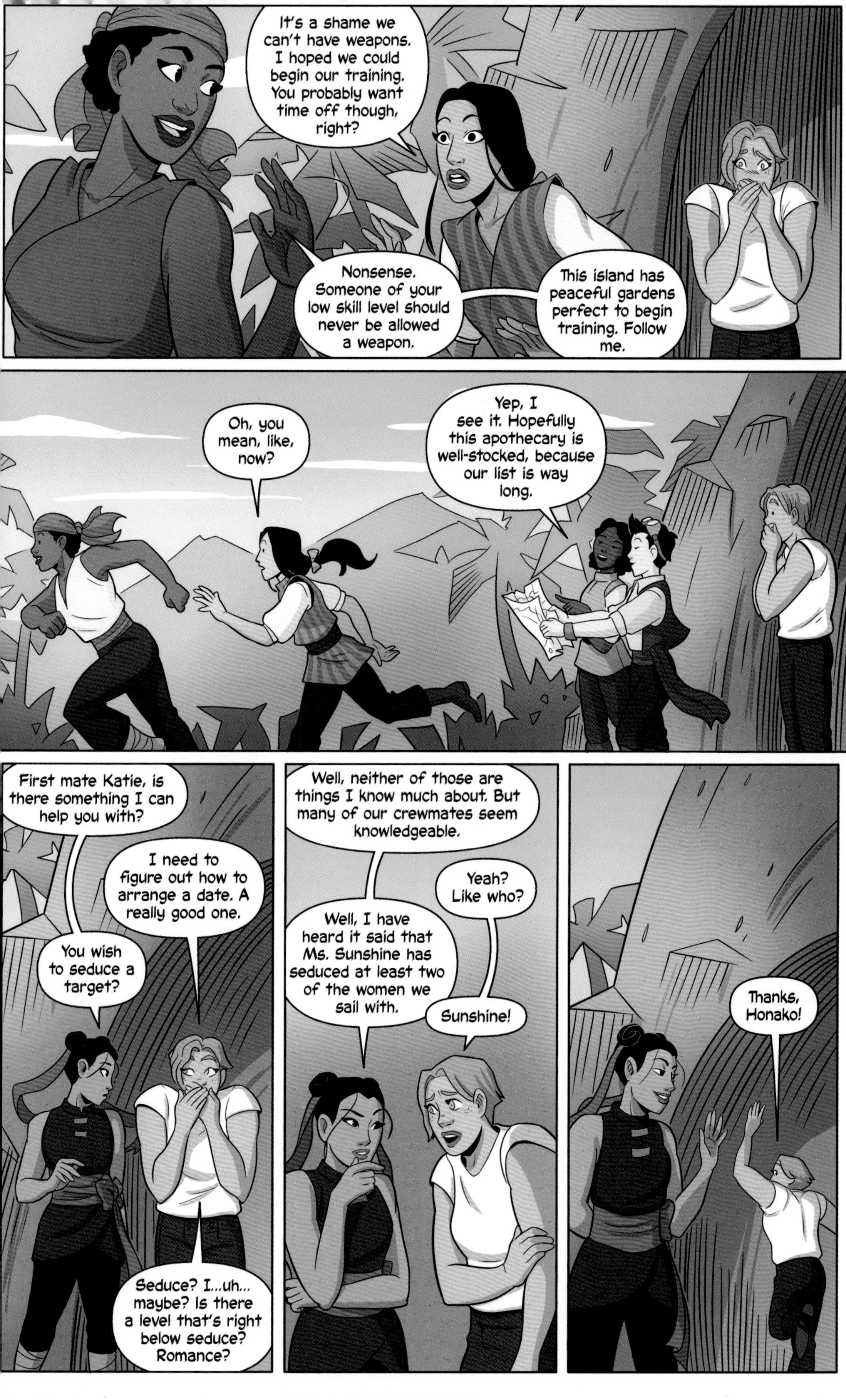
It's a shame we can't have weapons. I hoped we could begin our training. You probably want time off though, right?
Nonsense. Someone of your low skill level should never be allowed a weapon.
This island has peaceful gardens perfect to begin training. Follow me.
Oh, you mean, like, now?
Yep, I see it. Hopefully this apothecary is well-stocked, because our list is way long.
First mate Katie, is there something I can help you with?
I need to figure out how to arrange a date. A really good one.
You wish to seduce a target?
Seduce? I...uh... maybe? Is there a level that's right below seduce? Romance?
Well, neither of those are things I know much about. But many of our crewmates seem knowledgeable.
Yeah? Like who?
Well, I have heard it said that Ms. Sunshine has seduced at least two of the women we sail with.
Sunshine!
Thanks, Honako!

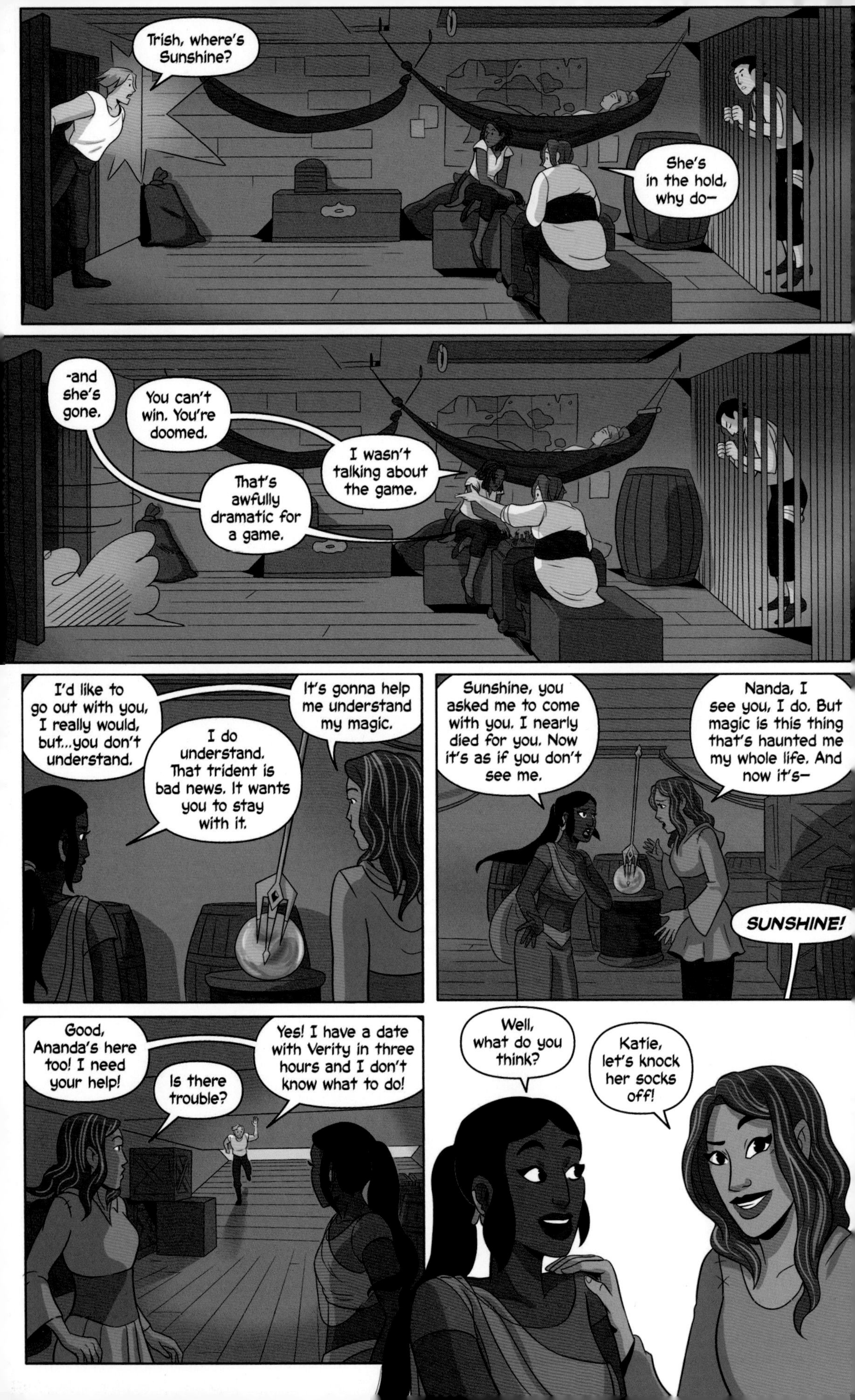

Trish, where's Sunshine?
She's in the hold, why do—
-and she's gone.
You can't win. You're doomed.
I wasn't talking about the game.
That's awfully dramatic for a game.
I'd like to go out with you, I really would, but...you don't understand.
It's gonna help me understand my magic.
I do understand. That trident is bad news. It wants you to stay with it.
Sunshine, you asked me to come with you. I nearly died for you. Now it's as if you don't see me.
Nanda, I see you, I do. But magic is this thing that's haunted me my whole life. And now it's—
SUNSHINE!
Good, Ananda's here too! I need your help!
Yes! I have a date with Verity in three hours and I don't know what to do!
Is there trouble?
Well, what do you think?
Katie, let's knock her socks off!

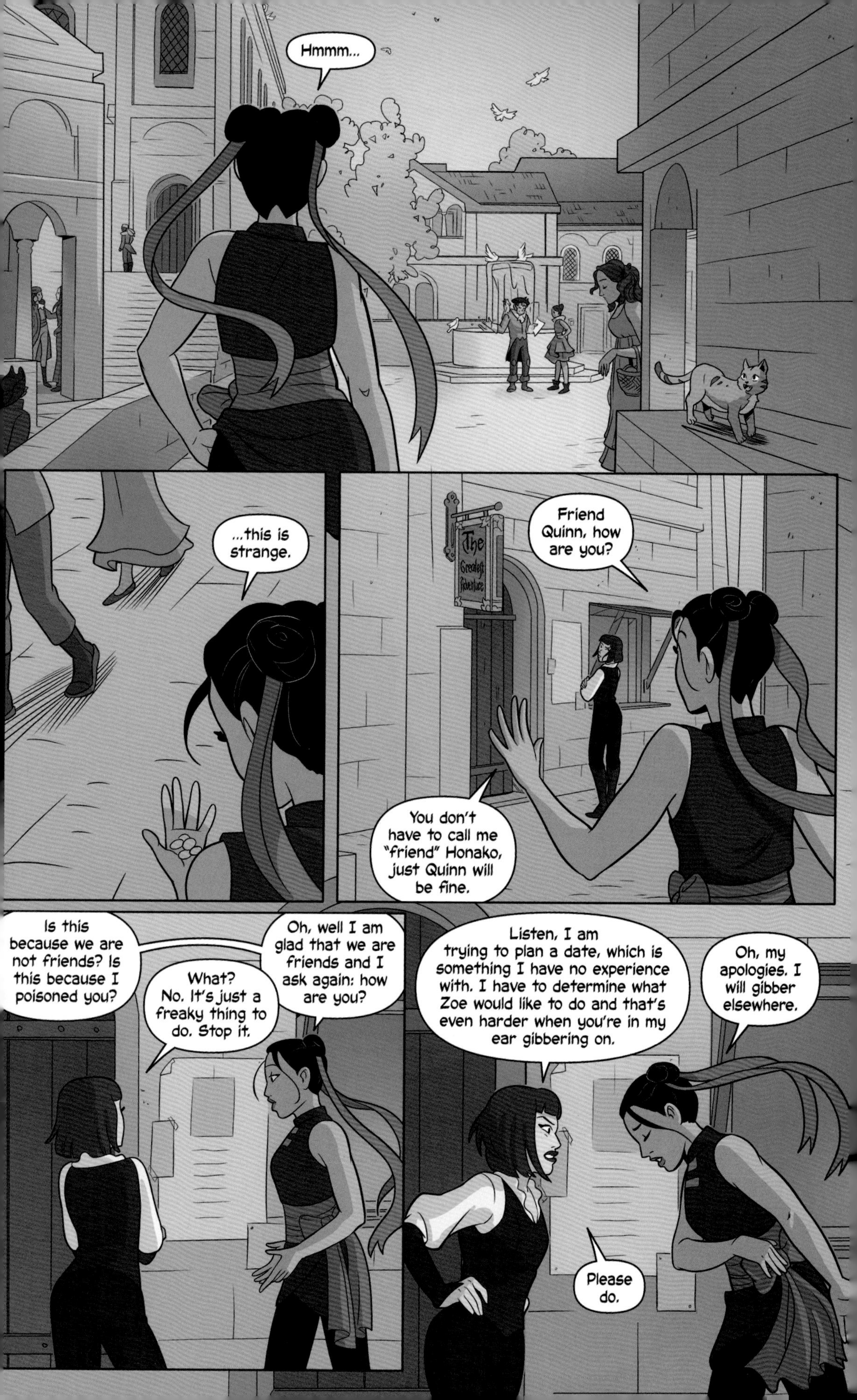
Hmmm...
...this is strange.
Friend Quinn, how are you?
The Greatest Adventure
You don't have to call me "friend" Honako, just Quinn will be fine.
Is this because we are not friends? Is this because I poisoned you?
What? No. It's just a freaky thing to do. Stop it.
Oh, well I am glad that we are friends and I ask again: how are you?
Listen, I am trying to plan a date, which is something I have no experience with. I have to determine what Zoe would like to do and that's even harder when you're in my ear gibbering on.
Oh, my apologies. I will gibber elsewhere.
Please do.

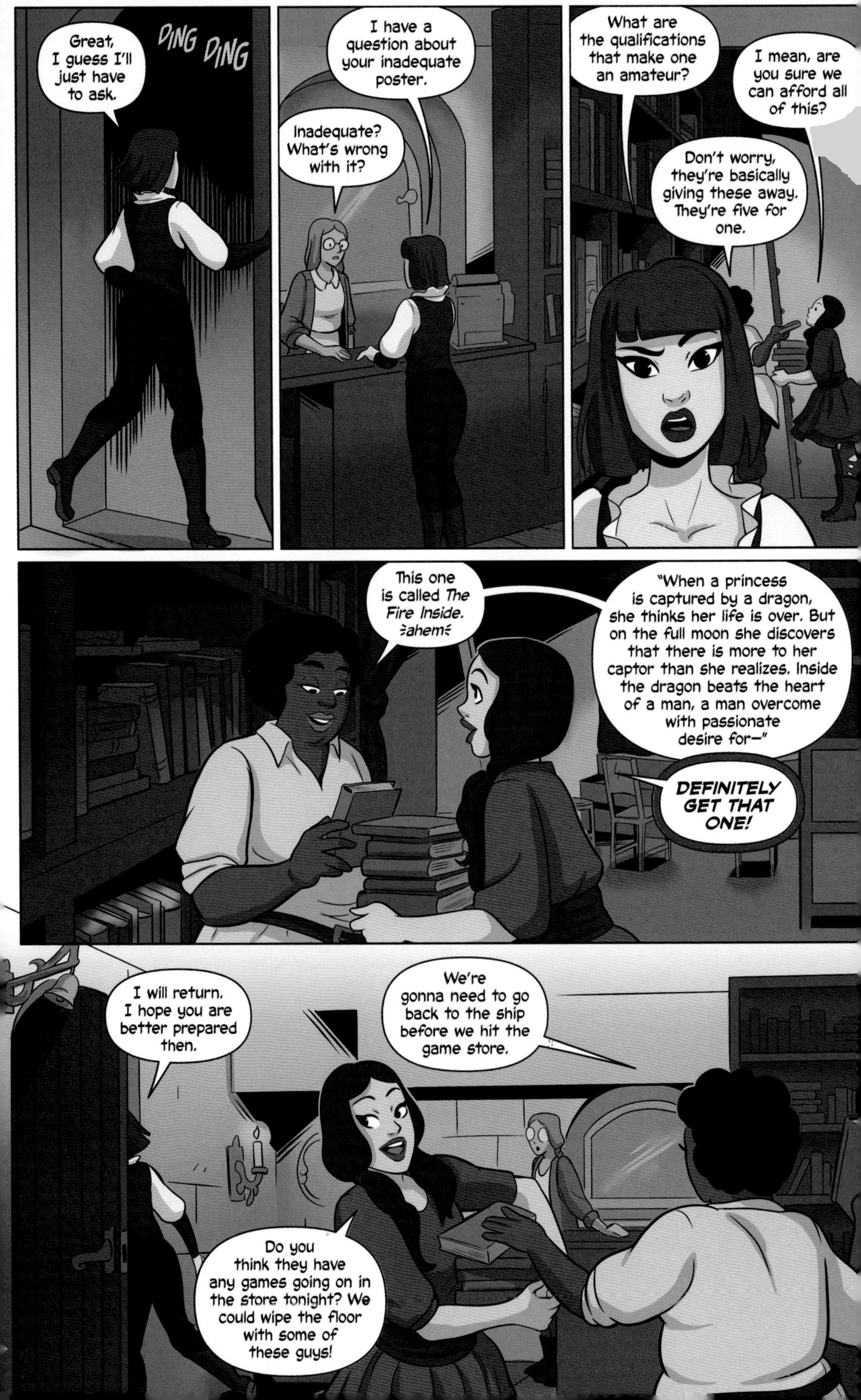

Great, I guess I'll just have to ask.
DING DING
I have a question about your inadequate poster.
Inadequate? What's wrong with it?
What are the qualifications that make one an amateur?
I mean, are you sure we can afford all of this?
Don't worry, they're basically giving these away. They're five for one.
This one is called *The Fire Inside.* ahem
"When a princess is captured by a dragon, she thinks her life is over. But on the full moon she discovers that there is more to her captor than she realizes. Inside the dragon beats the heart of a man, a man overcome with passionate desire for—"
DEFINITELY GET THAT ONE!
I will return. I hope you are better prepared then.
We're gonna need to go back to the ship before we hit the game store.
Do you think they have any games going on in the store tonight? We could wipe the floor with some of these guys!

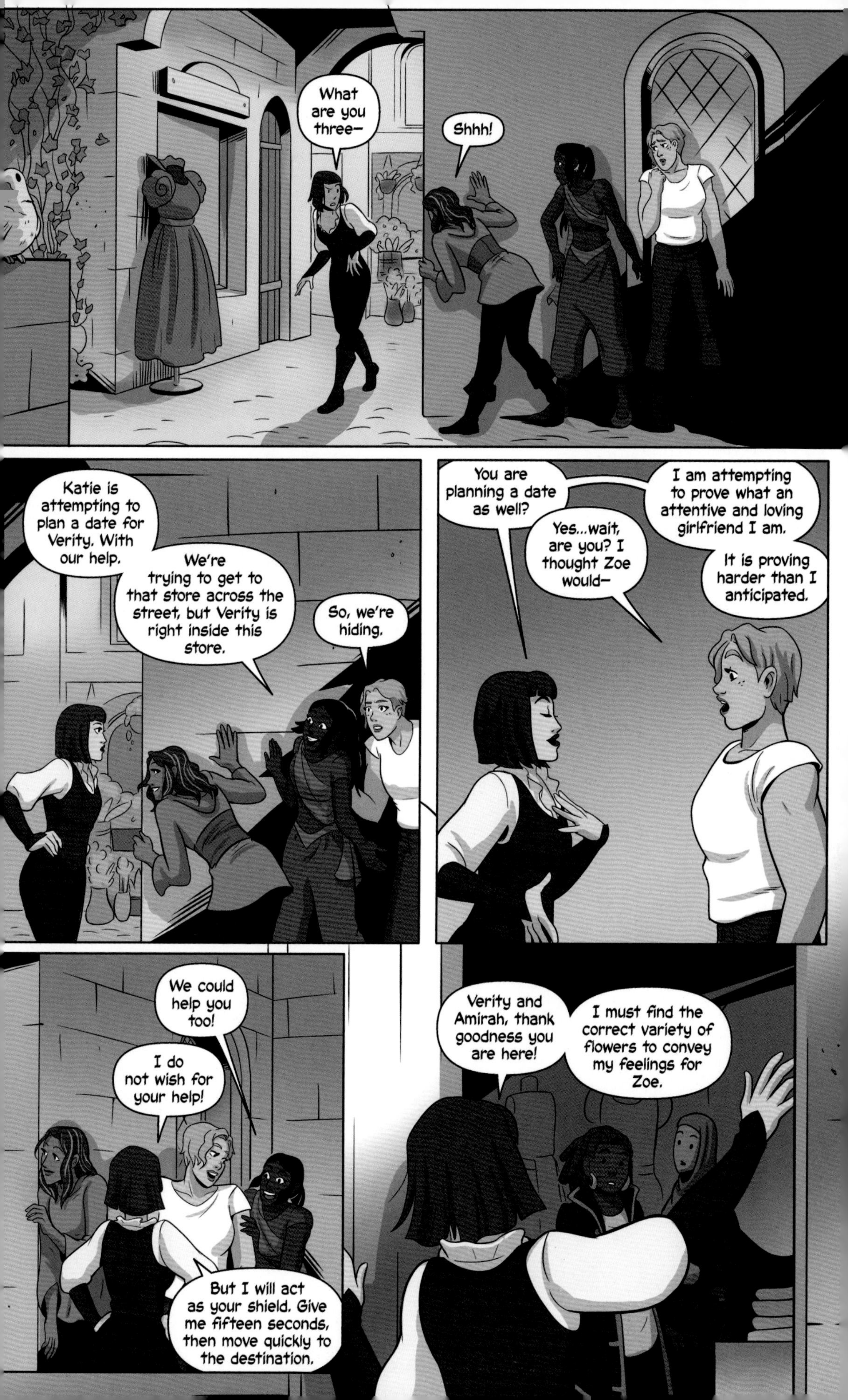
What are you three—
Shhh!
Katie is attempting to plan a date for Verity. With our help.
We're trying to get to that store across the street, but Verity is right inside this store.
So, we're hiding.
You are planning a date as well?
Yes...wait, are you? I thought Zoe would—
I am attempting to prove what an attentive and loving girlfriend I am.
It is proving harder than I anticipated.
We could help you too!
I do not wish for your help!
But I will act as your shield. Give me fifteen seconds, then move quickly to the destination.
Verity and Amirah, thank goodness you are here!
I must find the correct variety of flowers to convey my feelings for Zoe.

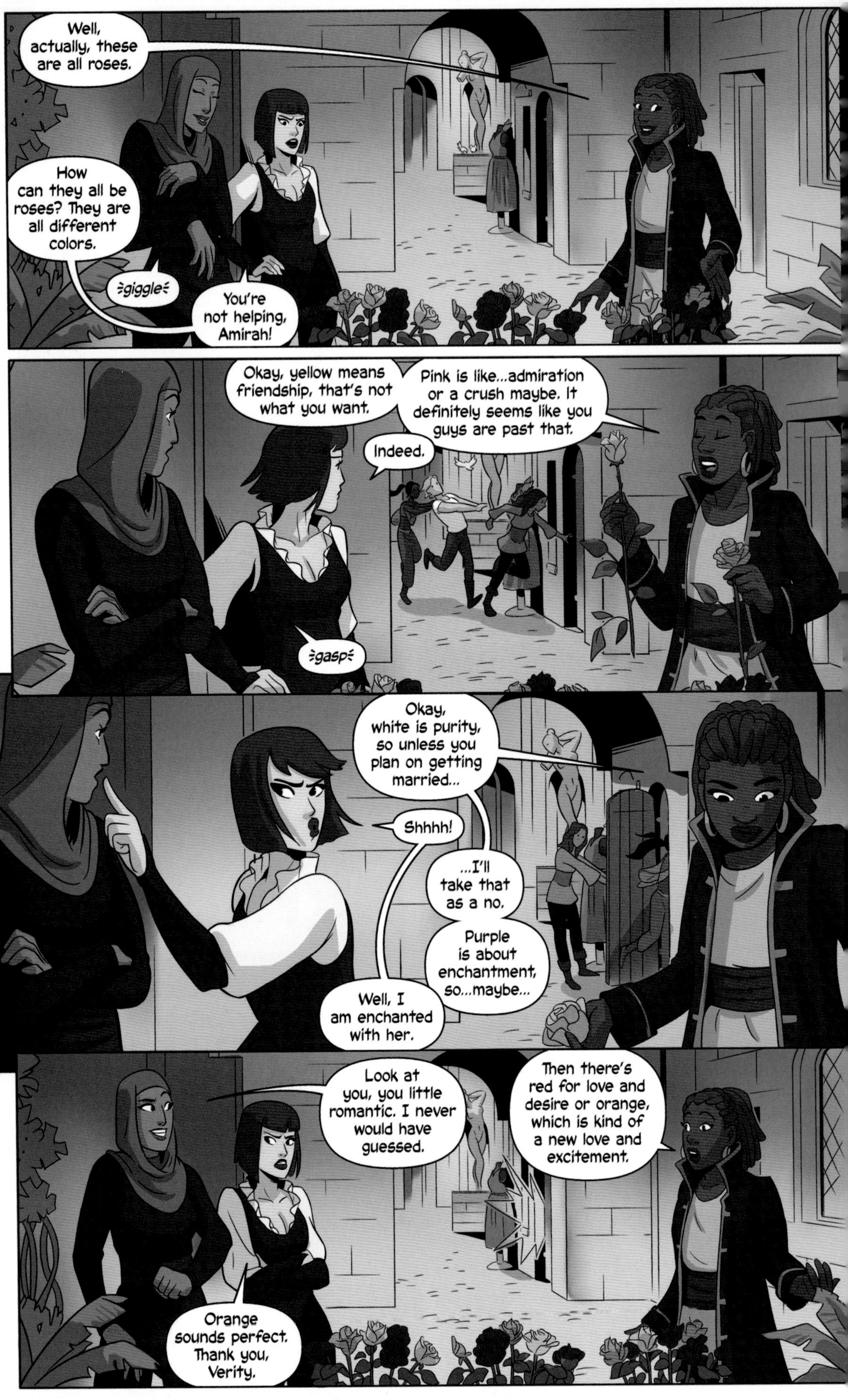
Well, actually, these are all roses.
How can they all be roses? They are all different colors.
≡giggle≡
You're not helping, Amirah!
Okay, yellow means friendship, that's not what you want.
Pink is like...admiration or a crush maybe. It definitely seems like you guys are past that.
Indeed.
≡gasp≡
Okay, white is purity, so unless you plan on getting married...
Shhhh!
...I'll take that as a no.
Purple is about enchantment, so...maybe...
Well, I am enchanted with her.
Look at you, you little romantic. I never would have guessed.
Then there's red for love and desire or orange, which is kind of a new love and excitement.
Orange sounds perfect. Thank you, Verity.

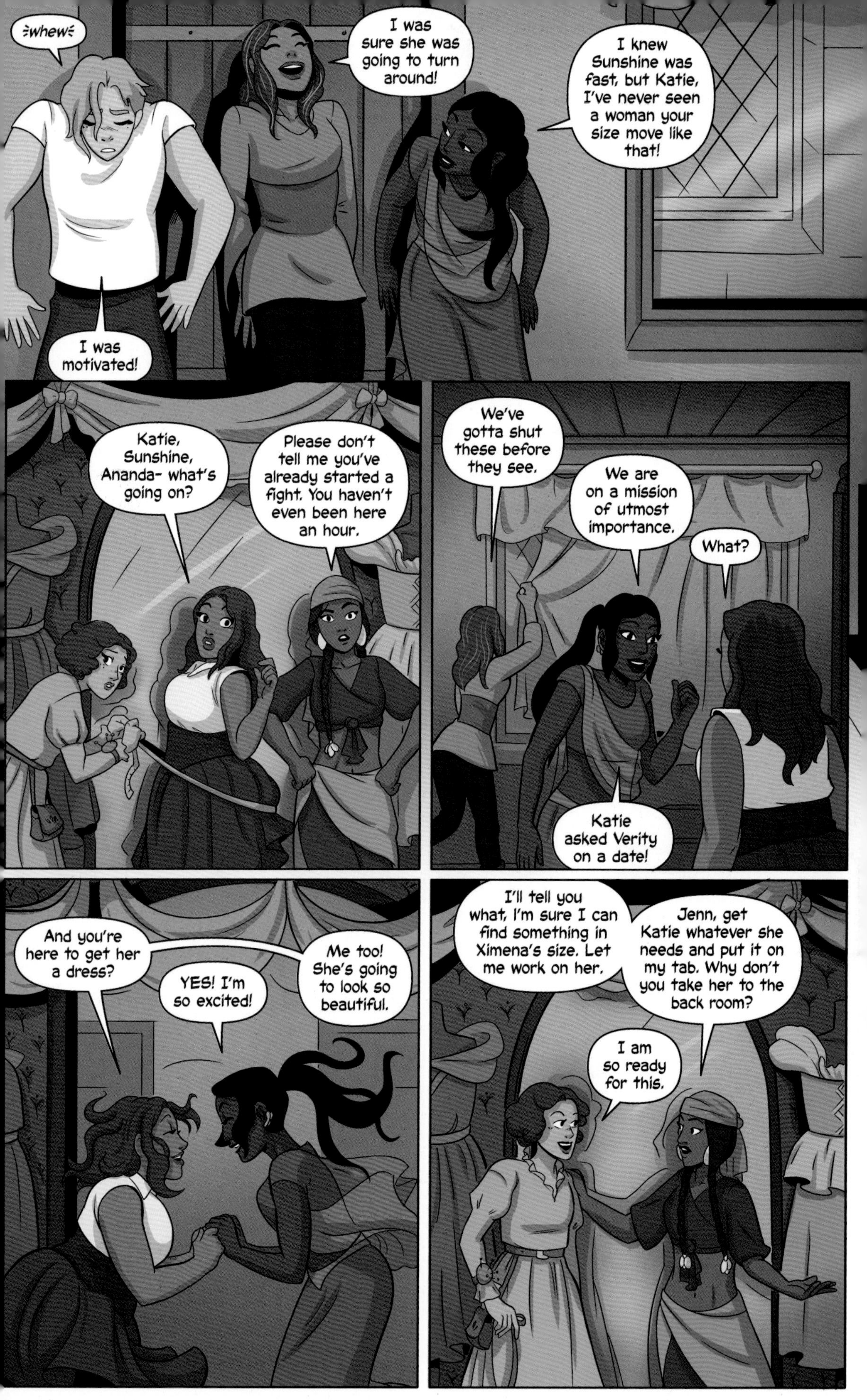

≑whew≑
I was sure she was going to turn around!
I knew Sunshine was fast, but Katie, I've never seen a woman your size move like that!
I was motivated!
Katie, Sunshine, Ananda- what's going on?
Please don't tell me you've already started a fight. You haven't even been here an hour.
We've gotta shut these before they see.
We are on a mission of utmost importance.
What?
Katie asked Verity on a date!
And you're here to get her a dress?
YES! I'm so excited!
Me too! She's going to look so beautiful.
I'll tell you what, I'm sure I can find something in Ximena's size. Let me work on her.
Jenn, get Katie whatever she needs and put it on my tab. Why don't you take her to the back room?
I am so ready for this.

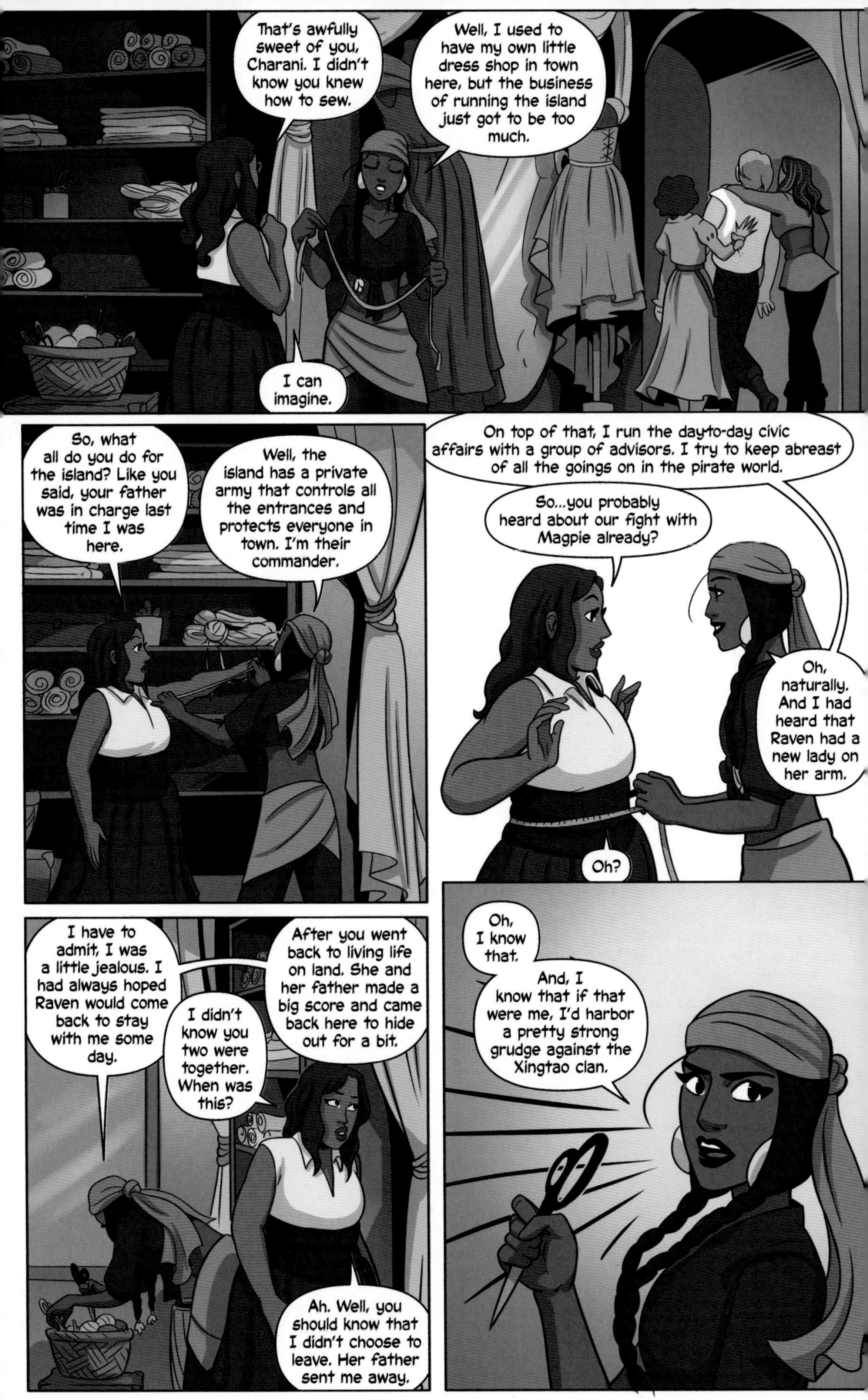
That's awfully sweet of you, Charani. I didn't know you knew how to sew.
Well, I used to have my own little dress shop in town here, but the business of running the island just got to be too much.
I can imagine.
So, what all do you do for the island? Like you said, your father was in charge last time I was here.
Well, the island has a private army that controls all the entrances and protects everyone in town. I'm their commander.
On top of that, I run the day-to-day civic affairs with a group of advisors. I try to keep abreast of all the goings on in the pirate world.
So...you probably heard about our fight with Magpie already?
Oh, naturally. And I had heard that Raven had a new lady on her arm.
Oh?
I have to admit, I was a little jealous. I had always hoped Raven would come back to stay with me some day.
I didn't know you two were together. When was this?
After you went back to living life on land. She and her father made a big score and came back here to hide out for a bit.
Ah. Well, you should know that I didn't choose to leave. Her father sent me away.
Oh, I know that.
And, I know that if that were me, I'd harbor a pretty strong grudge against the Xingtao clan.

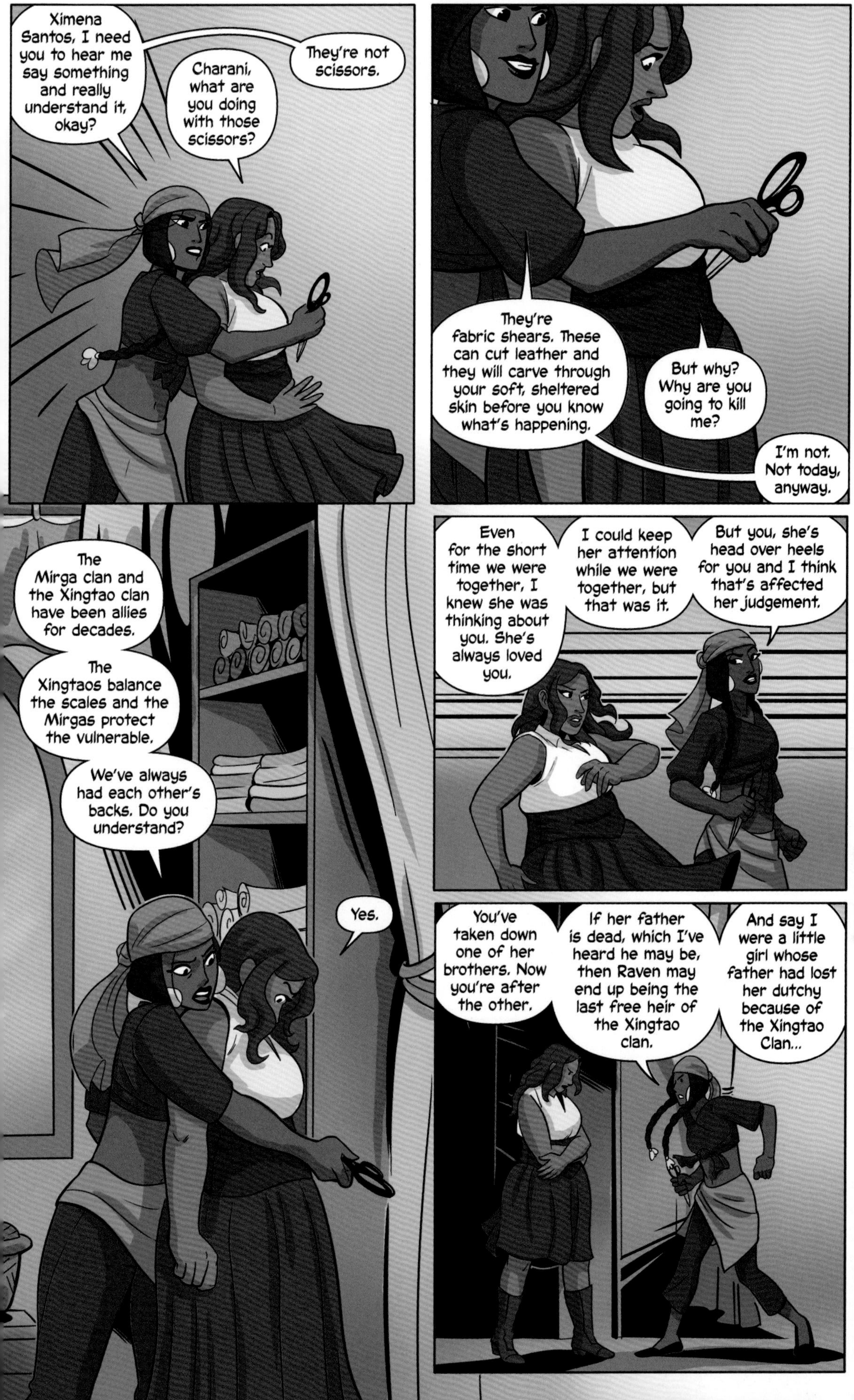
Ximena Santos, I need you to hear me say something and really understand it, okay?
Charani, what are you doing with those scissors?
They're not scissors.
They're fabric shears. These can cut leather and they will carve through your soft, sheltered skin before you know what's happening.
But why? Why are you going to kill me?
I'm not. Not today, anyway.
The Mirga clan and the Xingtao clan have been allies for decades.
The Xingtaos balance the scales and the Mirgas protect the vulnerable.
We've always had each other's backs. Do you understand?
Yes.
Even for the short time we were together, I knew she was thinking about you. She's always loved you.
I could keep her attention while we were together, but that was it.
But you, she's head over heels for you and I think that's affected her judgement.
You've taken down one of her brothers. Now you're after the other.
If her father is dead, which I've heard he may be, then Raven may end up being the last free heir of the Xingtao clan.
And say I were a little girl whose father had lost her dutchy because of the Xingtao Clan...

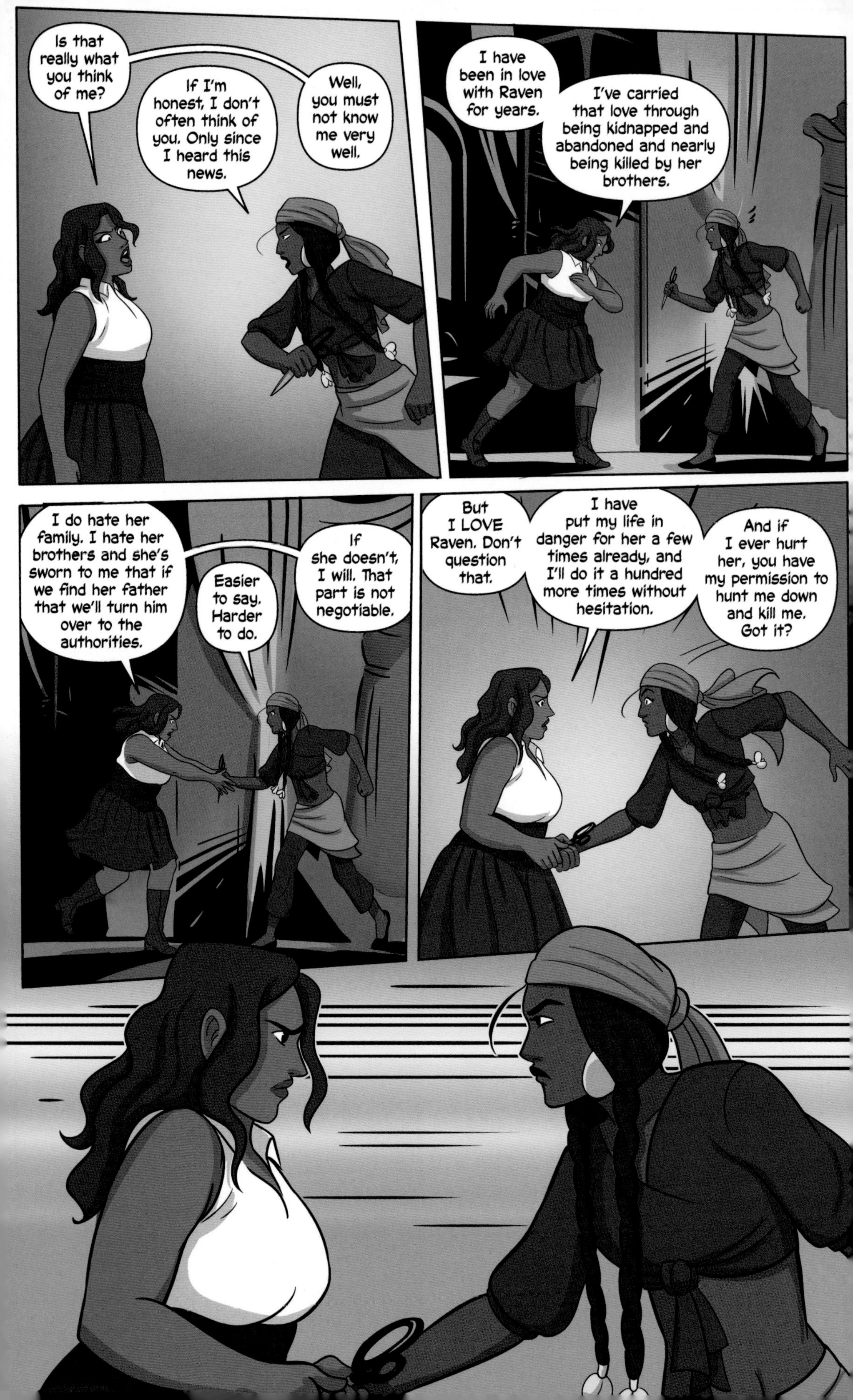
Is that really what you think of me?
If I'm honest, I don't often think of you. Only since I heard this news.
Well, you must not know me very well.
I have been in love with Raven for years.
I've carried that love through being kidnapped and abandoned and nearly being killed by her brothers.
I do hate her family. I hate her brothers and she's sworn to me that if we find her father that we'll turn him over to the authorities.
Easier to say. Harder to do.
If she doesn't, I will. That part is not negotiable.
But I LOVE Raven. Don't question that.
I have put my life in danger for her a few times already, and I'll do it a hundred more times without hesitation.
And if I ever hurt her, you have my permission to hunt me down and kill me. Got it?

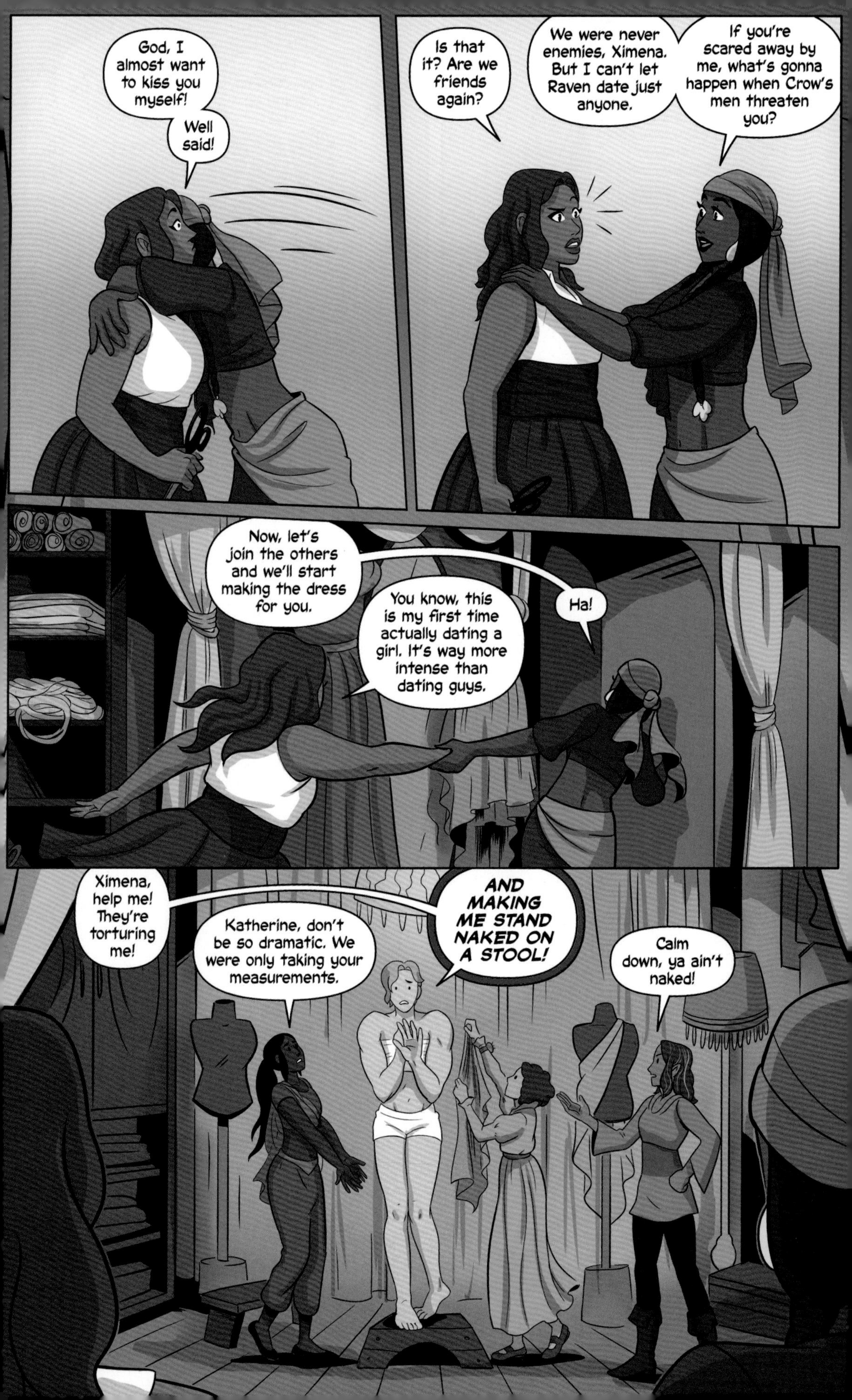
God, I almost want to kiss you myself!
Well said!
Is that it? Are we friends again?
We were never enemies, Ximena. But I can't let Raven date just anyone.
If you're scared away by me, what's gonna happen when Crow's men threaten you?
Now, let's join the others and we'll start making the dress for you.
Ha!
You know, this is my first time actually dating a girl. It's way more intense than dating guys.
Ximena, help me! They're torturing me!
Katherine, don't be so dramatic. We were only taking your measurements.
AND MAKING ME STAND NAKED ON A STOOL!
Calm down, ya ain't naked!

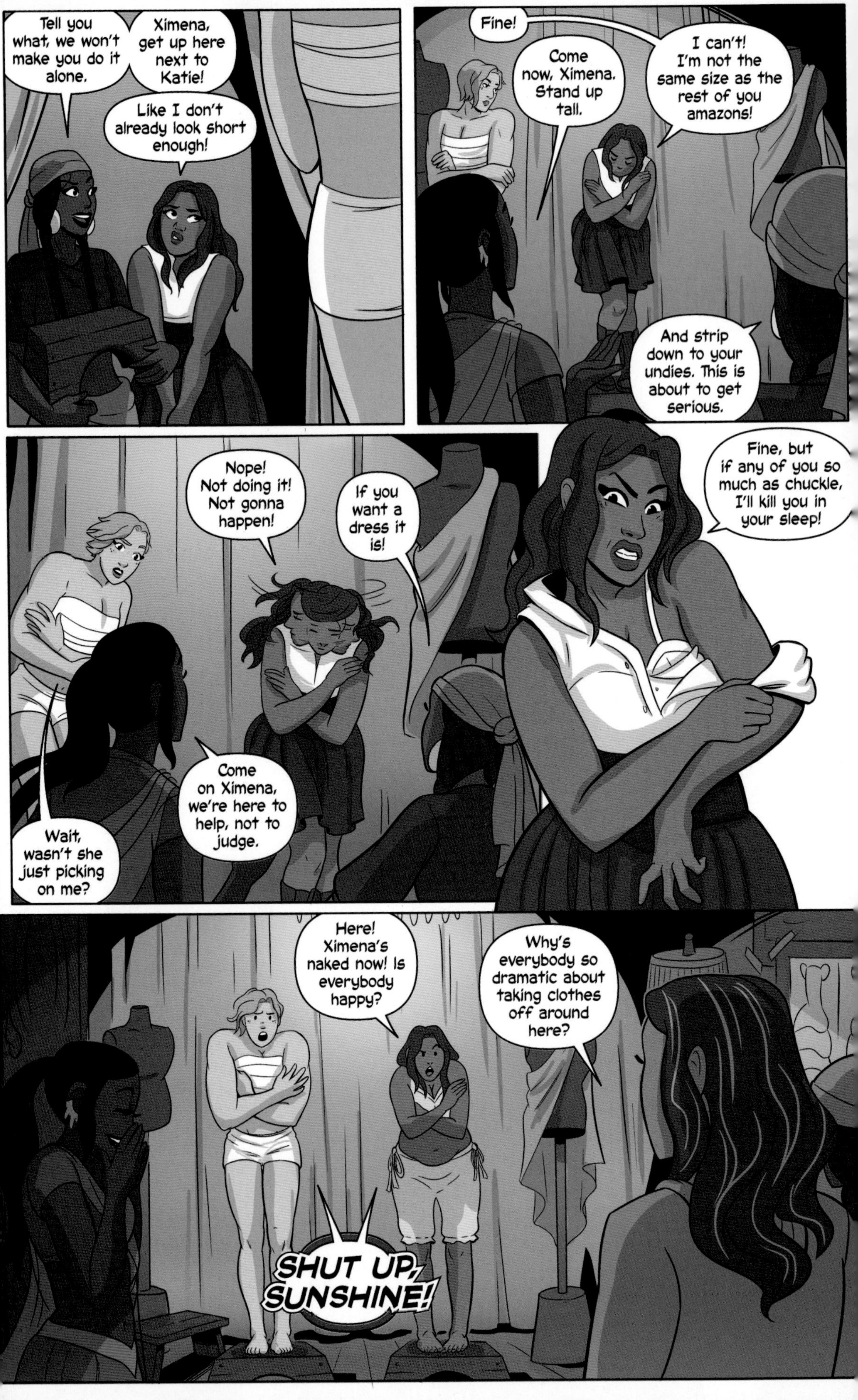
Tell you what, we won't make you do it alone.
Ximena, get up here next to Katie!
Like I don't already look short enough!
Fine!
Come now, Ximena. Stand up tall.
I can't! I'm not the same size as the rest of you amazons!
And strip down to your undies. This is about to get serious.
Nope! Not doing it! Not gonna happen!
If you want a dress it is!
Come on Ximena, we're here to help, not to judge.
Wait, wasn't she just picking on me?
Fine, but if any of you so much as chuckle, I'll kill you in your sleep!
Here! Ximena's naked now! Is everybody happy?
Why's everybody so dramatic about taking clothes off around here?
SHUT UP, SUNSHINE!

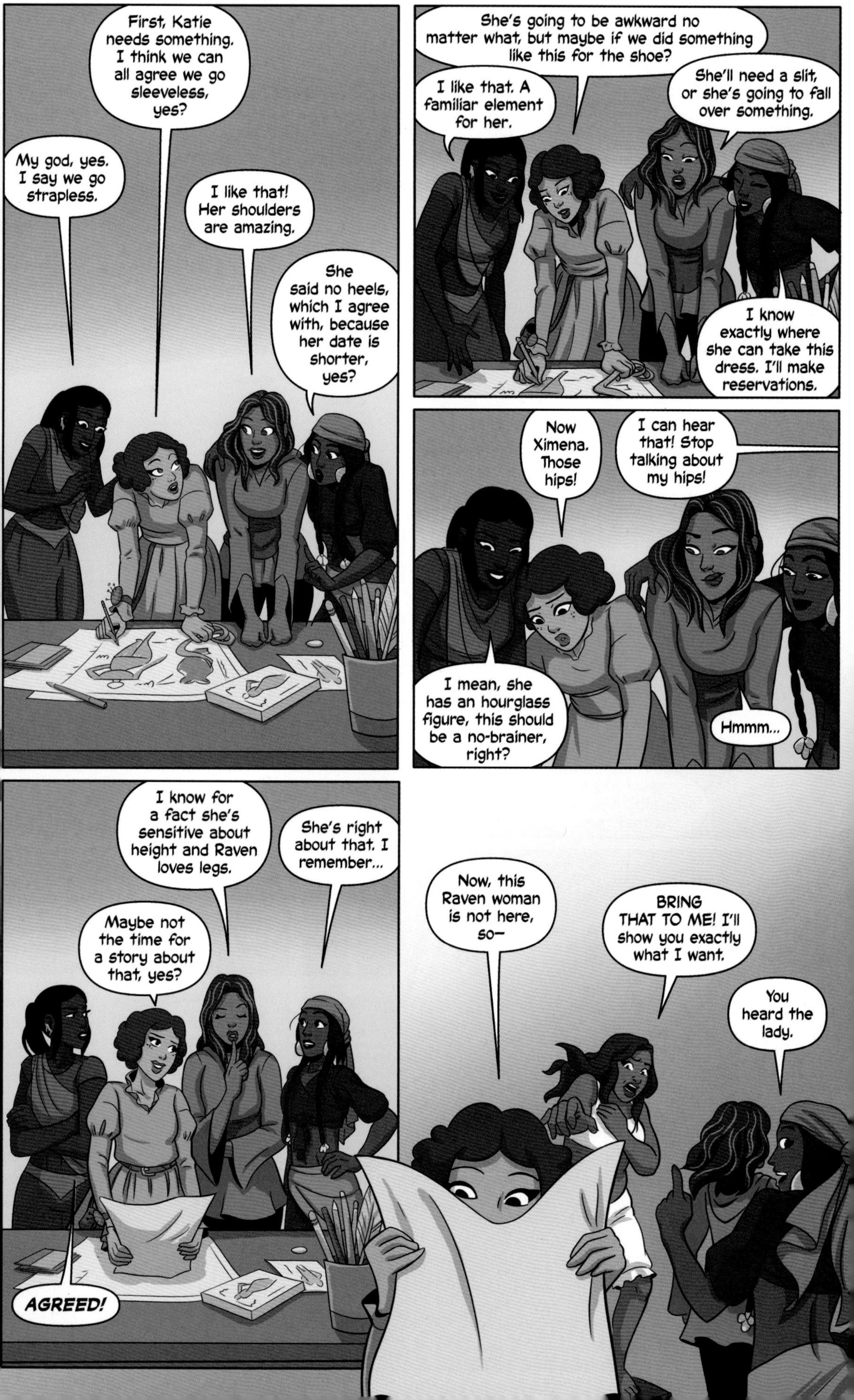
First, Katie needs something. I think we can all agree we go sleeveless, yes?
My god, yes. I say we go strapless.
I like that! Her shoulders are amazing.
She said no heels, which I agree with, because her date is shorter, yes?
She's going to be awkward no matter what, but maybe if we did something like this for the shoe?
I like that. A familiar element for her.
She'll need a slit, or she's going to fall over something.
I know exactly where she can take this dress. I'll make reservations.
Now Ximena. Those hips!
I can hear that! Stop talking about my hips!
I mean, she has an hourglass figure, this should be a no-brainer, right?
Hmmm...
I know for a fact she's sensitive about height and Raven loves legs.
She's right about that. I remember...
Maybe not the time for a story about that, yes?
AGREED!
Now, this Raven woman is not here, so—
BRING THAT TO ME! I'll show you exactly what I want.
You heard the lady.

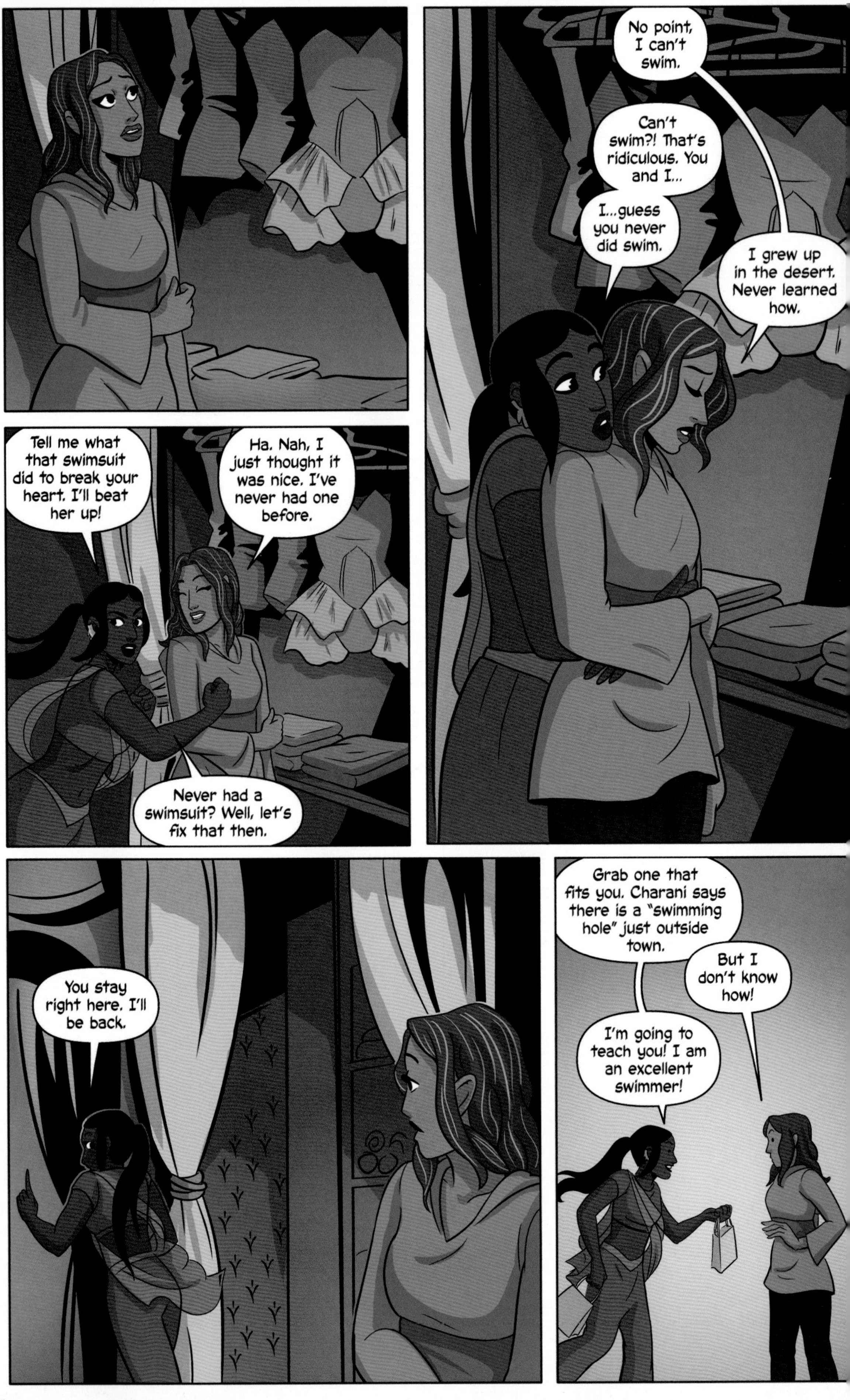
No point, I can't swim.
Can't swim?! That's ridiculous. You and I...
I...guess you never did swim.
I grew up in the desert. Never learned how.
Tell me what that swimsuit did to break your heart. I'll beat her up!
Ha. Nah, I just thought it was nice. I've never had one before.
Never had a swimsuit? Well, let's fix that then.
You stay right here. I'll be back.
Grab one that fits you. Charani says there is a "swimming hole" just outside town.
But I don't know how!
I'm going to teach you! I am an excellent swimmer!

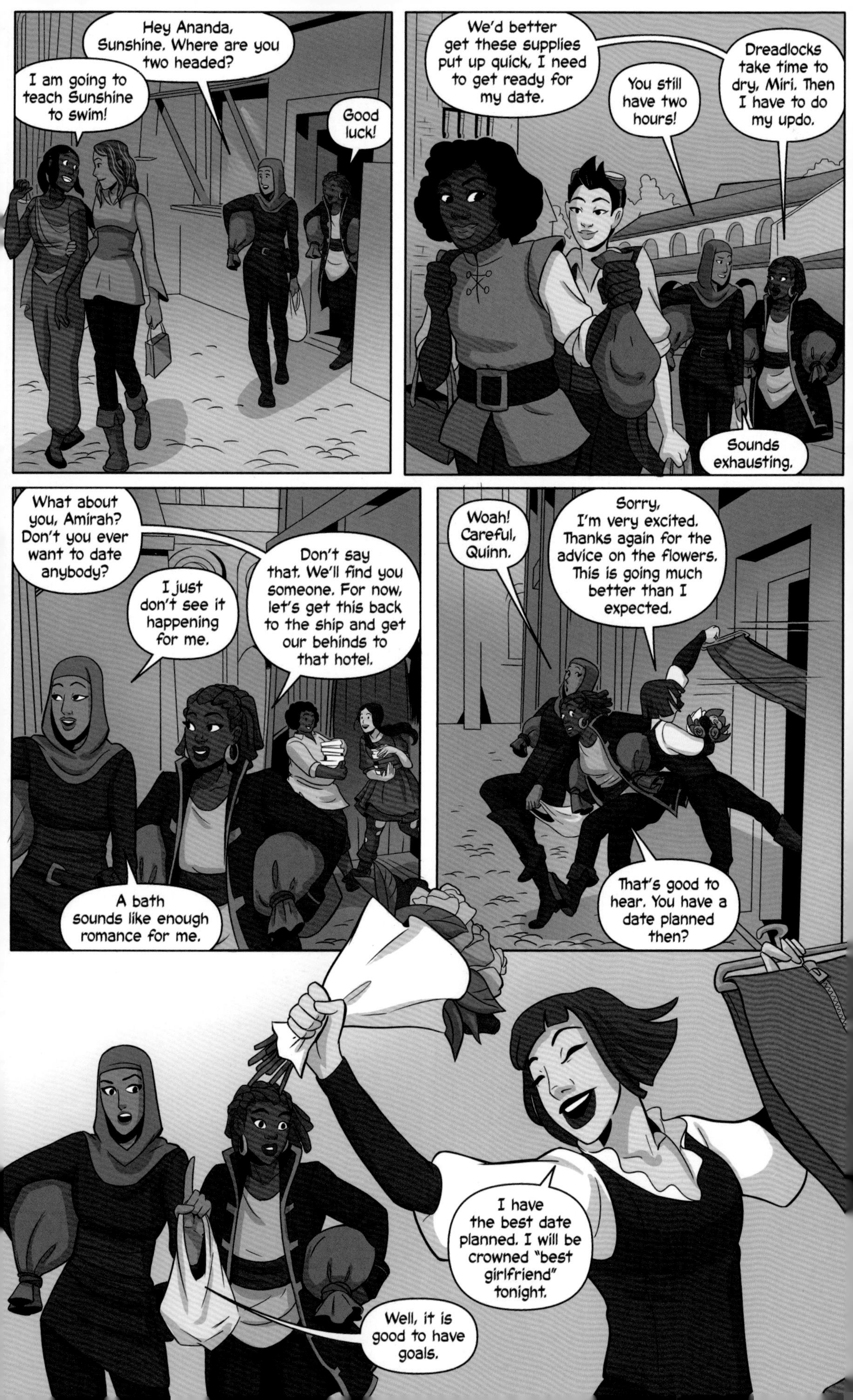
Hey Ananda, Sunshine. Where are you two headed?
I am going to teach Sunshine to swim!
Good luck!
We'd better get these supplies put up quick, I need to get ready for my date.
You still have two hours!
Dreadlocks take time to dry, Miri. Then I have to do my updo.
Sounds exhausting.
What about you, Amirah? Don't you ever want to date anybody?
I just don't see it happening for me.
Don't say that. We'll find you someone. For now, let's get this back to the ship and get our behinds to that hotel.
A bath sounds like enough romance for me.
Woah! Careful, Quinn.
Sorry, I'm very excited. Thanks again for the advice on the flowers. This is going much better than I expected.
That's good to hear. You have a date planned then?
I have the best date planned. I will be crowned "best girlfriend" tonight.
Well, it is good to have goals.

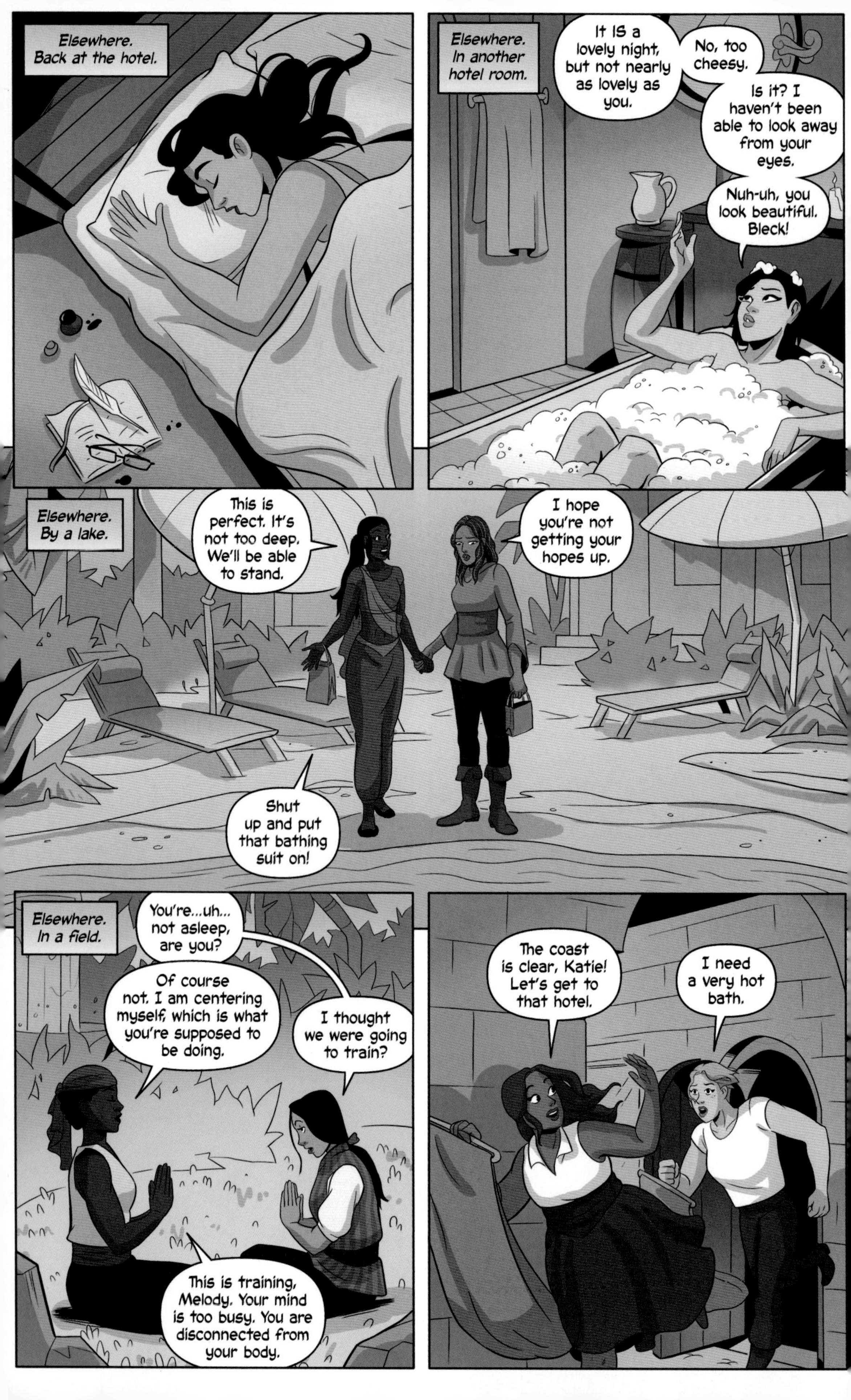
Elsewhere. Back at the hotel.
Elsewhere. In another hotel room.
It IS a lovely night, but not nearly as lovely as you.
No, too cheesy.
Is it? I haven't been able to look away from your eyes.
Nuh-uh, you look beautiful. Bleck!
Elsewhere. By a lake.
This is perfect. It's not too deep. We'll be able to stand.
I hope you're not getting your hopes up.
Shut up and put that bathing suit on!
Elsewhere. In a field.
You're...uh... not asleep, are you?
Of course not. I am centering myself, which is what you're supposed to be doing.
I thought we were going to train?
This is training, Melody. Your mind is too busy. You are disconnected from your body.
The coast is clear, Katie! Let's get to that hotel.
I need a very hot bath.

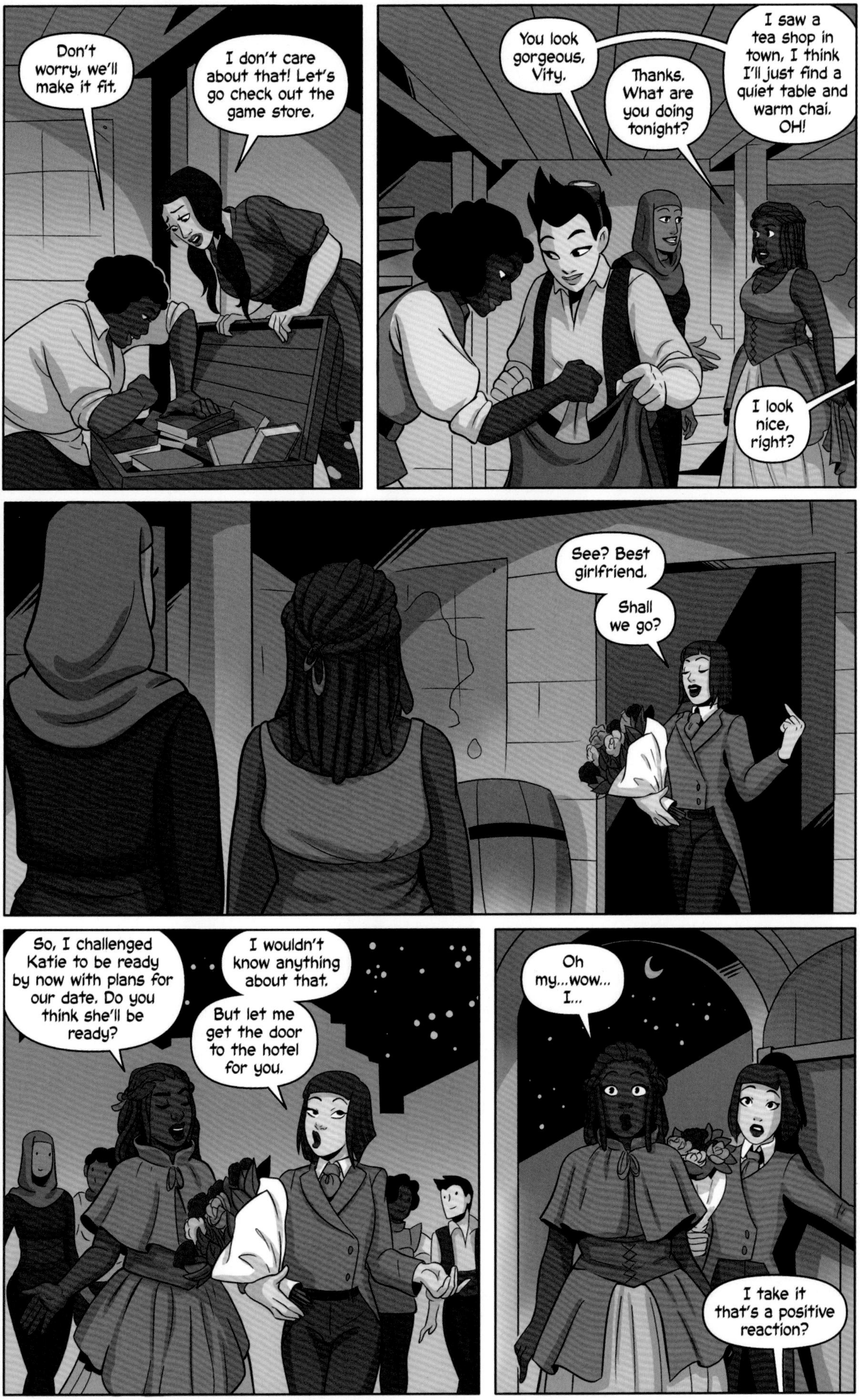
Don't worry, we'll make it fit.
I don't care about that! Let's go check out the game store.
You look gorgeous, Vity.
Thanks. What are you doing tonight?
I saw a tea shop in town, I think I'll just find a quiet table and warm chai. OH!
I look nice, right?
See? Best girlfriend.
Shall we go?
So, I challenged Katie to be ready by now with plans for our date. Do you think she'll be ready?
I wouldn't know anything about that.
But let me get the door to the hotel for you.
Oh my...wow... I...
I take it that's a positive reaction?

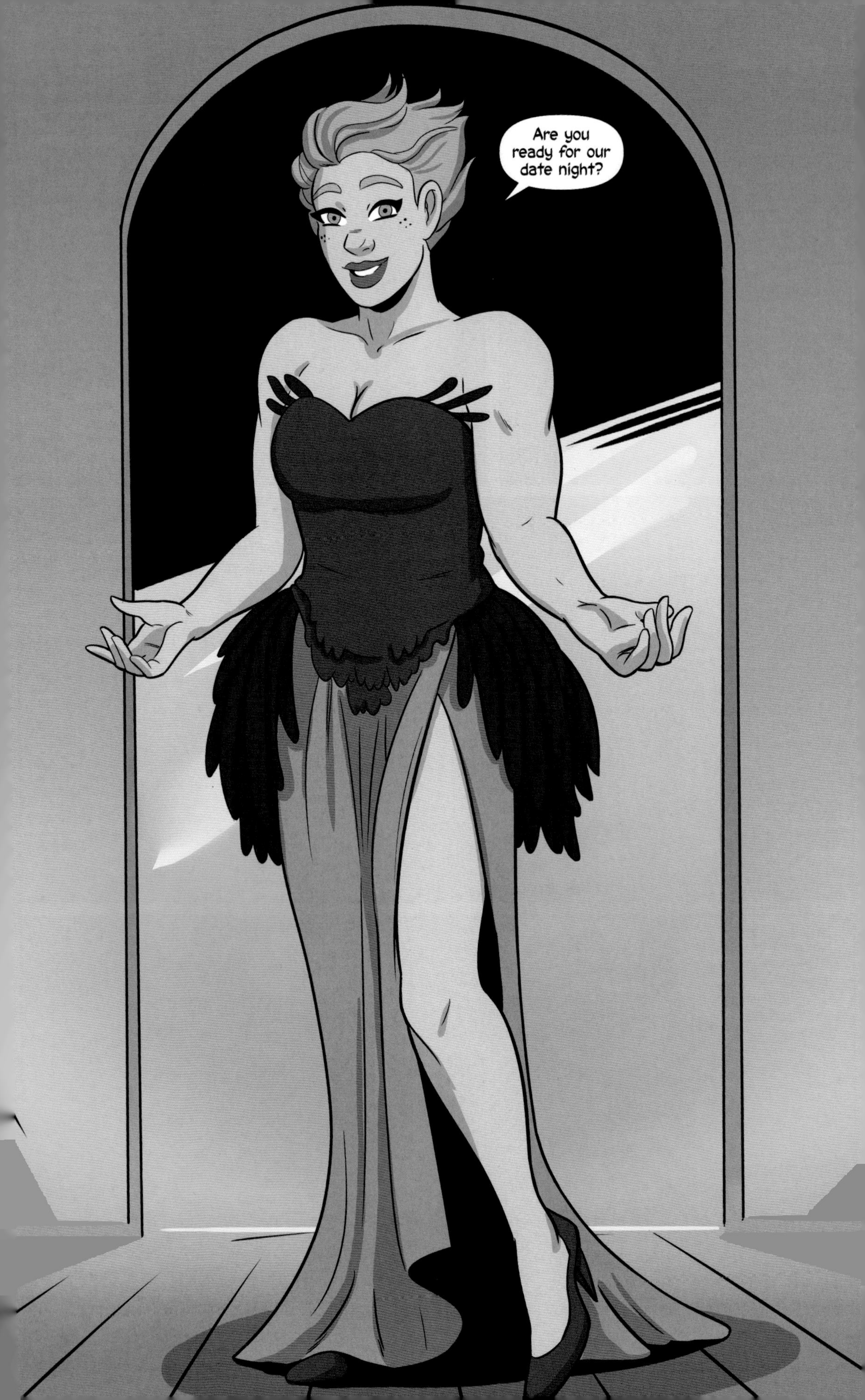
Are you ready for our date night?

Princeless

Raven

The Pirate Princess

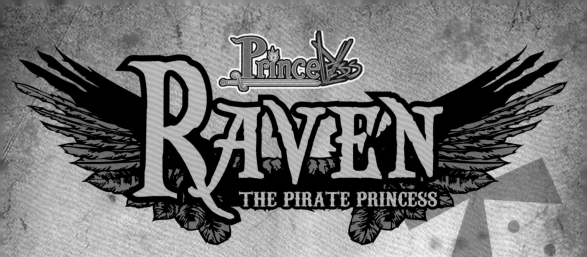

Year Three: Monsters of the Deep

Chapter Three: Date Night Part 3

Written By: Jeremy Whitley

Pencils By: Xenia Pamfil

Inks By: Christine Hipp

Colors By: Lexillo

Lettered By: Alex Scherkenbach

Edited By: Nicole D'Andria

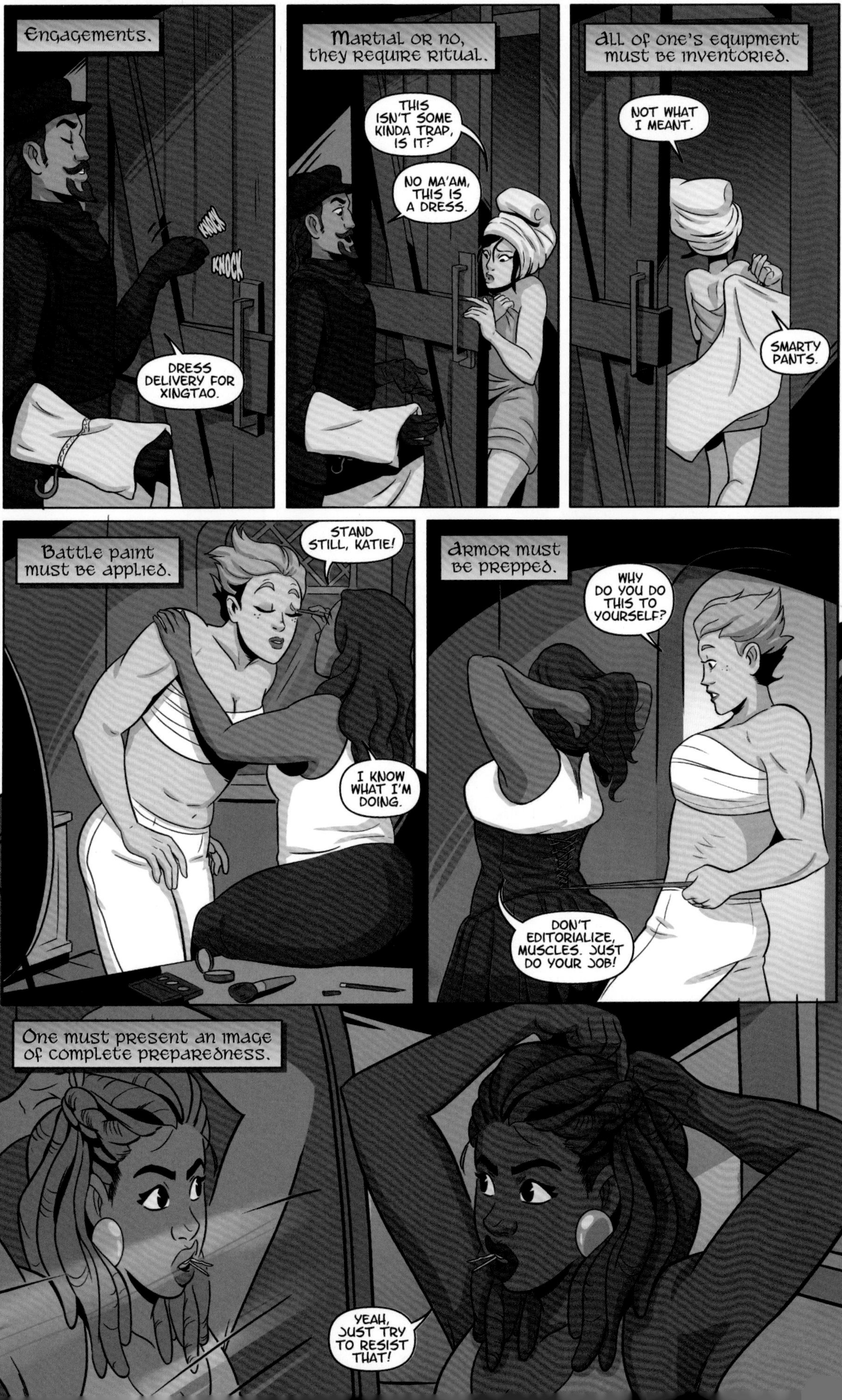
Engagements.
KNOCK
KNOCK
DRESS DELIVERY FOR XINGTAO.
Martial or no, they require ritual.
THIS ISN'T SOME KINDA TRAP, IS IT?
NO MA'AM, THIS IS A DRESS.
All of one's equipment must be inventoried.
NOT WHAT I MEANT.
SMARTY PANTS.
Battle paint must be applied.
STAND STILL, KATIE!
I KNOW WHAT I'M DOING.
Armor must be prepped.
WHY DO YOU DO THIS TO YOURSELF?
DON'T EDITORIALIZE, MUSCLES. JUST DO YOUR JOB!
One must present an image of complete preparedness.
YEAH, JUST TRY TO RESIST THAT!

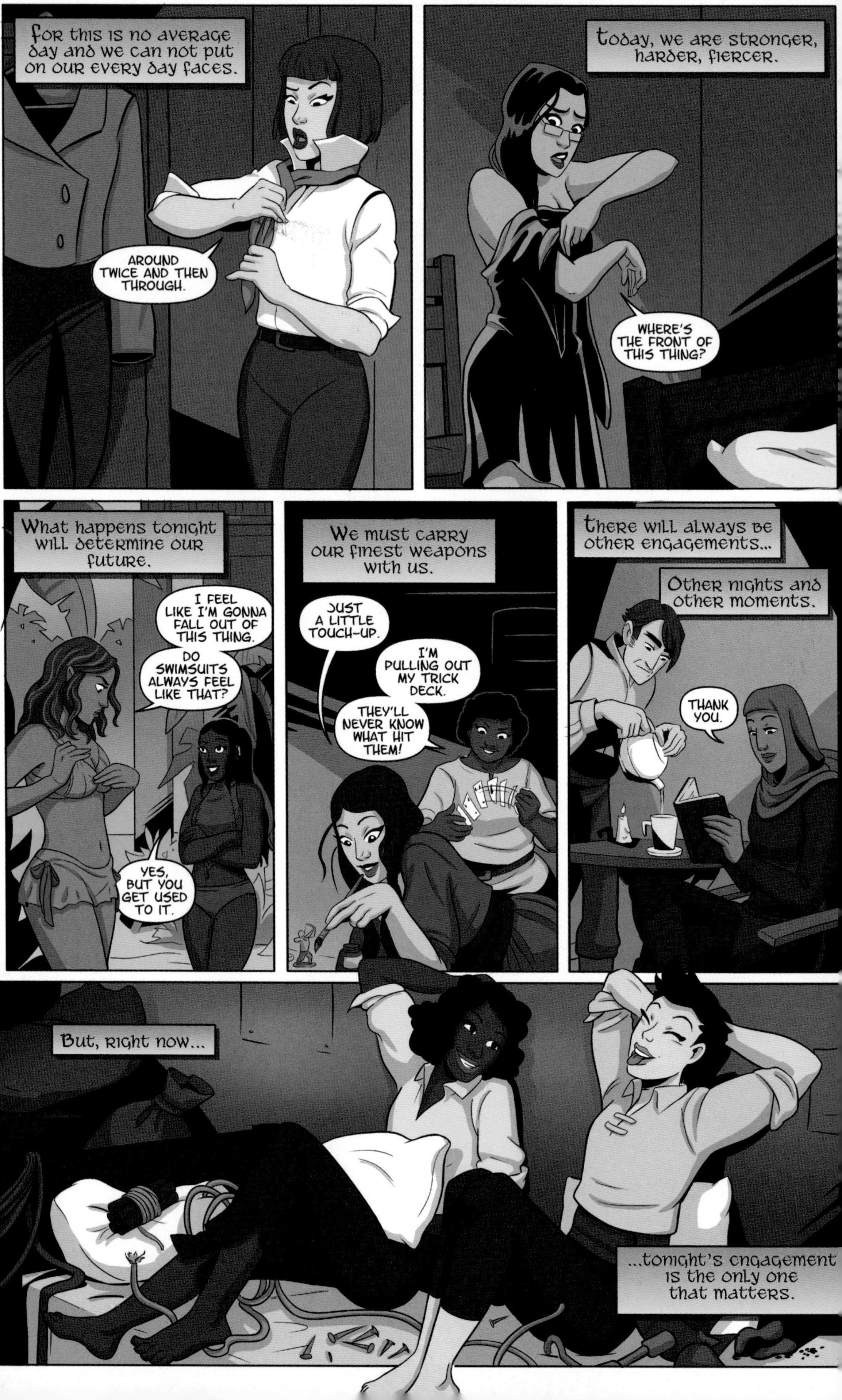
for this is no average day and we can not put on our every day faces.
AROUND TWICE AND THEN THROUGH.
today, we are stronger, harder, fiercer.
WHERE'S THE FRONT OF THIS THING?
What happens tonight will determine our future.
I FEEL LIKE I'M GONNA FALL OUT OF THIS THING.
DO SWIMSUITS ALWAYS FEEL LIKE THAT?
YES, BUT YOU GET USED TO IT.
We must carry our finest weapons with us.
JUST A LITTLE TOUCH-UP.
I'M PULLING OUT MY TRICK DECK.
THEY'LL NEVER KNOW WHAT HIT THEM!
there will always be other engagements...
Other nights and other moments.
THANK YOU.
But, right now...
...tonight's engagement is the only one that matters.

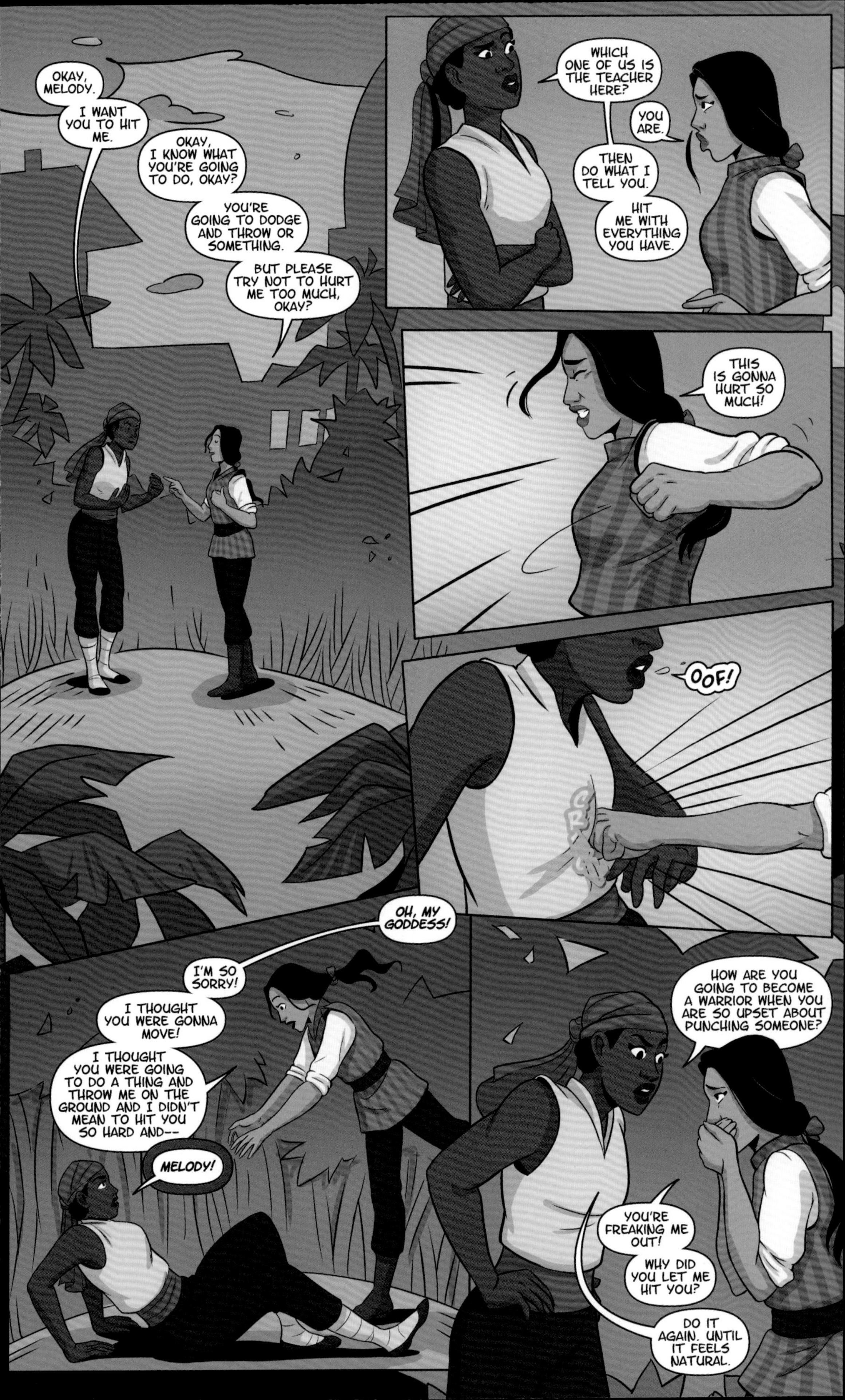
OKAY, MELODY.
I WANT YOU TO HIT ME.
OKAY, I KNOW WHAT YOU'RE GOING TO DO, OKAY?
YOU'RE GOING TO DODGE AND THROW OR SOMETHING.
BUT PLEASE TRY NOT TO HURT ME TOO MUCH, OKAY?
WHICH ONE OF US IS THE TEACHER HERE?
YOU ARE.
THEN DO WHAT I TELL YOU.
HIT ME WITH EVERYTHING YOU HAVE.
THIS IS GONNA HURT SO MUCH!
OOF!
OH, MY GODDESS!
I'M SO SORRY!
I THOUGHT YOU WERE GONNA MOVE!
I THOUGHT YOU WERE GOING TO DO A THING AND THROW ME ON THE GROUND AND I DIDN'T MEAN TO HIT YOU SO HARD AND--
MELODY!
HOW ARE YOU GOING TO BECOME A WARRIOR WHEN YOU ARE SO UPSET ABOUT PUNCHING SOMEONE?
YOU'RE FREAKING ME OUT!
WHY DID YOU LET ME HIT YOU?
DO IT AGAIN. UNTIL IT FEELS NATURAL.

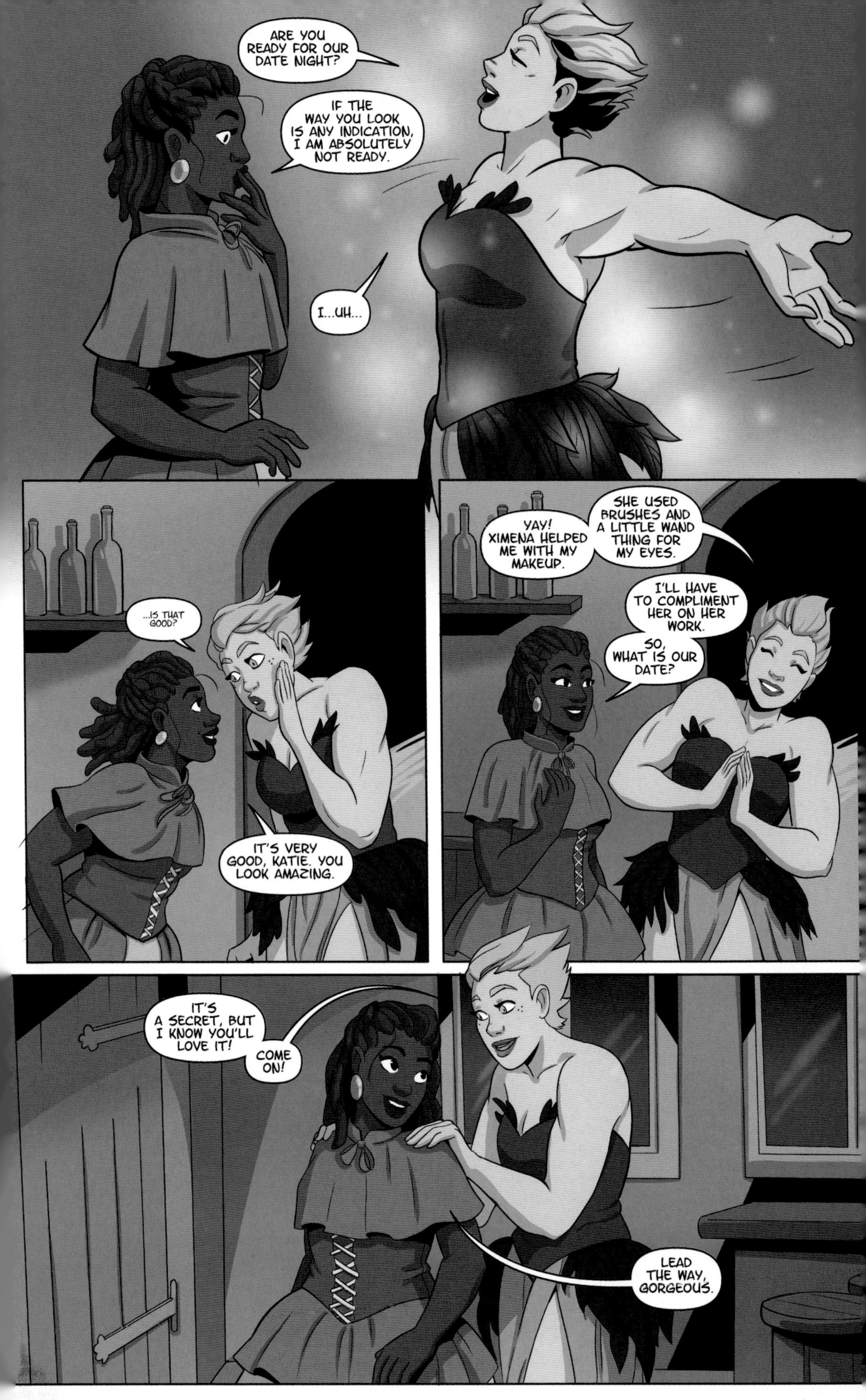
ARE YOU READY FOR OUR DATE NIGHT?
IF THE WAY YOU LOOK IS ANY INDICATION, I AM ABSOLUTELY NOT READY.
I...UH...
...IS THAT GOOD?
IT'S VERY GOOD, KATIE. YOU LOOK AMAZING.
YAY! XIMENA HELPED ME WITH MY MAKEUP.
SHE USED BRUSHES AND A LITTLE WAND THING FOR MY EYES.
I'LL HAVE TO COMPLIMENT HER ON HER WORK.
SO, WHAT IS OUR DATE?
IT'S A SECRET, BUT I KNOW YOU'LL LOVE IT!
COME ON!
LEAD THE WAY, GORGEOUS.

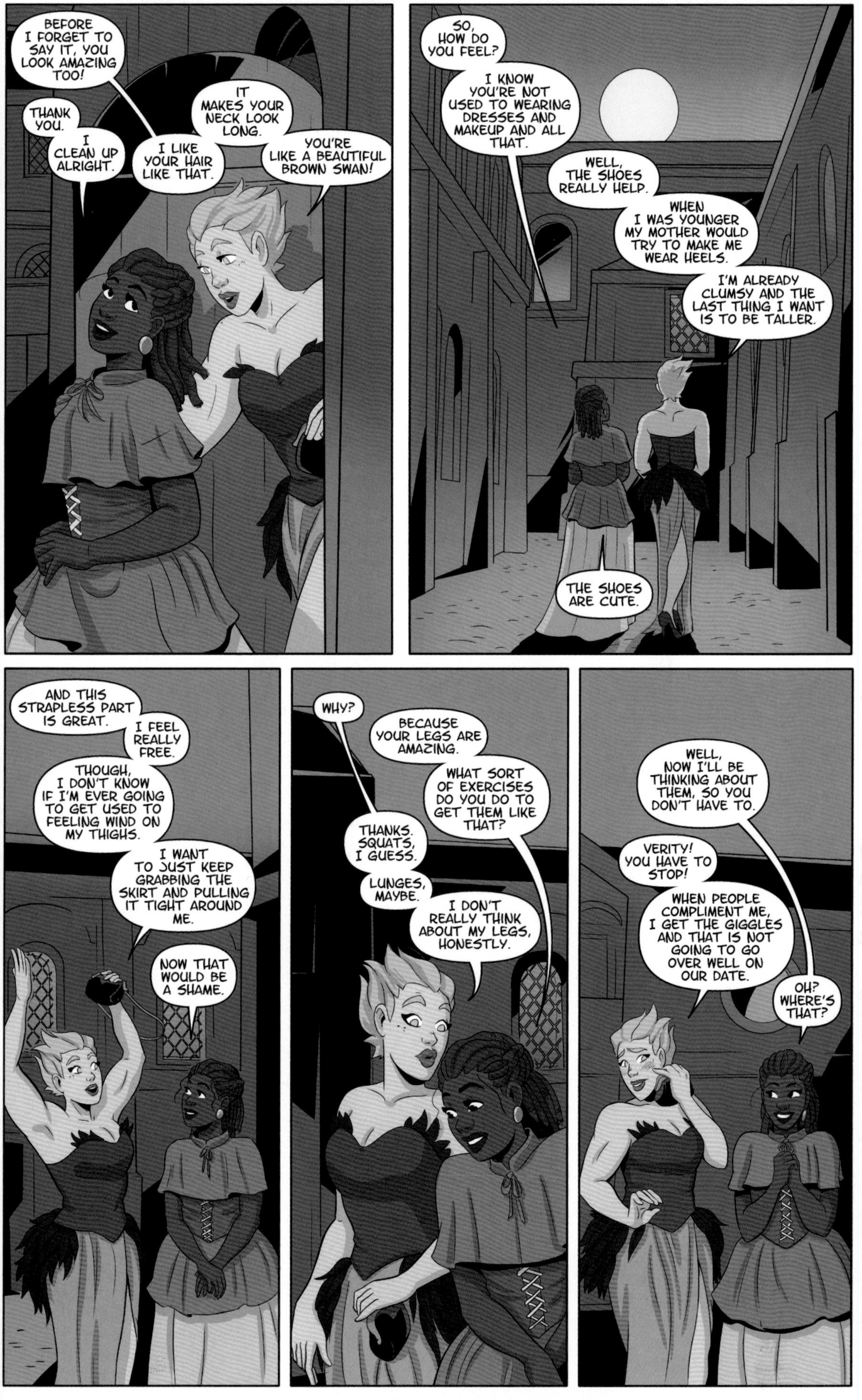
BEFORE I FORGET TO SAY IT, YOU LOOK AMAZING TOO!
THANK YOU.
I CLEAN UP ALRIGHT.
I LIKE YOUR HAIR LIKE THAT.
IT MAKES YOUR NECK LOOK LONG.
YOU'RE LIKE A BEAUTIFUL BROWN SWAN!
SO, HOW DO YOU FEEL?
I KNOW YOU'RE NOT USED TO WEARING DRESSES AND MAKEUP AND ALL THAT.
WELL, THE SHOES REALLY HELP.
WHEN I WAS YOUNGER MY MOTHER WOULD TRY TO MAKE ME WEAR HEELS.
I'M ALREADY CLUMSY AND THE LAST THING I WANT IS TO BE TALLER.
THE SHOES ARE CUTE.
AND THIS STRAPLESS PART IS GREAT.
I FEEL REALLY FREE.
THOUGH, I DON'T KNOW IF I'M EVER GOING TO GET USED TO FEELING WIND ON MY THIGHS.
I WANT TO JUST KEEP GRABBING THE SKIRT AND PULLING IT TIGHT AROUND ME.
NOW THAT WOULD BE A SHAME.
WHY?
BECAUSE YOUR LEGS ARE AMAZING.
WHAT SORT OF EXERCISES DO YOU DO TO GET THEM LIKE THAT?
THANKS. SQUATS, I GUESS.
LUNGES, MAYBE.
I DON'T REALLY THINK ABOUT MY LEGS, HONESTLY.
WELL, NOW I'LL BE THINKING ABOUT THEM, SO YOU DON'T HAVE TO.
VERITY! YOU HAVE TO STOP!
WHEN PEOPLE COMPLIMENT ME, I GET THE GIGGLES AND THAT IS NOT GOING TO GO OVER WELL ON OUR DATE.
OH? WHERE'S THAT?

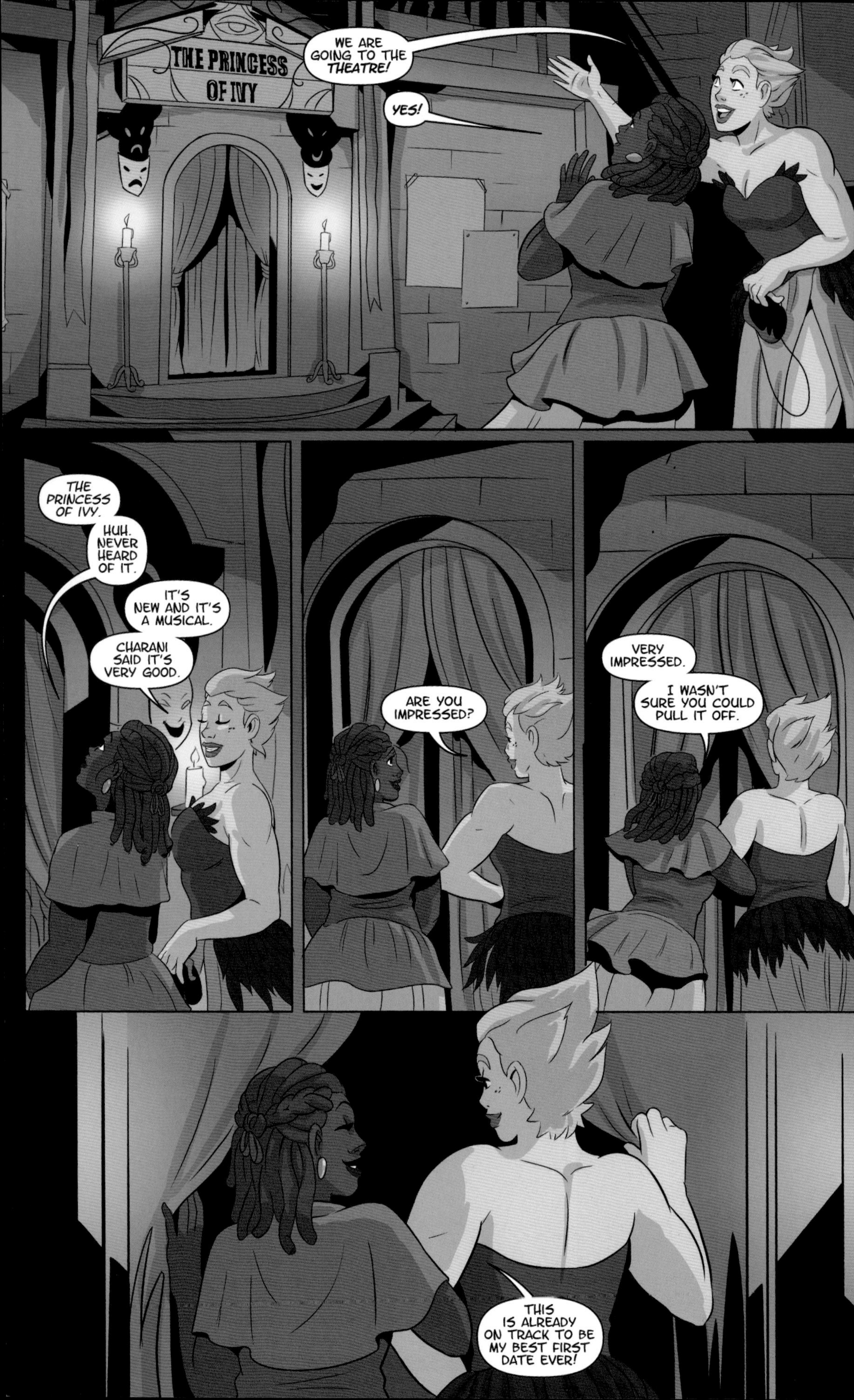
THE PRINCESS OF IVY
WE ARE GOING TO THE *THEATRE!*
YES!
THE PRINCESS OF IVY.
HUH. NEVER HEARD OF IT.
IT'S NEW AND IT'S A MUSICAL.
CHARANI SAID IT'S VERY GOOD.
ARE YOU IMPRESSED?
VERY IMPRESSED.
I WASN'T SURE YOU COULD PULL IT OFF.
THIS IS ALREADY ON TRACK TO BE MY BEST FIRST DATE EVER!

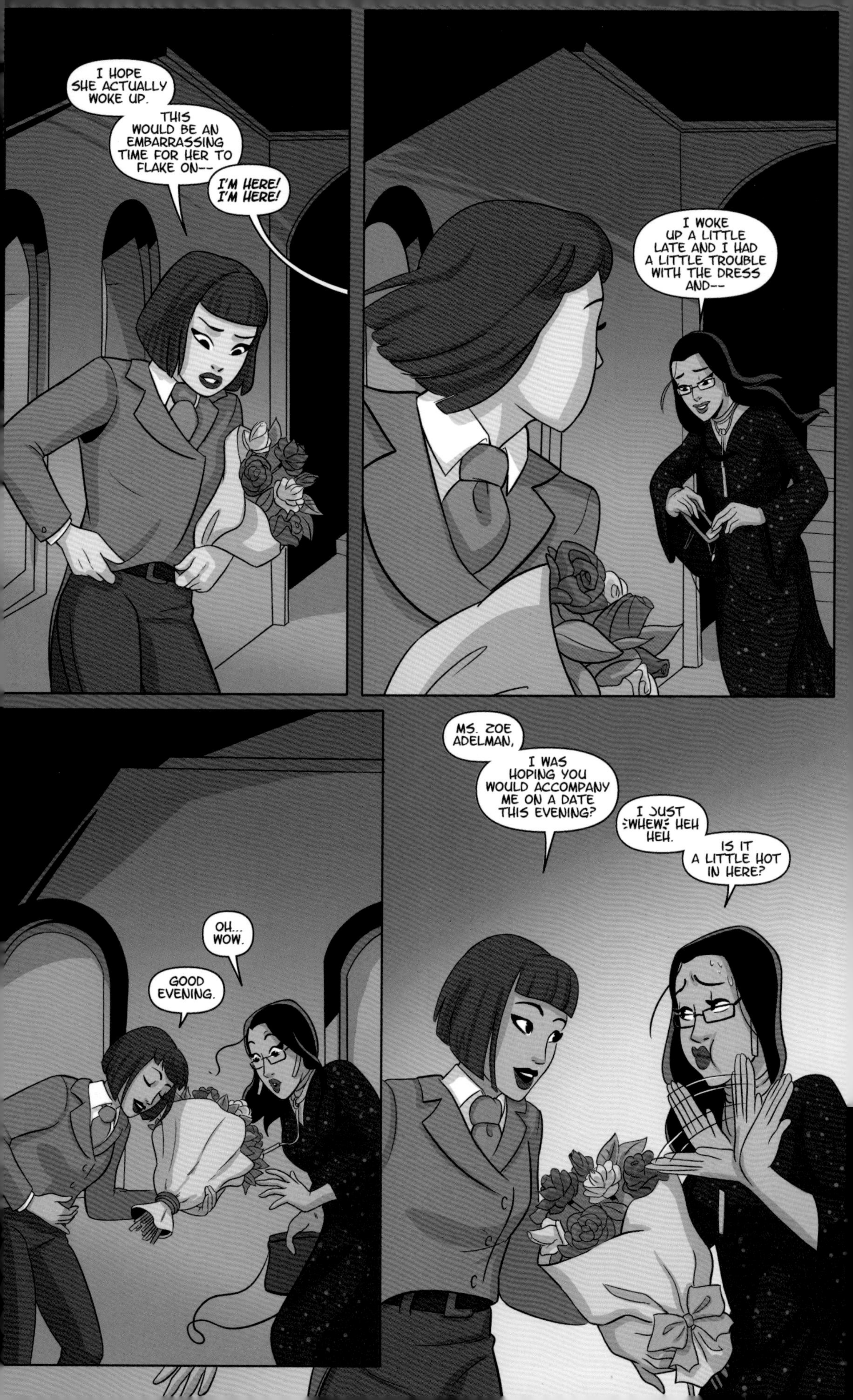

I HOPE SHE ACTUALLY WOKE UP.
THIS WOULD BE AN EMBARRASSING TIME FOR HER TO FLAKE ON--
I'M HERE! I'M HERE!
I WOKE UP A LITTLE LATE AND I HAD A LITTLE TROUBLE WITH THE DRESS AND--
GOOD EVENING.
OH... WOW.
MS. ZOE ADELMAN,
I WAS HOPING YOU WOULD ACCOMPANY ME ON A DATE THIS EVENING?
I JUST WHEW. HEH HEH.
IS IT A LITTLE HOT IN HERE?

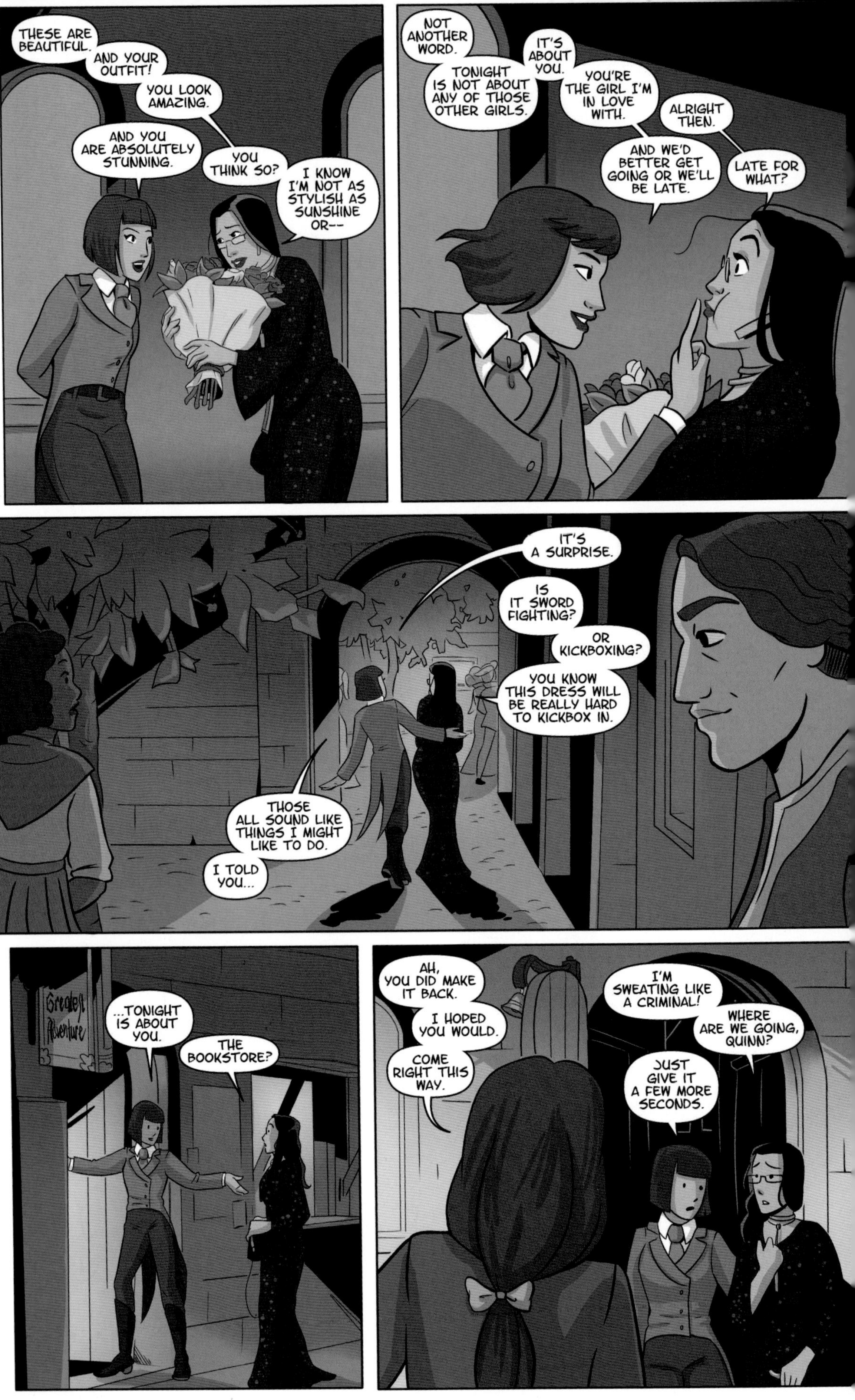
THESE ARE BEAUTIFUL.
AND YOUR OUTFIT!
YOU LOOK AMAZING.
AND YOU ARE ABSOLUTELY STUNNING.
YOU THINK SO?
I KNOW I'M NOT AS STYLISH AS SUNSHINE OR--
NOT ANOTHER WORD.
TONIGHT IS NOT ABOUT ANY OF THOSE OTHER GIRLS.
IT'S ABOUT YOU.
YOU'RE THE GIRL I'M IN LOVE WITH.
ALRIGHT THEN.
AND WE'D BETTER GET GOING OR WE'LL BE LATE.
LATE FOR WHAT?
IT'S A SURPRISE.
IS IT SWORD FIGHTING?
OR KICKBOXING?
YOU KNOW THIS DRESS WILL BE REALLY HARD TO KICKBOX IN.
THOSE ALL SOUND LIKE THINGS I MIGHT LIKE TO DO.
I TOLD YOU...
Greatest Adventure
...TONIGHT IS ABOUT YOU.
THE BOOKSTORE?
AH, YOU DID MAKE IT BACK.
I HOPED YOU WOULD.
COME RIGHT THIS WAY.
I'M SWEATING LIKE A CRIMINAL!
WHERE ARE WE GOING, QUINN?
JUST GIVE IT A FEW MORE SECONDS.

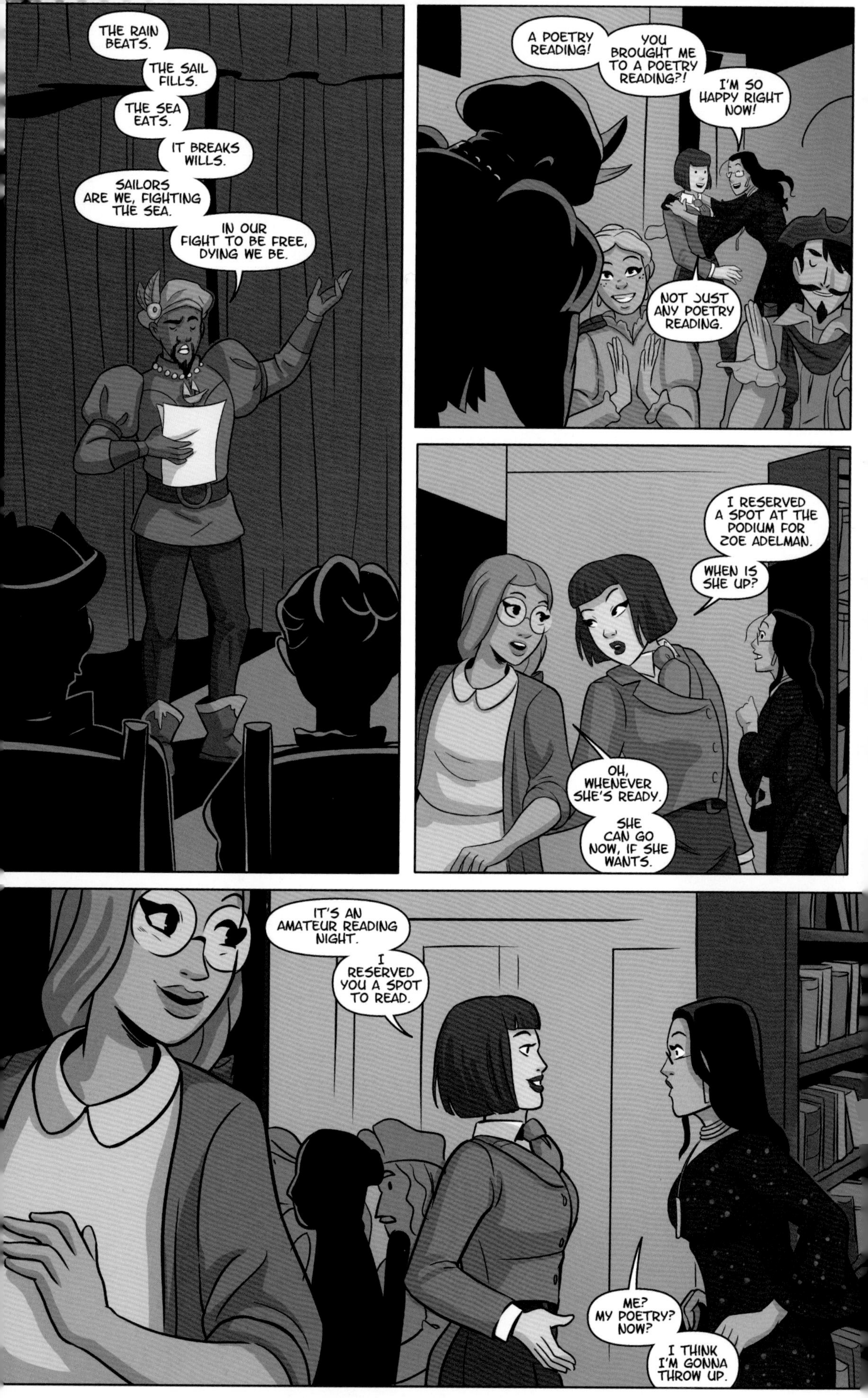
THE RAIN BEATS.
THE SAIL FILLS.
THE SEA EATS.
IT BREAKS WILLS.
SAILORS ARE WE, FIGHTING THE SEA.
IN OUR FIGHT TO BE FREE, DYING WE BE.
A POETRY READING!
YOU BROUGHT ME TO A POETRY READING?!
I'M SO HAPPY RIGHT NOW!
NOT JUST ANY POETRY READING.
I RESERVED A SPOT AT THE PODIUM FOR ZOE ADELMAN.
WHEN IS SHE UP?
OH, WHENEVER SHE'S READY.
SHE CAN GO NOW, IF SHE WANTS.
IT'S AN AMATEUR READING NIGHT.
I RESERVED YOU A SPOT TO READ.
ME? MY POETRY? NOW?
I THINK I'M GONNA THROW UP.

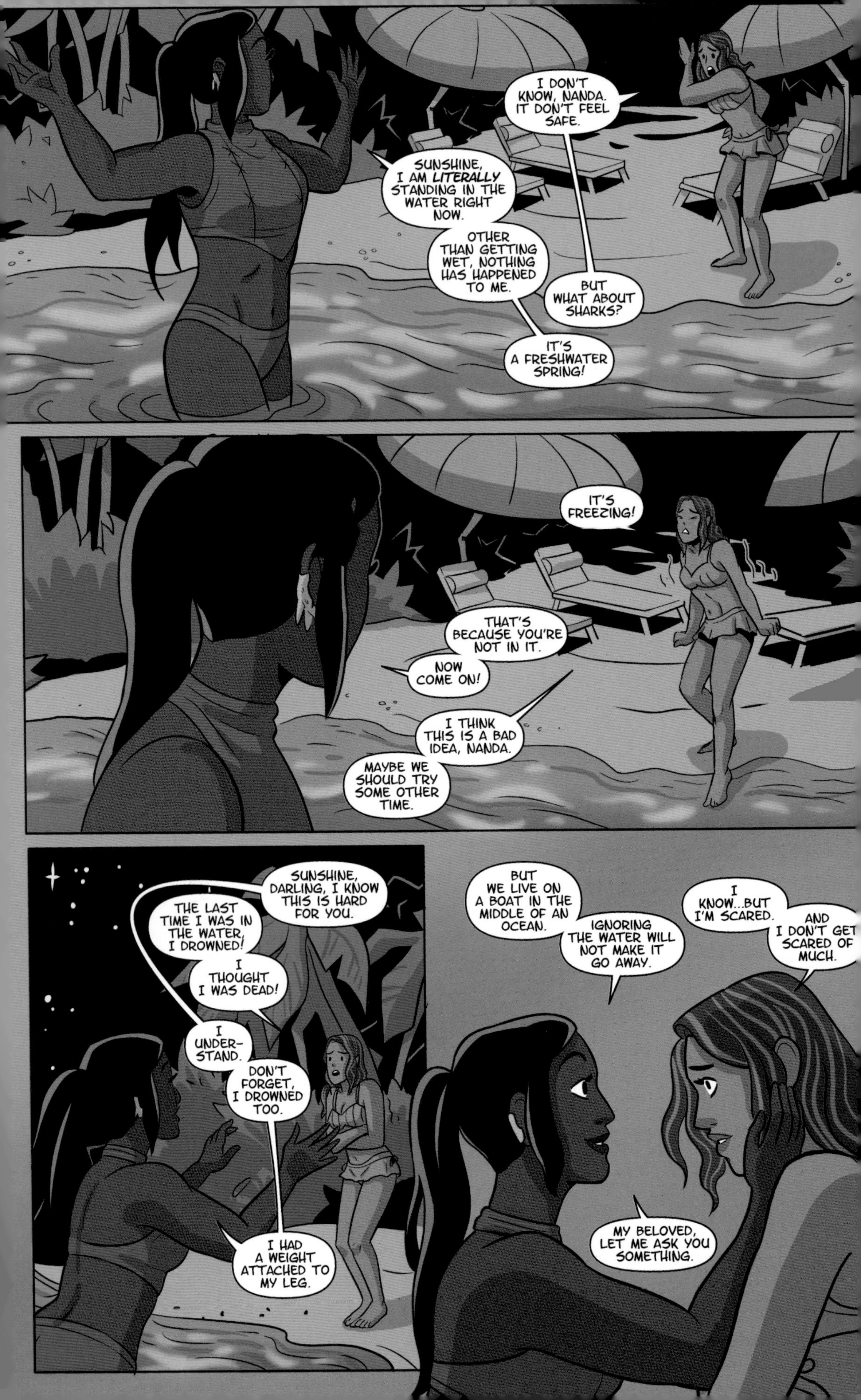
I DON'T KNOW, NANDA. IT DON'T FEEL SAFE.
SUNSHINE, I AM LITERALLY STANDING IN THE WATER RIGHT NOW.
OTHER THAN GETTING WET, NOTHING HAS HAPPENED TO ME.
BUT WHAT ABOUT SHARKS?
IT'S A FRESHWATER SPRING!
IT'S FREEZING!
THAT'S BECAUSE YOU'RE NOT IN IT.
NOW COME ON!
I THINK THIS IS A BAD IDEA, NANDA.
MAYBE WE SHOULD TRY SOME OTHER TIME.
SUNSHINE, DARLING, I KNOW THIS IS HARD FOR YOU.
THE LAST TIME I WAS IN THE WATER, I DROWNED!
I THOUGHT I WAS DEAD!
I UNDER-STAND.
DON'T FORGET, I DROWNED TOO.
I HAD A WEIGHT ATTACHED TO MY LEG.
BUT WE LIVE ON A BOAT IN THE MIDDLE OF AN OCEAN.
IGNORING THE WATER WILL NOT MAKE IT GO AWAY.
I KNOW...BUT I'M SCARED.
AND I DON'T GET SCARED OF MUCH.
MY BELOVED, LET ME ASK YOU SOMETHING.

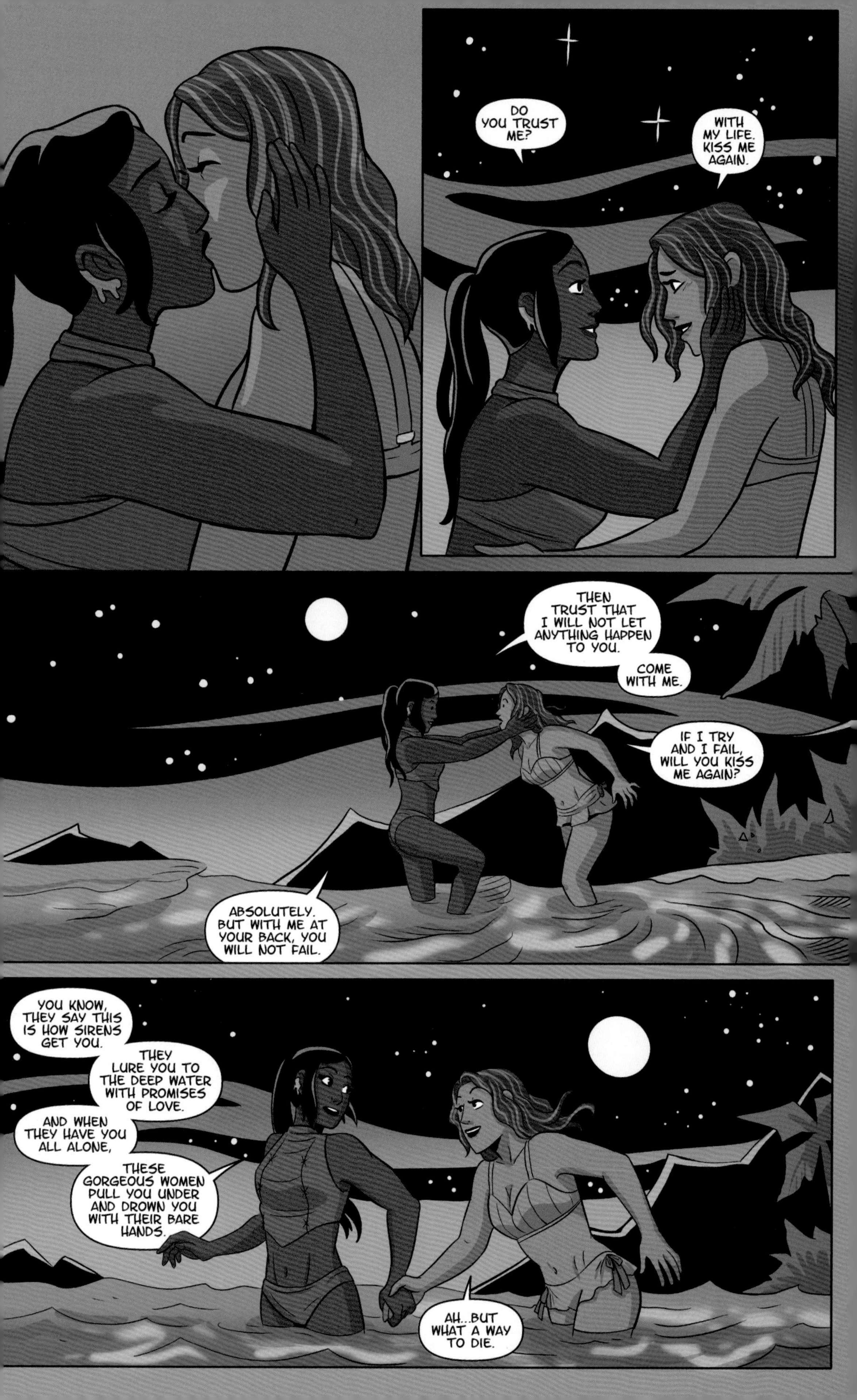
DO YOU TRUST ME?
WITH MY LIFE. KISS ME AGAIN.
THEN TRUST THAT I WILL NOT LET ANYTHING HAPPEN TO YOU.
COME WITH ME.
IF I TRY AND I FAIL, WILL YOU KISS ME AGAIN?
ABSOLUTELY. BUT WITH ME AT YOUR BACK, YOU WILL NOT FAIL.
YOU KNOW, THEY SAY THIS IS HOW SIRENS GET YOU.
THEY LURE YOU TO THE DEEP WATER WITH PROMISES OF LOVE.
AND WHEN THEY HAVE YOU ALL ALONE,
THESE GORGEOUS WOMEN PULL YOU UNDER AND DROWN YOU WITH THEIR BARE HANDS.
AH...BUT WHAT A WAY TO DIE.

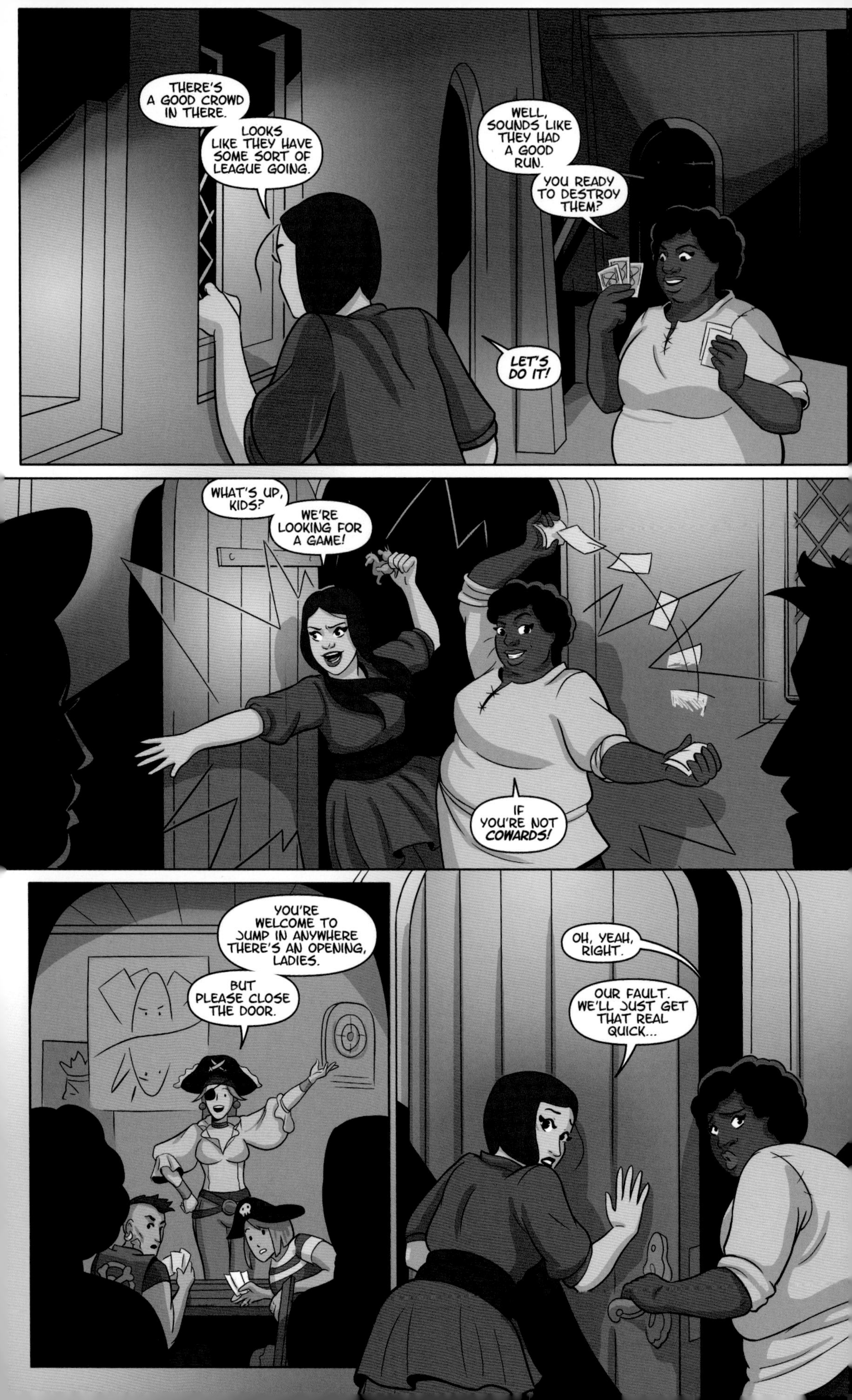
THERE'S A GOOD CROWD IN THERE.
LOOKS LIKE THEY HAVE SOME SORT OF LEAGUE GOING.
WELL, SOUNDS LIKE THEY HAD A GOOD RUN.
YOU READY TO DESTROY THEM?
LET'S DO IT!
WHAT'S UP, KIDS?
WE'RE LOOKING FOR A GAME!
IF YOU'RE NOT COWARDS!
YOU'RE WELCOME TO JUMP IN ANYWHERE THERE'S AN OPENING, LADIES.
BUT PLEASE CLOSE THE DOOR.
OH, YEAH, RIGHT.
OUR FAULT. WE'LL JUST GET THAT REAL QUICK...

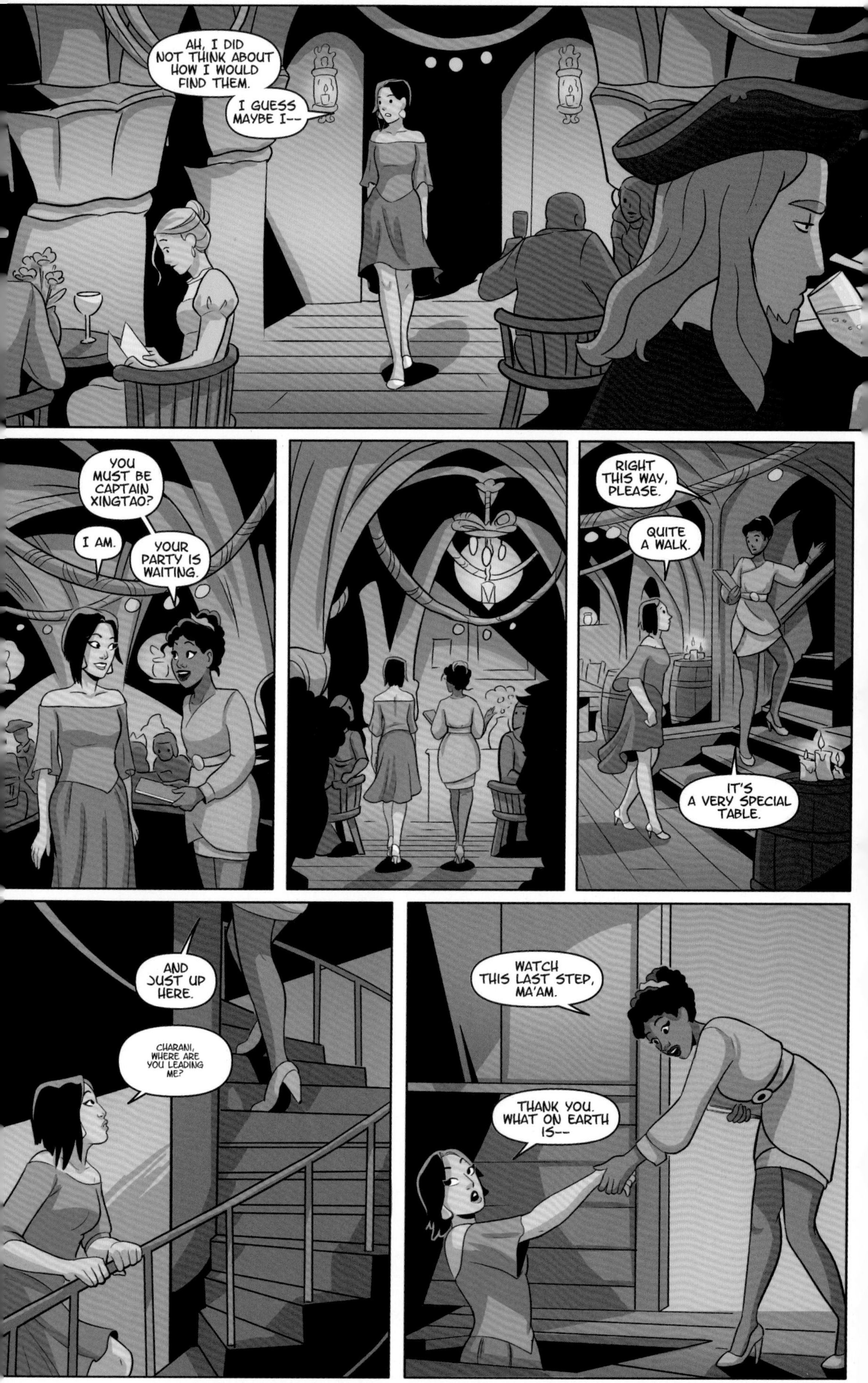

AH, I DID NOT THINK ABOUT HOW I WOULD FIND THEM.
I GUESS MAYBE I--
YOU MUST BE CAPTAIN XINGTAO?
I AM.
YOUR PARTY IS WAITING.
RIGHT THIS WAY, PLEASE.
QUITE A WALK.
IT'S A VERY SPECIAL TABLE.
AND JUST UP HERE.
CHARANI, WHERE ARE YOU LEADING ME?
WATCH THIS LAST STEP, MA'AM.
THANK YOU. WHAT ON EARTH IS--

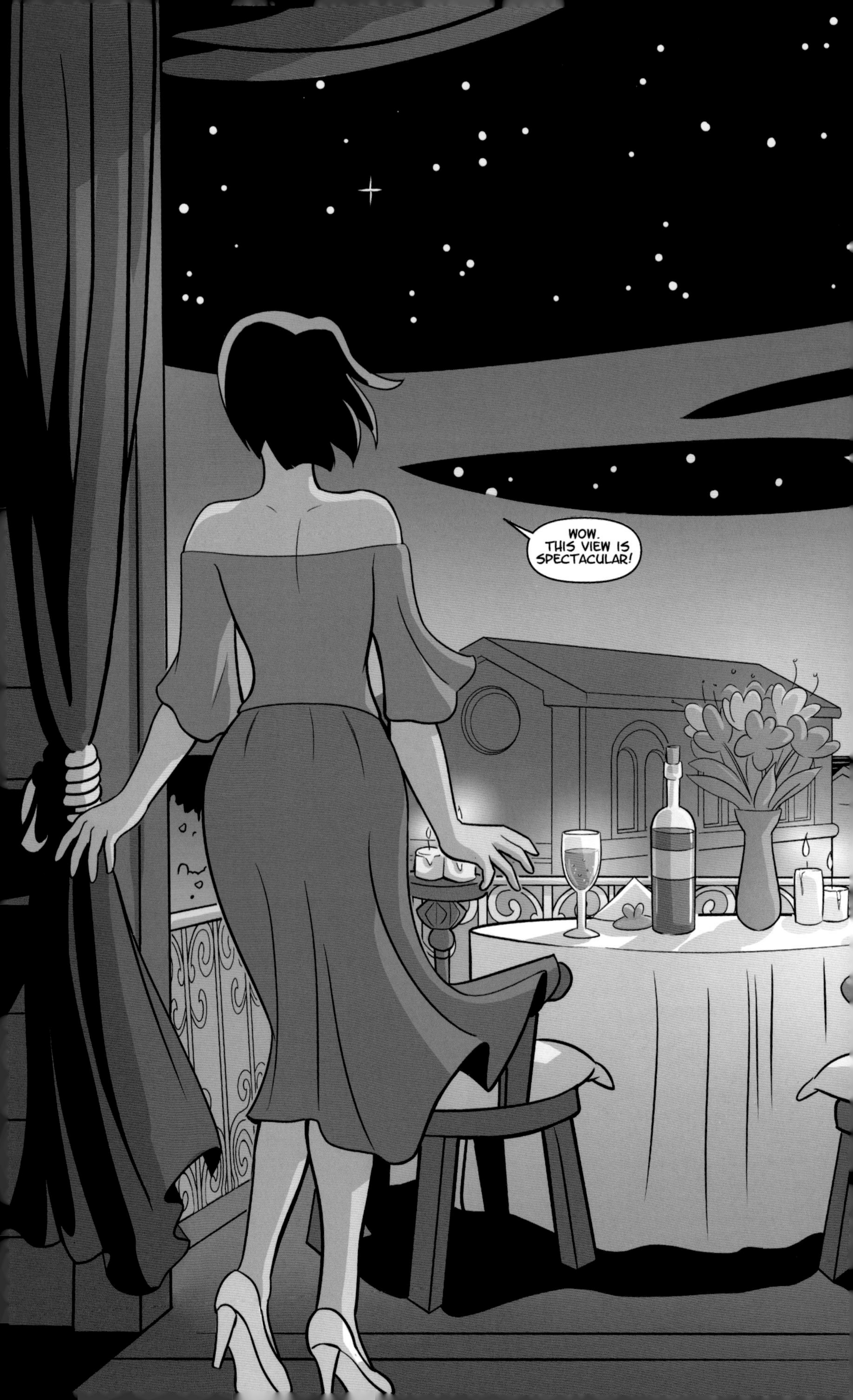
WOW. THIS VIEW IS SPECTACULAR!

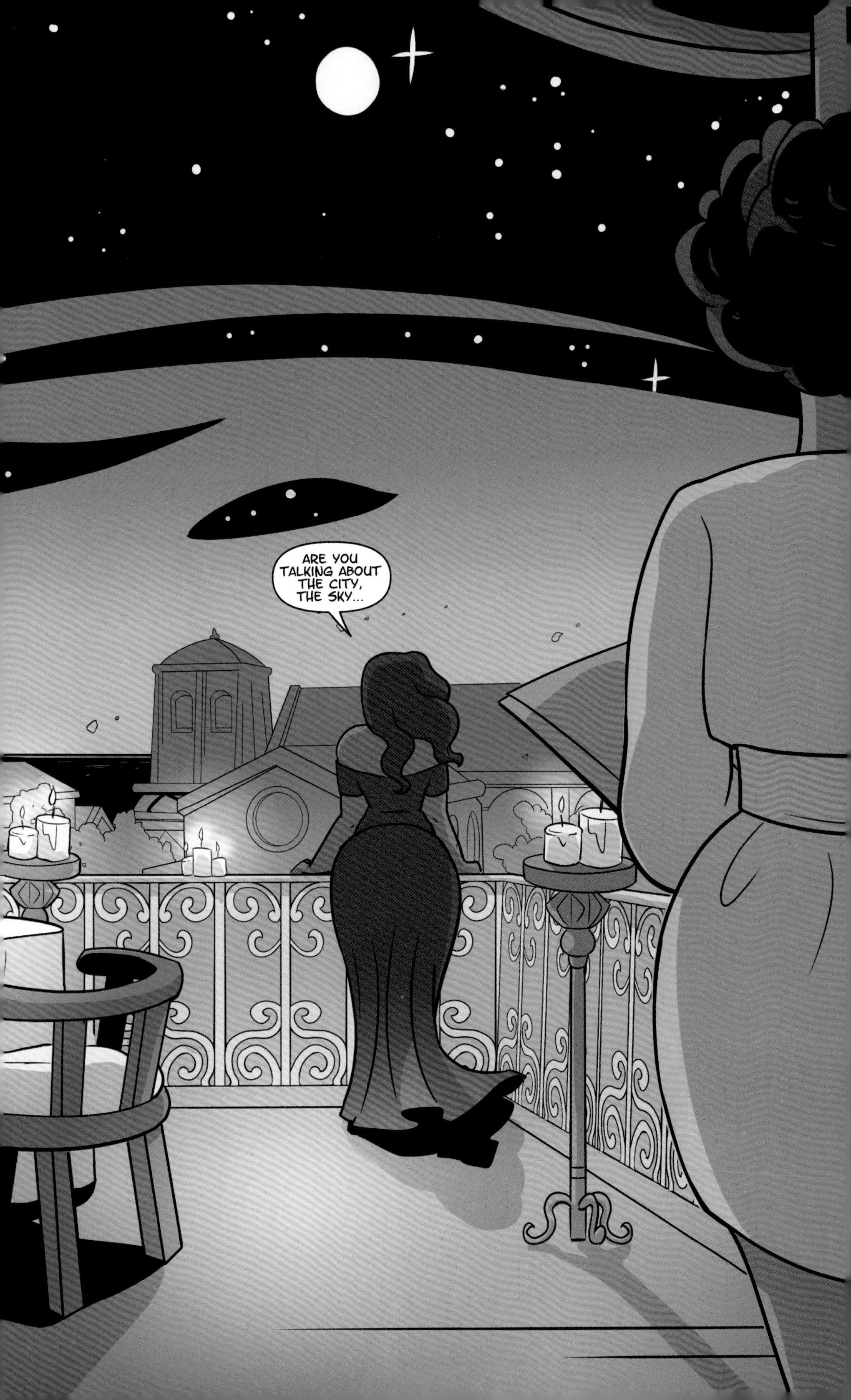
ARE YOU TALKING ABOUT THE CITY, THE SKY...

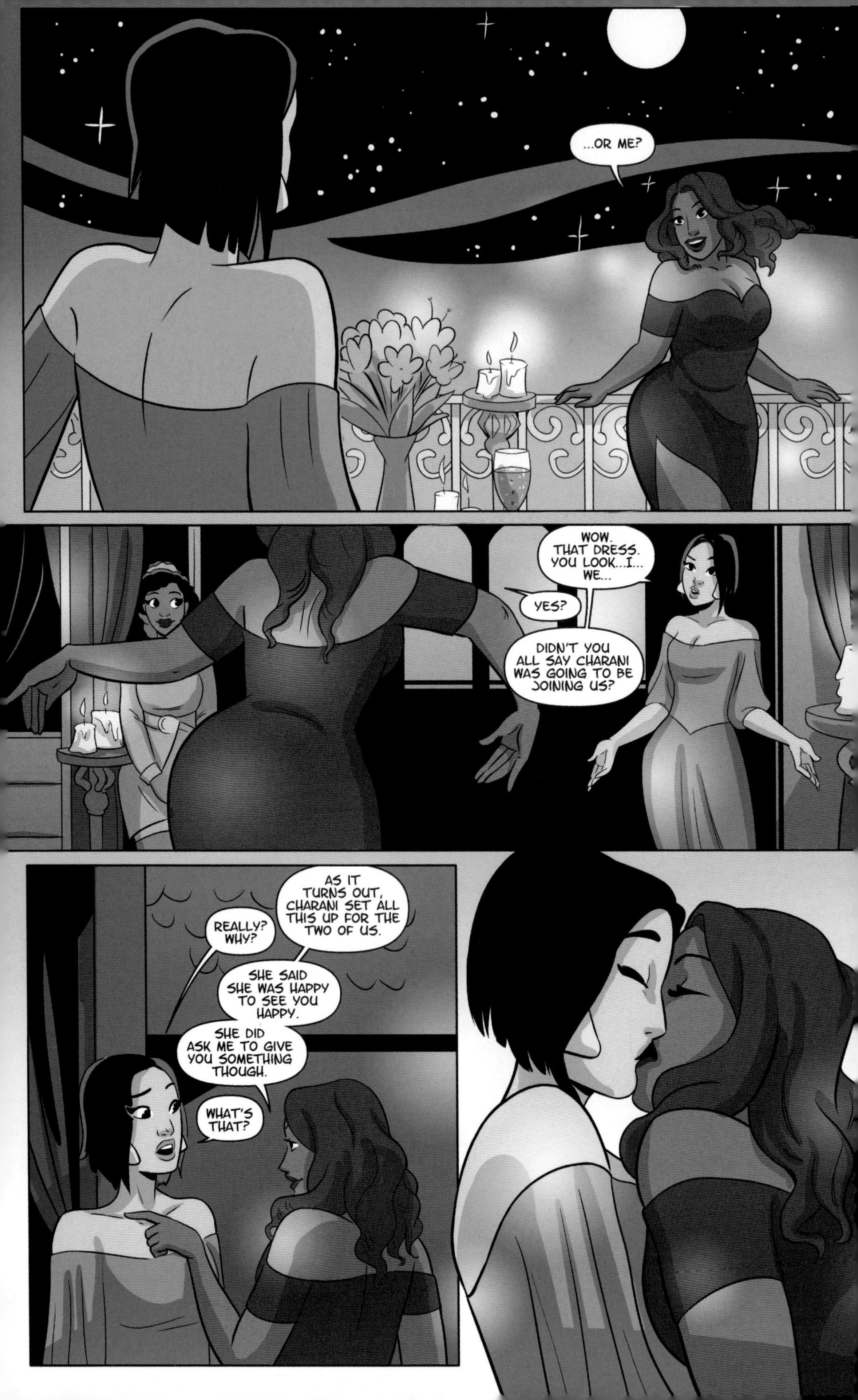
...OR ME?
WOW. THAT DRESS. YOU LOOK...I... WE...
YES?
DIDN'T YOU ALL SAY CHARANI WAS GOING TO BE JOINING US?
AS IT TURNS OUT, CHARANI SET ALL THIS UP FOR THE TWO OF US.
REALLY? WHY?
SHE SAID SHE WAS HAPPY TO SEE YOU HAPPY.
SHE DID ASK ME TO GIVE YOU SOMETHING THOUGH.
WHAT'S THAT?

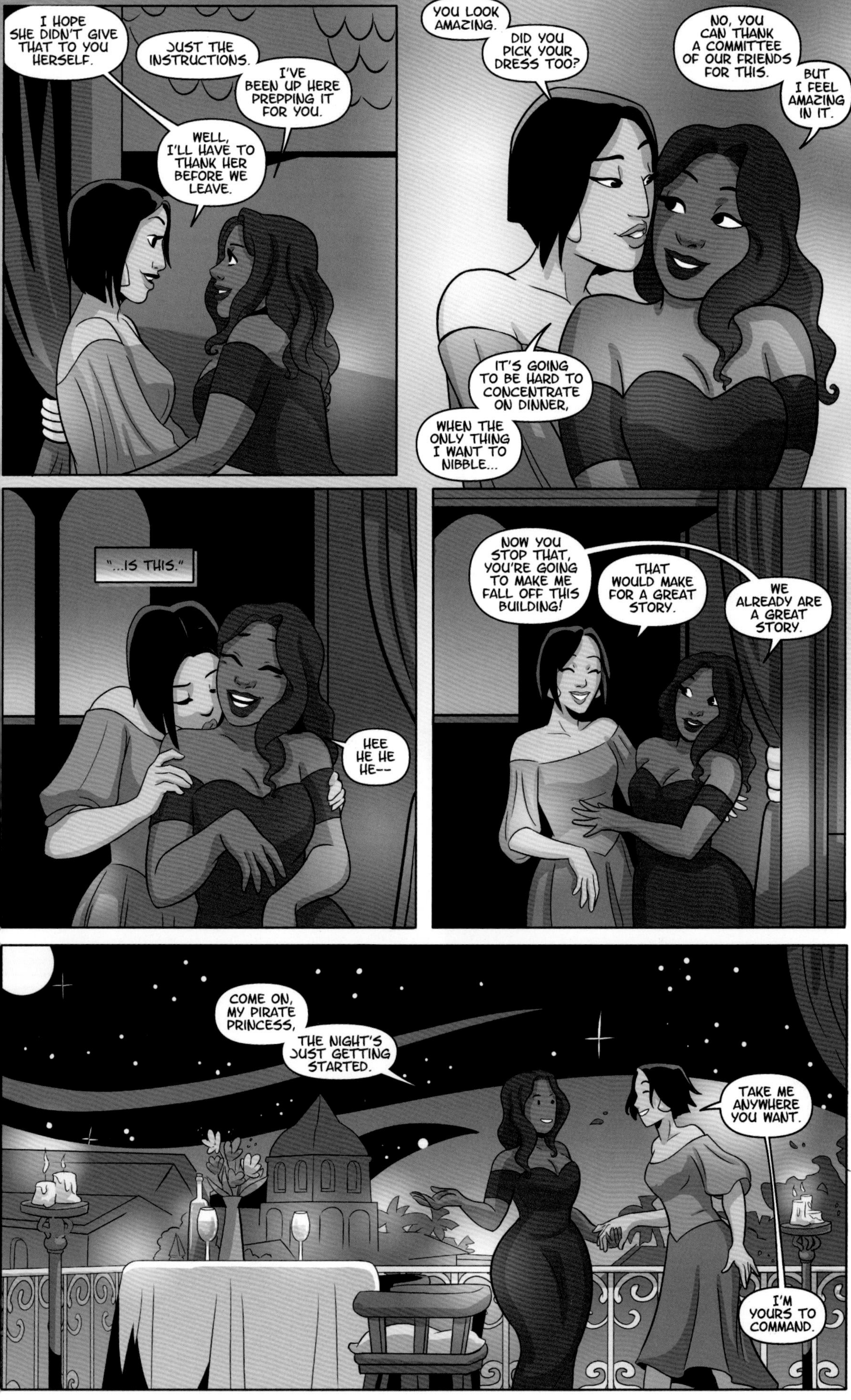
I HOPE SHE DIDN'T GIVE THAT TO YOU HERSELF.
JUST THE INSTRUCTIONS.
I'VE BEEN UP HERE PREPPING IT FOR YOU.
WELL, I'LL HAVE TO THANK HER BEFORE WE LEAVE.
YOU LOOK AMAZING.
DID YOU PICK YOUR DRESS TOO?
NO, YOU CAN THANK A COMMITTEE OF OUR FRIENDS FOR THIS.
BUT I FEEL AMAZING IN IT.
IT'S GOING TO BE HARD TO CONCENTRATE ON DINNER,
WHEN THE ONLY THING I WANT TO NIBBLE...
"...IS THIS."
HEE HE HE HE--
NOW YOU STOP THAT, YOU'RE GOING TO MAKE ME FALL OFF THIS BUILDING!
THAT WOULD MAKE FOR A GREAT STORY.
WE ALREADY ARE A GREAT STORY.
COME ON, MY PIRATE PRINCESS,
THE NIGHT'S JUST GETTING STARTED.
TAKE ME ANYWHERE YOU WANT.
I'M YOURS TO COMMAND.

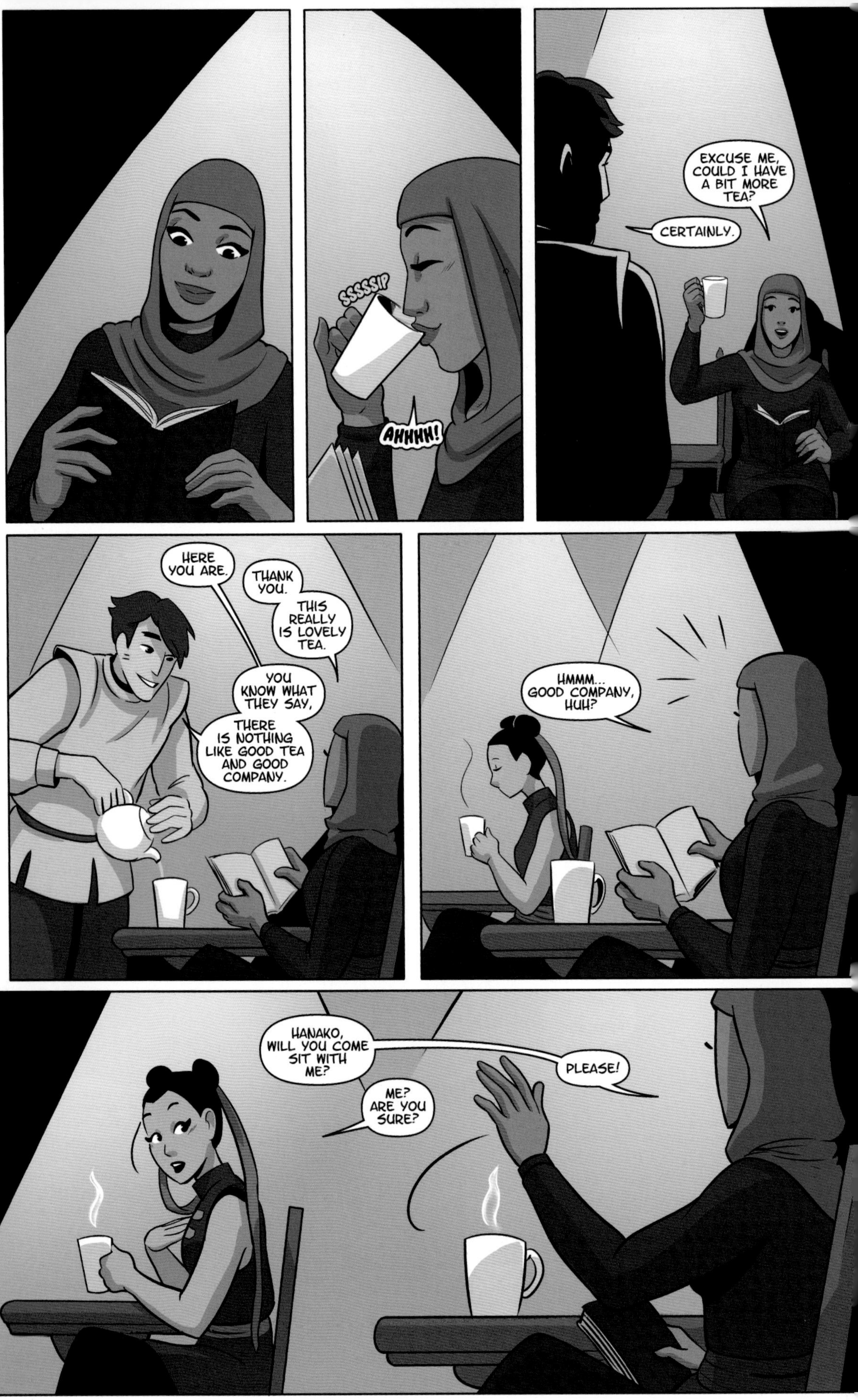
SSSSSIP
AHHHH!
EXCUSE ME, COULD I HAVE A BIT MORE TEA?
CERTAINLY.
HERE YOU ARE.
THANK YOU.
THIS REALLY IS LOVELY TEA.
YOU KNOW WHAT THEY SAY,
THERE IS NOTHING LIKE GOOD TEA AND GOOD COMPANY.
HMMM... GOOD COMPANY, HUH?
HANAKO, WILL YOU COME SIT WITH ME?
PLEASE!
ME? ARE YOU SURE?

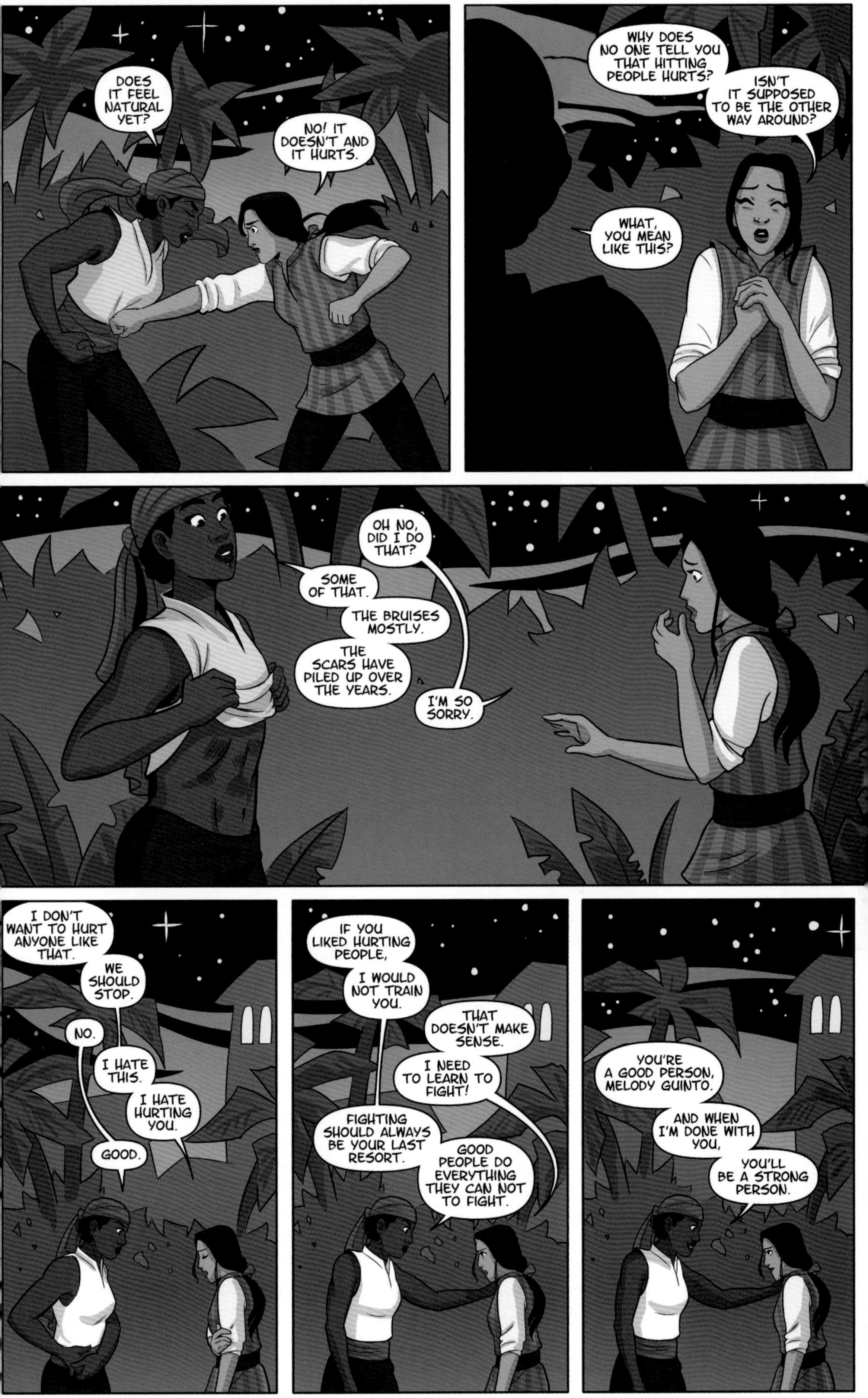
DOES IT FEEL NATURAL YET?
NO! IT DOESN'T AND IT HURTS.
WHY DOES NO ONE TELL YOU THAT HITTING PEOPLE HURTS?
ISN'T IT SUPPOSED TO BE THE OTHER WAY AROUND?
WHAT, YOU MEAN LIKE THIS?
OH NO, DID I DO THAT?
SOME OF THAT.
THE BRUISES MOSTLY.
THE SCARS HAVE PILED UP OVER THE YEARS.
I'M SO SORRY.
I DON'T WANT TO HURT ANYONE LIKE THAT.
WE SHOULD STOP.
NO.
I HATE THIS.
I HATE HURTING YOU.
GOOD.
IF YOU LIKED HURTING PEOPLE,
I WOULD NOT TRAIN YOU.
THAT DOESN'T MAKE SENSE.
I NEED TO LEARN TO FIGHT!
FIGHTING SHOULD ALWAYS BE YOUR LAST RESORT.
GOOD PEOPLE DO EVERYTHING THEY CAN NOT TO FIGHT.
YOU'RE A GOOD PERSON, MELODY GUINTO.
AND WHEN I'M DONE WITH YOU,
YOU'LL BE A STRONG PERSON.

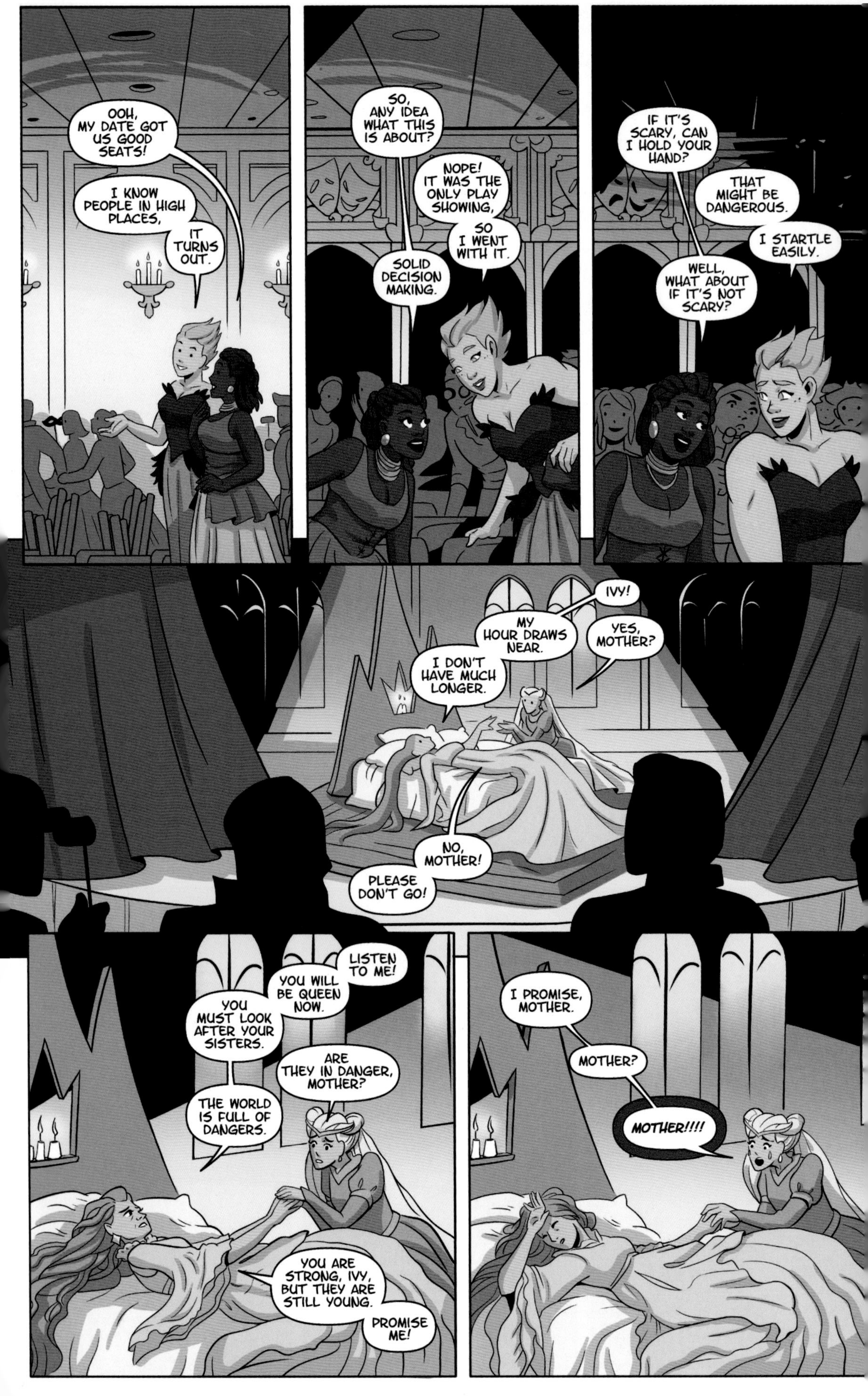
OOH, MY DATE GOT US GOOD SEATS!
I KNOW PEOPLE IN HIGH PLACES,
IT TURNS OUT.
SO, ANY IDEA WHAT THIS IS ABOUT?
NOPE! IT WAS THE ONLY PLAY SHOWING,
SO I WENT WITH IT.
SOLID DECISION MAKING.
IF IT'S SCARY, CAN I HOLD YOUR HAND?
THAT MIGHT BE DANGEROUS.
I STARTLE EASILY.
WELL, WHAT ABOUT IF IT'S NOT SCARY?
IVY!
MY HOUR DRAWS NEAR.
YES, MOTHER?
I DON'T HAVE MUCH LONGER.
NO, MOTHER!
PLEASE DON'T GO!
LISTEN TO ME!
YOU WILL BE QUEEN NOW.
YOU MUST LOOK AFTER YOUR SISTERS.
ARE THEY IN DANGER, MOTHER?
THE WORLD IS FULL OF DANGERS.
YOU ARE STRONG, IVY, BUT THEY ARE STILL YOUNG.
PROMISE ME!
I PROMISE, MOTHER.
MOTHER?
MOTHER!!!!

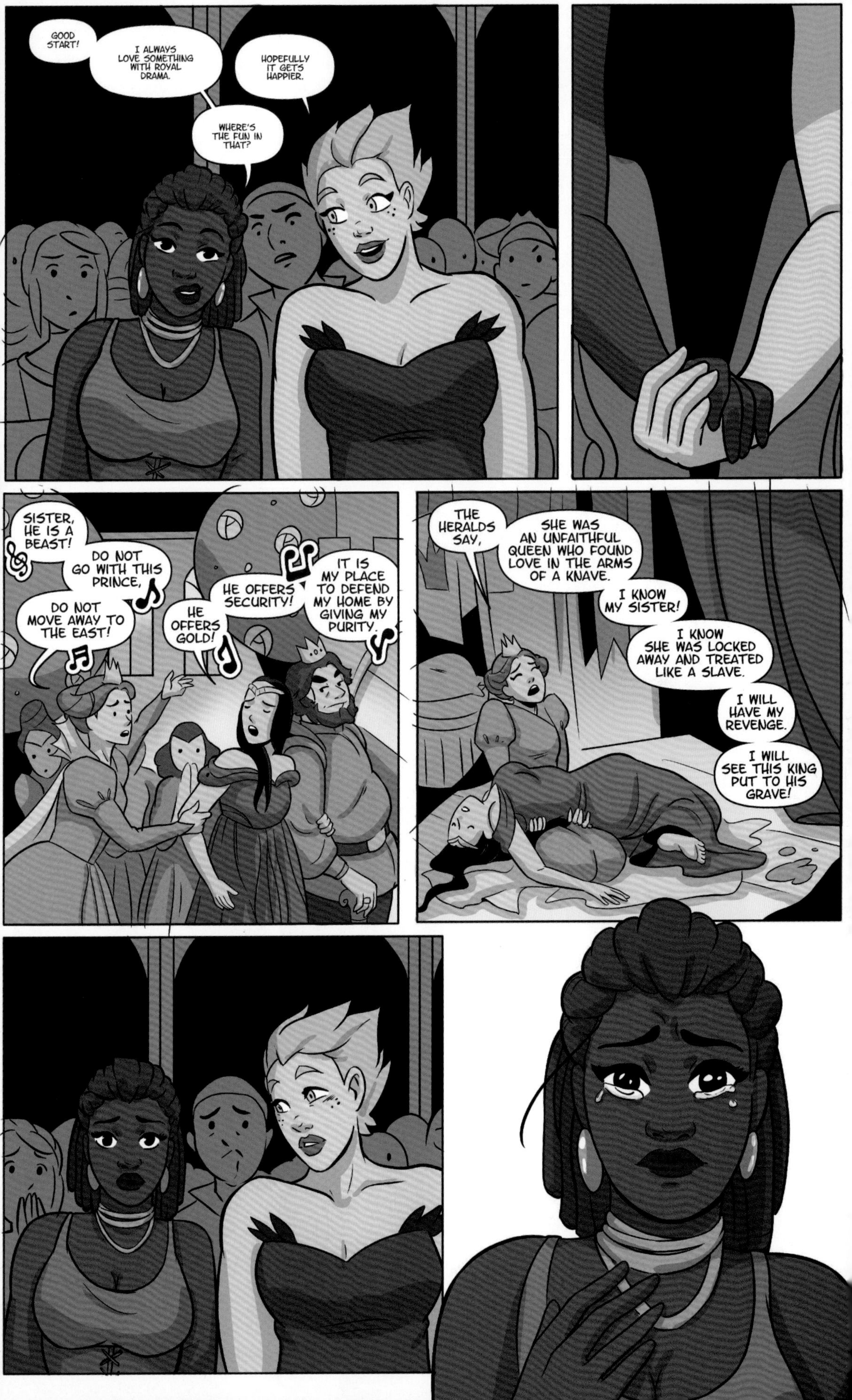
GOOD START!
I ALWAYS LOVE SOMETHING WITH ROYAL DRAMA.
WHERE'S THE FUN IN THAT?
HOPEFULLY IT GETS HAPPIER.
SISTER, HE IS A BEAST!
DO NOT GO WITH THIS PRINCE,
DO NOT MOVE AWAY TO THE EAST!
HE OFFERS GOLD!
HE OFFERS SECURITY!
IT IS MY PLACE TO DEFEND MY HOME BY GIVING MY PURITY.
THE HERALDS SAY,
SHE WAS AN UNFAITHFUL QUEEN WHO FOUND LOVE IN THE ARMS OF A KNAVE.
I KNOW MY SISTER!
I KNOW SHE WAS LOCKED AWAY AND TREATED LIKE A SLAVE.
I WILL HAVE MY REVENGE.
I WILL SEE THIS KING PUT TO HIS GRAVE!

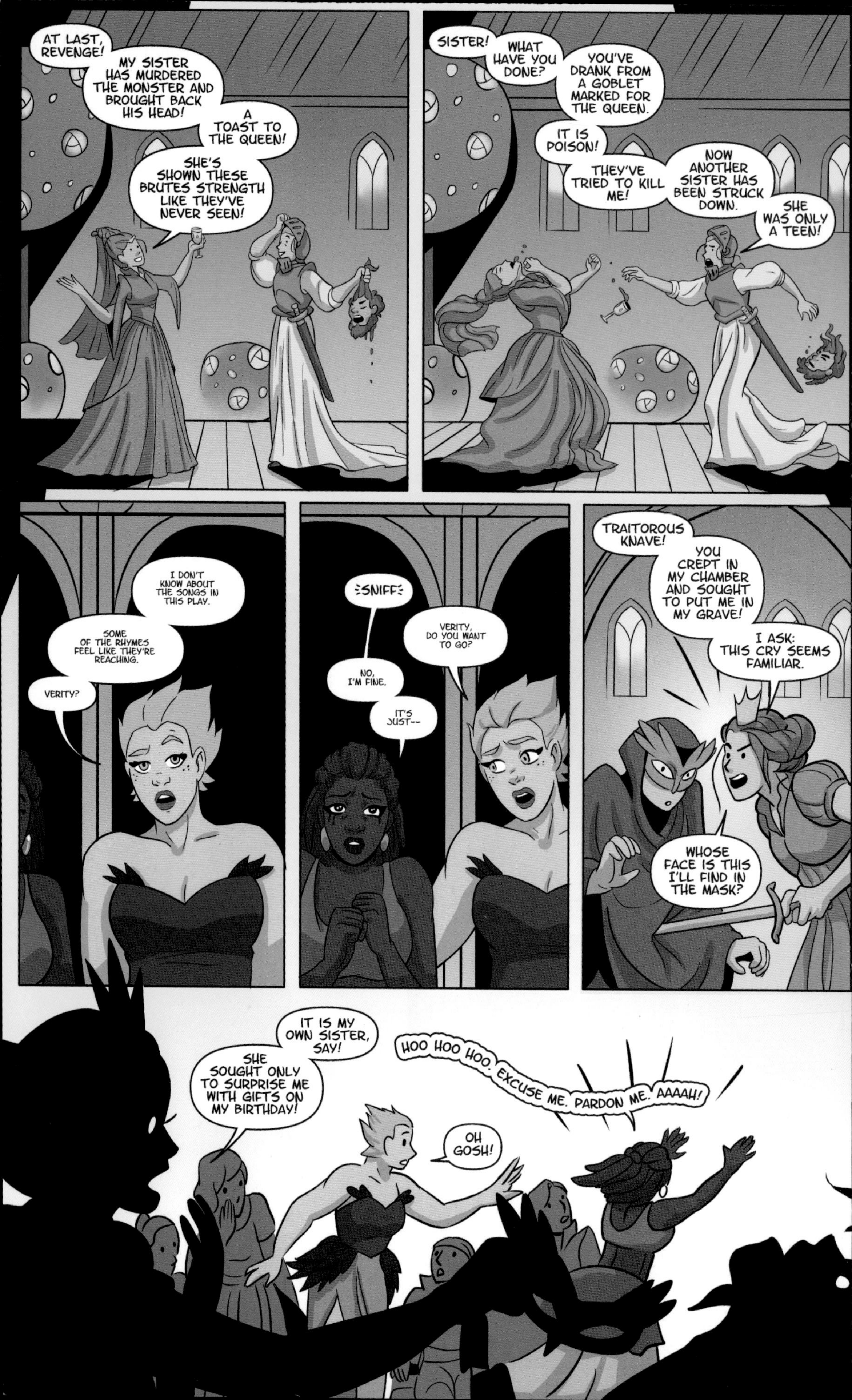
AT LAST, REVENGE!
MY SISTER HAS MURDERED THE MONSTER AND BROUGHT BACK HIS HEAD!
A TOAST TO THE QUEEN!
SHE'S SHOWN THESE BRUTES STRENGTH LIKE THEY'VE NEVER SEEN!
SISTER!
WHAT HAVE YOU DONE?
YOU'VE DRANK FROM A GOBLET MARKED FOR THE QUEEN.
IT IS POISON!
THEY'VE TRIED TO KILL ME!
NOW ANOTHER SISTER HAS BEEN STRUCK DOWN.
SHE WAS ONLY A TEEN!
I DON'T KNOW ABOUT THE SONGS IN THIS PLAY.
SOME OF THE RHYMES FEEL LIKE THEY'RE REACHING.
VERITY?
SNIFF
VERITY, DO YOU WANT TO GO?
NO, I'M FINE.
IT'S JUST--
TRAITOROUS KNAVE!
YOU CREPT IN MY CHAMBER AND SOUGHT TO PUT ME IN MY GRAVE!
I ASK: THIS CRY SEEMS FAMILIAR.
WHOSE FACE IS THIS I'LL FIND IN THE MASK?
IT IS MY OWN SISTER, SAY!
SHE SOUGHT ONLY TO SURPRISE ME WITH GIFTS ON MY BIRTHDAY!
OH GOSH!
HOO HOO HOO. EXCUSE ME. PARDON ME. AAAAH!

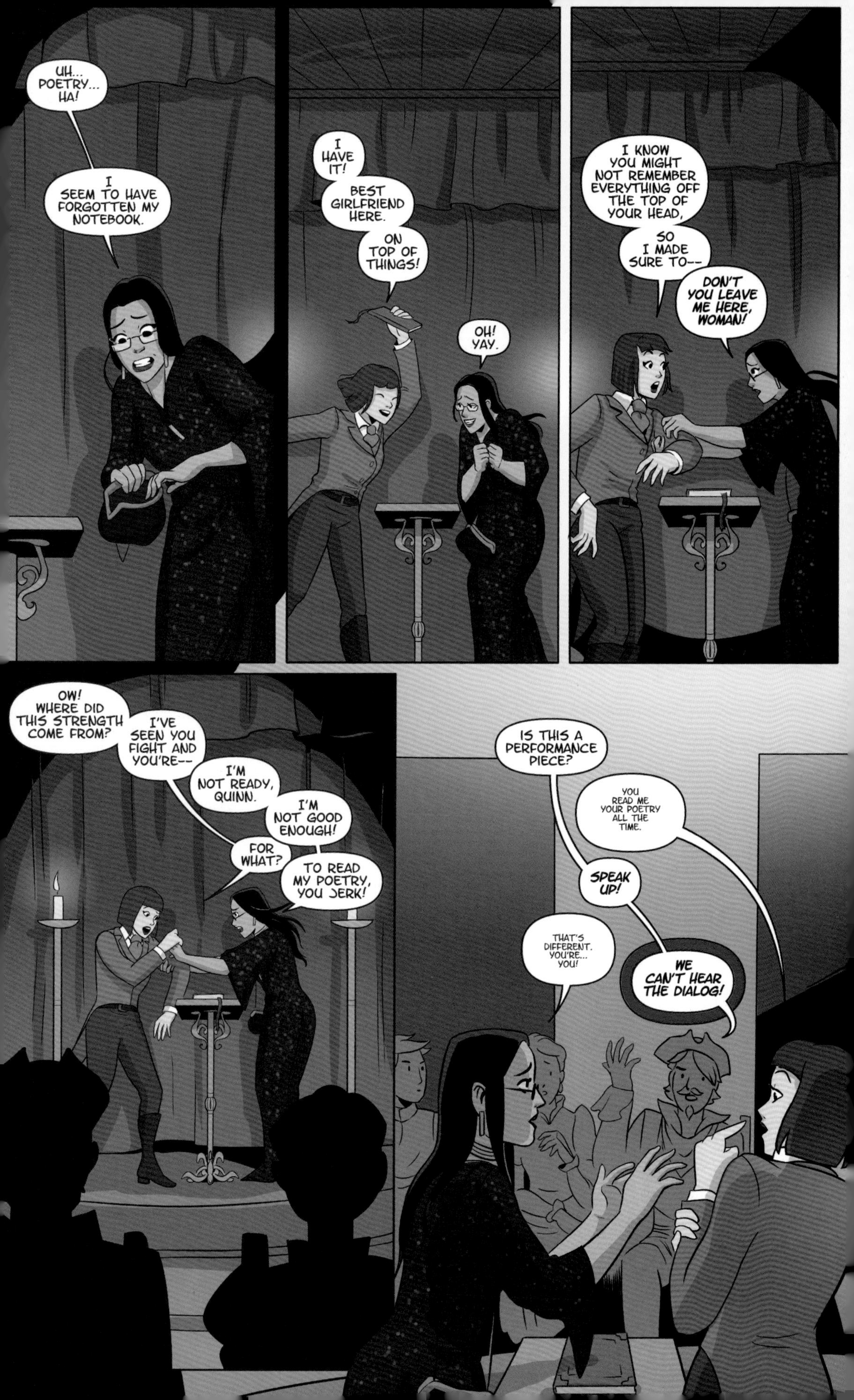
UH... POETRY... HA!
I SEEM TO HAVE FORGOTTEN MY NOTEBOOK.
I HAVE IT!
BEST GIRLFRIEND HERE.
ON TOP OF THINGS!
OH! YAY.
I KNOW YOU MIGHT NOT REMEMBER EVERYTHING OFF THE TOP OF YOUR HEAD,
SO I MADE SURE TO--
DON'T YOU LEAVE ME HERE, WOMAN!
OW! WHERE DID THIS STRENGTH COME FROM?
I'VE SEEN YOU FIGHT AND YOU'RE--
I'M NOT READY, QUINN.
I'M NOT GOOD ENOUGH!
FOR WHAT?
TO READ MY POETRY, YOU JERK!
IS THIS A PERFORMANCE PIECE?
YOU READ ME YOUR POETRY ALL THE TIME.
SPEAK UP!
THAT'S DIFFERENT. YOU'RE... YOU!
WE CAN'T HEAR THE DIALOG!

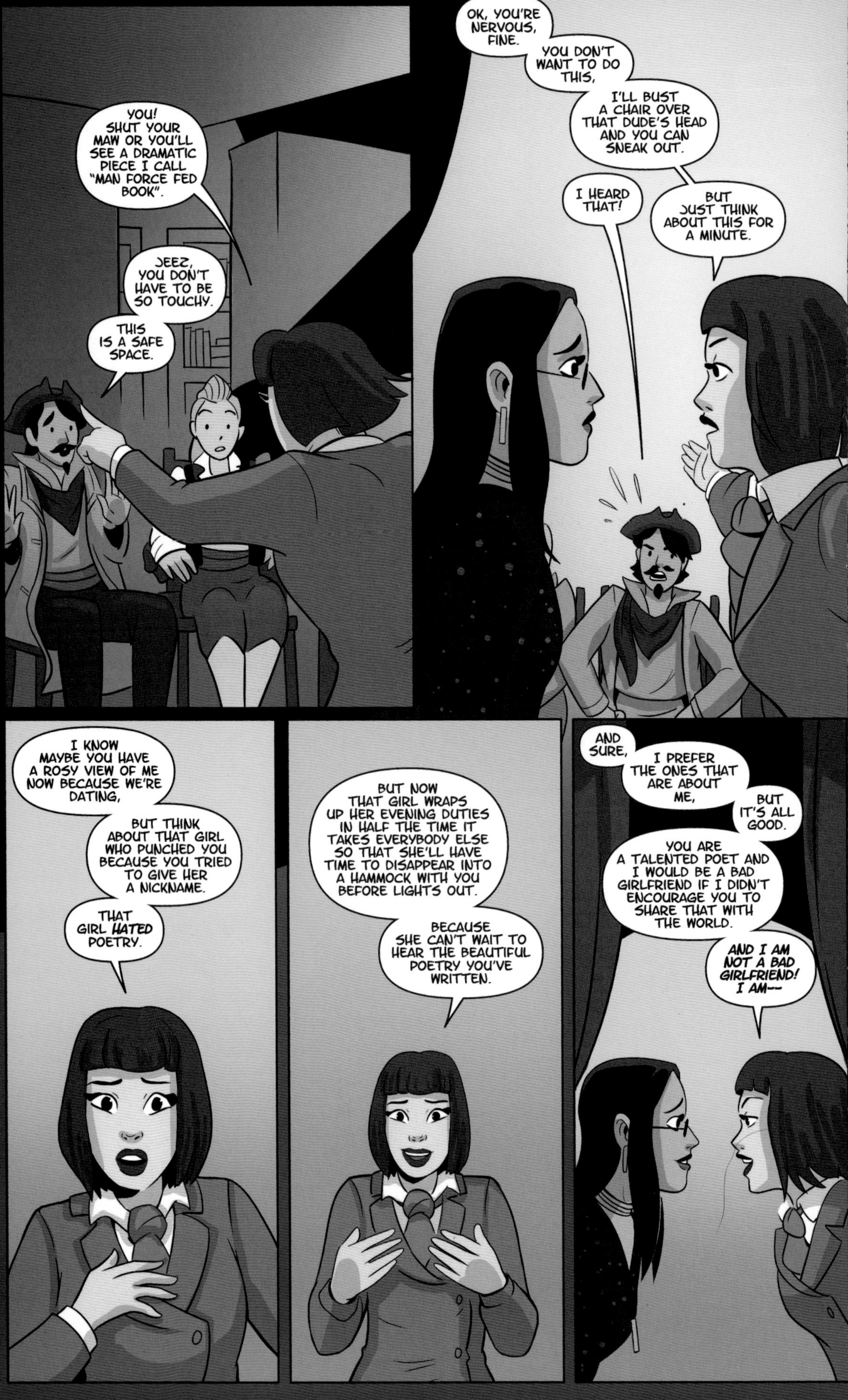
YOU! SHUT YOUR MAW OR YOU'LL SEE A DRAMATIC PIECE I CALL "MAN FORCE FED BOOK".
JEEZ, YOU DON'T HAVE TO BE SO TOUCHY.
THIS IS A SAFE SPACE.
OK, YOU'RE NERVOUS, FINE.
YOU DON'T WANT TO DO THIS,
I'LL BUST A CHAIR OVER THAT DUDE'S HEAD AND YOU CAN SNEAK OUT.
I HEARD THAT!
BUT JUST THINK ABOUT THIS FOR A MINUTE.
I KNOW MAYBE YOU HAVE A ROSY VIEW OF ME NOW BECAUSE WE'RE DATING,
BUT THINK ABOUT THAT GIRL WHO PUNCHED YOU BECAUSE YOU TRIED TO GIVE HER A NICKNAME.
THAT GIRL HATED POETRY.
BUT NOW THAT GIRL WRAPS UP HER EVENING DUTIES IN HALF THE TIME IT TAKES EVERYBODY ELSE SO THAT SHE'LL HAVE TIME TO DISAPPEAR INTO A HAMMOCK WITH YOU BEFORE LIGHTS OUT.
BECAUSE SHE CAN'T WAIT TO HEAR THE BEAUTIFUL POETRY YOU'VE WRITTEN.
AND SURE,
I PREFER THE ONES THAT ARE ABOUT ME,
BUT IT'S ALL GOOD.
YOU ARE A TALENTED POET AND I WOULD BE A BAD GIRLFRIEND IF I DIDN'T ENCOURAGE YOU TO SHARE THAT WITH THE WORLD.
AND I AM NOT A BAD GIRLFRIEND! I AM--

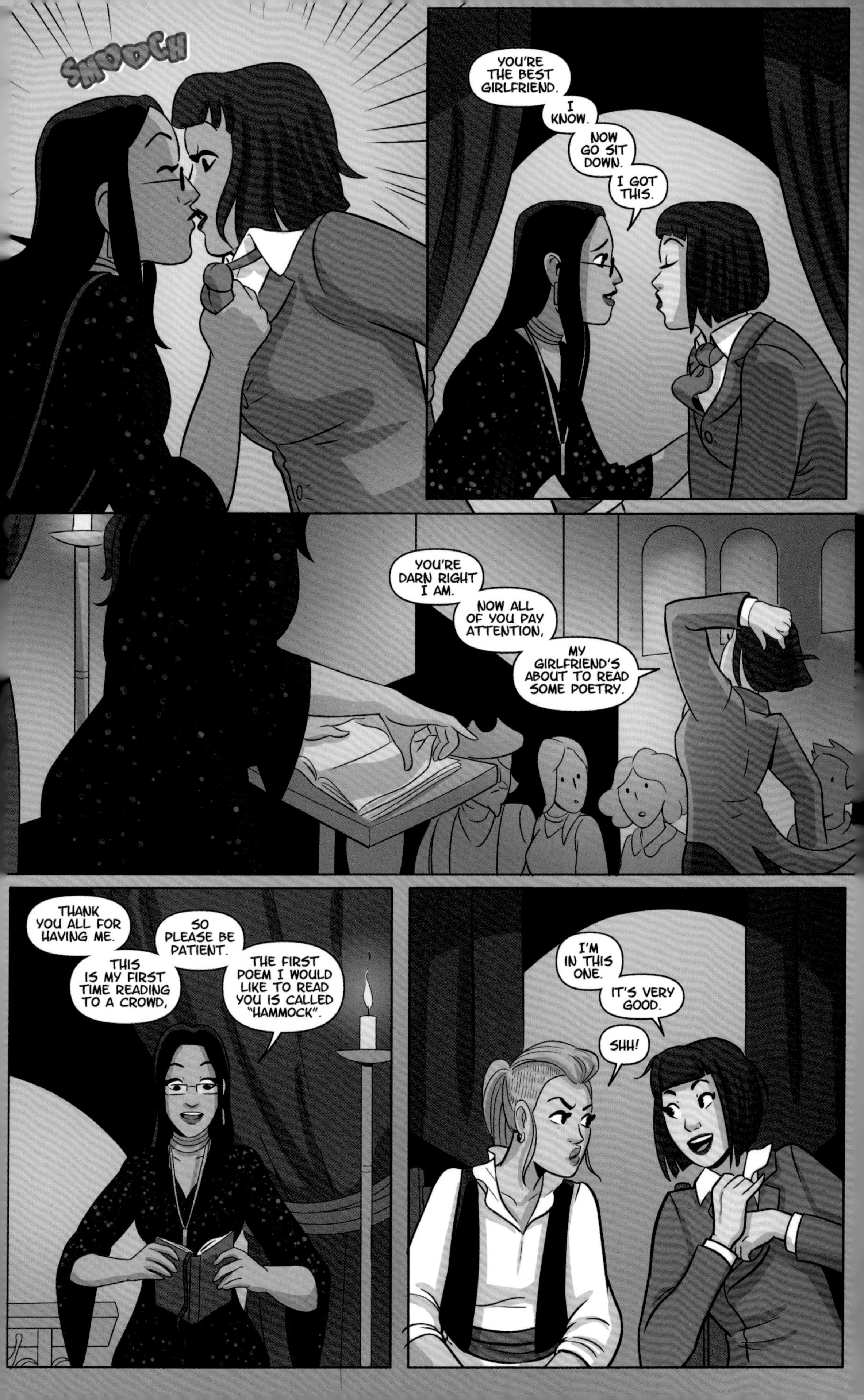
SMOOCH
YOU'RE THE BEST GIRLFRIEND.
I KNOW.
NOW GO SIT DOWN.
I GOT THIS.
YOU'RE DARN RIGHT I AM.
NOW ALL OF YOU PAY ATTENTION,
MY GIRLFRIEND'S ABOUT TO READ SOME POETRY.
THANK YOU ALL FOR HAVING ME.
THIS IS MY FIRST TIME READING TO A CROWD,
SO PLEASE BE PATIENT.
THE FIRST POEM I WOULD LIKE TO READ YOU IS CALLED "HAMMOCK".
I'M IN THIS ONE.
IT'S VERY GOOD.
SHH!

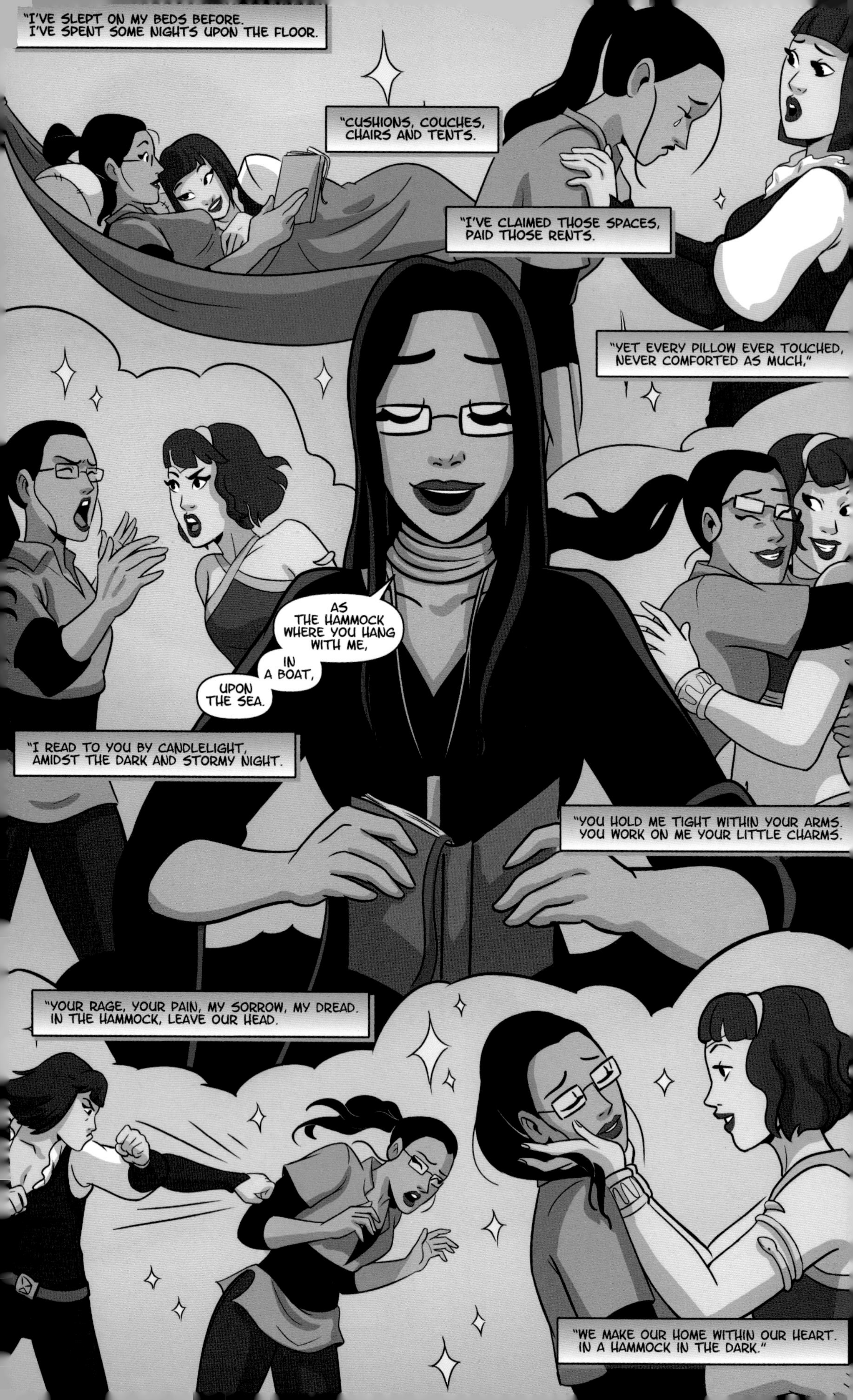
"I'VE SLEPT ON MY BEDS BEFORE. I'VE SPENT SOME NIGHTS UPON THE FLOOR.
"CUSHIONS, COUCHES, CHAIRS AND TENTS.
"I'VE CLAIMED THOSE SPACES, PAID THOSE RENTS.
"YET EVERY PILLOW EVER TOUCHED, NEVER COMFORTED AS MUCH,"
AS THE HAMMOCK WHERE YOU HANG WITH ME,
IN A BOAT,
UPON THE SEA.
"I READ TO YOU BY CANDLELIGHT, AMIDST THE DARK AND STORMY NIGHT.
"YOU HOLD ME TIGHT WITHIN YOUR ARMS. YOU WORK ON ME YOUR LITTLE CHARMS.
"YOUR RAGE, YOUR PAIN, MY SORROW, MY DREAD. IN THE HAMMOCK, LEAVE OUR HEAD.
"WE MAKE OUR HOME WITHIN OUR HEART. IN A HAMMOCK IN THE DARK."

Princess Raven: The Pirate Princess

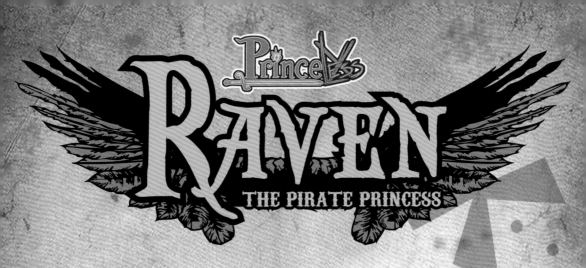

Year Three: Monsters of the Deep

Chapter Four: Date Night Part 4

Written By: Jeremy Whitley

Pencils By: Telênia Albuquerque

Inks By: Christine Hipp

Colors By: Lexillo

Lettered By: Alex Scherkenbach

Edited By: Nicole D'Andria

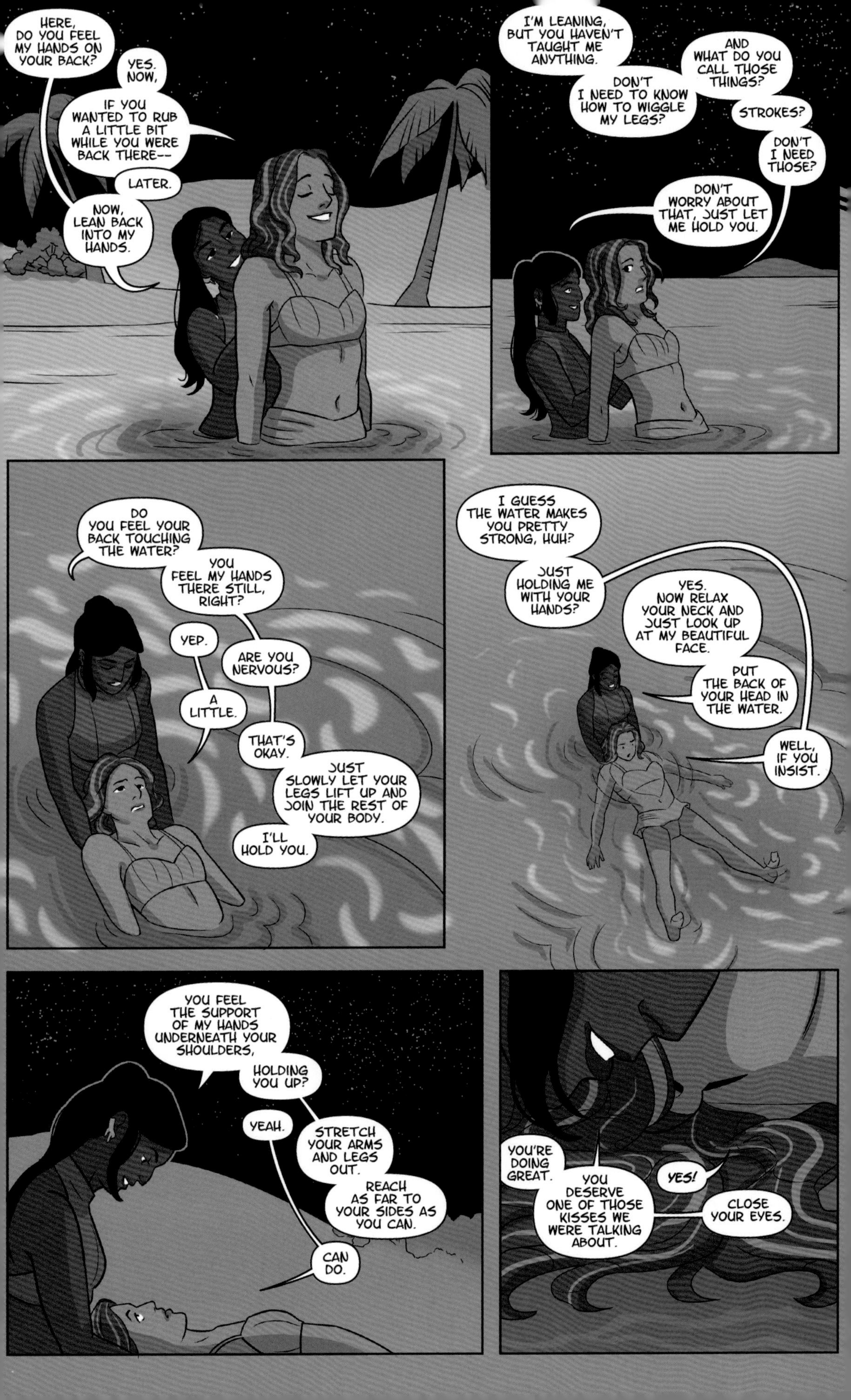
HERE, DO YOU FEEL MY HANDS ON YOUR BACK?
YES. NOW,
IF YOU WANTED TO RUB A LITTLE BIT WHILE YOU WERE BACK THERE--
LATER.
NOW, LEAN BACK INTO MY HANDS.
I'M LEANING, BUT YOU HAVEN'T TAUGHT ME ANYTHING.
DON'T I NEED TO KNOW HOW TO WIGGLE MY LEGS?
AND WHAT DO YOU CALL THOSE THINGS?
STROKES?
DON'T I NEED THOSE?
DON'T WORRY ABOUT THAT, JUST LET ME HOLD YOU.
DO YOU FEEL YOUR BACK TOUCHING THE WATER?
YOU FEEL MY HANDS THERE STILL, RIGHT?
YEP.
ARE YOU NERVOUS?
A LITTLE.
THAT'S OKAY.
JUST SLOWLY LET YOUR LEGS LIFT UP AND JOIN THE REST OF YOUR BODY.
I'LL HOLD YOU.
I GUESS THE WATER MAKES YOU PRETTY STRONG, HUH?
JUST HOLDING ME WITH YOUR HANDS?
YES. NOW RELAX YOUR NECK AND JUST LOOK UP AT MY BEAUTIFUL FACE.
PUT THE BACK OF YOUR HEAD IN THE WATER.
WELL, IF YOU INSIST.
YOU FEEL THE SUPPORT OF MY HANDS UNDERNEATH YOUR SHOULDERS,
HOLDING YOU UP?
YEAH.
STRETCH YOUR ARMS AND LEGS OUT.
REACH AS FAR TO YOUR SIDES AS YOU CAN.
CAN DO.
YOU'RE DOING GREAT.
YOU DESERVE ONE OF THOSE KISSES WE WERE TALKING ABOUT.
YES!
CLOSE YOUR EYES.

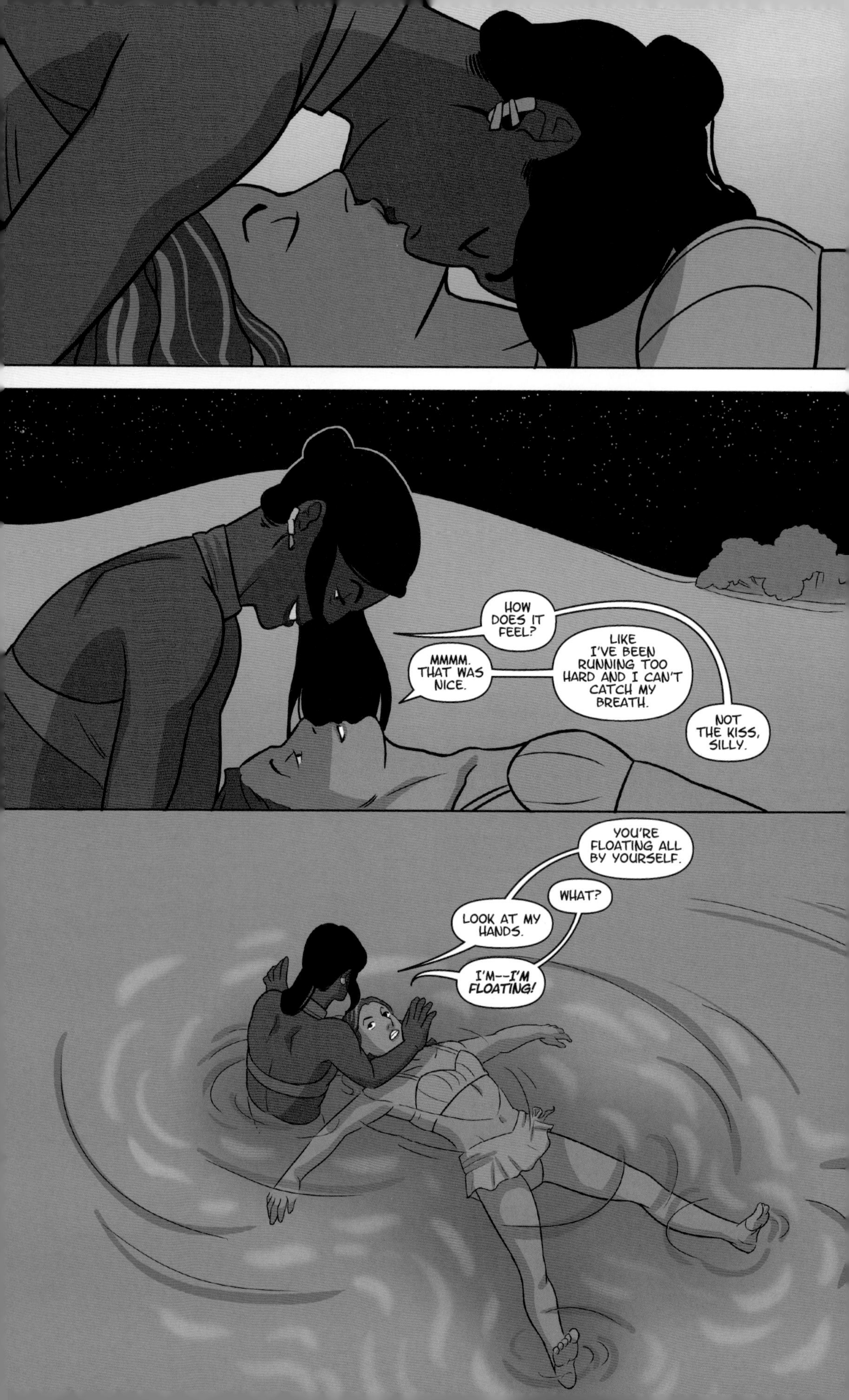
HOW DOES IT FEEL?
MMMM. THAT WAS NICE.
LIKE I'VE BEEN RUNNING TOO HARD AND I CAN'T CATCH MY BREATH.
NOT THE KISS, SILLY.
YOU'RE FLOATING ALL BY YOURSELF.
WHAT?
LOOK AT MY HANDS.
I'M--I'M *FLOATING!*

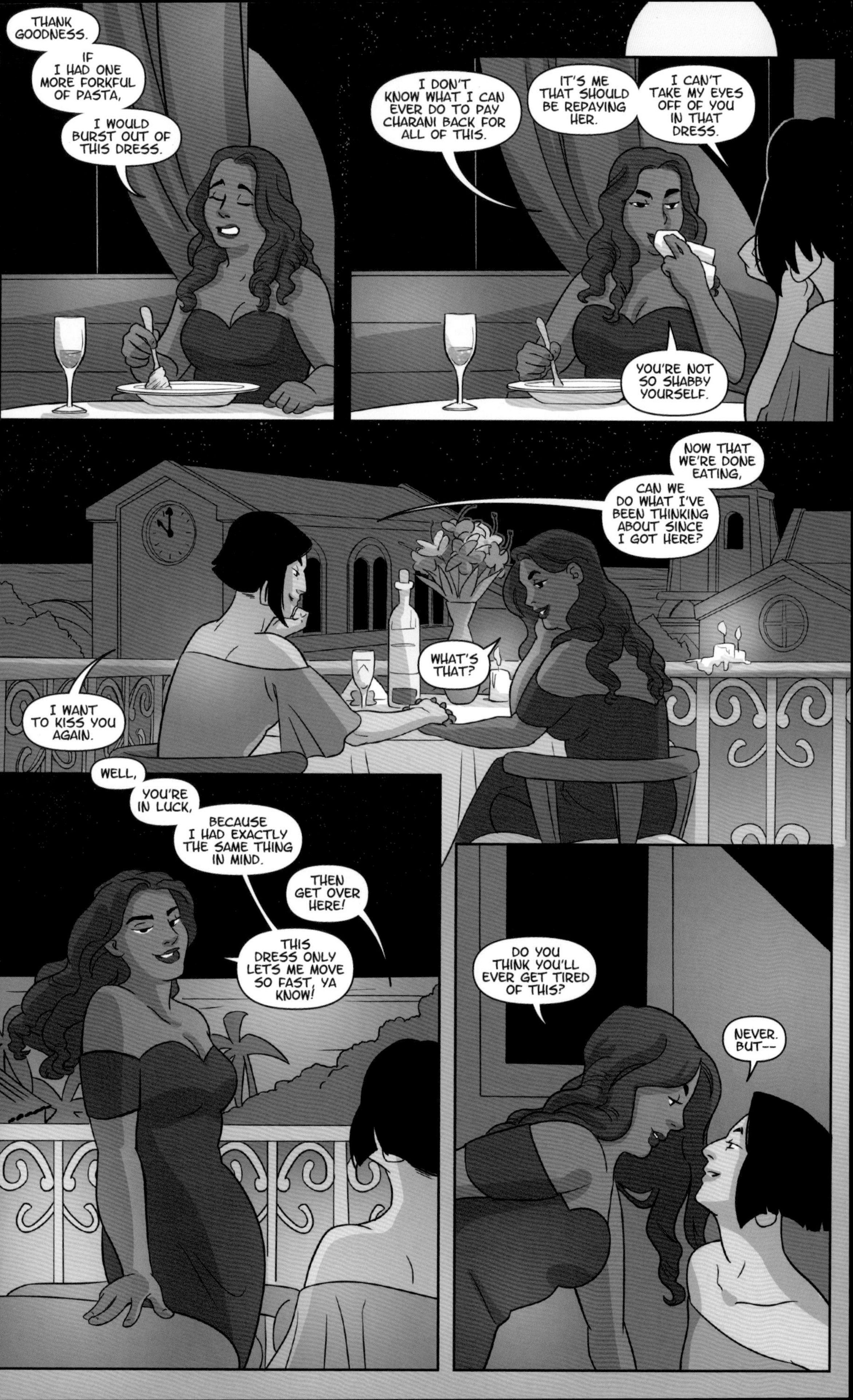

THANK GOODNESS.
IF I HAD ONE MORE FORKFUL OF PASTA,
I WOULD BURST OUT OF THIS DRESS.
I DON'T KNOW WHAT I CAN EVER DO TO PAY CHARANI BACK FOR ALL OF THIS.
IT'S ME THAT SHOULD BE REPAYING HER.
I CAN'T TAKE MY EYES OFF OF YOU IN THAT DRESS.
YOU'RE NOT SO SHABBY YOURSELF.
NOW THAT WE'RE DONE EATING,
CAN WE DO WHAT I'VE BEEN THINKING ABOUT SINCE I GOT HERE?
WHAT'S THAT?
I WANT TO KISS YOU AGAIN.
WELL,
YOU'RE IN LUCK,
BECAUSE I HAD EXACTLY THE SAME THING IN MIND.
THEN GET OVER HERE!
THIS DRESS ONLY LETS ME MOVE SO FAST, YA KNOW!
DO YOU THINK YOU'LL EVER GET TIRED OF THIS?
NEVER. BUT--

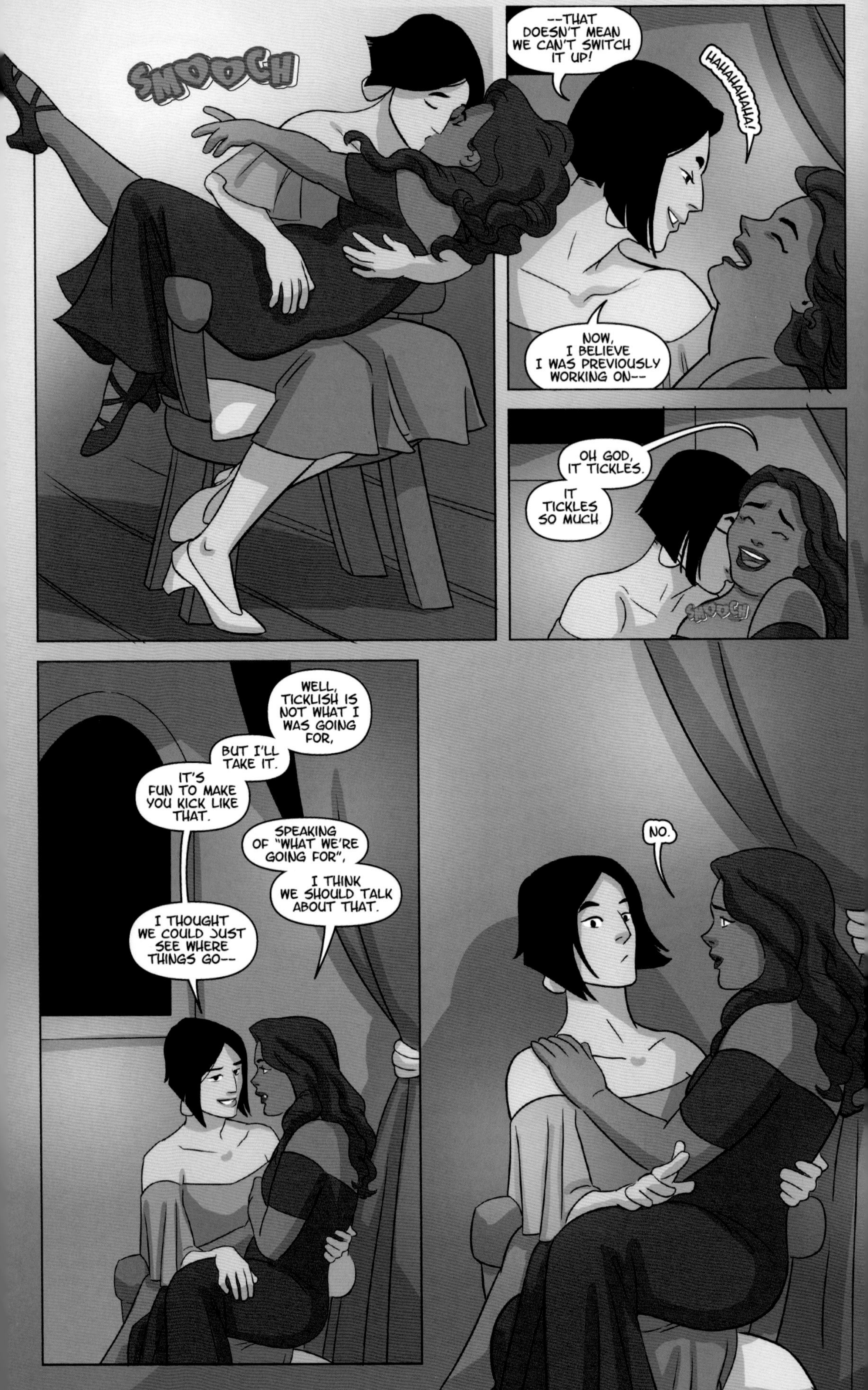
SMOOCH
--THAT DOESN'T MEAN WE CAN'T SWITCH IT UP!
HAHAHAHAHA!
NOW, I BELIEVE I WAS PREVIOUSLY WORKING ON--
OH GOD, IT TICKLES.
IT TICKLES SO MUCH.
SMOOCH
WELL, TICKLISH IS NOT WHAT I WAS GOING FOR,
BUT I'LL TAKE IT.
IT'S FUN TO MAKE YOU KICK LIKE THAT.
SPEAKING OF "WHAT WE'RE GOING FOR",
I THINK WE SHOULD TALK ABOUT THAT.
I THOUGHT WE COULD JUST SEE WHERE THINGS GO--
NO.

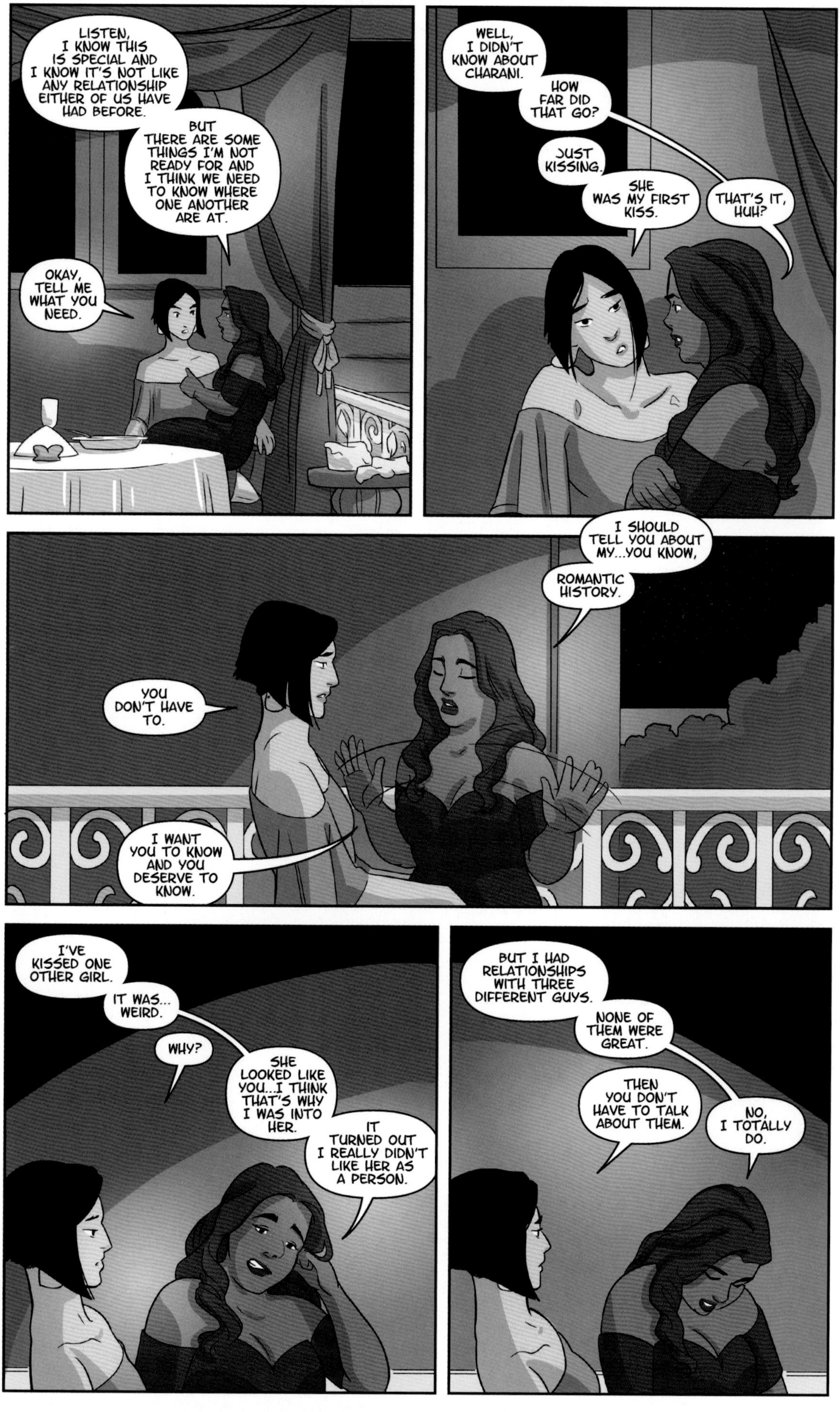
LISTEN, I KNOW THIS IS SPECIAL AND I KNOW IT'S NOT LIKE ANY RELATIONSHIP EITHER OF US HAVE HAD BEFORE.
BUT THERE ARE SOME THINGS I'M NOT READY FOR AND I THINK WE NEED TO KNOW WHERE ONE ANOTHER ARE AT.
OKAY, TELL ME WHAT YOU NEED.
WELL, I DIDN'T KNOW ABOUT CHARANI.
HOW FAR DID THAT GO?
JUST KISSING.
SHE WAS MY FIRST KISS.
THAT'S IT, HUH?
I SHOULD TELL YOU ABOUT MY...YOU KNOW,
ROMANTIC HISTORY.
YOU DON'T HAVE TO.
I WANT YOU TO KNOW AND YOU DESERVE TO KNOW.
I'VE KISSED ONE OTHER GIRL.
IT WAS... WEIRD.
WHY?
SHE LOOKED LIKE YOU...I THINK THAT'S WHY I WAS INTO HER.
IT TURNED OUT I REALLY DIDN'T LIKE HER AS A PERSON.
BUT I HAD RELATIONSHIPS WITH THREE DIFFERENT GUYS.
NONE OF THEM WERE GREAT.
THEN YOU DON'T HAVE TO TALK ABOUT THEM.
NO, I TOTALLY DO.

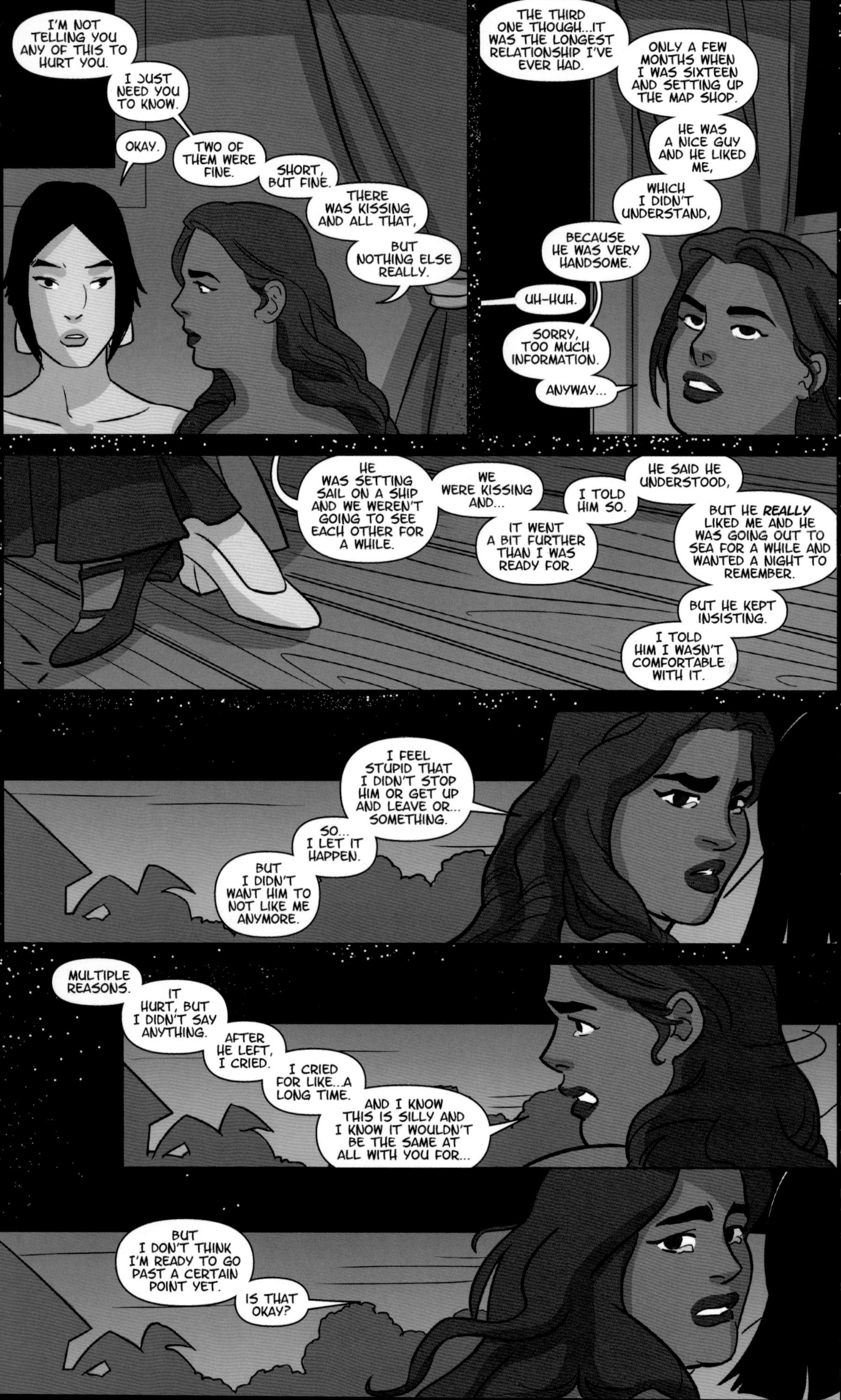

I'M NOT TELLING YOU ANY OF THIS TO HURT YOU.
I JUST NEED YOU TO KNOW.
OKAY.
TWO OF THEM WERE FINE.
SHORT, BUT FINE.
THERE WAS KISSING AND ALL THAT,
BUT NOTHING ELSE REALLY.
THE THIRD ONE THOUGH...IT WAS THE LONGEST RELATIONSHIP I'VE EVER HAD.
ONLY A FEW MONTHS WHEN I WAS SIXTEEN AND SETTING UP THE MAP SHOP.
HE WAS A NICE GUY AND HE LIKED ME,
WHICH I DIDN'T UNDERSTAND,
BECAUSE HE WAS VERY HANDSOME.
UH-HUH.
SORRY, TOO MUCH INFORMATION.
ANYWAY...
HE WAS SETTING SAIL ON A SHIP AND WE WEREN'T GOING TO SEE EACH OTHER FOR A WHILE.
WE WERE KISSING AND...
IT WENT A BIT FURTHER THAN I WAS READY FOR.
I TOLD HIM SO.
HE SAID HE UNDERSTOOD,
BUT HE *REALLY* LIKED ME AND HE WAS GOING OUT TO SEA FOR A WHILE AND WANTED A NIGHT TO REMEMBER.
BUT HE KEPT INSISTING.
I TOLD HIM I WASN'T COMFORTABLE WITH IT.
I FEEL STUPID THAT I DIDN'T STOP HIM OR GET UP AND LEAVE OR... SOMETHING.
SO... I LET IT HAPPEN.
BUT I DIDN'T WANT HIM TO NOT LIKE ME ANYMORE.
MULTIPLE REASONS.
IT HURT, BUT I DIDN'T SAY ANYTHING.
AFTER HE LEFT, I CRIED.
I CRIED FOR LIKE...A LONG TIME.
AND I KNOW THIS IS SILLY AND I KNOW IT WOULDN'T BE THE SAME AT ALL WITH YOU FOR...
BUT I DON'T THINK I'M READY TO GO PAST A CERTAIN POINT YET.
IS THAT OKAY?

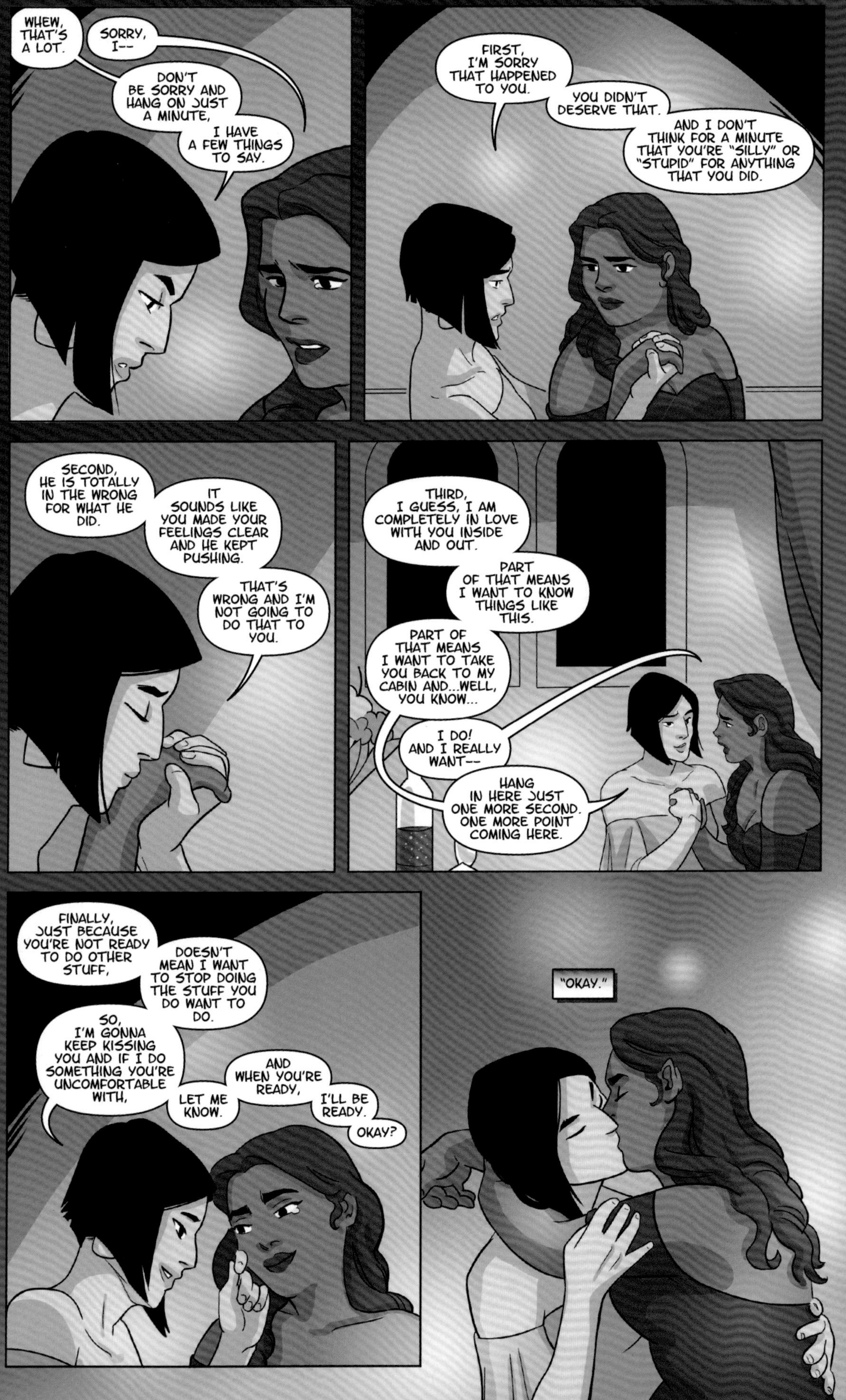
WHEW, THAT'S A LOT.
SORRY, I--
DON'T BE SORRY AND HANG ON JUST A MINUTE,
I HAVE A FEW THINGS TO SAY.
FIRST, I'M SORRY THAT HAPPENED TO YOU.
YOU DIDN'T DESERVE THAT.
AND I DON'T THINK FOR A MINUTE THAT YOU'RE "SILLY" OR "STUPID" FOR ANYTHING THAT YOU DID.
SECOND, HE IS TOTALLY IN THE WRONG FOR WHAT HE DID.
IT SOUNDS LIKE YOU MADE YOUR FEELINGS CLEAR AND HE KEPT PUSHING.
THAT'S WRONG AND I'M NOT GOING TO DO THAT TO YOU.
THIRD, I GUESS, I AM COMPLETELY IN LOVE WITH YOU INSIDE AND OUT.
PART OF THAT MEANS I WANT TO KNOW THINGS LIKE THIS.
PART OF THAT MEANS I WANT TO TAKE YOU BACK TO MY CABIN AND...WELL, YOU KNOW...
I DO! AND I REALLY WANT--
HANG IN HERE JUST ONE MORE SECOND. ONE MORE POINT COMING HERE.
FINALLY, JUST BECAUSE YOU'RE NOT READY TO DO OTHER STUFF,
DOESN'T MEAN I WANT TO STOP DOING THE STUFF YOU DO WANT TO DO.
SO, I'M GONNA KEEP KISSING YOU AND IF I DO SOMETHING YOU'RE UNCOMFORTABLE WITH,
LET ME KNOW.
AND WHEN YOU'RE READY,
I'LL BE READY.
OKAY?
"OKAY."

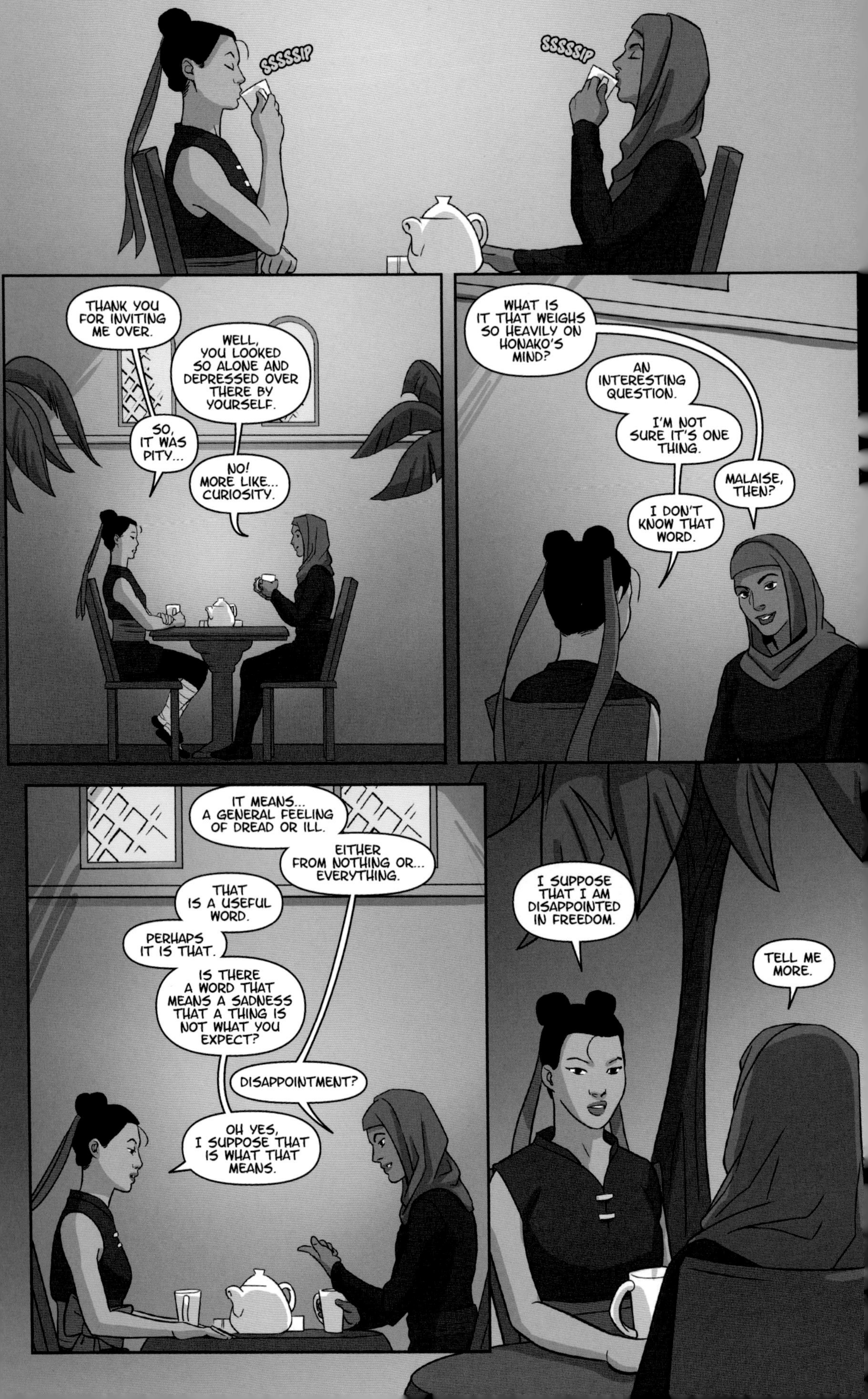
SSSSSIP
SSSSSIP
THANK YOU FOR INVITING ME OVER.
WELL, YOU LOOKED SO ALONE AND DEPRESSED OVER THERE BY YOURSELF.
SO, IT WAS PITY...
NO! MORE LIKE... CURIOSITY.
WHAT IS IT THAT WEIGHS SO HEAVILY ON HONAKO'S MIND?
AN INTERESTING QUESTION.
I'M NOT SURE IT'S ONE THING.
MALAISE, THEN?
I DON'T KNOW THAT WORD.
IT MEANS... A GENERAL FEELING OF DREAD OR ILL.
EITHER FROM NOTHING OR... EVERYTHING.
THAT IS A USEFUL WORD.
PERHAPS IT IS THAT.
IS THERE A WORD THAT MEANS A SADNESS THAT A THING IS NOT WHAT YOU EXPECT?
DISAPPOINTMENT?
OH YES, I SUPPOSE THAT IS WHAT THAT MEANS.
I SUPPOSE THAT I AM DISAPPOINTED IN FREEDOM.
TELL ME MORE.

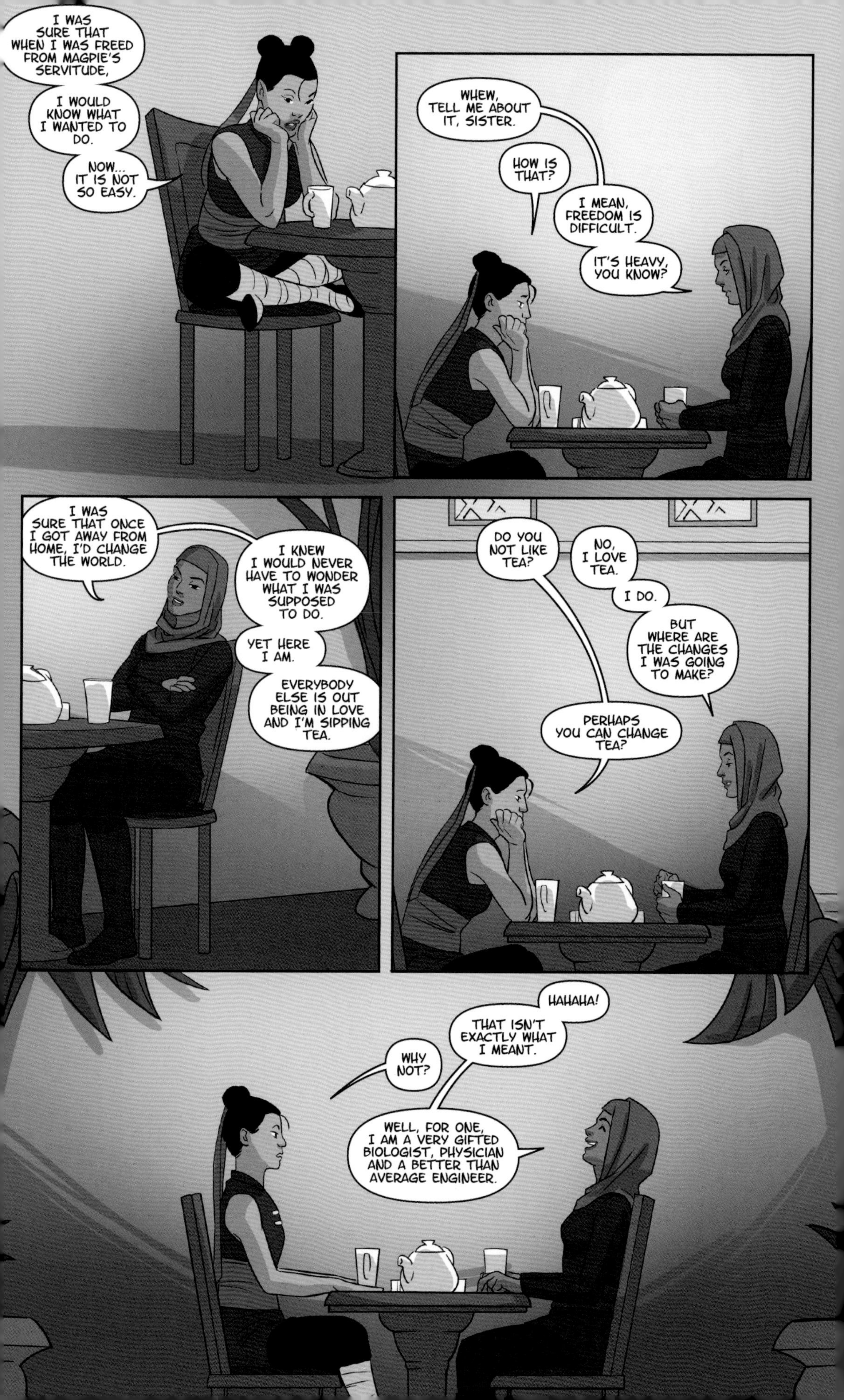
I WAS SURE THAT WHEN I WAS FREED FROM MAGPIE'S SERVITUDE,
I WOULD KNOW WHAT I WANTED TO DO.
NOW... IT IS NOT SO EASY.
WHEW, TELL ME ABOUT IT, SISTER.
HOW IS THAT?
I MEAN, FREEDOM IS DIFFICULT.
IT'S HEAVY, YOU KNOW?
I WAS SURE THAT ONCE I GOT AWAY FROM HOME, I'D CHANGE THE WORLD.
I KNEW I WOULD NEVER HAVE TO WONDER WHAT I WAS SUPPOSED TO DO.
YET HERE I AM.
EVERYBODY ELSE IS OUT BEING IN LOVE AND I'M SIPPING TEA.
DO YOU NOT LIKE TEA?
NO, I LOVE TEA.
I DO.
BUT WHERE ARE THE CHANGES I WAS GOING TO MAKE?
PERHAPS YOU CAN CHANGE TEA?
HAHAHA!
THAT ISN'T EXACTLY WHAT I MEANT.
WHY NOT?
WELL, FOR ONE, I AM A VERY GIFTED BIOLOGIST, PHYSICIAN AND A BETTER THAN AVERAGE ENGINEER.

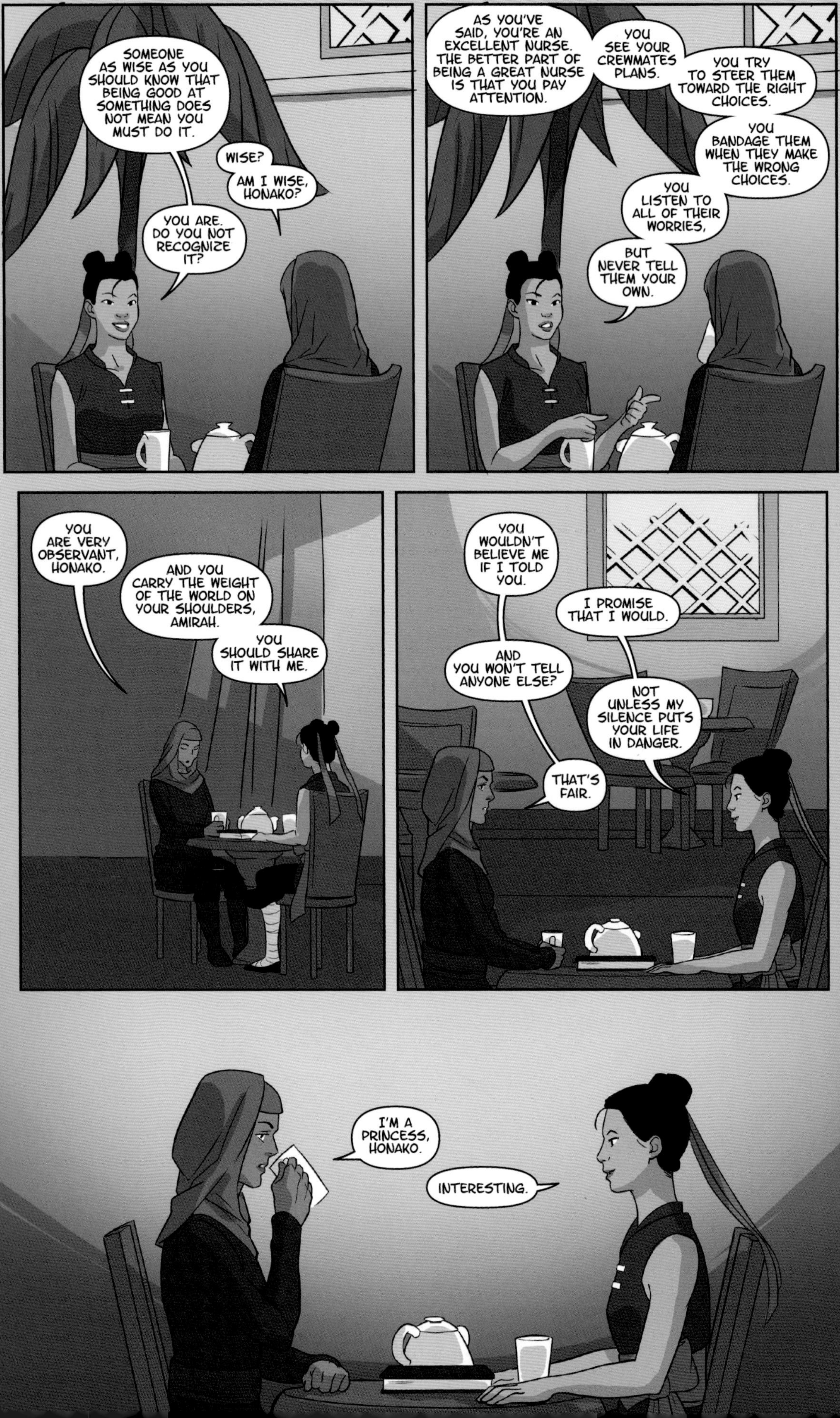
SOMEONE AS WISE AS YOU SHOULD KNOW THAT BEING GOOD AT SOMETHING DOES NOT MEAN YOU MUST DO IT.
WISE?
AM I WISE, HONAKO?
YOU ARE. DO YOU NOT RECOGNIZE IT?
AS YOU'VE SAID, YOU'RE AN EXCELLENT NURSE. THE BETTER PART OF BEING A GREAT NURSE IS THAT YOU PAY ATTENTION.
YOU SEE YOUR CREWMATES PLANS.
YOU TRY TO STEER THEM TOWARD THE RIGHT CHOICES.
YOU BANDAGE THEM WHEN THEY MAKE THE WRONG CHOICES.
YOU LISTEN TO ALL OF THEIR WORRIES,
BUT NEVER TELL THEM YOUR OWN.
YOU ARE VERY OBSERVANT, HONAKO.
AND YOU CARRY THE WEIGHT OF THE WORLD ON YOUR SHOULDERS, AMIRAH.
YOU SHOULD SHARE IT WITH ME.
YOU WOULDN'T BELIEVE ME IF I TOLD YOU.
I PROMISE THAT I WOULD.
AND YOU WON'T TELL ANYONE ELSE?
NOT UNLESS MY SILENCE PUTS YOUR LIFE IN DANGER.
THAT'S FAIR.
I'M A PRINCESS, HONAKO.
INTERESTING.

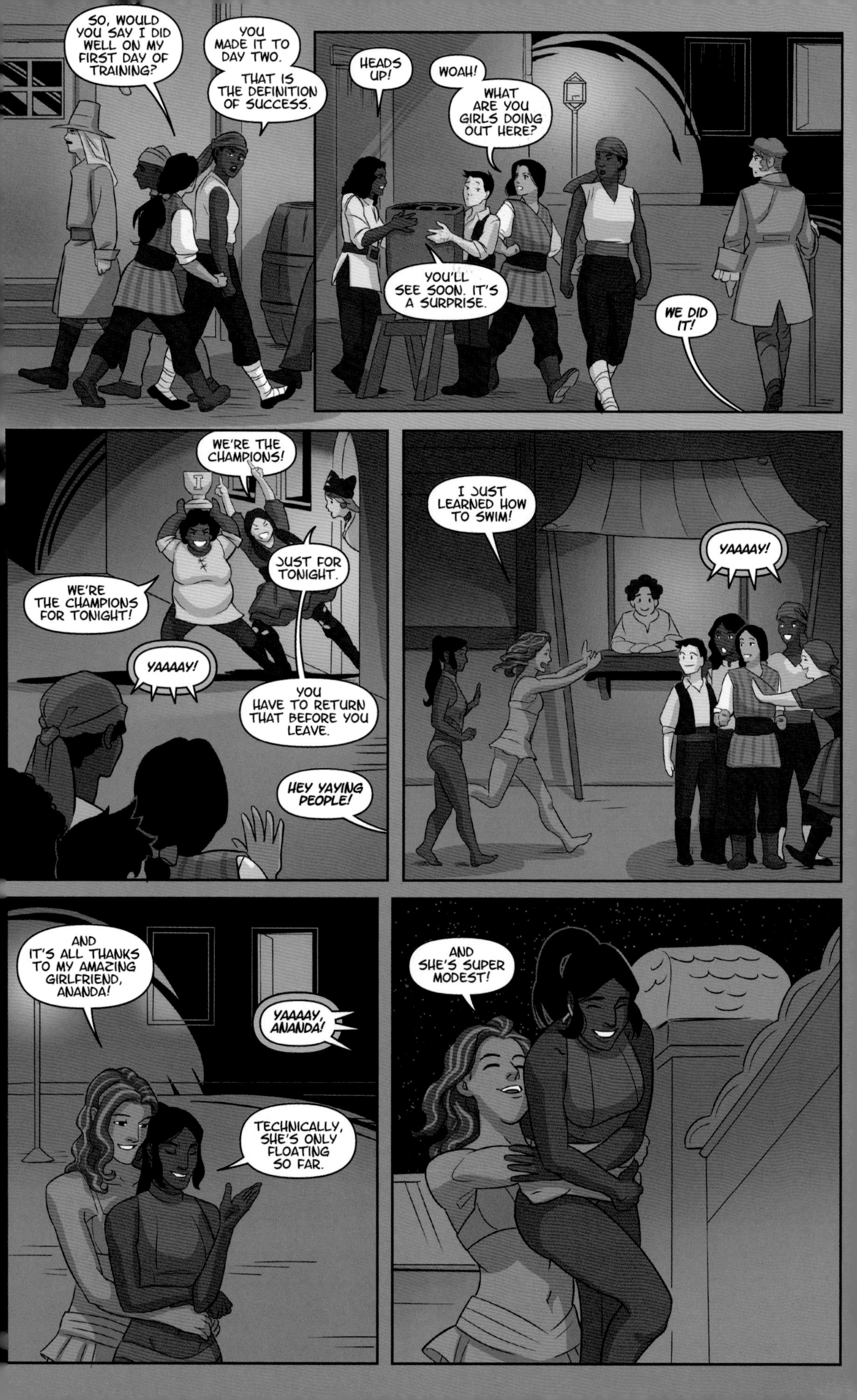
SO, WOULD YOU SAY I DID WELL ON MY FIRST DAY OF TRAINING?
YOU MADE IT TO DAY TWO.
THAT IS THE DEFINITION OF SUCCESS.
HEADS UP!
WOAH!
WHAT ARE YOU GIRLS DOING OUT HERE?
YOU'LL SEE SOON. IT'S A SURPRISE.
WE DID IT!
WE'RE THE CHAMPIONS!
WE'RE THE CHAMPIONS FOR TONIGHT!
JUST FOR TONIGHT.
YAAAAY!
YOU HAVE TO RETURN THAT BEFORE YOU LEAVE.
HEY YAYING PEOPLE!
I JUST LEARNED HOW TO SWIM!
YAAAAY!
AND IT'S ALL THANKS TO MY AMAZING GIRLFRIEND, ANANDA!
YAAAAY, ANANDA!
TECHNICALLY, SHE'S ONLY FLOATING SO FAR.
AND SHE'S SUPER MODEST!

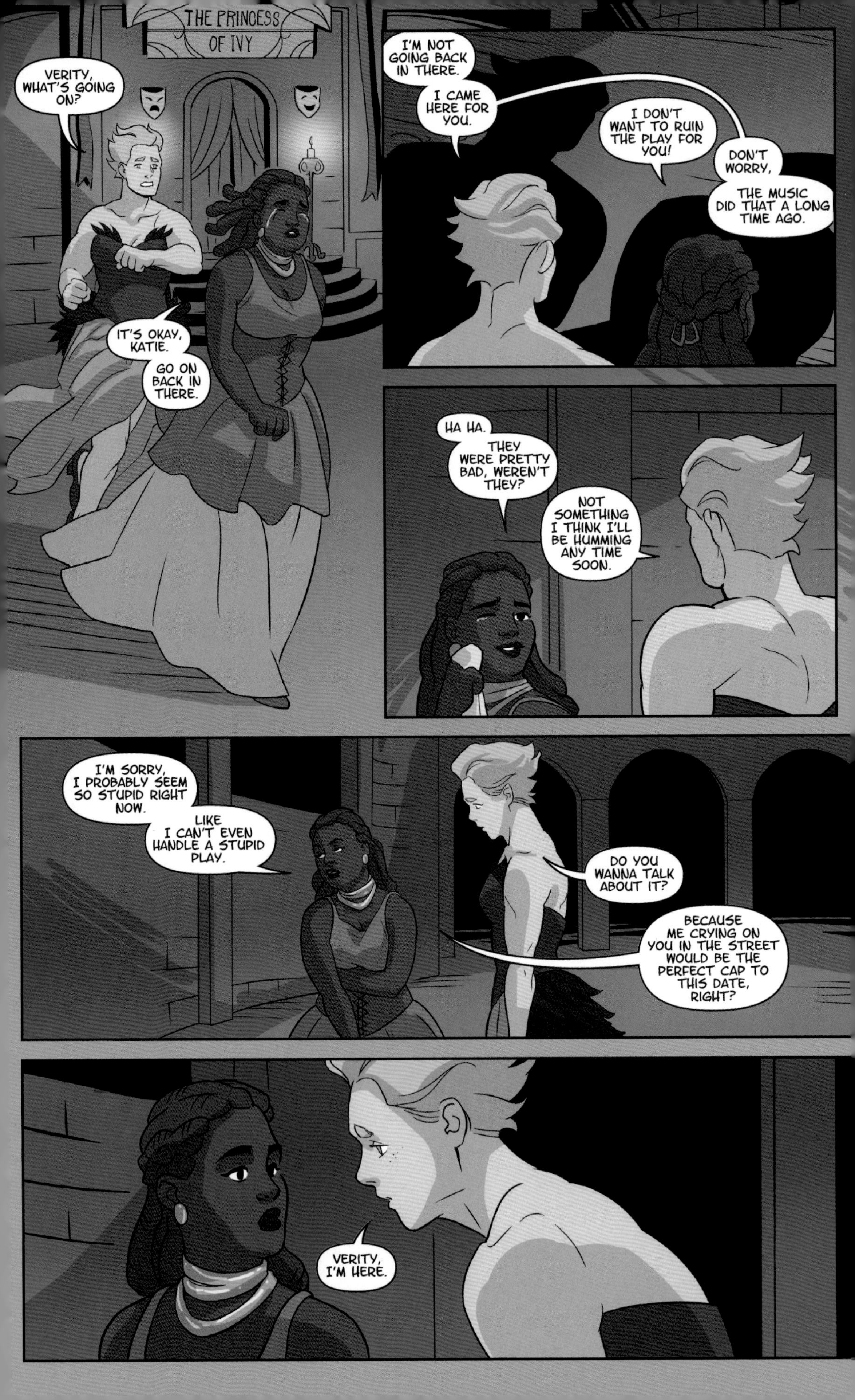
THE PRINCESS OF IVY
VERITY, WHAT'S GOING ON?
IT'S OKAY, KATIE.
GO ON BACK IN THERE.
I'M NOT GOING BACK IN THERE.
I CAME HERE FOR YOU.
I DON'T WANT TO RUIN THE PLAY FOR YOU!
DON'T WORRY,
THE MUSIC DID THAT A LONG TIME AGO.
HA HA.
THEY WERE PRETTY BAD, WEREN'T THEY?
NOT SOMETHING I THINK I'LL BE HUMMING ANY TIME SOON.
I'M SORRY, I PROBABLY SEEM SO STUPID RIGHT NOW.
LIKE I CAN'T EVEN HANDLE A STUPID PLAY.
DO YOU WANNA TALK ABOUT IT?
BECAUSE ME CRYING ON YOU IN THE STREET WOULD BE THE PERFECT CAP TO THIS DATE, RIGHT?
VERITY, I'M HERE.

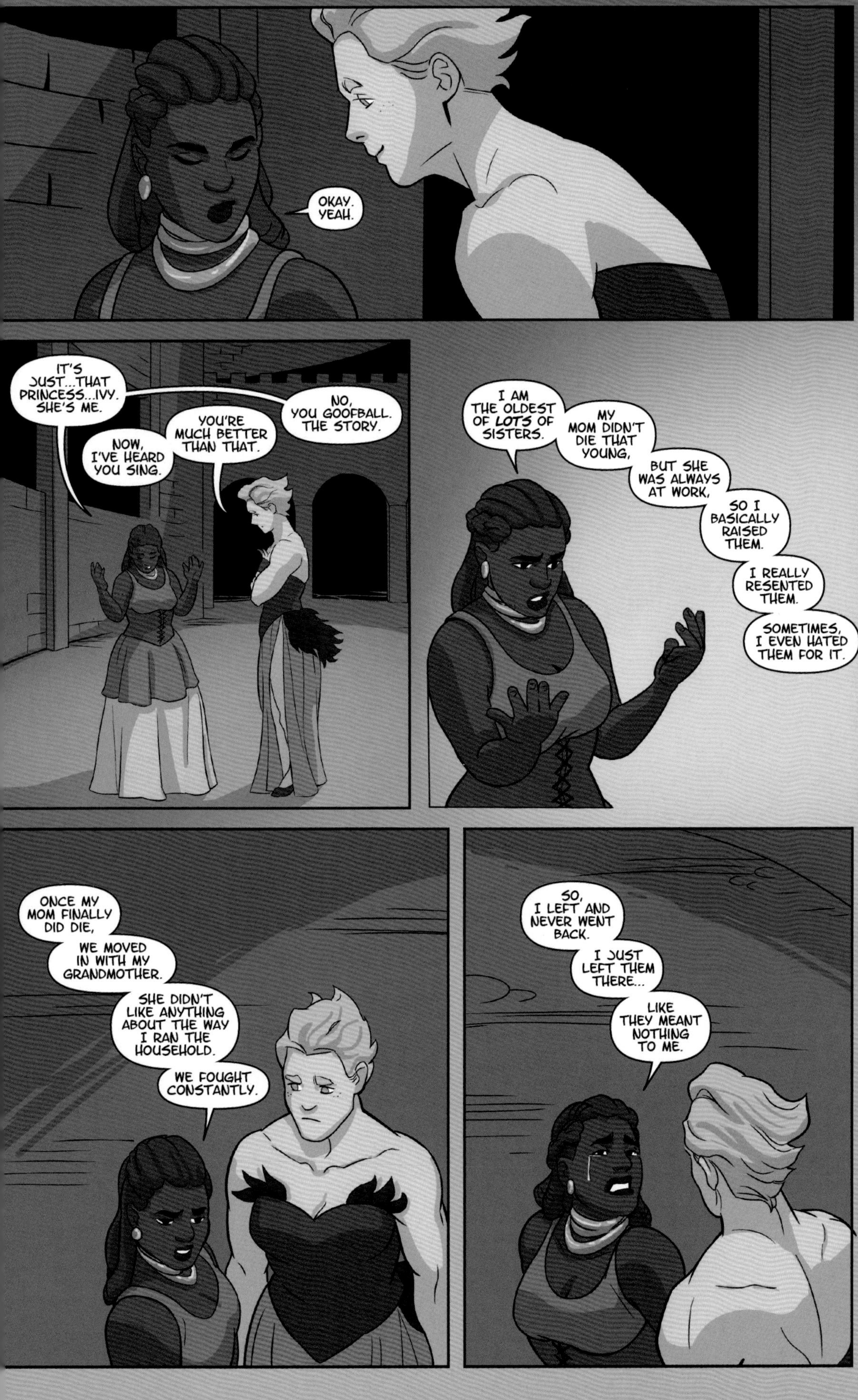
OKAY. YEAH.
IT'S JUST...THAT PRINCESS...IVY. SHE'S ME.
NO, YOU GOOFBALL. THE STORY.
NOW, I'VE HEARD YOU SING.
YOU'RE MUCH BETTER THAN THAT.
I AM THE OLDEST OF LOTS OF SISTERS.
MY MOM DIDN'T DIE THAT YOUNG,
BUT SHE WAS ALWAYS AT WORK,
SO I BASICALLY RAISED THEM.
I REALLY RESENTED THEM.
SOMETIMES, I EVEN HATED THEM FOR IT.
ONCE MY MOM FINALLY DID DIE,
WE MOVED IN WITH MY GRANDMOTHER.
SHE DIDN'T LIKE ANYTHING ABOUT THE WAY I RAN THE HOUSEHOLD.
WE FOUGHT CONSTANTLY.
SO, I LEFT AND NEVER WENT BACK.
I JUST LEFT THEM THERE...
LIKE THEY MEANT NOTHING TO ME.

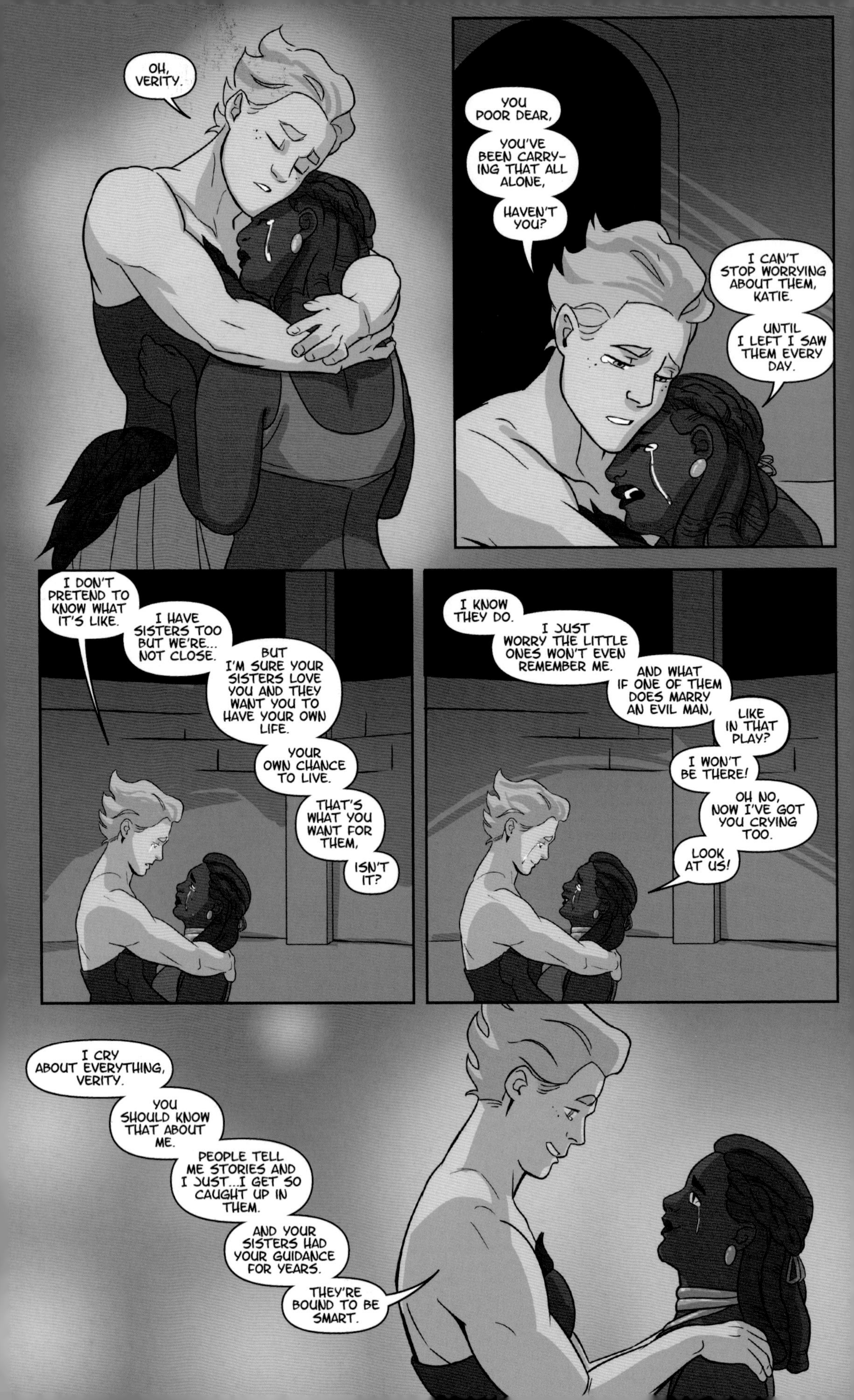
OH, VERITY.
YOU POOR DEAR,
YOU'VE BEEN CARRY-ING THAT ALL ALONE,
HAVEN'T YOU?
I CAN'T STOP WORRYING ABOUT THEM, KATIE.
UNTIL I LEFT I SAW THEM EVERY DAY.
I DON'T PRETEND TO KNOW WHAT IT'S LIKE.
I HAVE SISTERS TOO BUT WE'RE... NOT CLOSE.
BUT I'M SURE YOUR SISTERS LOVE YOU AND THEY WANT YOU TO HAVE YOUR OWN LIFE.
YOUR OWN CHANCE TO LIVE.
THAT'S WHAT YOU WANT FOR THEM,
ISN'T IT?
I KNOW THEY DO.
I JUST WORRY THE LITTLE ONES WON'T EVEN REMEMBER ME.
AND WHAT IF ONE OF THEM DOES MARRY AN EVIL MAN,
LIKE IN THAT PLAY?
I WON'T BE THERE!
OH NO, NOW I'VE GOT YOU CRYING TOO.
LOOK AT US!
I CRY ABOUT EVERYTHING, VERITY.
YOU SHOULD KNOW THAT ABOUT ME.
PEOPLE TELL ME STORIES AND I JUST...I GET SO CAUGHT UP IN THEM.
AND YOUR SISTERS HAD YOUR GUIDANCE FOR YEARS.
THEY'RE BOUND TO BE SMART.

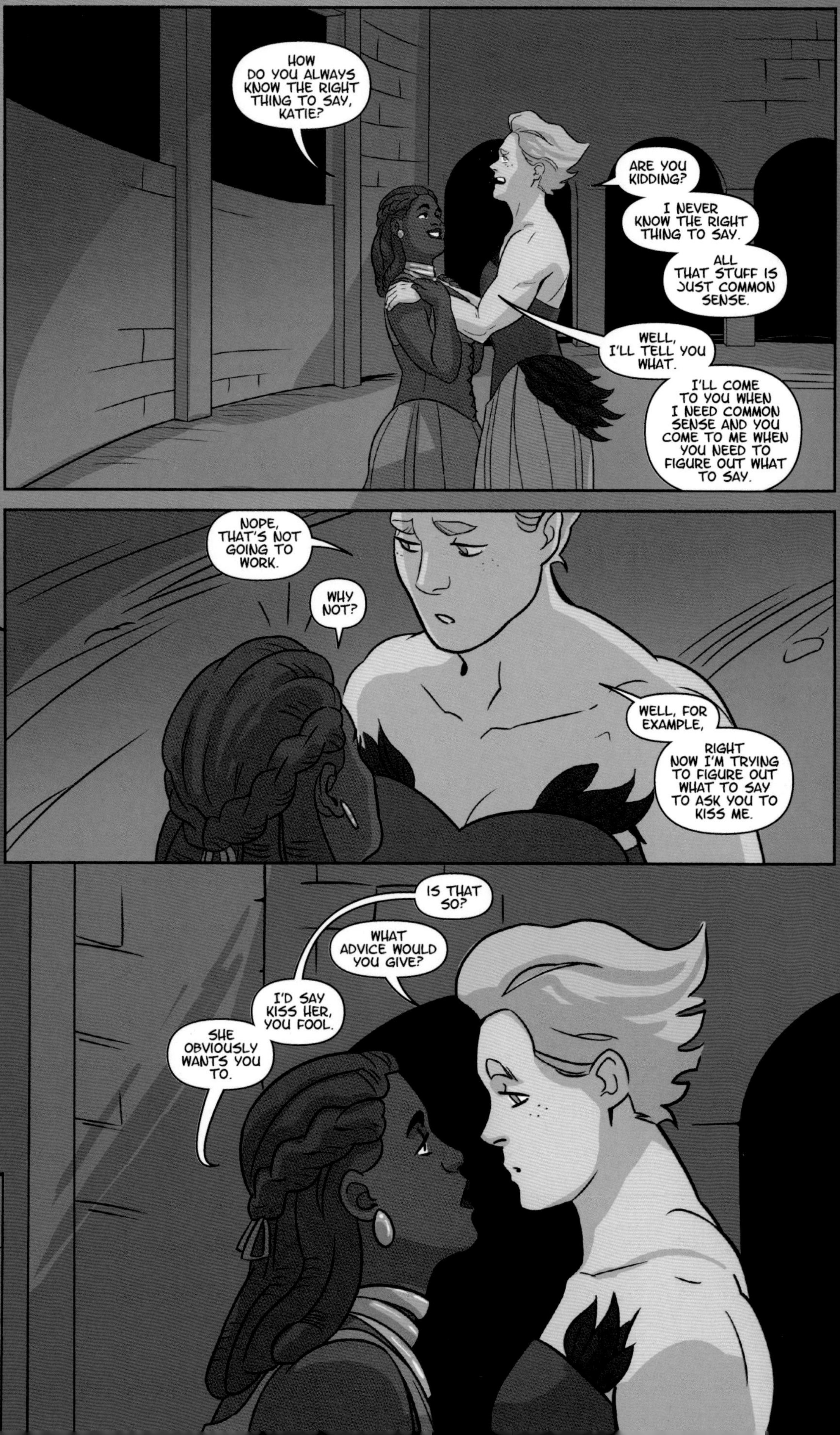
HOW DO YOU ALWAYS KNOW THE RIGHT THING TO SAY, KATIE?
ARE YOU KIDDING?
I NEVER KNOW THE RIGHT THING TO SAY.
ALL THAT STUFF IS JUST COMMON SENSE.
WELL, I'LL TELL YOU WHAT.
I'LL COME TO YOU WHEN I NEED COMMON SENSE AND YOU COME TO ME WHEN YOU NEED TO FIGURE OUT WHAT TO SAY.
NOPE, THAT'S NOT GOING TO WORK.
WHY NOT?
WELL, FOR EXAMPLE,
RIGHT NOW I'M TRYING TO FIGURE OUT WHAT TO SAY TO ASK YOU TO KISS ME.
IS THAT SO?
WHAT ADVICE WOULD YOU GIVE?
I'D SAY KISS HER, YOU FOOL.
SHE OBVIOUSLY WANTS YOU TO.

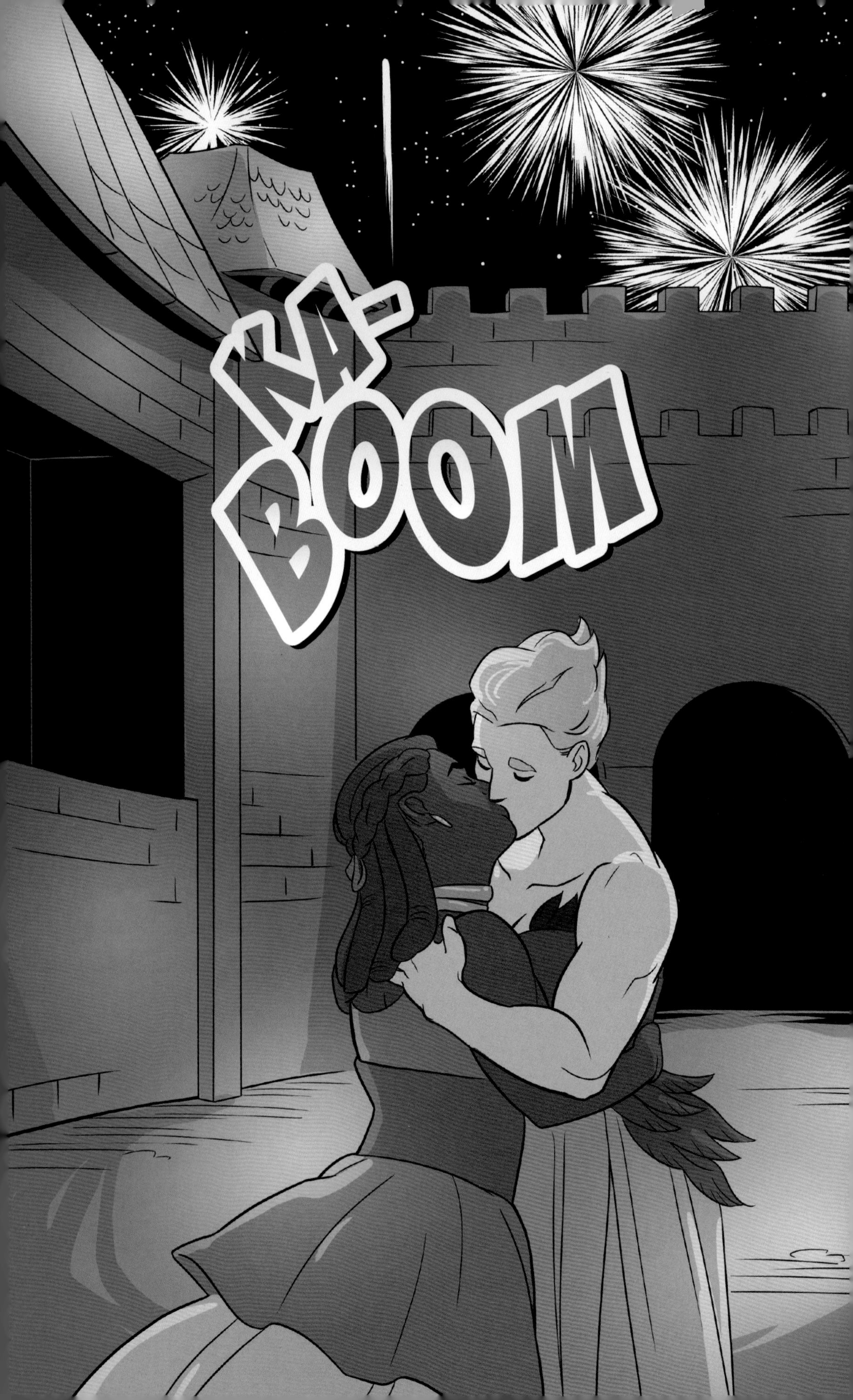
KA-BOOM

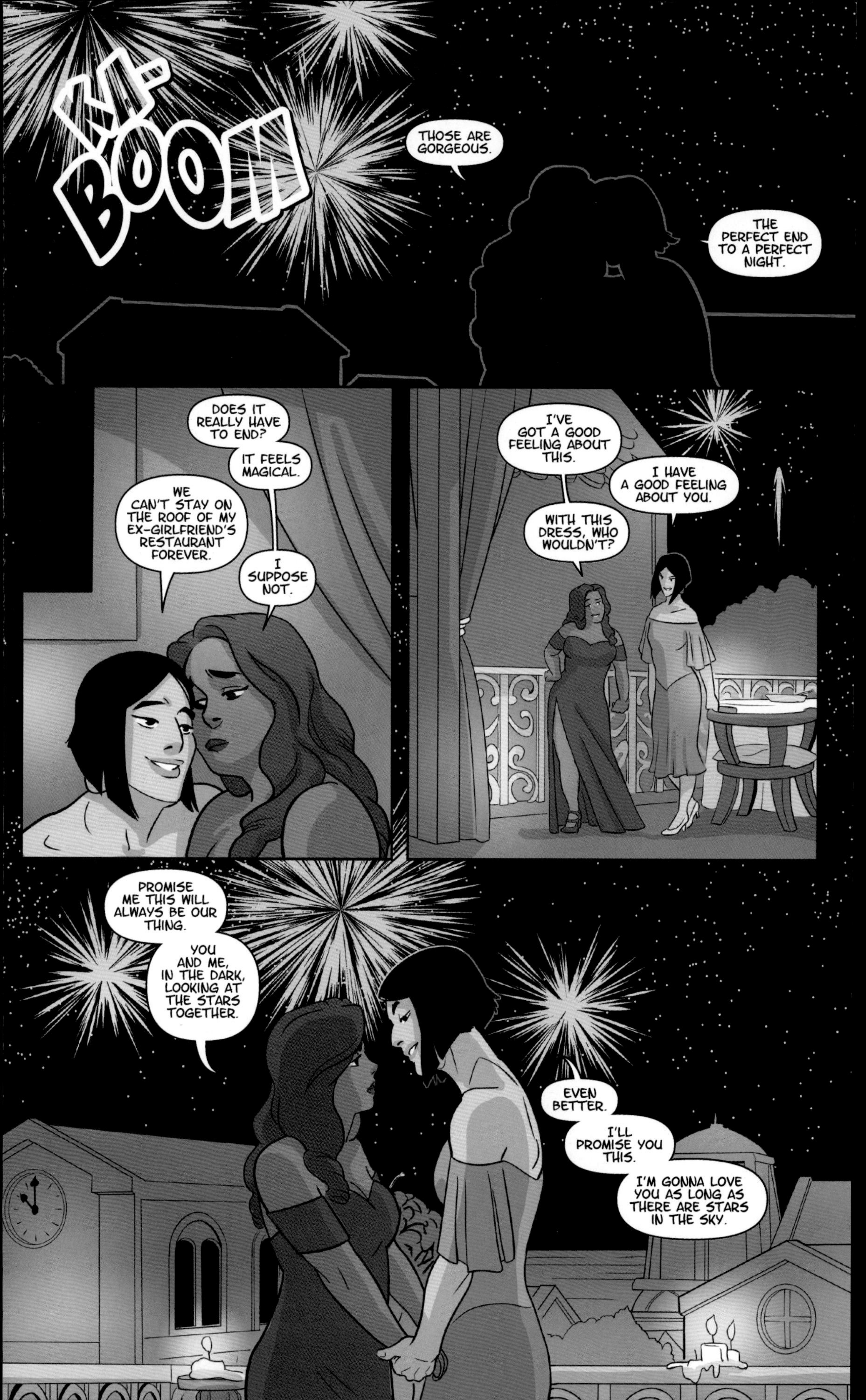
KA-BOOM
THOSE ARE GORGEOUS.
THE PERFECT END TO A PERFECT NIGHT.
DOES IT REALLY HAVE TO END?
IT FEELS MAGICAL.
WE CAN'T STAY ON THE ROOF OF MY EX-GIRLFRIEND'S RESTAURANT FOREVER.
I SUPPOSE NOT.
I'VE GOT A GOOD FEELING ABOUT THIS.
WITH THIS DRESS, WHO WOULDN'T?
I HAVE A GOOD FEELING ABOUT YOU.
PROMISE ME THIS WILL ALWAYS BE OUR THING.
YOU AND ME, IN THE DARK, LOOKING AT THE STARS TOGETHER.
EVEN BETTER.
I'LL PROMISE YOU THIS.
I'M GONNA LOVE YOU AS LONG AS THERE ARE STARS IN THE SKY.

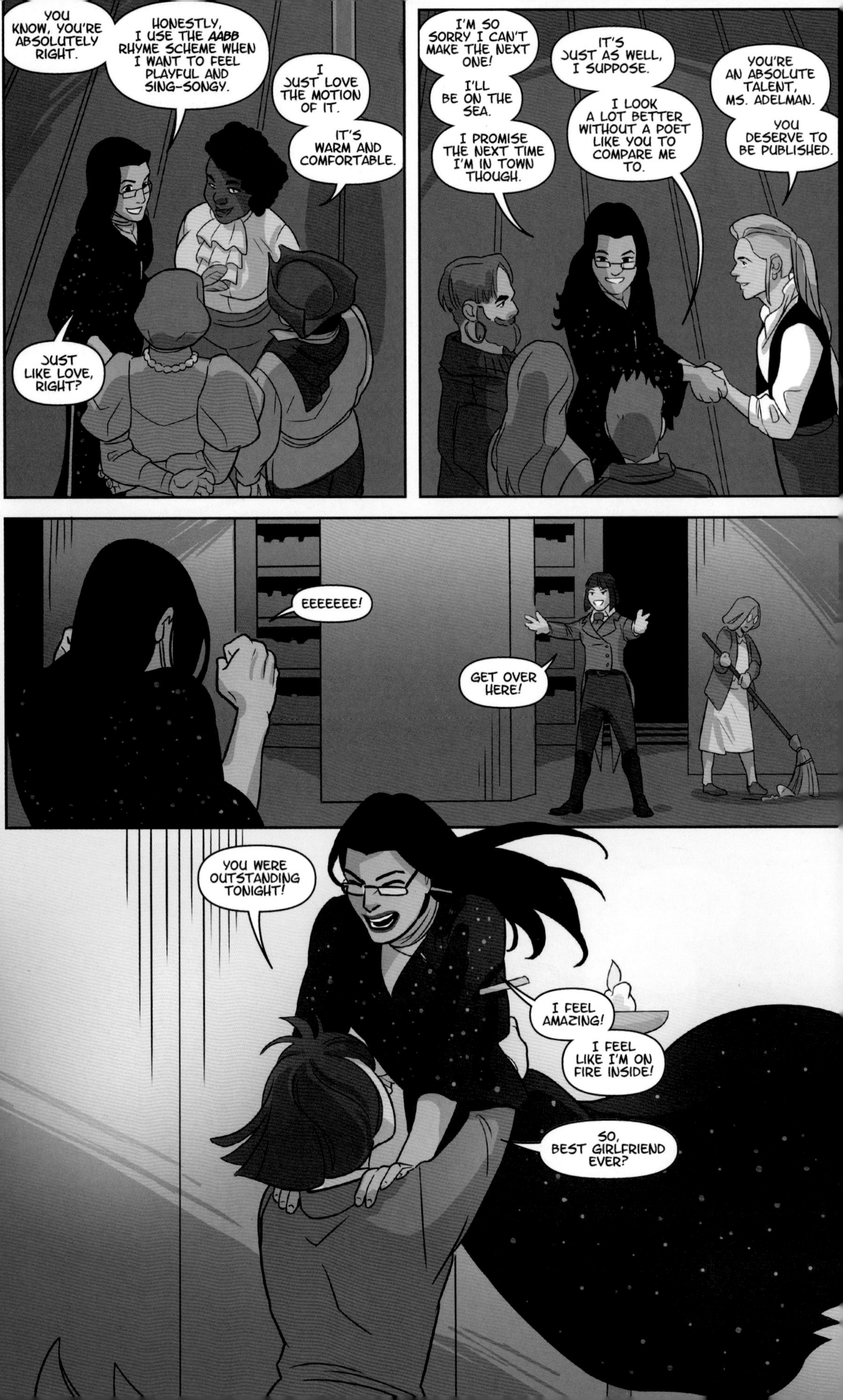
YOU KNOW, YOU'RE ABSOLUTELY RIGHT.
HONESTLY, I USE THE AABB RHYME SCHEME WHEN I WANT TO FEEL PLAYFUL AND SING-SONGY.
I JUST LOVE THE MOTION OF IT.
IT'S WARM AND COMFORTABLE.
JUST LIKE LOVE, RIGHT?
I'M SO SORRY I CAN'T MAKE THE NEXT ONE!
I'LL BE ON THE SEA.
I PROMISE THE NEXT TIME I'M IN TOWN THOUGH.
IT'S JUST AS WELL, I SUPPOSE.
I LOOK A LOT BETTER WITHOUT A POET LIKE YOU TO COMPARE ME TO.
YOU'RE AN ABSOLUTE TALENT, MS. ADELMAN.
YOU DESERVE TO BE PUBLISHED.
EEEEEEE!
GET OVER HERE!
YOU WERE OUTSTANDING TONIGHT!
I FEEL AMAZING!
I FEEL LIKE I'M ON FIRE INSIDE!
SO, BEST GIRLFRIEND EVER?

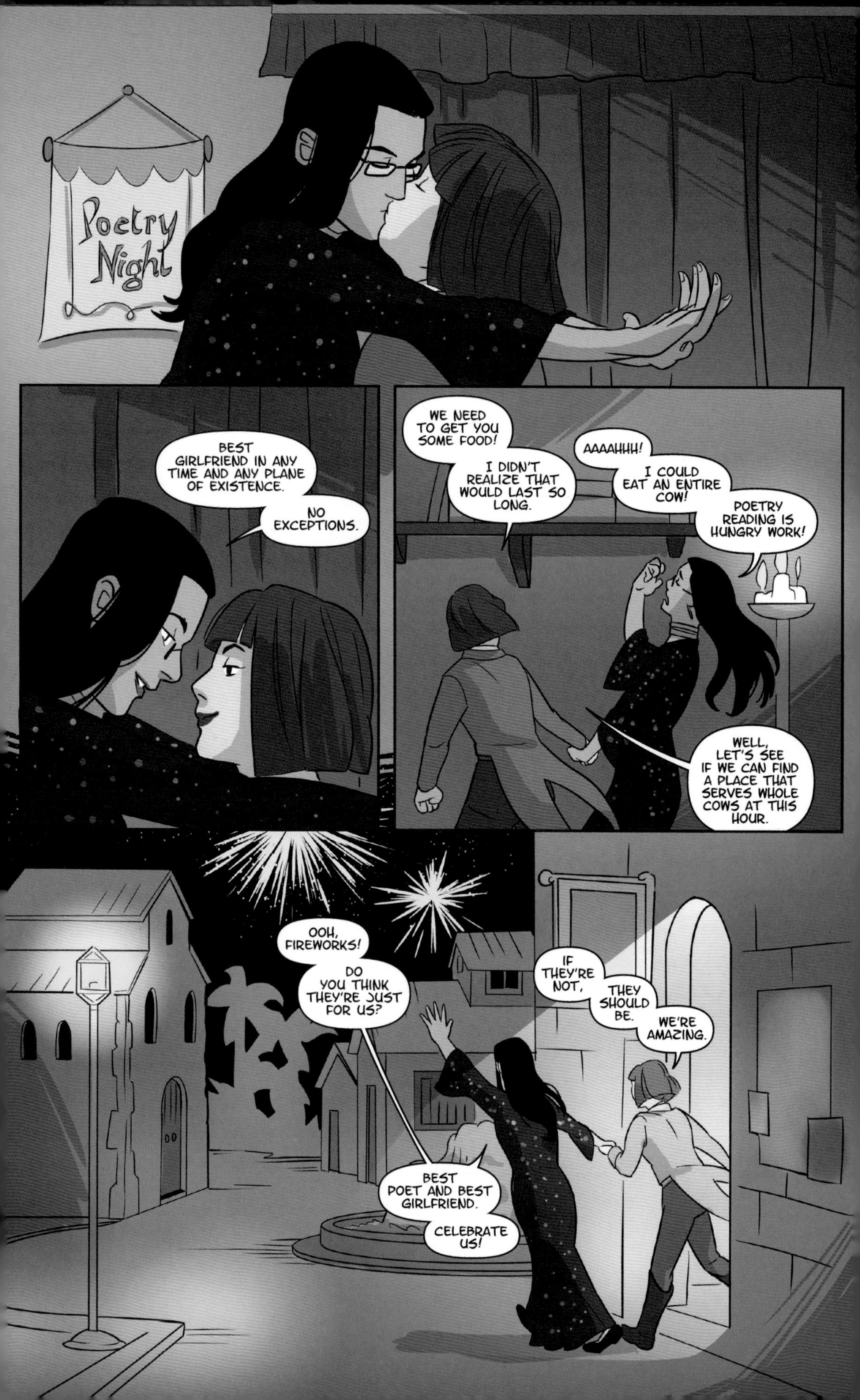
Poetry Night
BEST GIRLFRIEND IN ANY TIME AND ANY PLANE OF EXISTENCE.
NO EXCEPTIONS.
WE NEED TO GET YOU SOME FOOD!
I DIDN'T REALIZE THAT WOULD LAST SO LONG.
AAAAHHH!
I COULD EAT AN ENTIRE COW!
POETRY READING IS HUNGRY WORK!
WELL, LET'S SEE IF WE CAN FIND A PLACE THAT SERVES WHOLE COWS AT THIS HOUR.
OOH, FIREWORKS!
DO YOU THINK THEY'RE JUST FOR US?
IF THEY'RE NOT,
THEY SHOULD BE.
WE'RE AMAZING.
BEST POET AND BEST GIRLFRIEND.
CELEBRATE US!

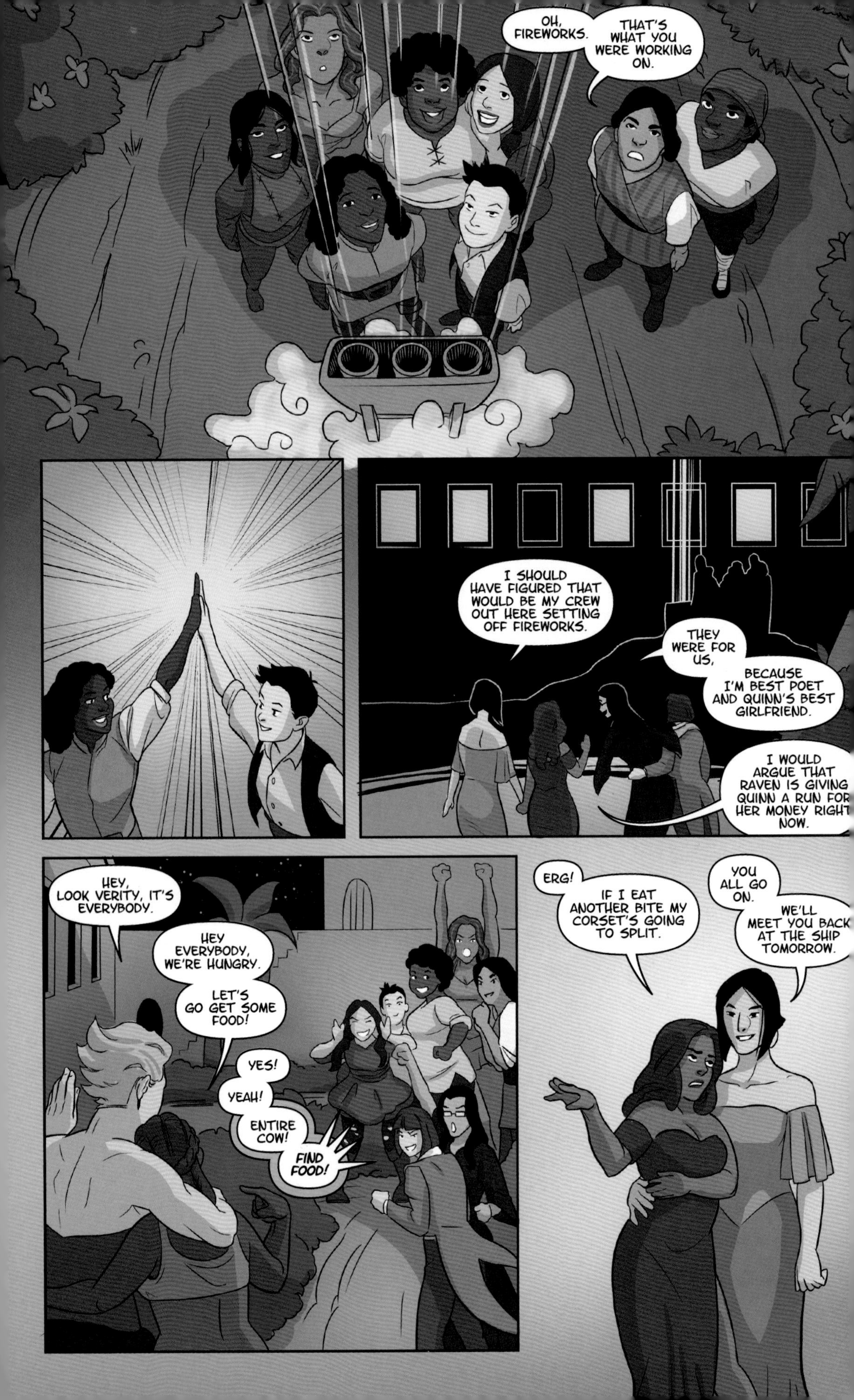
OH, FIREWORKS.
THAT'S WHAT YOU WERE WORKING ON.
I SHOULD HAVE FIGURED THAT WOULD BE MY CREW OUT HERE SETTING OFF FIREWORKS.
THEY WERE FOR US,
BECAUSE I'M BEST POET AND QUINN'S BEST GIRLFRIEND.
I WOULD ARGUE THAT RAVEN IS GIVING QUINN A RUN FOR HER MONEY RIGHT NOW.
HEY, LOOK VERITY, IT'S EVERYBODY.
HEY EVERYBODY, WE'RE HUNGRY.
LET'S GO GET SOME FOOD!
YES!
YEAH!
ENTIRE COW!
FIND FOOD!
ERG!
IF I EAT ANOTHER BITE MY CORSET'S GOING TO SPLIT.
YOU ALL GO ON.
WE'LL MEET YOU BACK AT THE SHIP TOMORROW.

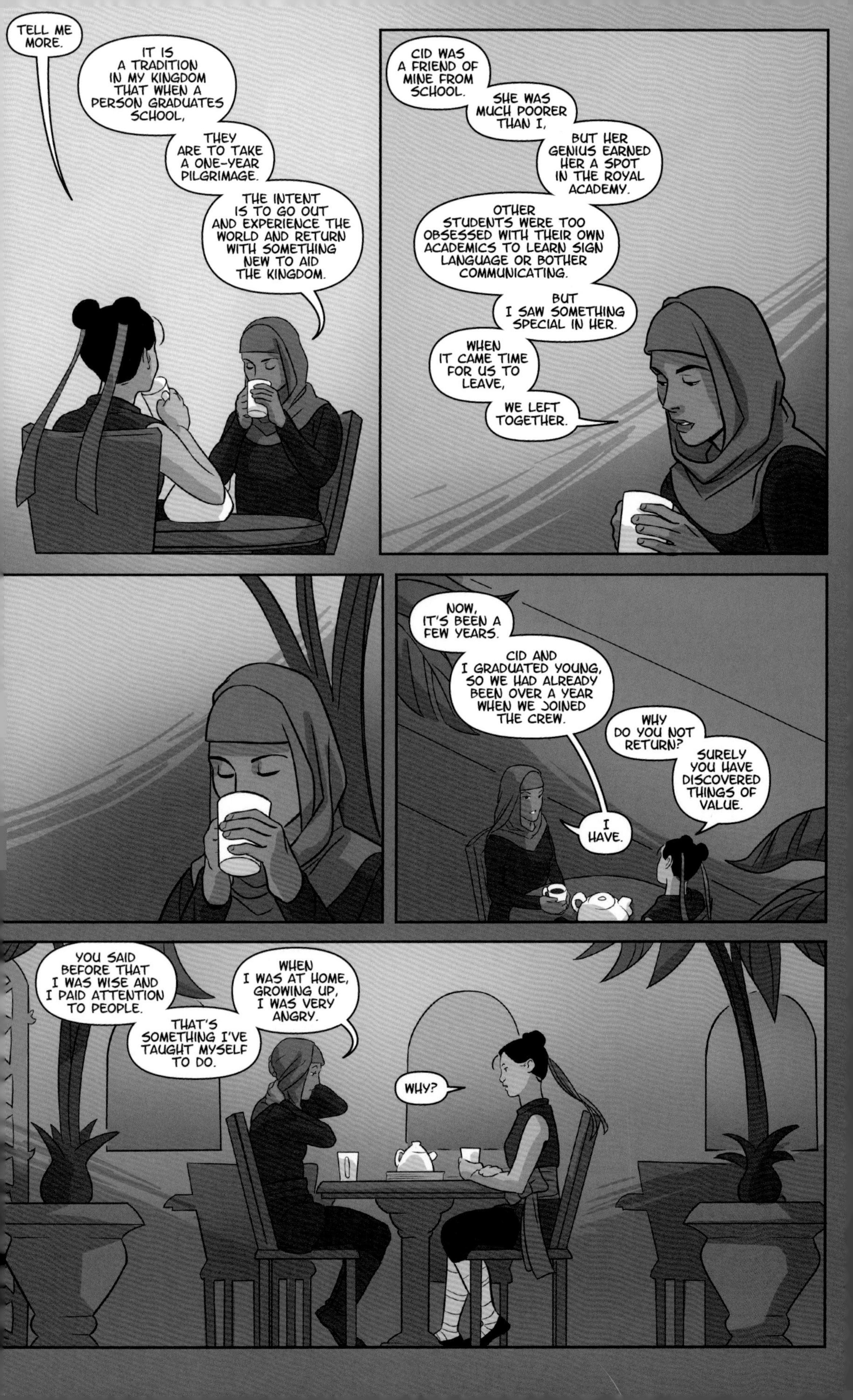
TELL ME MORE.
IT IS A TRADITION IN MY KINGDOM THAT WHEN A PERSON GRADUATES SCHOOL,
THEY ARE TO TAKE A ONE-YEAR PILGRIMAGE.
THE INTENT IS TO GO OUT AND EXPERIENCE THE WORLD AND RETURN WITH SOMETHING NEW TO AID THE KINGDOM.
CID WAS A FRIEND OF MINE FROM SCHOOL.
SHE WAS MUCH POORER THAN I,
BUT HER GENIUS EARNED HER A SPOT IN THE ROYAL ACADEMY.
OTHER STUDENTS WERE TOO OBSESSED WITH THEIR OWN ACADEMICS TO LEARN SIGN LANGUAGE OR BOTHER COMMUNICATING.
BUT I SAW SOMETHING SPECIAL IN HER.
WHEN IT CAME TIME FOR US TO LEAVE,
WE LEFT TOGETHER.
NOW, IT'S BEEN A FEW YEARS.
CID AND I GRADUATED YOUNG, SO WE HAD ALREADY BEEN OVER A YEAR WHEN WE JOINED THE CREW.
WHY DO YOU NOT RETURN?
SURELY YOU HAVE DISCOVERED THINGS OF VALUE.
I HAVE.
YOU SAID BEFORE THAT I WAS WISE AND I PAID ATTENTION TO PEOPLE.
THAT'S SOMETHING I'VE TAUGHT MYSELF TO DO.
WHEN I WAS AT HOME, GROWING UP, I WAS VERY ANGRY.
WHY?

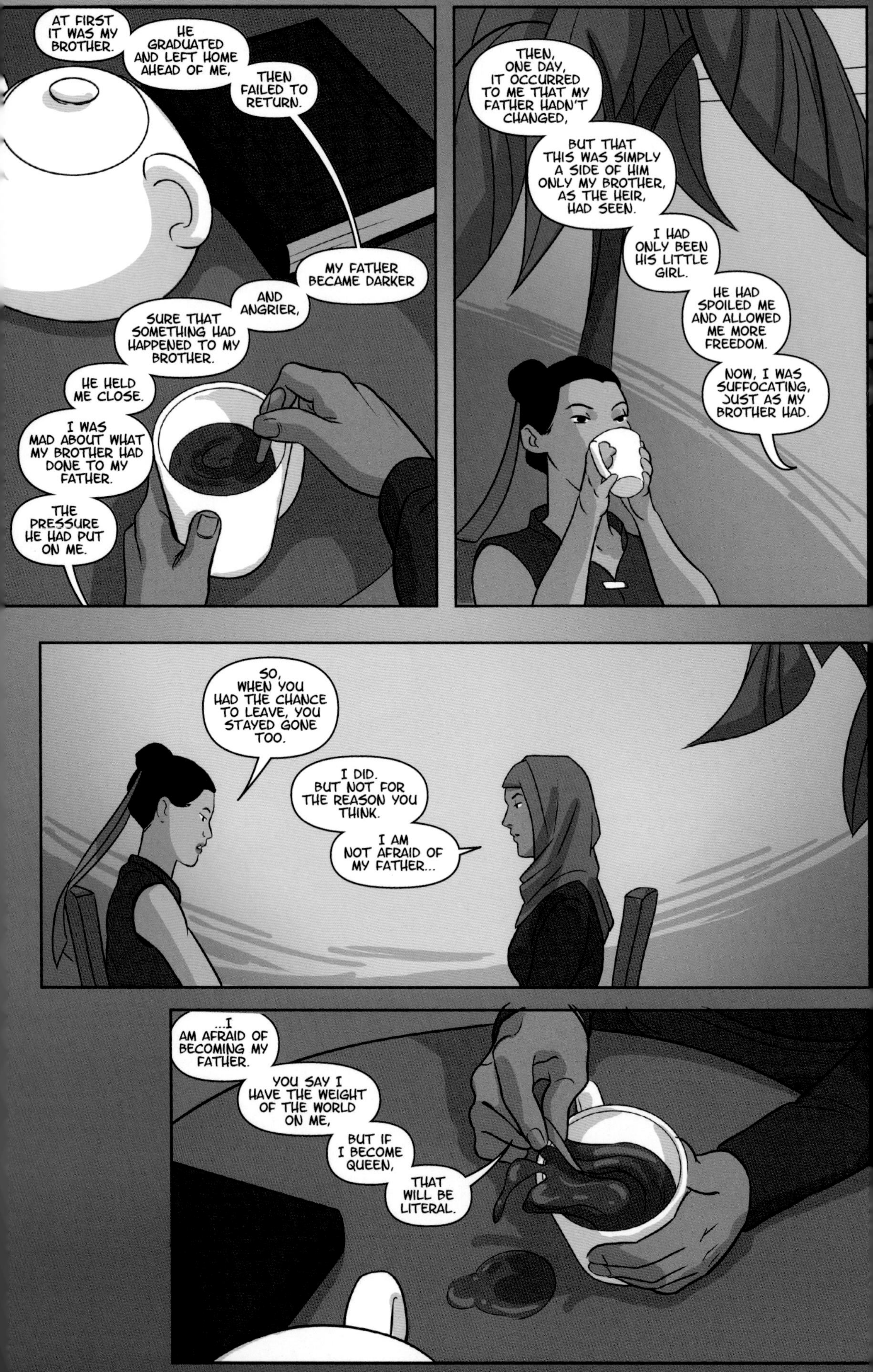
AT FIRST IT WAS MY BROTHER.
HE GRADUATED AND LEFT HOME AHEAD OF ME,
THEN FAILED TO RETURN.
MY FATHER BECAME DARKER
AND ANGRIER,
SURE THAT SOMETHING HAD HAPPENED TO MY BROTHER.
HE HELD ME CLOSE.
I WAS MAD ABOUT WHAT MY BROTHER HAD DONE TO MY FATHER.
THE PRESSURE HE HAD PUT ON ME.
THEN, ONE DAY, IT OCCURRED TO ME THAT MY FATHER HADN'T CHANGED,
BUT THAT THIS WAS SIMPLY A SIDE OF HIM ONLY MY BROTHER, AS THE HEIR, HAD SEEN.
I HAD ONLY BEEN HIS LITTLE GIRL.
HE HAD SPOILED ME AND ALLOWED ME MORE FREEDOM.
NOW, I WAS SUFFOCATING, JUST AS MY BROTHER HAD.
SO, WHEN YOU HAD THE CHANCE TO LEAVE, YOU STAYED GONE TOO.
I DID. BUT NOT FOR THE REASON YOU THINK.
I AM NOT AFRAID OF MY FATHER...
...I AM AFRAID OF BECOMING MY FATHER.
YOU SAY I HAVE THE WEIGHT OF THE WORLD ON ME,
BUT IF I BECOME QUEEN,
THAT WILL BE LITERAL.

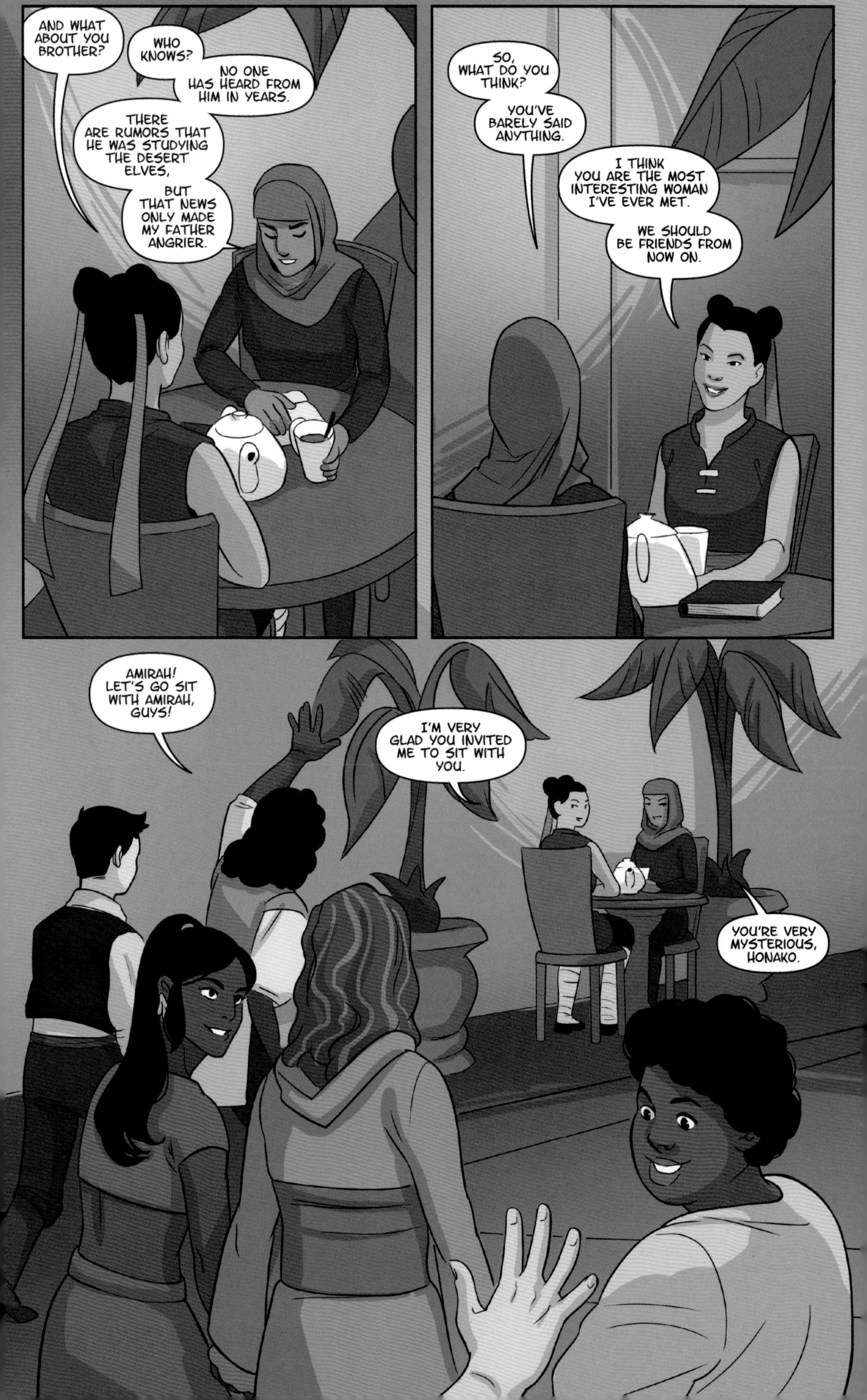
AND WHAT ABOUT YOU BROTHER?
WHO KNOWS?
NO ONE HAS HEARD FROM HIM IN YEARS.
THERE ARE RUMORS THAT HE WAS STUDYING THE DESERT ELVES,
BUT THAT NEWS ONLY MADE MY FATHER ANGRIER.
SO, WHAT DO YOU THINK?
YOU'VE BARELY SAID ANYTHING.
I THINK YOU ARE THE MOST INTERESTING WOMAN I'VE EVER MET.
WE SHOULD BE FRIENDS FROM NOW ON.
AMIRAH! LET'S GO SIT WITH AMIRAH, GUYS!
I'M VERY GLAD YOU INVITED ME TO SIT WITH YOU.
YOU'RE VERY MYSTERIOUS, HONAKO.

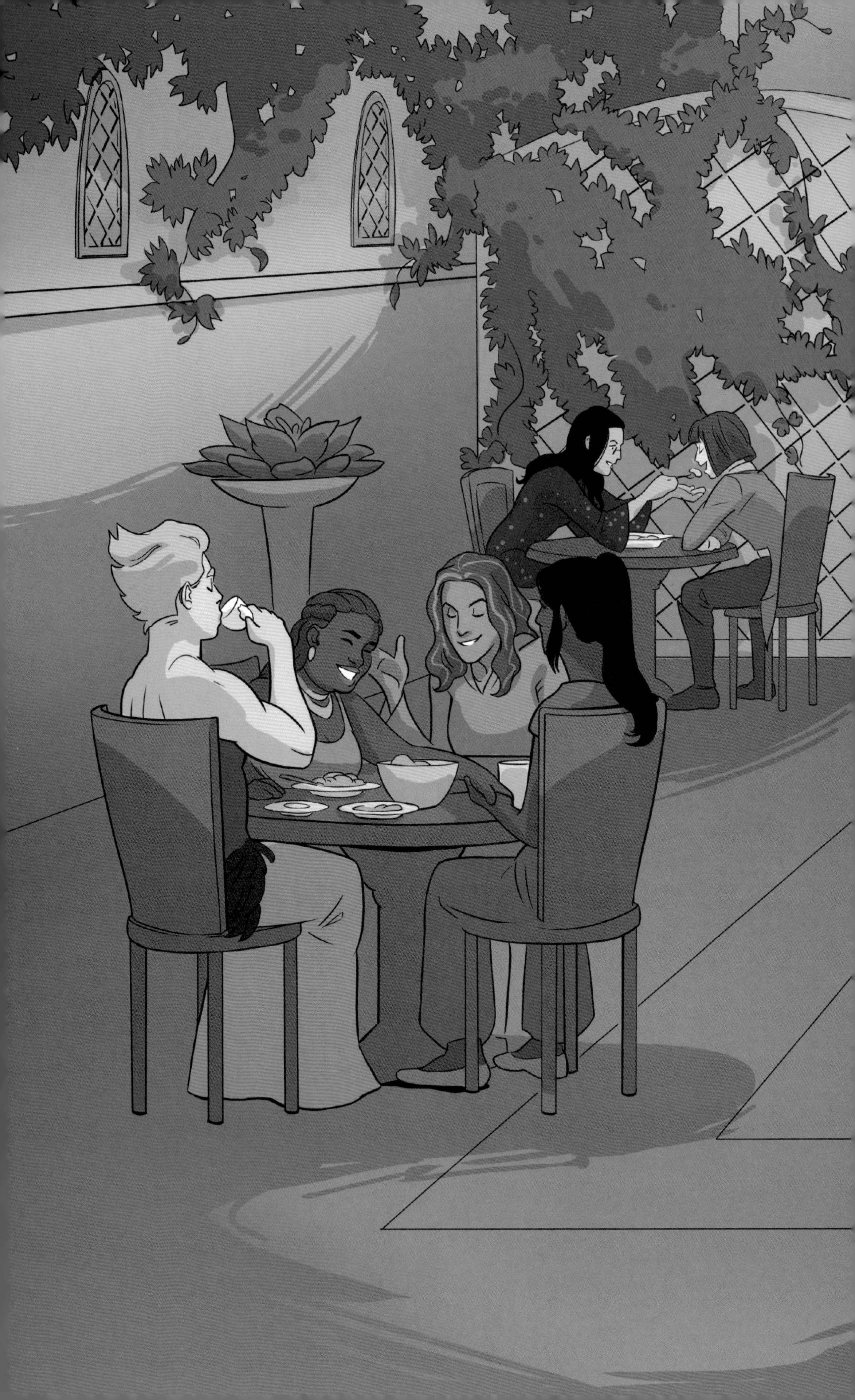

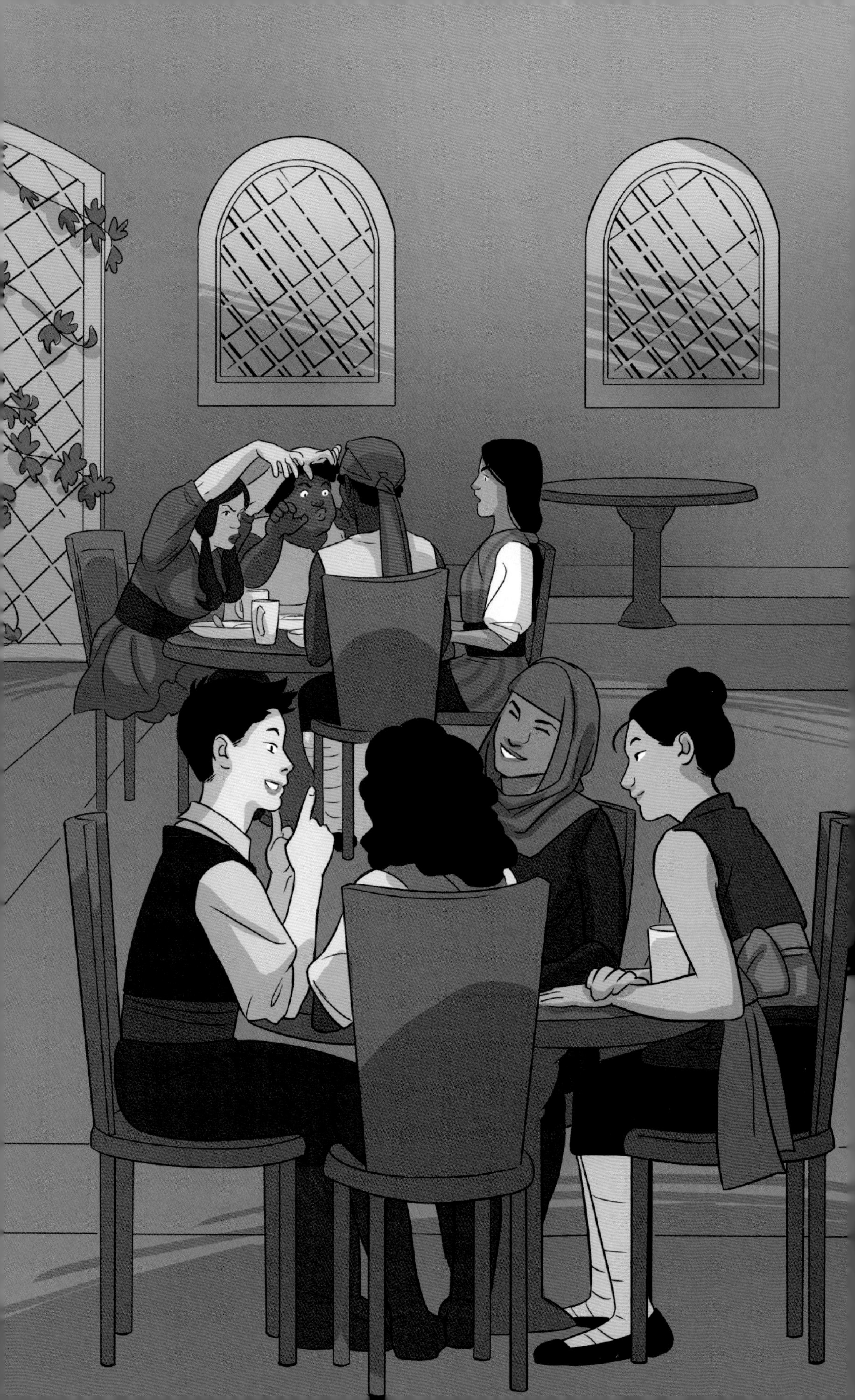

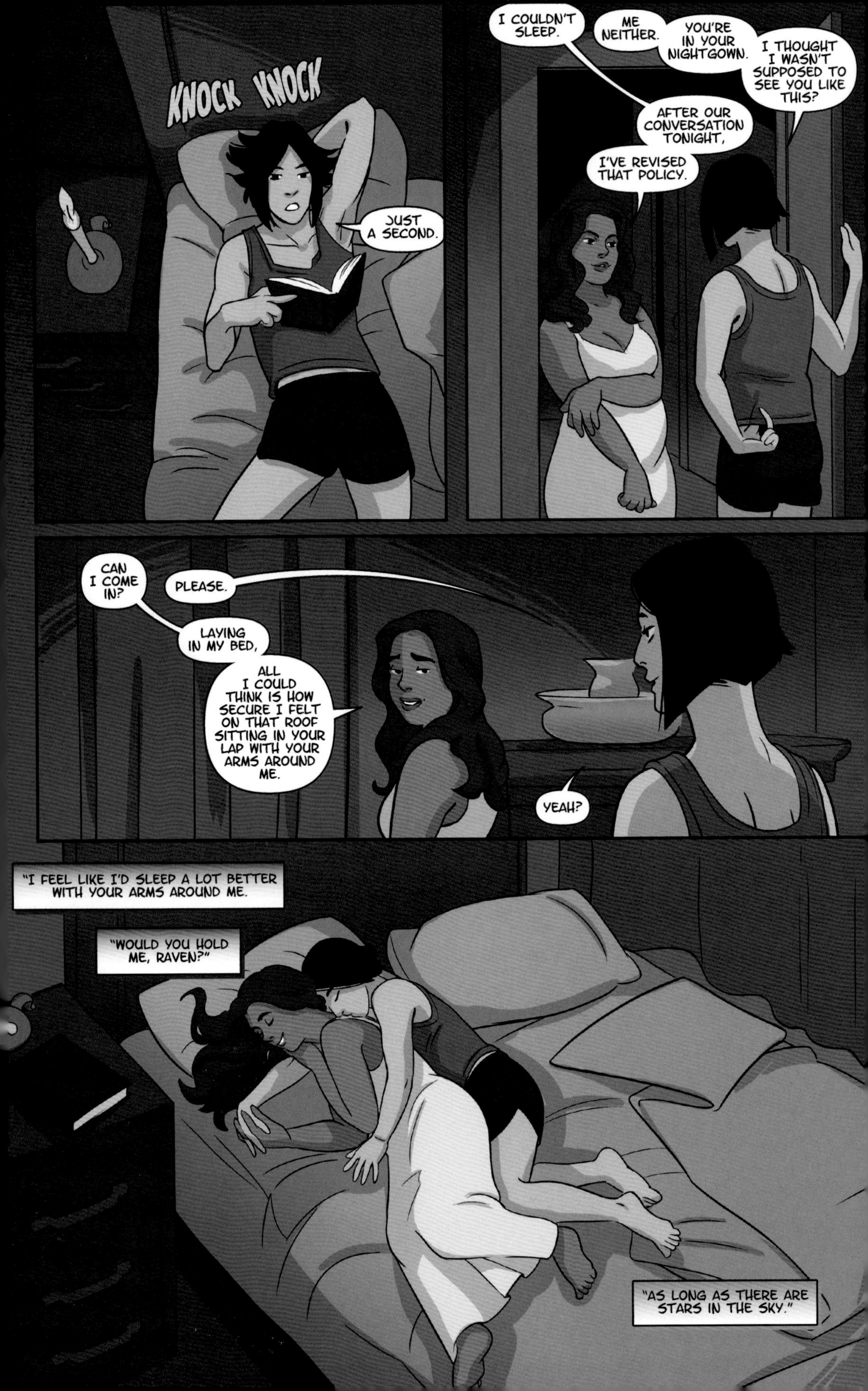
KNOCK KNOCK
JUST A SECOND.
I COULDN'T SLEEP.
ME NEITHER.
YOU'RE IN YOUR NIGHTGOWN.
I THOUGHT I WASN'T SUPPOSED TO SEE YOU LIKE THIS?
AFTER OUR CONVERSATION TONIGHT,
I'VE REVISED THAT POLICY.
CAN I COME IN?
PLEASE.
LAYING IN MY BED,
ALL I COULD THINK IS HOW SECURE I FELT ON THAT ROOF SITTING IN YOUR LAP WITH YOUR ARMS AROUND ME.
YEAH?
"I FEEL LIKE I'D SLEEP A LOT BETTER WITH YOUR ARMS AROUND ME.
"WOULD YOU HOLD ME, RAVEN?"
"AS LONG AS THERE ARE STARS IN THE SKY."

Princess

RAVEN

THE PIRATE PRINCESS

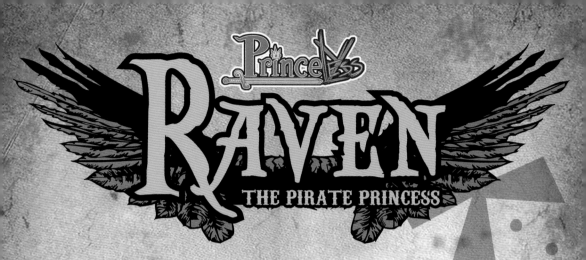

Year Three: Monsters of the Deep

Halloween ComicFest: The Drowned Witches' Offer

Written By: Jeremy Whitley

Art By: Megan Huang

Lettered By: Justin Birch

Edited By: Nicole D'Andria

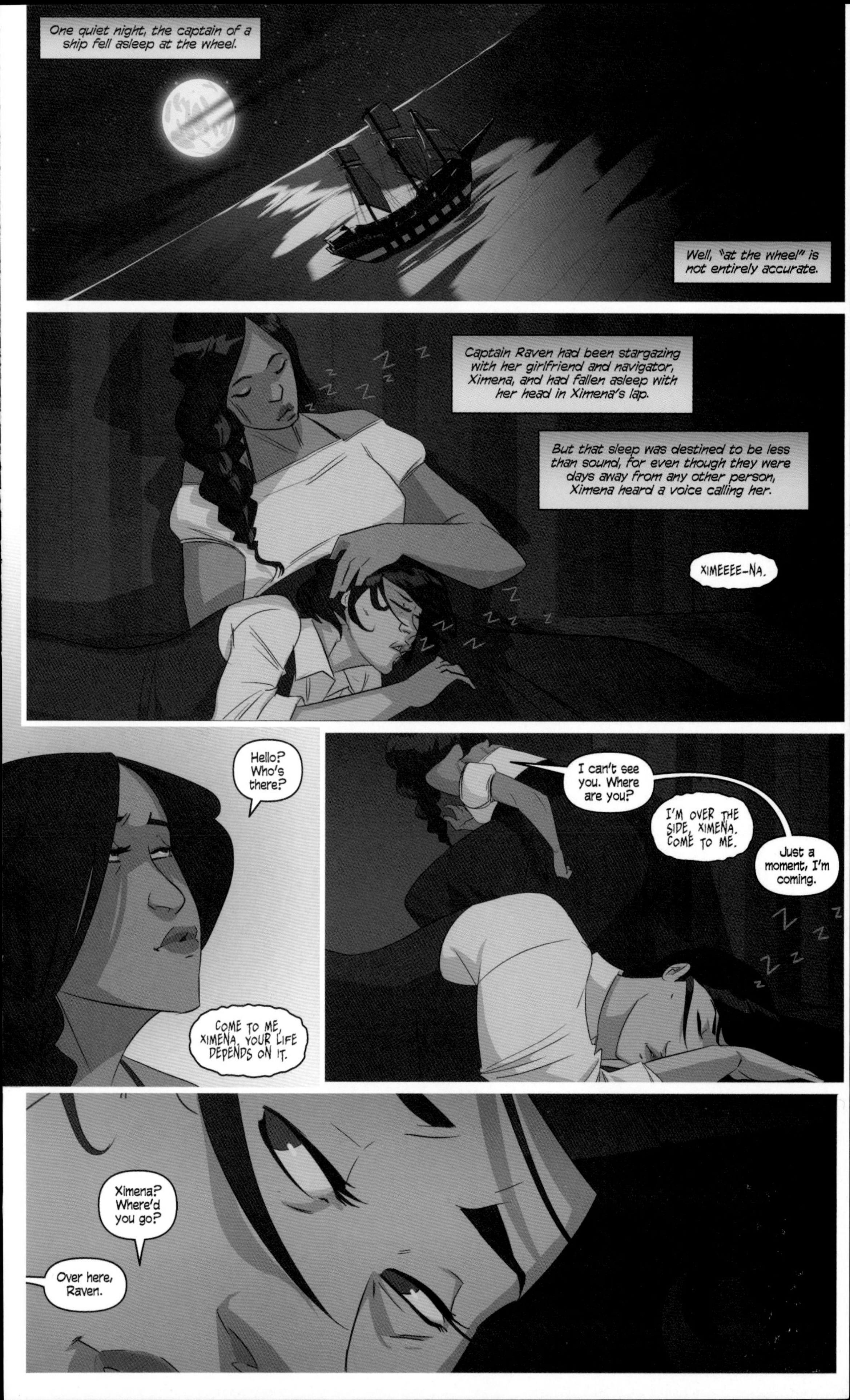
One quiet night, the captain of a ship fell asleep at the wheel.
Well, "at the wheel" is not entirely accurate.
Captain Raven had been stargazing with her girlfriend and navigator, Ximena, and had fallen asleep with her head in Ximena's lap.
But that sleep was destined to be less than sound, for even though they were days away from any other person, Ximena heard a voice calling her.
XIMEEEE-NA.
Hello? Who's there?
COME TO ME, XIMENA. YOUR LIFE DEPENDS ON IT.
I can't see you. Where are you?
I'M OVER THE SIDE, XIMENA. COME TO ME.
Just a moment, I'm coming.
Ximena? Where'd you go?
Over here, Raven.

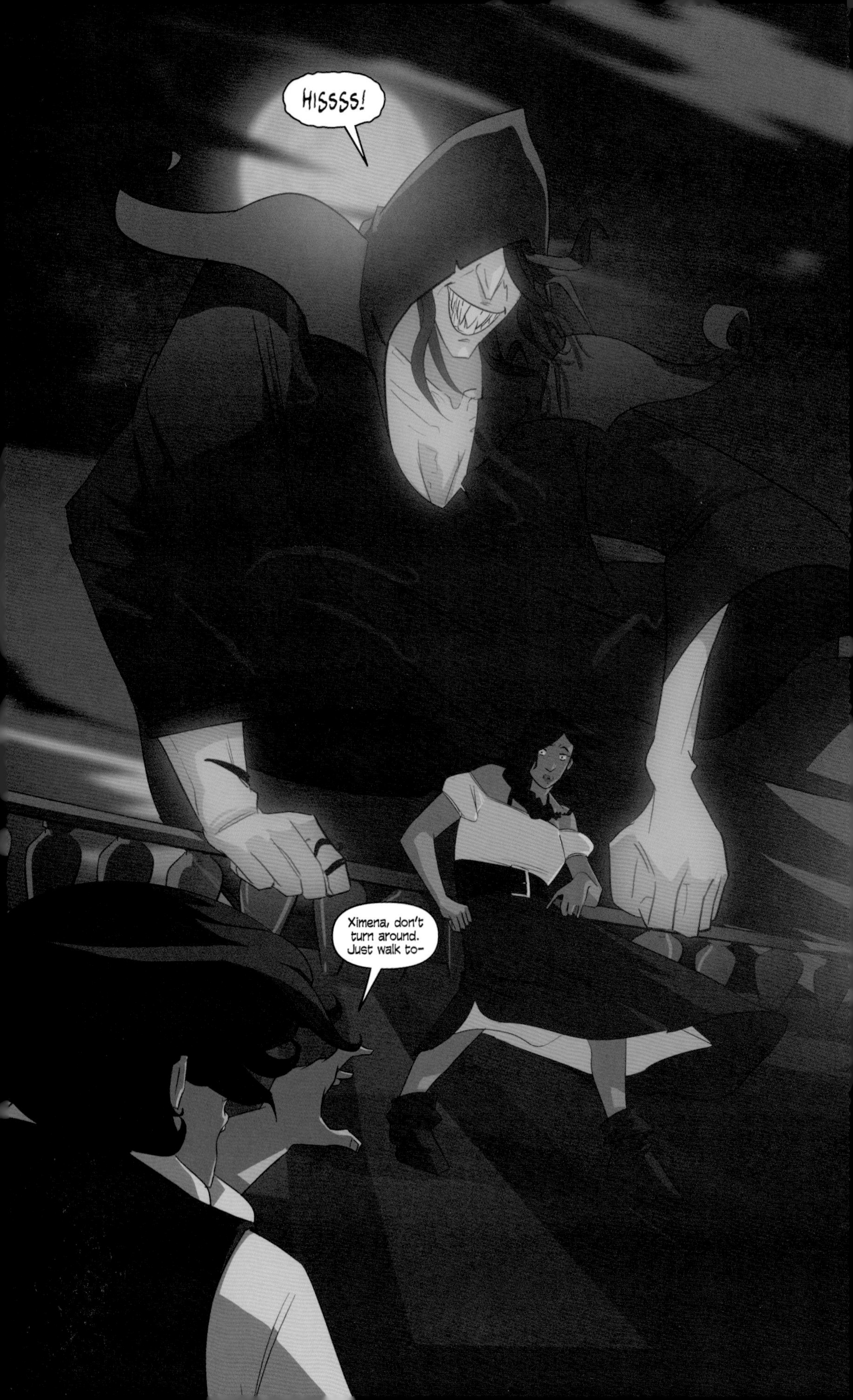
HISSSS!
Ximena, don't turn around. Just walk to-

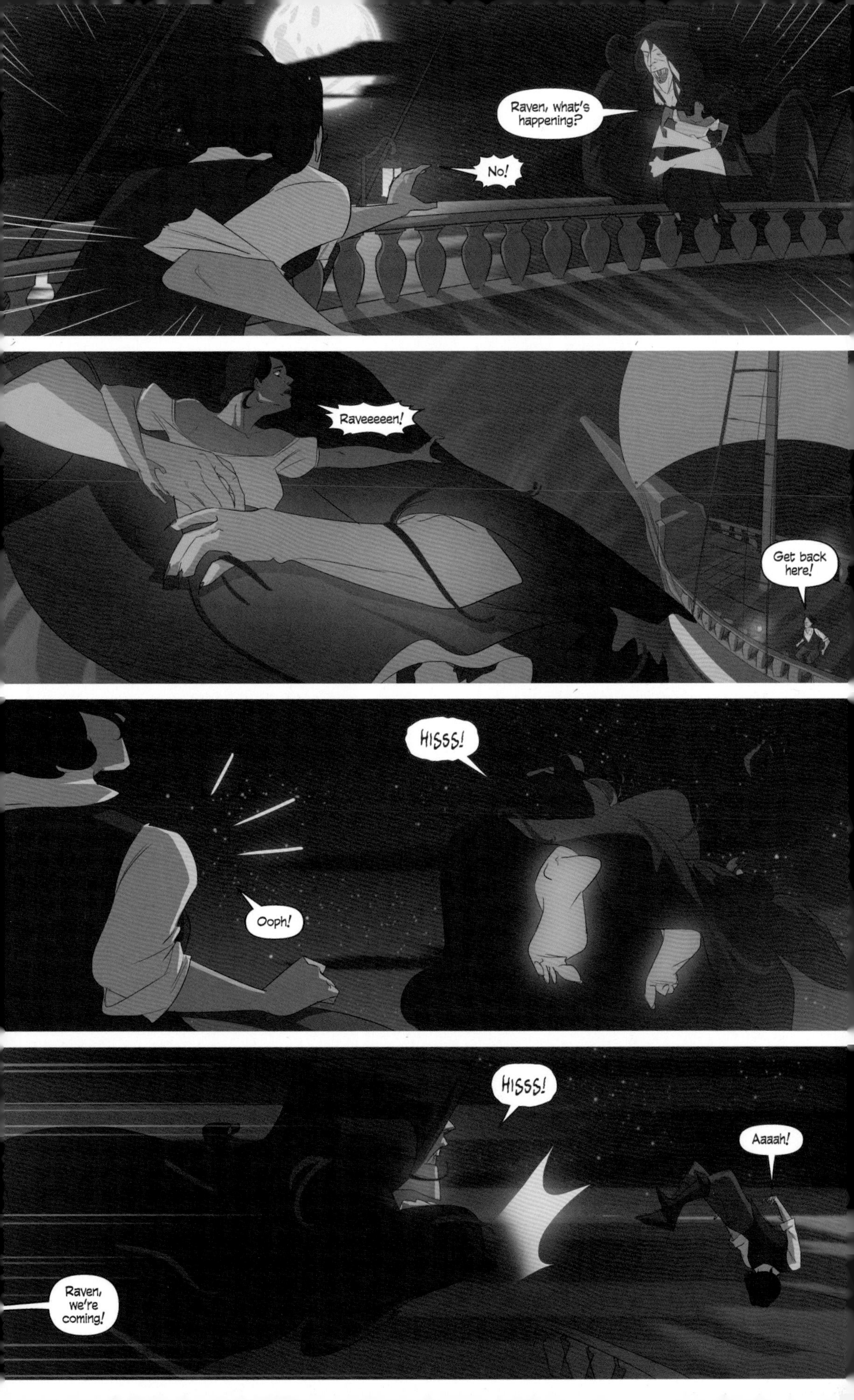
Raven, what's happening?
No!
Raveeeeen!
Get back here!
HISSS!
Ooph!
HISSS!
Aaaah!
Raven, we're coming!

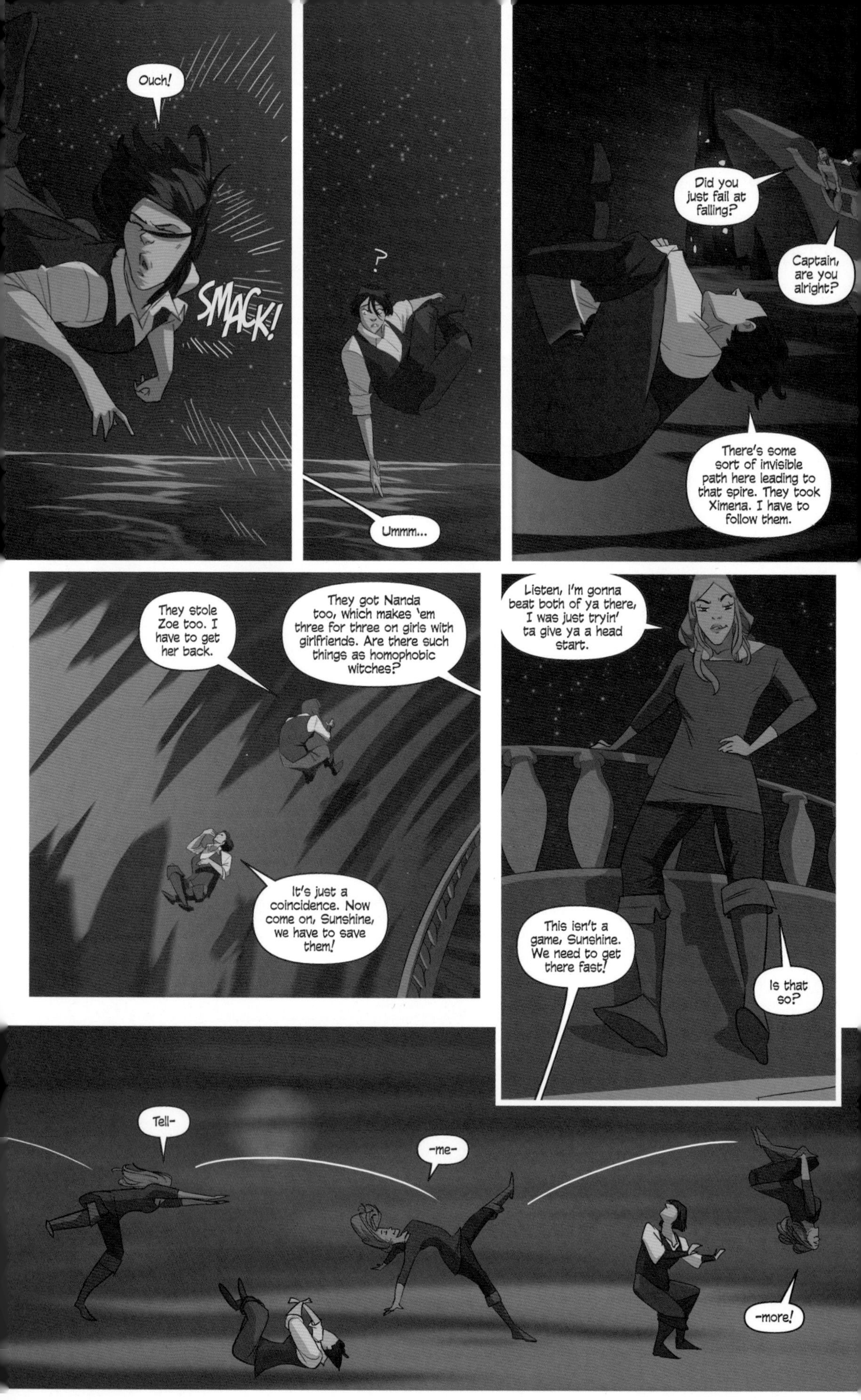
Ouch!
SMACK!
?
Ummm...
Did you just fail at falling?
Captain, are you alright?
There's some sort of invisible path here leading to that spire. They took Ximena. I have to follow them.
They stole Zoe too. I have to get her back.
They got Nanda too, which makes 'em three for three on girls with girlfriends. Are there such things as homophobic witches?
It's just a coincidence. Now come on, Sunshine, we have to save them!
Listen, I'm gonna beat both of ya there, I was just tryin' ta give ya a head start.
This isn't a game, Sunshine. We need to get there fast!
Is that so?
Tell-
-me-
-more!

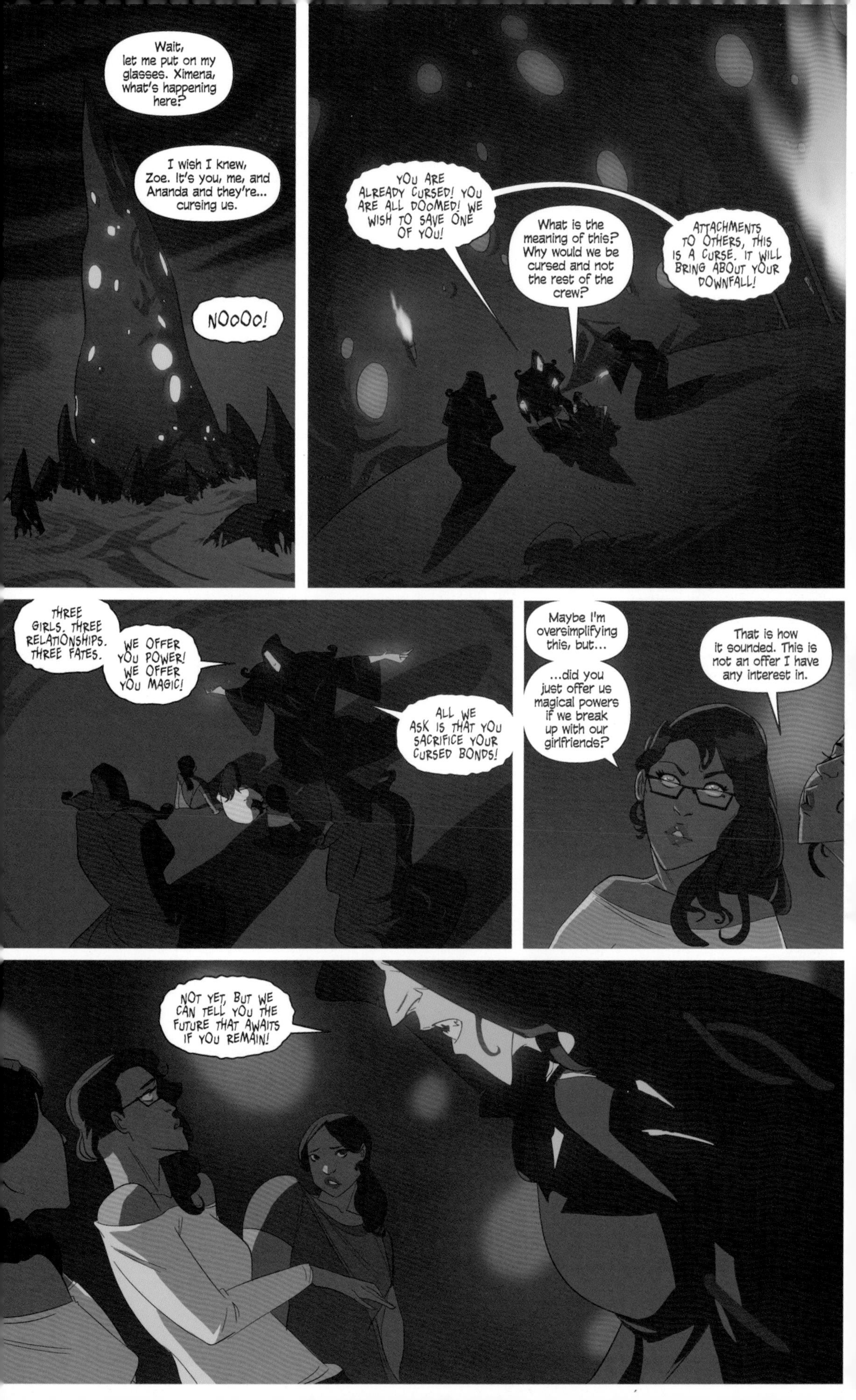
Wait, let me put on my glasses. Ximena, what's happening here?
I wish I knew, Zoe. It's you, me, and Ananda and they're... cursing us.
NOoOo!
YOU ARE ALREADY CURSED! YOU ARE ALL DOOMED! WE WISH TO SAVE ONE OF YOU!
What is the meaning of this? Why would we be cursed and not the rest of the crew?
ATTACHMENTS TO OTHERS, THIS IS A CURSE. IT WILL BRING ABOUT YOUR DOWNFALL!
THREE GIRLS. THREE RELATIONSHIPS. THREE FATES.
WE OFFER YOU POWER! WE OFFER YOU MAGIC!
ALL WE ASK IS THAT YOU SACRIFICE YOUR CURSED BONDS!
Maybe I'm oversimplifying this, but...
...did you just offer us magical powers if we break up with our girlfriends?
That is how it sounded. This is not an offer I have any interest in.
NOT YET, BUT WE CAN TELL YOU THE FUTURE THAT AWAITS IF YOU REMAIN!

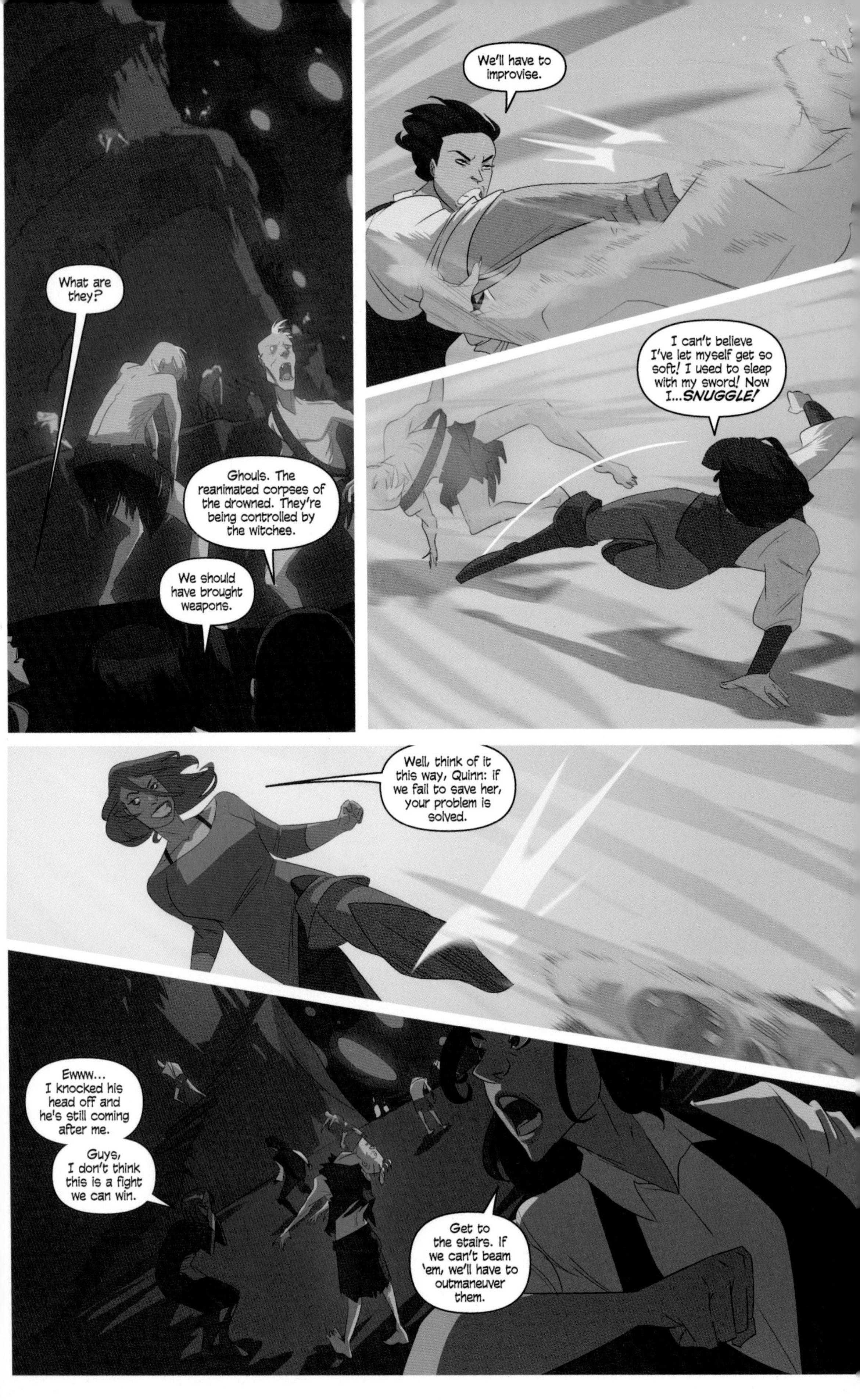
What are they?
Ghouls. The reanimated corpses of the drowned. They're being controlled by the witches.
We should have brought weapons.
We'll have to improvise.
I can't believe I've let myself get so soft! I used to sleep with my sword! Now I...SNUGGLE!
Well, think of it this way, Quinn: if we fail to save her, your problem is solved.
Ewww... I knocked his head off and he's still coming after me.
Guys, I don't think this is a fight we can win.
Get to the stairs. If we can't beam 'em, we'll have to outmaneuver them.

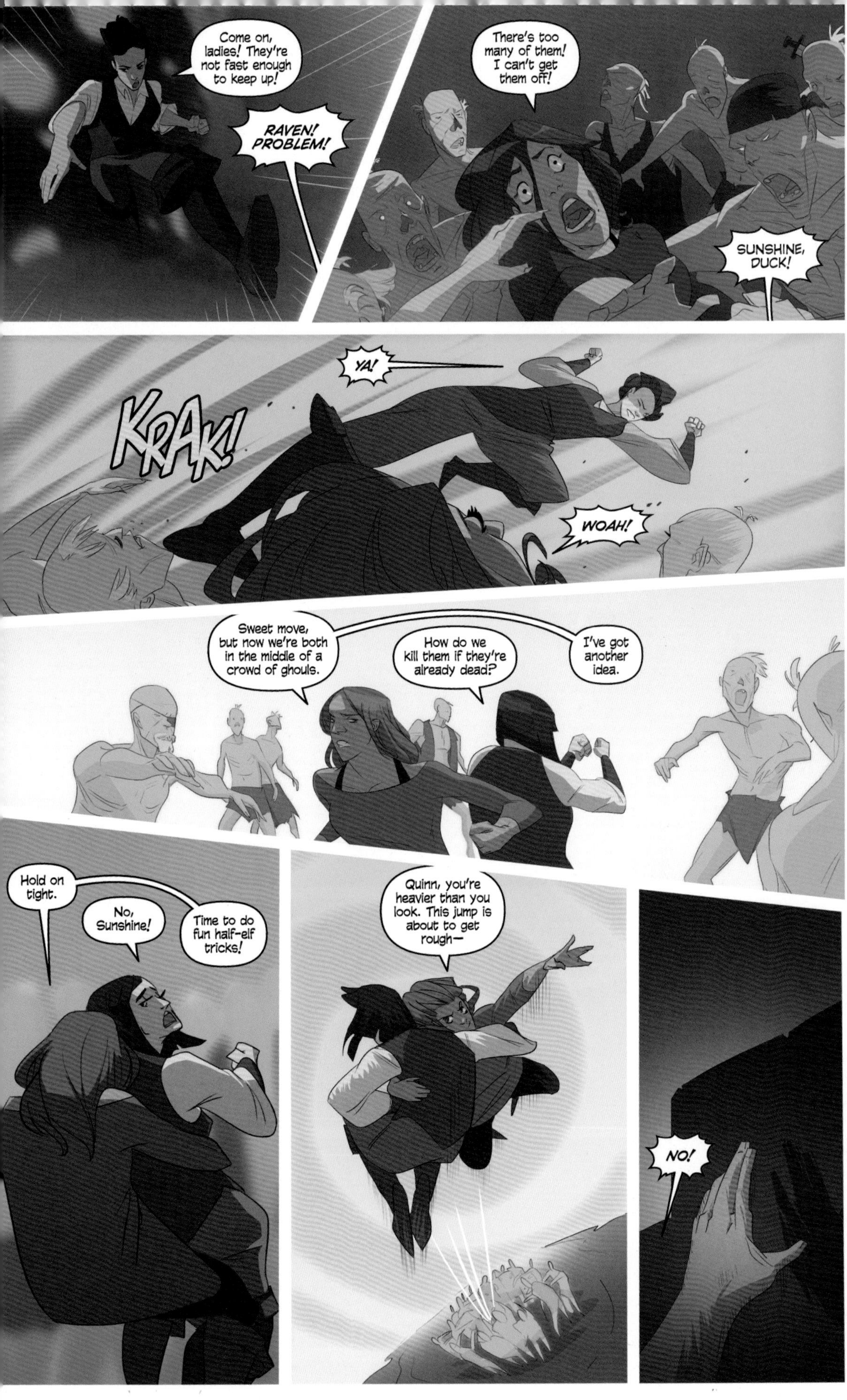

Come on, ladies! They're not fast enough to keep up!
RAVEN! PROBLEM!
There's too many of them! I can't get them off!
SUNSHINE, DUCK!
YA!
KRAK!
WOAH!
Sweet move, but now we're both in the middle of a crowd of ghouls.
How do we kill them if they're already dead?
I've got another idea.
Hold on tight.
No, Sunshine!
Time to do fun half-elf tricks!
Quinn, you're heavier than you look. This jump is about to get rough—
NO!

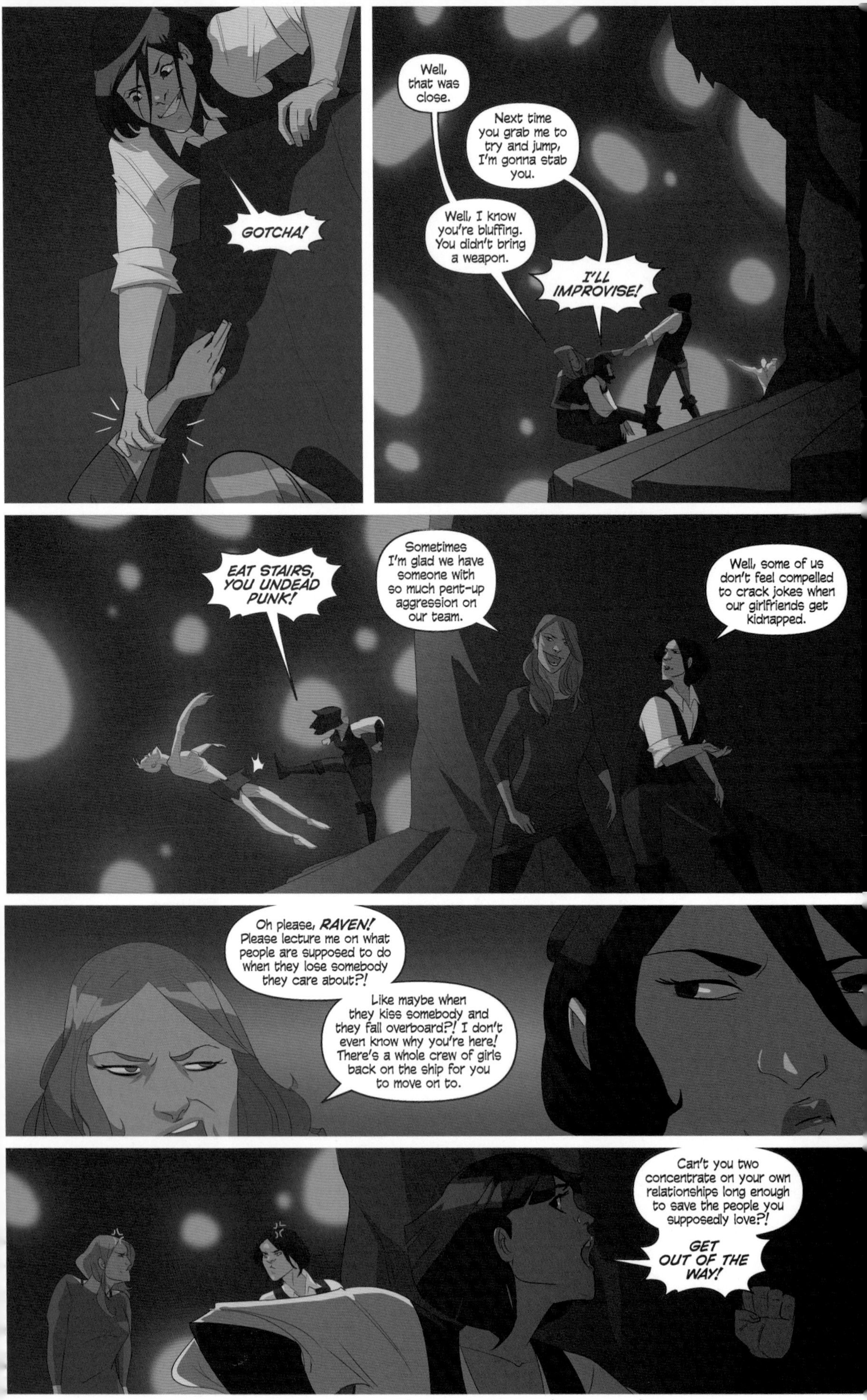
GOTCHA!
Well, that was close.
Next time you grab me to try and jump, I'm gonna stab you.
Well, I know you're bluffing. You didn't bring a weapon.
I'LL IMPROVISE!
EAT STAIRS, YOU UNDEAD PUNK!
Sometimes I'm glad we have someone with so much pent-up aggression on our team.
Well, some of us don't feel compelled to crack jokes when our girlfriends get kidnapped.
Oh please, RAVEN! Please lecture me on what people are supposed to do when they lose somebody they care about?!
Like maybe when they kiss somebody and they fall overboard?! I don't even know why you're here! There's a whole crew of girls back on the ship for you to move on to.
Can't you two concentrate on your own relationships long enough to save the people you supposedly love?!
GET OUT OF THE WAY!

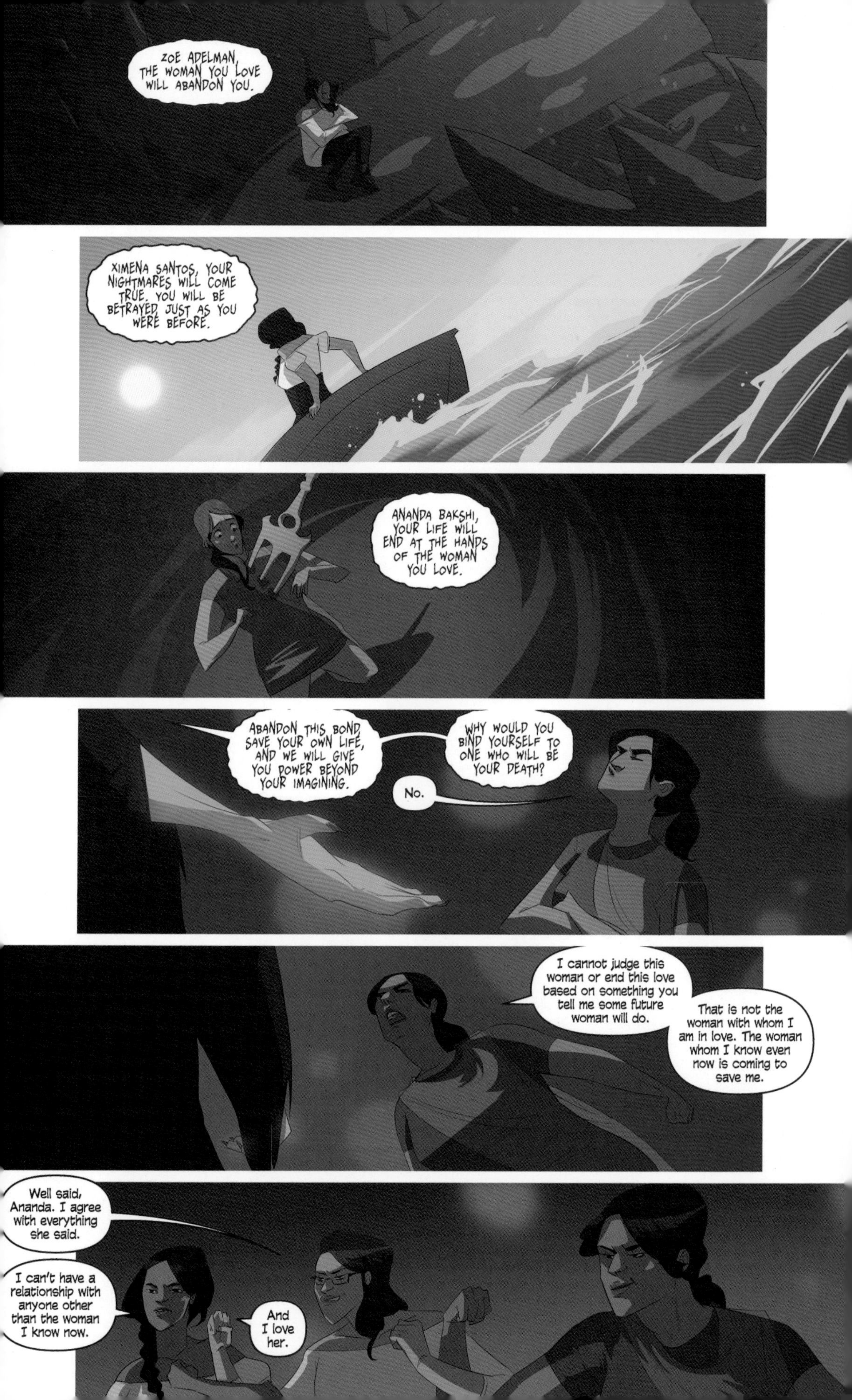
ZOE ADELMAN, THE WOMAN YOU LOVE WILL ABANDON YOU.
XIMENA SANTOS, YOUR NIGHTMARES WILL COME TRUE. YOU WILL BE BETRAYED JUST AS YOU WERE BEFORE.
ANANDA BAKSHI, YOUR LIFE WILL END AT THE HANDS OF THE WOMAN YOU LOVE.
ABANDON THIS BOND, SAVE YOUR OWN LIFE, AND WE WILL GIVE YOU POWER BEYOND YOUR IMAGINING.
WHY WOULD YOU BIND YOURSELF TO ONE WHO WILL BE YOUR DEATH?
No.
I cannot judge this woman or end this love based on something you tell me some future woman will do.
That is not the woman with whom I am in love. The woman whom I know even now is coming to save me.
Well said, Ananda. I agree with everything she said.
I can't have a relationship with anyone other than the woman I know now.
And I love her.

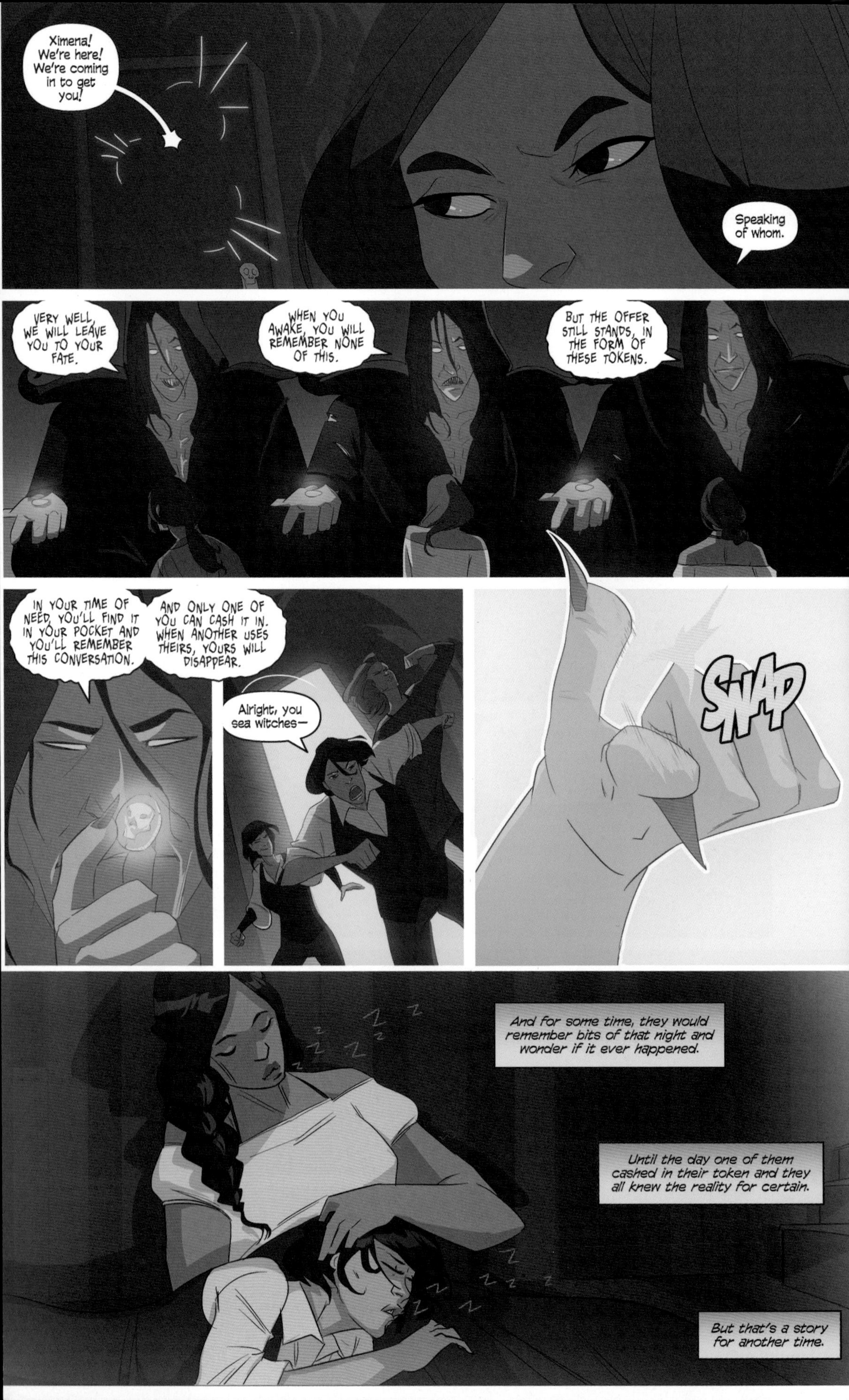
Ximena! We're here! We're coming in to get you!
Speaking of whom.
VERY WELL, WE WILL LEAVE YOU TO YOUR FATE.
WHEN YOU AWAKE, YOU WILL REMEMBER NONE OF THIS.
BUT THE OFFER STILL STANDS, IN THE FORM OF THESE TOKENS.
IN YOUR TIME OF NEED, YOU'LL FIND IT IN YOUR POCKET AND YOU'LL REMEMBER THIS CONVERSATION.
AND ONLY ONE OF YOU CAN CASH IT IN. WHEN ANOTHER USES THEIRS, YOURS WILL DISAPPEAR.
Alright, you sea witches—
SNAP
And for some time, they would remember bits of that night and wonder if it ever happened.
Until the day one of them cashed in their token and they all knew the reality for certain.
But that's a story for another time.

Issue 3, Page 17 Progression

Page 17:

Panel 1: They pull apart. Raven smiles at Ximena. Ximena bites her lip.

RAVEN
I hope she didn't give that to you herself.

XIMENA
Just the instructions. I've been up here prepping it for you.

RAVEN
Well, I'll have to thank her before we leave.

Panel 2: Raven whispers in Ximena's ear.

RAVEN
You look amazing. Did you pick your dress too?

XIMENA
No, you can thank a committee of our friends for this. But I feel amazing in it.

RAVEN
It's going to be hard to concentrate on dinner, when the only thing I want to nibble—

Panel 3: Raven nibbles on Ximena's neck. Ximena giggles.

RAVEN (CAPTION)
--is this.

XIMENA
Hee he he he—

Panel 4: Ximena playfully bats Raven away from her.

XIMENA
Now you stop that, you're going to make me fall off this building!

RAVEN
That would make for a great story.

XIMENA
We already are a great story.

Panel 5: Ximena pulls Raven down the widow's walk to the table.
The stars shine brightly around them.

XIMENA
Come on, my pirate princess, the night's just getting started.

RAVEN
Take me anywhere you want. I'm yours to command.

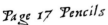

Page 17 Inks

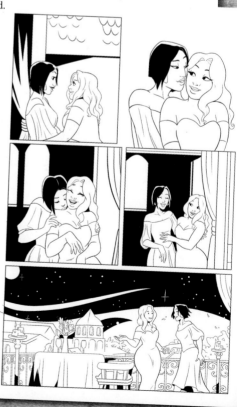

Page 17 Pencils

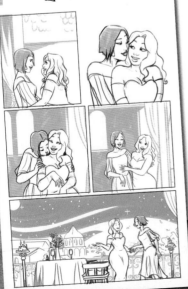

Issue 3, Page 17 Progression

Page 17 Colors

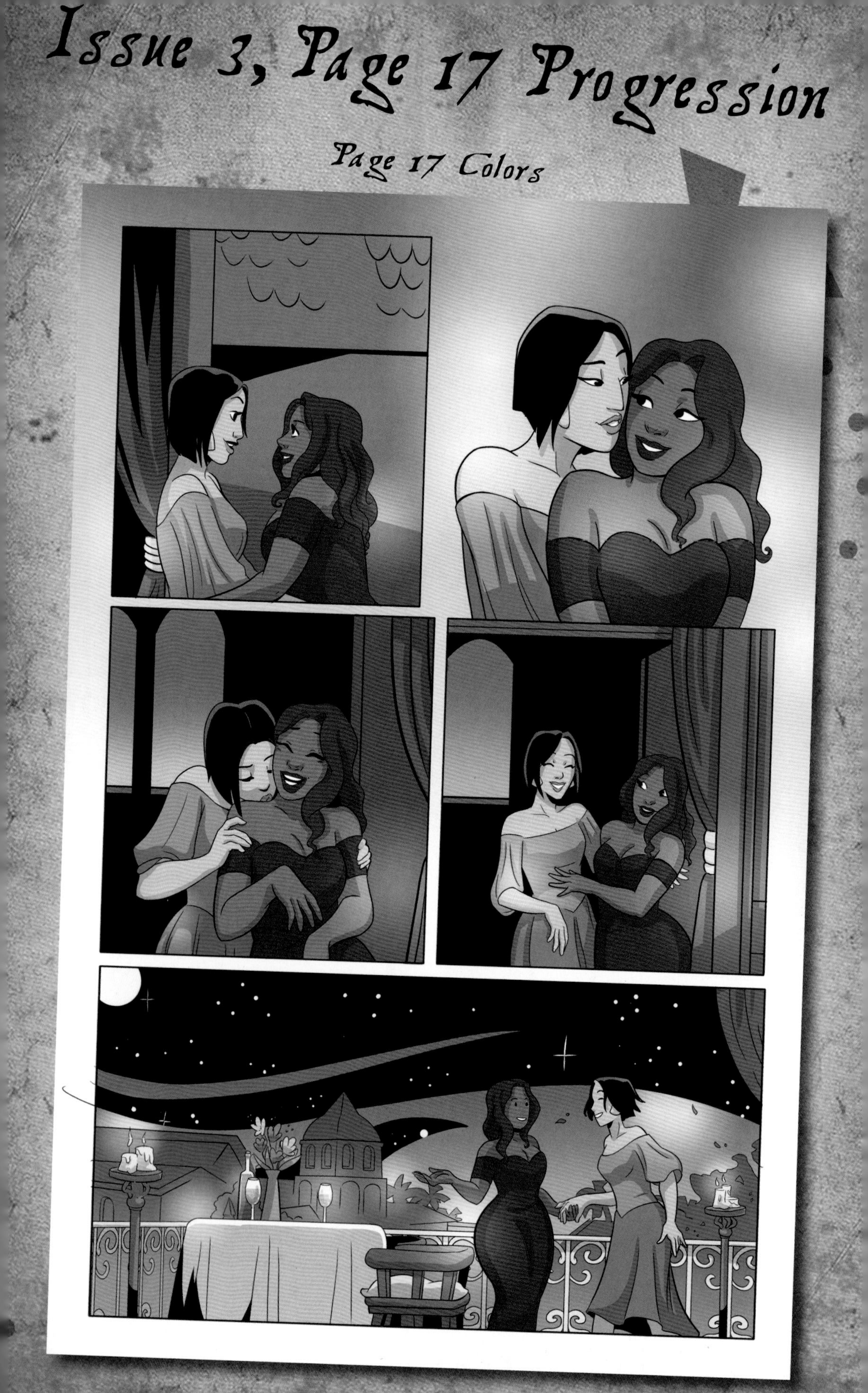

Issue 3, Page 21 Progression

Page 21:

Panel 1: Verity leans over to Katie, smiling.

VERITY
Good start! I always love something with royal drama.

KATIE
Hopefully it gets happier.

VERITY
Where's the fun in that?

Panel 2: Katie and Verity hold hands.

Panel 3: Ivy is struggling to keep another princess from going with an older king.

IVY (MUSICAL)
Sister, he is a beast! Do not go with this prince, do not move away to the east!

SISTER (MUSICAL)
He offers gold! He offers security! It is my place to defend my home by giving my purity.

Panel 4: Ivy holds her sister's body. Her dress is stained in blood.

IVY
The heralds say, she was an unfaithful queen who found love in the arms of a knave.
I know my sister! I know she was locked away and treated like a slave.
I will have my revenge. I will see this King put to his grave!

Panel 5: Katie looks at Verity, trying to judge reaction.

Panel 6: Verity is crying.

Page 21 Inks

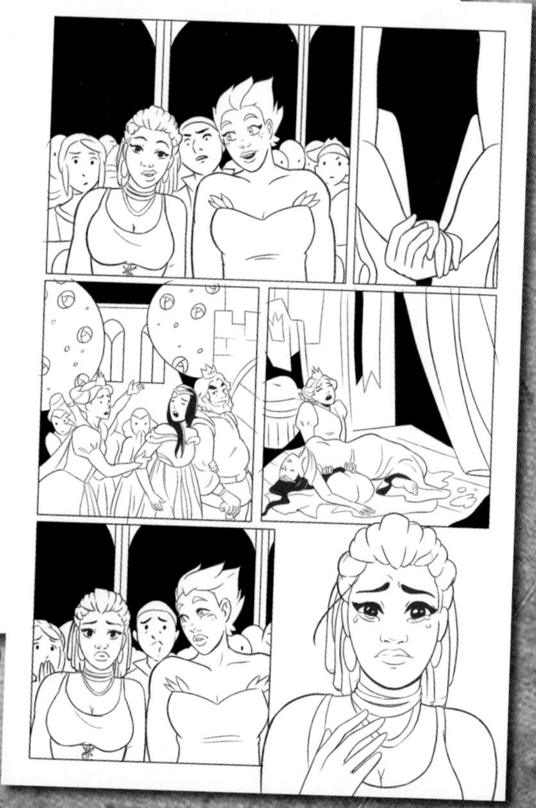

Page 21 Pencils

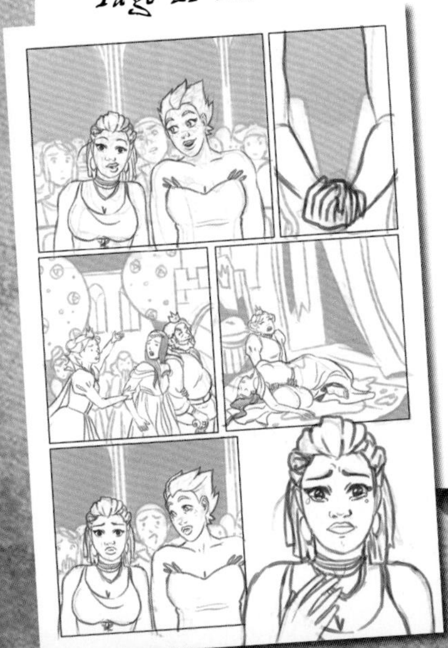

Issue 3, Page 21 Progression

Page 21 Colors

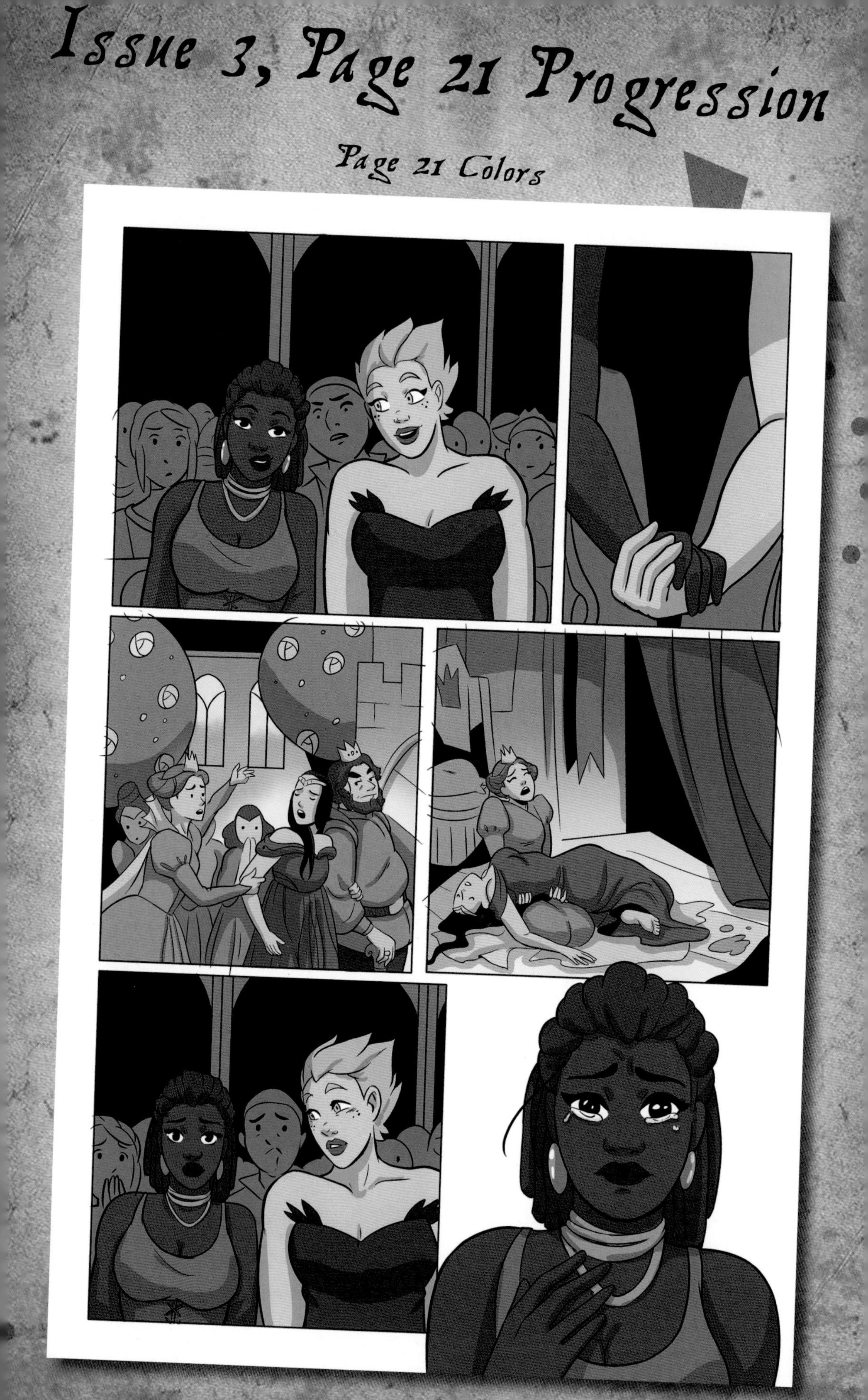

Issue 4, Page 20 Progression

Page 20:

Panel 1: Jayla and Cid stand with their device, fireworks exploding overhead. Around them Ananda, Sunshine, Ophelia, Pirate, Melody, and Valentina stand.

MELODY
Oh, fireworks. That's what you were working on.

Panel 2: Jayla and Cid high five.

Panel 3: Raven and Ximena meet Quinn and Zoe in the middle of the road approaching the rest of the group.

RAVEN
I should have figured that would be my crew out here setting off fireworks.

ZOE
They were for us, because I'm best poet and Quinn's best girlfriend.

XIMENA
I would argue that Raven is giving Quinn a run for her money right now.

Panel 4: Katie and Verity wander up from another side. Verity is snuggled closed to Katie.

KATIE
Hey, look Verity, it's everybody.

VERITY
Hey everybody, we're hungry. Let's go get some food!

REST OF CROWD
Yes!
Yeah!
Entire cow!
FIND FOOD!

Panel 5: Raven and Ximena wave the rest of them on.

XIMENA
Erg! If I eat another bite my corset's going to split.

RAVEN
You all go on. We'll meet you back at the ship tomorrow.

Page 20 Inks

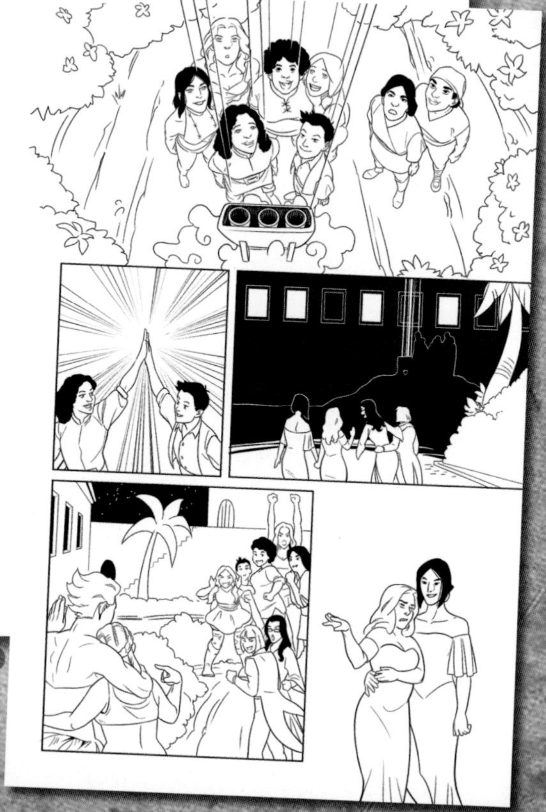

Page 20 Pencils

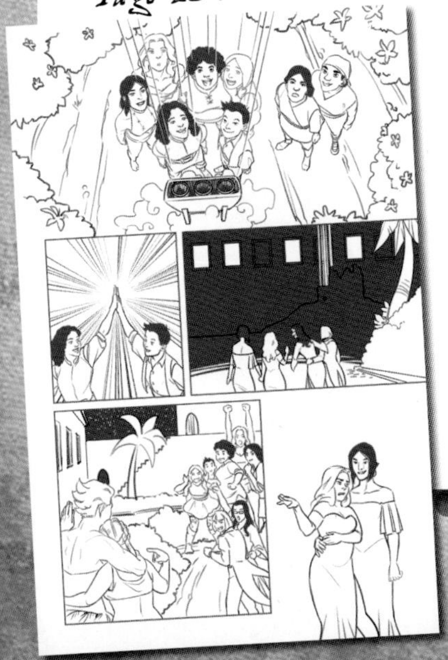

Issue 4, Page 20 Progression

Page 20 Colors

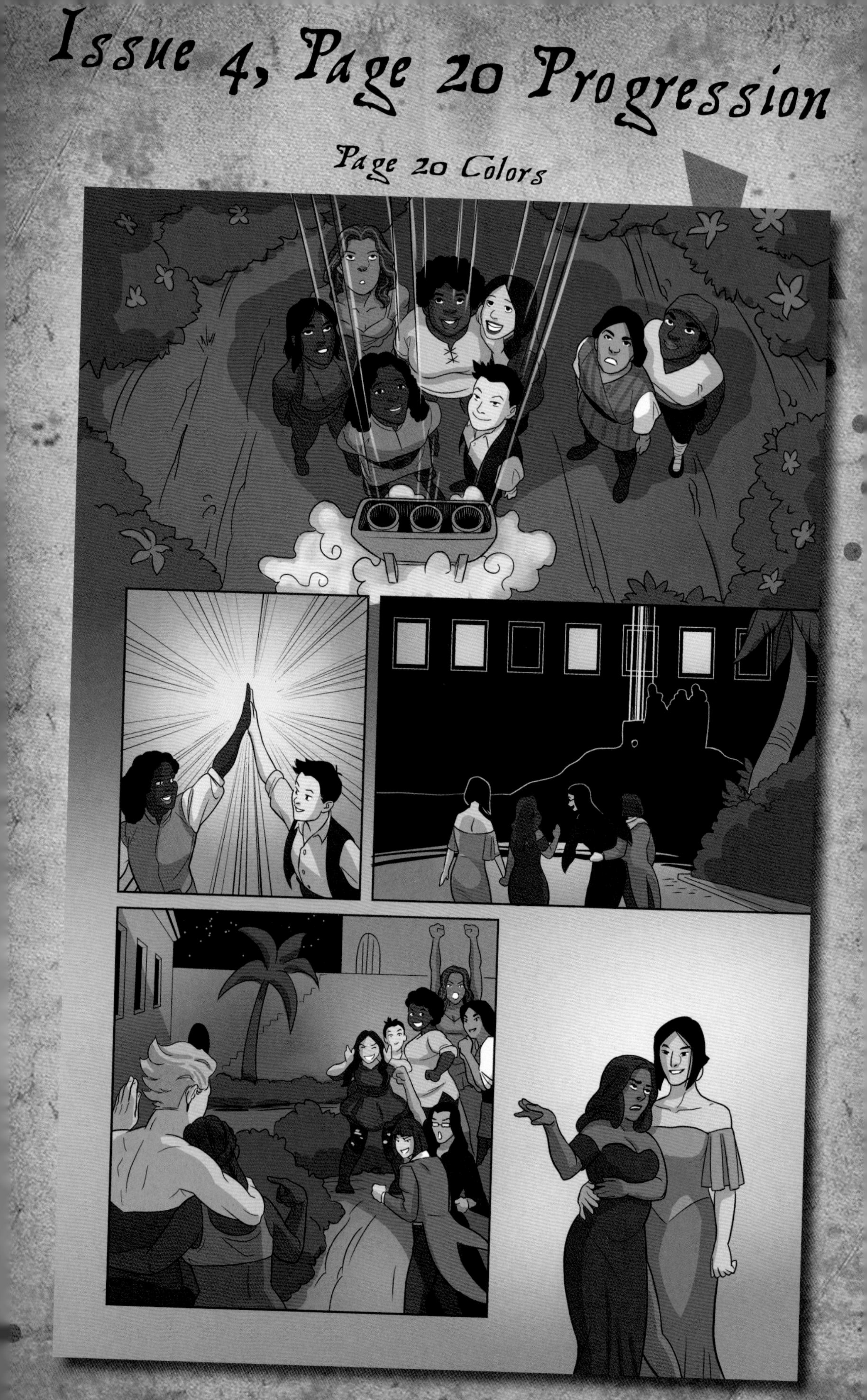

Issue 4, Page 26 Progression

Page 26:

Panel 1: Raven lays on her bed wearing her usual nighttime shorts and tanktop, next to a small candle. She is reading a book. There is a knock at the door.

SFX
Knock knock.

RAVEN
Just a second.

Panel 2: Raven opens the door. Ximena is there in her nightgown.

XIMENA
I couldn't sleep.

RAVEN
Me neither.

RAVEN
You're in your nightgown. I thought I wasn't supposed to see you like this?

XIMENA
After our conversation tonight, I've revised that policy.

Panel 3: Ximena enters. Raven allows her in.

XIMENA
Can I come in?

RAVEN
Please.

XIMENA
Laying in my bed, all I could think is how secure I felt on that roof sitting in your lap with your arms around me.

RAVEN
Yeah?

Panel 4: Raven and Ximena lie together in bed. They are still dressed in their respective pajamas. Raven spoons Ximena, with her arm around her. They are both asleep.

XIMENA (CAPTION)
I feel like I'd sleep a lot better with your arms around me.
Would you hold me, Raven?

RAVEN (CAPTION)
As long as there are stars in the sky.

Page 26 Inks

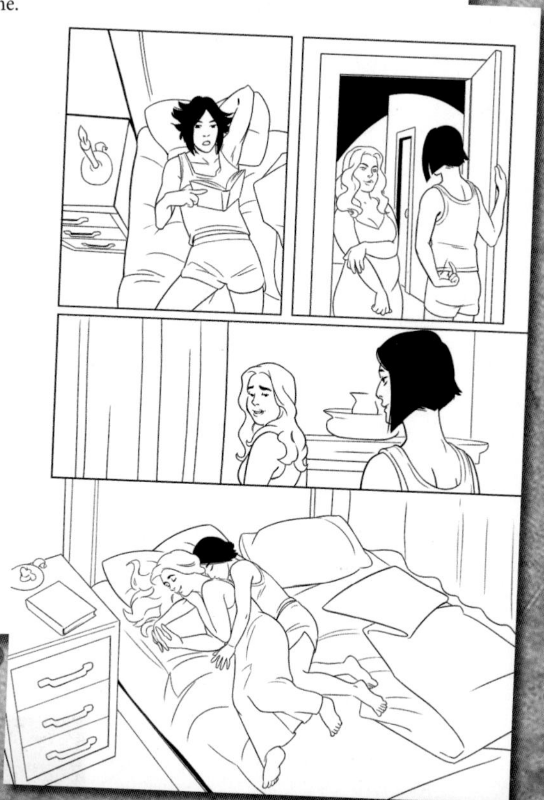

Page 26 Pencils

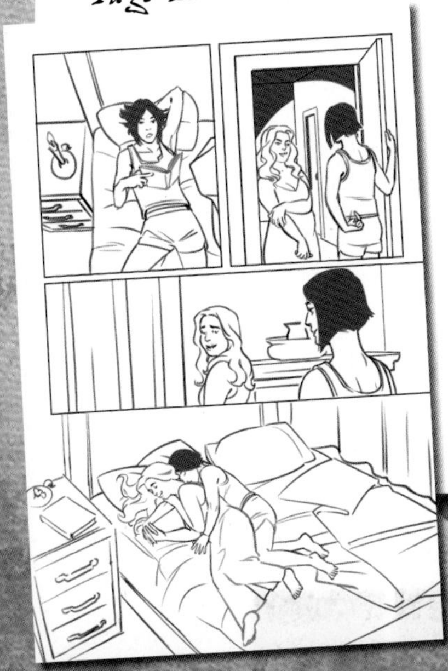

Issue 4, Page 26 Progression

Page 26 Colors

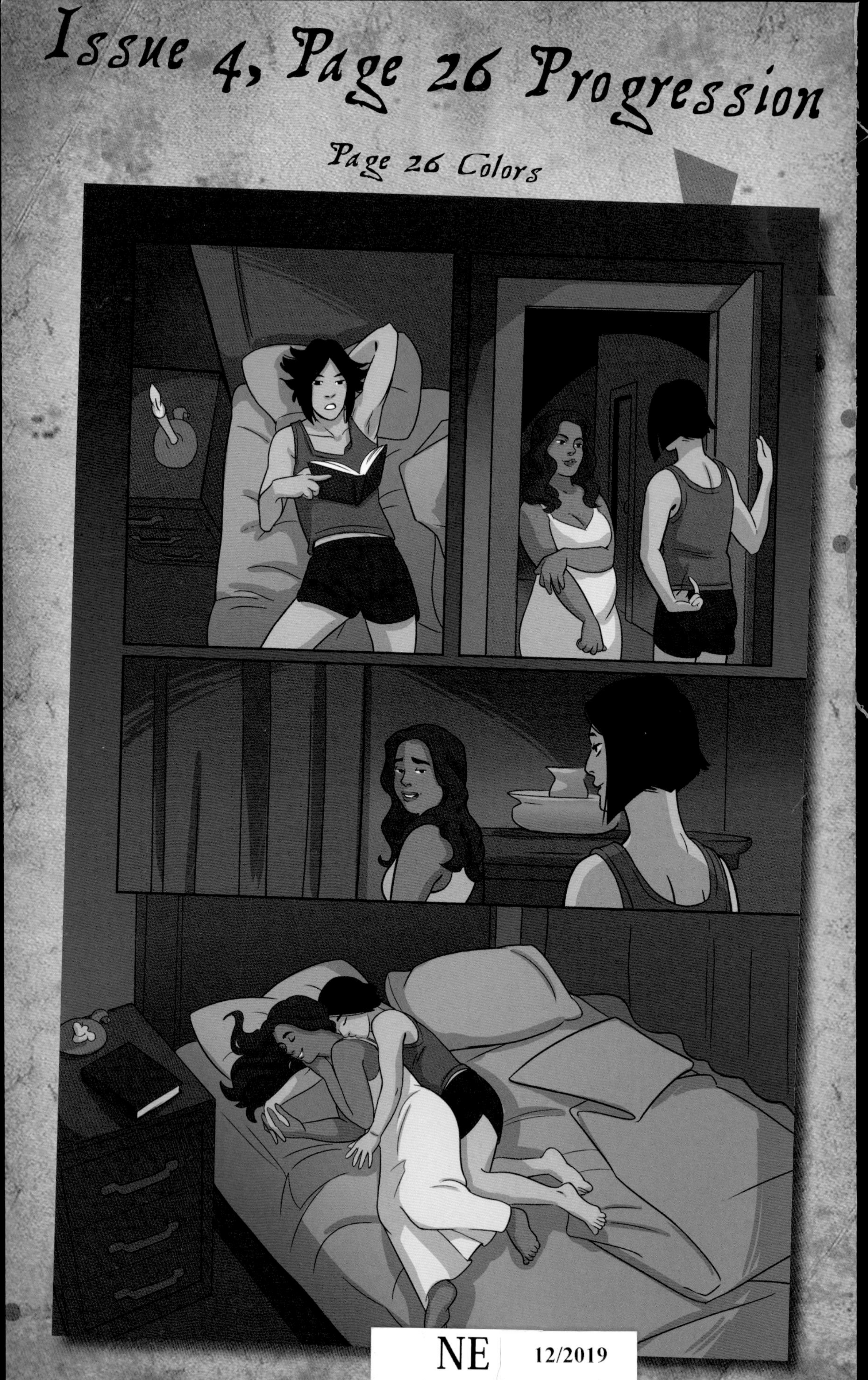